D0878257

SOME LIKE THEM DEAD

James Davidson II

AuthorHouse™
1663 Liberty Drive
Bloomington, IN 47403
www.authorhouse.com
Phone: 1-800-839-8640

First published by AuthorHouse 07/21/2011

ISBN: 978-1-4567-6308-4 (sc)
ISBN: 978-1-4567-6307-7 (ebk)

Library of Congress Control Number: 2011913165

Printed in the United States of America

To Carolyn

Whose insight, editing, and creative additions gave this project closure. Can't wait till our next chapter....

Chapter One

The chamber was moist and cool but not uncomfortable. The air was alive with a rhythmic current, ebbing and flowing, stronger than a draft but not quite a breeze. It was as if some gargantuan, slumbering, beast was providing a gentle breath to caress and calm the weary subterranean traveler. The walls of the chamber were wet with condensation and streaked with milky, green, limestone deposits. A mineral odor, damp and stagnant, permeated the place. The overall feeling was that of being in a cave, but it was actually a large, domed, underground room.

The room was furnished with twenty gray metal desks and matching chairs constructed with the dull efficiency expected of government furniture manufactured during the Cold War era, neither pleasing to the eye nor particularly ugly. They were just desks and chairs with no distinctive design or marking, welded together to provide only a modicum of comfort to underpaid government cave dwellers. The walls were lined with empty consoles, each with its own swivel stool, memorials to the ghosts of command post workers who had gone about the daily business of nuclear deterrence.

The furniture was also covered in slick limestone droppings from the ceiling.

Outside of the chamber's unlikely location, the only thing remarkable about it was one of the desks, which was unremarkable in and of itself. What set it apart from the others was the small form resting on its back in the center, a small child, his face relaxed and serene. His cheeks were pale from the cool air. The day before that same face had been flushed from the warmth of the sun, the cheeks ruddy from the carefree exertions of a child hard at play.

As the sun retired for the day, and the air in the cavern began to mirror the temperature of the cooling concrete shroud above, the face would loose the illusion of being in comfortable repose. The blood remaining in the diminutive body, having recently lost the use of a beating heart to force it along its not so perpetual route, would settle to the bottom of the shell. As post mortem lividity set in, the pearly inner flesh of bloodless wounds would start to contrast against the boy's pale blue skin. In time, the body would begin its metamorphosis into the dust from which it had come. Before that happened, however, it would spend some time looking exactly like what it was...the body of a small boy, mutilated and alone.

Chapter Two

Elliot had his own internal theme music, an edgy rock and roll action hero score that generally played in a continuous loop inside his head whenever he was doing something he thought was particularly cool, which was often the case. Not that he was often doing something particularly cool, but the narcissist in him liked to think everything he did was cool. His theme music, however, stopped abruptly when he looked down and realized he was covered in blood. As the crashing cadence of his heart slowed and the adrenaline faded, he turned his consciousness inward and tried to determine if any his aches and pains needed immediate medical attention. He'd heard stories about soldiers who suffered fatal wounds but still continued to fight. They didn't even realize they were hurt until the surge of adrenaline abated, and they dropped dead. He suspected dropping dead sucked; he didn't think he would allow the dropping dead thing to happen tonight.

Satisfied with his quick self-examination, and a prognosis of not dropping dead in the immediate future, he bent to take a look at the freshly dead and oozing carcass at his feet.

Most of the blood on him had splashed out of it. In life, this newly rendered pile of goo had been a biker who went by the gentle moniker of "Hatchet". He suspected this wasn't a given name and, although he didn't know what Hatchet had done to earn it, he was pretty sure it was indeed *earned,* and had likely involved a *hatchet.*

In life Hatchet hadn't been much to look at. He was the poster boy for outlaw bikers: fat, hairy, filthy, and rank. Now he was bloody, fat, hairy, filthy and rank; and he was missing half his face. That part, Elliot mused, was actually an improvement.

Hatchet's bowels had loosed after Elliot pressed his government-issued 9mm to his head, pulled the trigger, and given him a bloody lobotomy. The smell of shit was in the air. Elliot's face was covered in a fine crimson mist from the blowback. *Yuck!* Who knew what manner of disease Hatchet had been carrying? Fucker was probably a disease playground. He hoped the biker didn't have any of the three H's (the HIV, the HERP, or the HEP), because he, himself, hadn't come out of the scuffle completely unscathed. He'd sustained a number of small cuts and abrasions, and his right eye was starting to swell shut. Hatchet didn't just look like a grizzly bear, he also hit like one. There had been more than a small amount of bodily fluids exchanged while he and Hatchet battled for survival. Hell, he would have exchanged less body fluid if he had fucked him. Killing someone up close and personal was much more intimate than sex. You could have sex with a person many times over, but you could only kill a person once.

Hatchet was starting to smell worse in death than he had in life, but not by much. The smell of death, on top of being covered in Hatchet's coagulating blood, was making him nauseous…and thinking about Hatchet and sex in the same span brought up his gorge. He choked it down.

Note to self: Don't shoot anybody else in the face, at least not at close range. The thought made him giggle a little. He had to force himself to stop, and realized he was a hair's breath from hysteria. If he started laughing now he would loose his fucking mind.

Think, think, think.... think! He needed to clean up, but he should wait for back up. *Okay kids, one real dead biker, one blood drenched special agent, no backup, this was what was known in laymen's terms as a drug deal gone real bad.*

Where was his backup, anyway? He'd been about to buy five-hundred dollars worth of crystal-methamphetamine from Hatchet in the parking lot of the Crazy Bull Saloon and Pool Hall, which he had taken to calling Bull's Dingus Redneck Emporium (but only to other cops). This would have been just little starter purchase to build some mutual trust. Before he could pull out his wad of money, though, he had one of his flashes, a familiar feeling of *déjà vu.* Everything slowed down as he watched Hatchet, now in stark techno-colored relief, pull that big fucking knife he wore in a functional leather sheath on his right thigh and skewer him through the gut.

The premonition only took a second, and then Elliot was back, looking at Hatchet who was still standing in front of him, beaming his most disarming grin right at him. What Hatchet didn't know was that his face was simply not accustomed to smiling, and so his unpracticed muscles only managed to twist his ugly mug into a reasonable facsimile of a cheerful, deranged wolverine. Hatchet dropped all pretenses of friendliness, however, when he noticed Elliot noticing his insincerity and the resultant change in Elliot's demeanor. He reached for his companion, the aforementioned big ass knife. Elliot grabbed for Hatchet's knife hand, even as the biker formulated the best way to skewer him with the nasty, well-worn blade. Hatchet responded by hitting him across the face, and he just knew he'd be feeling *that* in the morning. He kicked the biker between his legs and, when Hatchet dropped his hands to cover his violated gonads, hit him in the head with his elbow. It wasn't pretty, but over the years of training in a variety of exotic fighting techniques all around the world, Elliot finally came to understand that, in a pinch, kicking a man in the balls and bopping him in the head with something was a flawless one-two combination.

The elbow to the head sent Hatchet to the ground, but since the big man's head wasn't a particularly sensitive vital organ, he managed to grab Elliot around the waist and drag him down with him.

As they rolled around grappling on the blacktop, Elliot had another flash: *Two in one night, the moon must be aligned or some shit. In another couple of seconds or so he's going to grab my gun and completely wreck my evening.* Elliot's gun was nestled snuggly inside his waistline in a concealed holster. He was on top of Hatchet, and in that instance, he realized he wouldn't get a better chance to end the fight and live to tell about it. He pulled his weapon and shot Hatchet point blank in the nose.

He noticed some bar patrons standing outside of the mock saloon doors of the club. They had gathered to watch the fight but couldn't be bothered to intervene. There would later be witnesses who would testify that Elliot had clearly achieved the upper hand, when, for no reason, he shot the dazed and defenseless biker in the face, than started to giggle a little. He could still hear the music coming from inside. The fact that there were folks still doing Friday night bar folk stuff while he sat on his haunches by a man whose face he'd just blown apart, was overpoweringly surreal, and a testament to the caliber of Bull's Dingus clientele.

As he watched in horror, the bar patrons faded and reformed in front of his eyes. They turned into an old

English tribunal, complete with white wigs and black robes. He looked down at Hatchet. He wasn't dead! He had to be dead! Half his brain was on the ground for crying out loud! Hatchet, face dripping, flecks of brain and bone falling off of his leather jacket, stood up. Towering over Elliot now, he cocked his arm back ready to finish what he started. He swung the blade *hey that thing looks like, well…a hatchet!* Elliot looked at the court smugly; *Do you see? Do you see why I had to kill him? This is what he planned to do. Do you fucking see? Sometimes, I just know!* The blade connected with his neck. He closed his eyes bracing himself for death, and…woke up.

"Sometimes I just know," he mumbled, but the dream had faded and the court could not hear his defense. The dream was an old and uninvited friend. He hadn't had it in months. Why now? *Must have been the booze*, Elliot concluded.

Why had he drunk so much? This was harder to answer, but finally Elliot came up with the penetrating insight of *Why not*?

Since Idaho he hadn't trusted in his natural talent, his training, or his experience. It had been two years and the inquiry was still going on. Who would have figured Hatchet was the idiot half brother of an Idaho Senator? Looking back, that was probably something that should have shown up during the investigation preceding the ill-fated buy/bust. Actually, a lot of things should have come up: like the fact that Hatchet was also a member of the Aryan Brotherhood. That might have clued Elliot in early to the fact that Hatchet wouldn't be inclined to merely *sell* drugs to a black guy. It was a wonder that Hatchet's penchant for being a double-crossing asshole, and his deep-seated hatred of all things not white, hadn't come up during one of the endless pre-operational briefings he had been forced to suffer through.

Briefings that had included every inconsequential detail the team could dredge up, to include (no shit) the fact that Hatchet was not circumcised. Now what the fuck did Elliot's crack team of special agents think he was going to do with that tidbit? For some bizarre reason, they thought that the esthetic appeal of Hatchet's dick was worth citing, but his raging racial bias hadn't even rated an honorable mention. That little bit of clarification would have saved him, and the biker, a lot of grief. Wasn't somebody supposed to research that stuff? He probably should have seen it coming, or taken the initiative and done a little extra research himself. After all, it was his ass on the line.

In the months that followed "the incident," Elliot had explained to various Air Force inquiry officers, over and over, the unclassified version of his story minus his "premonitions". He got to tell the real version to an intimidating group of people who only introduced themselves using first names like Bob or Mike in a windowless room on an Air Force installation that, as far as he could tell, didn't appear on any map. What made them truly scary was the fact that they didn't appear to have any sense of humor, or any human emotion he could discern. Elliot was convinced they were going to throw the book at him and he would spend a long time at Fort Leavenworth. The weird part was that they believed him, but they didn't know how to appease the politicians. They resorted to the world's oldest solution; *ignore it and hopes it goes away.* They let him keep his badge and found a nice carpet to hide him under in the form of a small OSI office in Colorado.

Elliot had bigger problems at the moment, however, because the sun, as indifferent to the comfort it provided as it was to the pain it could cause, had found Elliot's apartment and was searing through his Venetian blinds. It forced its way between his slit eyelids in a determined effort to fry his retinas.

Okay, judging by the feeling in his gut, he was dying. Things could be worse. He called on his gods, prayed to his ancestors, and whimpered a bit for his mother.

Someone must have heard his prayers because he was still alive. He didn't particularly want to be alive. At the moment 'alive' hurt. His body was drained. His senses, all six, were dulled and his spirit was weak. To make matters worse, his teeth felt hairy, alien, and somehow alive, as if they might decide they needed a life of their own, free from his abuses, and crawl out of his mouth to check out how the other half lived in the high rent district. They could find some nice yuppie mouth to live in, something with caps and a view, and an owner who drank bottled water instead of tequila. Elliot would be left toothless and blithering, and it would probably serve him right.

He didn't think he would have a headache. He had drunk plenty of water and popped five aspirin after he staggered in and before he passed out. But it was too soon to tell, because he couldn't feel his head. God! He had to stop drinking. He was thirty-five years old and becoming a walking cliché: the divorced, bitter, boozing, cop.

He remembered when it used to be one of his private jokes. If anyone asked him why he'd become an OSI special agent, he would tell them it was simple: he wanted to retire after twenty years of thankless service, three bad marriages, with a drinking problem and a beer gut. It wasn't a joke anymore. He was working hard on developing the drinking problem. He'd just finished one bad marriage. The beer gut was a long way off, but he definitely wasn't in peak fighting condition. He tried to inventory his senses, picking one at a time, concentrating; sight...check, hearing...check, smell...check, that other thing...check. He'd started doing the exercise as a teen and now he barely thought about it, just push the button and start the self-diagnostic.

Sensation was creeping back into his body. He could feel his head, which was starting to throb a bit and demanding to be felt. Now he cursed the gods for letting him live. He rolled out of bed onto the hardwood floor of his bedroom. *Hey, new perspective.* He reminded himself to buy some throw rugs, make the place look a little homier.

He lay with his cheek slowly conforming to the flatness of the hardwood bedroom floor, watching the dust-balls under the bed near his face dance to the rhythmic flow of his breath. He tried to lift his head, only to find his drool and sweat had somehow managed to bond his cheek to the floor like some foul epoxy. His own bodily fluids were conspiring against him. It was just as well. He wasn't sure he wanted to stand up anyway. Plus, if lying in a pool of drool on a dusty floor wasn't the right place to be and the right fucking time to be there, he didn't know what was.

After a while, strength and feeling started seeping back into his limbs. He was pretty sure he was alive and likely to stay that way. He pushed himself up to a sitting position by the side of the bed, and stood up on legs that were unsteady, but apparently still functioning. Convinced that his legs could walk as well as stand, he shuffled his way towards the bathroom.

He glanced at his bookcase out of habit, making sure his badge and gun were in their usual place, sandwiched between his books on Zen, horror novels, and criminal investigations. He shuffled over and picked up his badge case, and opened it to his credentials, which identified him as Elliot Turner, a Special Agent of the Air Force Office of Special Investigations. His photo stared out at him. It was an old photo. He'd been in the organization for well over ten years, and had only replaced the photo once, five years ago. He'd put on some miles since then. The photo showed a young black man, crew cut, and mustache, with the gleam of righteousness still in his eyes, trying to look professional and competent.

"We going to save the world today, Junior?" he asked his picture. As usual there was no response. He needed a new picture, one that was more responsive. "What the hell, we'll save it tomorrow." He tossed the badge case back onto the shelf then, out of habit, performed a quick functions check on his German made 9mm. Time to make the donuts.

Chapter Three

A hangover was an excellent excuse to wear a foul mood for the day. However, nature, in the form of a beautiful Colorado spring day, was engaged in a relentless campaign to cheer him up.

Fucking nature! A man should be able to wallow in his hangover. But no, here was the sun, high in the sky. Nor was it just any old sky; the cosmic forces had pulled out all the stops and thrown the grand champion of all deep blue skies at him. Where was the brown haze? That gaseous odorous entity, which normally covered the Denver valley like a filthy quilt? The haze would be good, Elliot concluded. Brown foul haze...hangover… the two just seemed to go together.

Elliot squinted upward. He sighed, "Fuckin' A."

Even his recently born again neighbor, Eric, was conspicuously absent. Eric lived in the apartment across the hall and usually accosted him on his way out the door to preach at him in a desperate attempt to save him from perdition. Elliot had nothing against religion in general. He was a progressive agnostic and even believed in God most of the time...kind of. Normally, Eric had an uncanny sense of Elliot's comings and goings, and in that irritating fashion that new Christians and door-to-door salesmen shared, he was a master of the casual intrusion. Clutching the gospel like a well-worn security blanket, he was eager to save the unwashed masses from their wicked ways, as if in so doing, he could ensure his own place in the afterlife. Elliot liked most of the unwashed masses - some of them were dead sexy. As for his personal wicked ways, he tried to leave them to their own devices so they would continue to comfort him in his times of need.

His car, old, foreign, and normally temperamental, sat quietly in the parking lot. Elliot usually had to coax the beastly car into life every morning through an elaborate ritual of pumping the clutch and grinding the transmission. But this morning it started on the first try and purred at him with smug condescension as if it realized he was trying to have a bad day and wanted no part of it.

He opened his glove box to look for his sunglasses, fully prepared not to find them. Then he would have to squint into the sun all the way to work, arriving with stinging eyes and a full-grown headache. Oh yes, that would put him into a righteously foul mood. His sunglasses were in the glove box where he left them nestled next to a twenty-dollar bill, which he had no idea would be there.

Okay, no use trying to swim against the cosmic currents. Elliot decided he might as well just enjoy the day, even if he hadn't earned it.

He drove to work the long way and stopped at a gas station to fill up and get a processed meat snack. Beef jerky and pickled sausage always cheered him up. Things seemed to be on the happy track anyway, so a little animal flesh - preserved past the point of actually being food - seemed to be just what the doctor ordered. Elliot had an old gumshoe attitude towards investigative work and food, and believed a good agent should be able to survive off of pickled sausages, beef jerky, chips, and donuts.

The radio was playing all his favorite songs, and he was starting to get into the whole feeling-good-thing. It was seven thirty when he pulled up to the main gate of Lowry Air Force Base. All vestiges of his hangover had fled in fear of his meat snacks and happy thoughts.

His duty day officially began at seven thirty, but his perception of time (which he referred to as EST - Elliot Standard Time) and his concept of what constituted "duty" where very subjective. He figured if he was doing something remotely investigative - or was at least was on the Air Force base by seven thirty - then he was on time. Since he recognized the gate guard, an airman who had expressed some interest in joining Elliot's organization, Elliot reasoned that talking to him definitely qualified as performing his official duties, and so he stopped to bullshit with the young man while he finished his meat snacks. They discussed everything from Elliot's ex-wife to the last movies they had seen: really, anything but the job. By the time Elliot ran out of things to procrastinate about, and finally managed to walk into his office, it was after eight.

His boss, Commander/Major/Special Agent George Devine, didn't live by EST, so Elliot prudently snuck in the back door of the office. He was convinced that his boss was an unmitigated prick, and that, if he could, he would make everyone address him by all three of his titles. Elliot, himself, only had two titles: Master Sergeant/Special Agent. Since rank could be a bit confusing in the Air Force Office of Special Investigations, universally referred to as the OSI, most agents just called their commanders "Boss". By regulation, an OSI agent's rank was considered sensitive information. The Boss appellation served the dual function of hiding the commanders' rank while still allowing subordinates to kiss his or her ass with a deferential status reference. Unlike its cousin the Naval Criminal Investigative Service (NCIS) which was entirely civilian, the OSI was made up of both Air Force military personnel and civilians: all of whom, regardless of their rank, were referred to only as Special Agent. Military agents didn't usually wear uniforms, but they were acutely aware of who outranked whom.

People unfamiliar with the organization had no idea what a strange hybrid the OSI truly was: the unholy offspring of civilian government and the military bureaucracy. The OSI was created in 1948 just after the Army Air Corps broke away from the Army and evolved into the separate entity that is currently the world's most advanced, feared, and in some countries, despised, Air Force.

Prior to 1948, the office of the Army Provost Marshall had been the primary investigative agency servicing the Army Air Corps. They were fully capable of handling routine criminal investigations, but were at a loss when it came to conducting investigations that were unique to the new Air Force. The Department of Defense decided the Air Force needed its own investigative arm; a cadre of skilled investigators, trained to handle criminal, counterintelligence, and economic investigations. A small OSI detachment was assigned to every major Air Force base. They only reported to OSI headquarters in Washington DC in order to maintain autonomy from local Air Base commanders.

The OSI had a simple but broad mission: investigate major criminal activity, white collar crimes, and crimes that affected national security (like espionage and sabotage). OSI personnel were card-carrying federal agents, but their jurisdiction was normally limited to matters that occurred on Air Force installations or property, crimes committed by Air Force personnel, or matters that could have a direct affect on the Air Force mission. One of the more unusual responsibilities of the OSI was to investigate UFO sightings. In fact, it was the OSI, whose agents were the original "men in black", that conducted the Roswell investigation. Even within the OSI, the unit that conducted these investigations was an enigma and the source of intense fascination among the other agents. Elliot didn't know how agents got assigned to that detachment, but he suspected it was by invitation only.

Elliot needn't have bothered sneaking in the back way. Devine wasn't around. He was almost disappointed. Thinking up new and increasingly more transparent excuses for being late had become a ritual between them. *Sorry boss, traffic accident, sorry boss, I lost my way, sorry boss, I had cancer this morning… but I got better.*

Sally's perfume greeted him before he entered the office they shared. His senses, dulled by an evening of drink, were coming back to him. He stopped and closed his eyes. Sandalwood, Sally's fragrance, when combined with her natural body chemistry, turned into something so intoxicating it practically assaulted him. He could smell it, taste it in the air, and feel it caressing his skin. He was certain he could see it swirling around - or was it just his imagination? These days he had to rely on life's little pleasures to get him out of bed and motivated, and just the thought of walking in the office and smelling Sally was enough to lure him out of the house for another day.

Sally, like always, was at her computer when he walked in.

"Good morning, Special Agent Dupree, nice perfume," he said, just a little too bubbly, hopped up on sunshine and pickled sausage.

"What's up?" She looked up from her computer. Elliot was wearing his normal uniform, blue jeans, black T-shirt, biker boots and leather jacket. He looked like a reject from a 1960's biker movie. Sally was convinced that everything Elliot knew about fashion he learned from Happy Days and 70s cop shows. He was a thirty-five year old black man with the fashion sense of a white teenage metal-head. Thing was, it actually seemed to work for him, but that was because his clothes molded tightly to his muscular frame. Despite his largely unhealthy lifestyle, he was a fanatic about exercise, and it showed with a flat stomach and large, sinewy muscles. He bulged in all the right places, too. On more than one occasion she had had impure thoughts about Elliot, which she fervently hoped he didn't pick up on. He had a knack for knowing what a person was thinking. She wondered if he ever felt as though he had just been licked whenever she looked at him.

She noticed his mood was even lighter than his normal the-world-is-my-blow-up-doll attitude, which made her suspicious and a little uneasy. She'd only been working with him for a year, but she already knew how to surf his moods. Elliot Turner didn't bubble. He was usually grinning about something or other, which she often suspected was sleazy, but he didn't bubble. She'd long since realized that mood swings with Elliot, good or bad, should be looked upon with suspicion and a little trepidation. Elliot was a slave to unseen forces Sally didn't even try to understand. He was a psychic barometer, and shit seemed to happen whenever his mood changed. She wasn't even sure if he was even aware of the phenomenon. Elliot was connected to the world in a way that made some people uncomfortable. Sally couldn't explain it, but when she was with him, she felt comfortably connected as well. Sometimes when he let his guard down, his eyes would cloud over and he seemed to stare out at her from some dark dimension. On those occasions, she saw him as a tragic character, a lost soul, brimming with mystery, despair, and danger. But most of the time he was just this guy, casual and quick to laugh, with the easy confidence of a man who'd learned that life was not a test so much as a carnival ride.

Sally didn't try to lie to herself. She often looked at Elliot and thought, "hmmm;" but she was married, and almost certain she still loved her husband. Anyway, Elliot was too busy playing the role of the agent-who-had-seen-too-much-to-care. Even if she wasn't married, Sally couldn't see how a relationship could possibly fit into the eccentric and sometimes schizophrenic self-image he had created for himself. They were both content to live with the tension of unconsummated lust, and to admire each other from a respectable distance. In a way it helped them to work better together. Neither felt the need to ruin their strange, but effective, symbiosis by taking it to the next level.

"Why are you looking at me like that?" Elliot said, his eyes twinkling, as he settled in behind his desk and put his feet up.

"I'm looking at you," Sally said, answering his question "because you're acting strange. That is, stranger than usual."

"I haven't been sitting here long enough for you to make that assessment," Elliot said, hoping to drag her into some inane, childish debate. "Matter of fact, let's examine that word, *strange*."

"Let's not and say we did," Sally said. She knew him well enough not to give him anything to play with when he was being weird.

"Can I help it if I'm having a good day?" he asked, still trying. "Do you define 'strange' as a person who greets you with a smile. If so, that's kind of sad."

"Um," she went back to the report she was working on, ignoring him.

She knew him so well, Elliot thought. He considered himself lucky to have Sally as a partner. OSI agents were not technically assigned partners; but since much investigative work required two persons - good cop, bad cop - for safety or administrative purposes, most agents found someone in the office they could work well with and adopted them. It wasn't easy finding someone to fill the unofficial partner slot. Agents tended to be highly individualistic, strongly opinionated, and as a rule rubbed one another the wrong way.

Sally and Elliot complemented each other. Elliot's investigative style was eclectic at best and manic on occasion. Sally was meticulous in her execution of all her duties. Elliot was a cynic. Sally thought she could still make a difference, which was ironic, because Elliot, who claimed not to care about anything or anyone, seemed to be gifted with an enviable natural empathy. He seemed to know instinctively how to comfort people, but he claimed it was all an act.

Perhaps the quality that endeared Elliot to Sally the most - outside of having a nice ass - was she didn't buy Elliot's rebel-without-a-clue act for one minute. Elliot gave up trying to engage Sally in annoying conversation and opted for a less cerebral approach. He was, after all, a man; and he'd learned everything he needed to know about dealing with women and romance during kindergarten. If you like a girl pull her braid or throw something at her. He was wadding up a piece of paper, contemplating its trajectory, when George Devine walked into the office. Charcoal gray suit, red power tie, quarter inch of white cuff peeking from each sleeve of his suit jacket, Devine was the consummate politician, an OSI fast burner.

He stopped just inside the door and surveyed the scene for anything he could bitch about. But Elliot, feet on desk, obviously getting ready to do something unprofessional with a wad of paper, made it too easy. It wasn't worth the breath anymore; and he was in a hurry. He looked pointedly at Elliot's feet on the desk and scowled, hoping that would get the point across. It didn't matter, though. Elliot already knew the point and purposefully ignored it. Whenever he was in the office he made a conscious effort to put his feet up on the desk. During training at the OSI academy, one of the instructors, to whom Elliot had taken an instant dislike, had a habit of prattling on about how the well trained (or to Elliot's mind "house trained") professional should act at all times. How a professional should refrain from such casual acts as showing up unexpectedly on a colleague's doorstep to discuss a case, or from propping one's feet up on the desk. Elliot was privately at war against anyone anywhere who was overly concerned about things which fell into the area of things he categorized as 'little shit'. Most things fell into that category for Elliot.

He refused to squeeze into anyone's preconceived model of a professional, and considered himself the scourge of conformity. Little acts of rebellion like putting his feet up on the desk (besides being a cool and comfortable way to sit) were his way of showing the world he lived by his beliefs-whatever they were this week. His logic was simple: I am a professional, so if I, as a professional, put my feet on the stinking desk…doesn't that make it the professional stinking thing to do?

Devine gave up on Elliot and turned his attention to Sally, who was hard at work. His scowl softened a bit, Dupree was a good agent, even if she seemed not to recognize that Turner was a fuck up.

"Listen up, Sally, E.T." E.T. was a nickname Elliot had been stuck with since coming into the organization. He didn't mind. He thought it was cool to be referred to by his initials. "We've got a six-case out at the missile fields." A 'six-case' was OSI speak for a death investigation. "I want you out there, E.T., because you're familiar with the silo area. I want you to go with him, Sally, to keep him from stepping on his dick."

Sally was accustomed to working in a male dominated profession and didn't flinch at the vulgarity. She was too much the seasoned agent. She looked Devine in the eye and said, "Yes, sir."

Devine nodded. As he turned to leave, he couldn't keep himself from snapping at Elliot. "Keep your feet off the desk. It's not professional."

With Devine gone, Elliot grinned at Sally wolfishly, "So, are you up to the task?"

"A six-case? Of course." She was shutting down her computer and getting her kit bag from under the desk.

"No, keeping me from stepping on my dick. It could be a tall order."

Sally slowly turned to face him, her expression deadpan, "Any man who can step on his own dick is okay by me. Matter of fact, I live for men who can step on their own dicks and lick their eyebrows. They make me feel funny."

"Oooo." Elliot loved it when she talked semi-dirty – it was a delicious departure from her normally staid behavior. Elliot grabbed his bag and followed Sally out the door. Sally, for her part, had already left their exchange behind and was thinking about Elliot's mood shift. Just like clockwork, shit was about to happen.

Chapter Four

They had been on the road heading north out of Denver since slightly before one o'clock. The Rocky Mountains rose majestically against the sky behind them, the snow-capped peaks bidding them farewell and Godspeed. The last of the Denver suburbs were twenty miles to the south, and they were heading into the brown barren plains that surrounded the Denver oasis.

Sally was reclining in her seat, eyes closed, lips slightly parted, breathing evenly, but Elliot sensed she wasn't asleep. He thought she was preparing herself for what they would find out at the crime scene. Actually, she was wondering what Elliot would look like naked.

Elliot had his window rolled down, left arm hanging out, enjoying the Colorado spring air. There was just the hint of a smile on his face. He was thinking about a beer commercial.

Although they were most likely on their way to see something horrible, Elliot was feeling happy and content. He treasured any time he could spend alone with Sally.

Outside of the occasional beer after work, they didn't spend much time together off duty.

They both knew that if they allowed themselves to spend too much time together, without a chaperone, they would end up screwing like rabid weasels and have to reevaluate their comfortable relationship. Which was something they both wanted but couldn't afford. No one said life and love was simple. Consequently, most of their time alone together was spent on the road in their unmarked government sedan.

"What did the boss mean about you "knowing" the silo area?" Sally asked, interrupting his basking.

"I ran an investigation out there about two years ago," then added, " It was before your time."

Sally had been in the organization only half as long as Elliot, and she'd been assigned to the Denver office for about one year. Elliot had been in Denver for just over two years.

"What kind of investigation? I've never heard you talk about it. Must not have been very memorable," she challenged. All agents figured each of their cases, even the most routine, were unique and special, and they wore them like badges of honor.

"I've never told you about my naked pictures of Nancy Reagan either. Doesn't mean I'm holding out on you; just means I haven't got around to it. But actually you're right. It wasn't that memorable. Some local juveniles were ripping off houses and stashing their goods in one of the abandoned silo complexes."

"You really have naked pictures of Nancy Reagan?"

"Sure. I got them from a Secret Service agent. I had to trade a naked Janet Reno and my Madelyn Albright in a G-String, but it was more than worth it for the pleasure they've brought." His eyes were still twinkling. "A good agent collects things over the years."

"Well...not that I believe you, you understand, but you can keep that dirty little secret to yourself."

When they arrived at the scene there was already a crowd of uniformed cops and white-coated crime scene technicians milling about. The missile fields were situated at the intersection of about three different police jurisdictions in Weld and Larimer counties. The land was owned by the state, but the county sheriff's office was responsible for overall patrol duties in the area. The silos themselves were owned by the Air Force, but they shared concurrent jurisdiction with the federal government. The FBI had the juice to take over just about any investigation on military property, but Elliot didn't see any FBI agents from the local field office in the crowd.

There were also officers from the local fish and wildlife office. During open season, the missile-fields were a popular deer hunting area. During the off-season, the fields were popular deer *poaching* areas.

Since the Air Force owned the silos, if the FBI didn't want the case, investigative responsibility would ultimately fall on the OSI. But the OSI generally worked well with the FBI, and Elliot knew they would be more than willing to provide him with any assistance he needed in the way of forensic and lab support.

There were five police cruisers and a large black panel van, which belonged to the crime scene technicians, parked in a semi-circle around a large natural depression in the earth. In the middle of the depression assorted prairie foliage had been pushed aside to reveal a concrete slab with a large metal handle set into the concrete. The slab looked like it weighed a few hundred pounds. A bright yellow nylon towrope was still attached to the metal handle. The other end of the towrope was hooked to a large pick-up truck against which two nervous but curious young cowboy types were leaning, watching Elliot and Sally approach.

The slab had been pulled aside, leaving a crescent shaped opening large enough for a big man to climb through comfortably.

A group of uniformed policemen, representative of the different jurisdictions, were loitering around, telling war stories, renewing old acquaintances, and having a generally good time.

Elliot recognized a few of them: Richard Diaz from the State Police, Bob Molina from Fish and Wildlife, and the County Sheriff, Ken Raymond. Most of the cops knew each other from either having grown up in the area together or from working cross-jurisdictional investigations in the past. During those investigations friendships were made, personal and business numbers were exchanged, and everyone always promised to 'get together and do lunch or something'. Rotating shifts and busy schedules seldom allowed for the promised get togethers. It wasn't unusual for the cops to go months and even years without seeing someone who in another time or place would have become a good friend. So, whenever a case brought them all together, there was the obligatory social hour prior to getting down to business.

Somewhere beneath their feet someone lay dead, but for the cops it was old home week, just another chance to catch up on each other's lives and apologize for promises never kept.

Sheriff Raymond spotted Elliot and Sally as they approached, and detached from the group. The Sheriff looked like the Marlboro man before he got weather beaten; jaw...lined, chin...cleft, skin...tanned, feet...booted. He didn't look a day over thirty, but he had been Sheriff for at least ten years. He was intelligent and well liked. Elliot figured they would have been fast friends in another time or place.

Ken smiled as Elliot and Sally approached. He let his smile linger on Sally just a heartbeat longer than necessary, telling her non-verbally that he respected her presence as a professional, but was well aware she was an attractive woman. Sally seemed to appreciate the attention, and Elliot made a mental note to learn how to do the whole sexy, macho, smile thing.

"Well, as I live and breath," Ken said, doing his best redneck sheriff imitation, "If it isn't regular agent E.T. Turner and his lovely sidekick. How's it hangin, Sally?"

Sally smiled, "Low and to the left, Ken. Been awhile, huh?"

"Too long, almost a year, since that thing. Can you still do that trick with your mouth?"

"Probably, but I don't think your heart could handle it. What are you now, fifty-five… sixty years old?" She asked.

"What trick?" Elliot asked, feeling left out and slightly jealous of their flirting.

"Wouldn't you like to know?" She said coyly, walking over to join the crowd of cops.

Raymond and Elliot watched her walk away.

"Nice ass," Raymond said. He looked at Elliot, and even before his smile faded, Elliot could see he was disturbed.

Raymond was chewing on his lower lip, and Elliot could almost hear him trying to organize his thoughts, so that he could give Elliot some sense of the events leading up to this moment.

"Just give me the Cliff notes," Elliot said. "I'll fill in the blanks as we go."

"White, male…five or six years old..."

"Oh, *shit*."

"Multiple stab wounds, evidence of cannibalism. The two cowboys over on the truck found the body." He motioned over to where the two teenagers, wearing cowboy boots, big brass belt buckles, and cowboy hats were leaning on the bed of the truck attached to the tow chain. The truck was complete with gun rack and confederate flag in the rear window. The teens were whispering excitedly, chewing tobacco and spitting expertly into the dirt.

"Don't let the cool act fool you," Raymond said. "The big one tossed his cookies..."

"Tossed his cookies? Is that Mayberry-speak for puked?"

"Yeah, puked. Over by the entrance."

"Have you been down?"

"Yeah. No rigor. I wouldn't be surprised if the kids passed the perp on the road out here somewhere."

"You said 'perp.' Say something else cop-like for me. Anyone down there right now?"

"Three state forensic guys, setting up lights and making the place a little more habitable."

"I don't see any of my bastard stepbrothers from the FBI. I guess this is ours, huh?"

"You can have it."

"I'm going down. I see the crime scene guys are already here, but I don't want them to start processing the scene without me. You going back down?"

"Nope, got kids of my own. I want to be able to sleep tonight."

Elliot wandered over to the group to retrieve Sally. She was the only woman at the scene, and she was making lots of new friends.

"Let's do this, Dupree," he said.

Cool, moist, stagnant, air wafted out of the half moon shaped opening. Elliot could swear the place was breathing. He didn't have any trouble imagining they had stumbled upon the resting place of one of the old gods from an H.P. Lovecraft tale; Chtlon, Chtulu, or some other equally unpronounceable creeping terror crouching in wait at the bottom of the pit. Beneath the concrete opening was a metal platform of the same honeycombed design as many of the fire escapes in the city.

From the platform, a spiral staircase of the same material descended into the bowels of the missile complex. Even with the sunlight shining through the crescent hole, the pit was so deep and the darkness so pervasive that light only illuminated the upper levels of the stairs. After about thirty feet they faded into darkness as if disappearing into another dimension.

Elliot thought about what they used to say about the old Air Force missile officers; "If you bury any animal in a hole long enough, it's bound to come out changed."

After the Atlas E missile program had been rendered obsolete by more advanced weapons of mass destruction; the missile silos were scavenged of all salvageable equipment and then sealed off to the world. Some of them were imploded and filled with dirt and concrete; others were sold commercially and to private citizens. Because the underground missile complexes were so large, filling them proved to be a costly and time-consuming task. Finally, the money people-the ubiquitous "money people"- decided to just seal off the entrances of the remaining complexes in the futile hope that they would just go away.

The Army Corp of Engineers covered the main entrances with concrete slabs weighing close to a ton. They reasoned, the more difficult the task of tampering, the less likely tampering would occur. Of course, when teenagers with empty time and idle minds were thrown into the equation, the most difficult task became simply a cool way to spend an afternoon.

The silo around which all the excitement was centered was located in the far northeast quadrant of the missile fields. The gullies and natural land depressions in the area kept all but the most adventurous away from the area. The local police agencies only ventured into the area when they were bored, or wanted to take a mid-day nap. The silo was nestled in a natural depression. A few decades worth of sagebrush added to the camouflage. There was no way of knowing it was there unless you were right on top of it; and then you would have to know what it was.

The odds of stumbling across it by chance were astronomical. Enter the teens. Spring break. The cowboys, Darryl Bartot and Clayton Taylor, were out four-wheeling in Clayton's dad's pick-up truck. The northeast quadrant of the missile fields had the best rises and dips. When they left home that morning they each had a six-pack of beer, and their twenty-two caliber rifles. They were planning on raising a little hell, and shooting a couple of rabbits or any other small furred or feathered creature that had the misfortune of crossing their path.

By the time they four-wheeled over a rise and almost landed right on top of the silo entrance, they were bored and slightly drunk. The timid plain's creatures had decided it wasn't a good day to die and made themselves scarce, and Daryl and Clayton had squeezed all the fun they could out of four-wheeling.

Most of the kids in the area knew about the deserted missile complexes. Many of the complexes had long since been discovered and claimed by the local teens. Some of them had become regular hangouts. They were a good place to take Peggy-Sue for some gratuitous heavy petting, and an excellent place to get drunk and tell horror stories.

For Clayton and Darryl finding a new complex was like a Texan striking oil in an area thought to be dry. No teenager worth his salt could resist a door leading underground into the unknown. Their adventure glands kicked into high gear, and they wasted no time doing what came naturally. They took the towrope from the truck's toolbox, secured it to the slab handle, hopped in the truck and went for broke.

Had they known the reward for their explorations would be a lifetime of nightmares, they would have just finished their beer and gone home.

Chapter Five

Elliot had never become accustomed to the face of death, not even when he had been its cause-especially then.

Like every other cop he tried to hide his unease behind dark humor and banal remarks; but when death was in the air, he could feel his own mortality biting at his heels. Early in his career after a seminar on the legalities surrounding death investigations, complete with plenty of graphic photos (graphic photos held the cops' interest), he had developed an intense fear of dying. But it was more than that. Seeing soulless shell after soulless shell had given him a disturbing glimpse into his own future. Because of his unique gift of empathy and heightened sensibilities, he felt keenly the emptiness in the shells of the unanimated. He saw clearly his own shell for what it was, a barely contained bag of flesh and fluid, ill equipped to deal with the hazards of the modern world. Guns, knives, car accidents, plane crashes, natural disasters, hell, just slipping on the ice; all could reduce a person to a lifeless shell in a heartbeat. Had he not proven how fragile it all was by taking the life from others, who thought themselves immortal?

He'd felt himself becoming increasingly agoraphobic, and just leaving the house for work took a supreme act of will. He thought he could have benefited from professional help but he didn't trust the organization not to overreact if they thought he was mental. In the end he had just dealt with his developing psychosis one day at a time until it went away on its own. Over the years he had become acclimated to all the death food groups: homicide, suicide, accident, other; but he still found dead things more gross than fascinating.

They were in a large domed chamber. It could have been an office bullpen or conference room. There were a number of desks in the room, but only one interested Elliot.

Displayed in the center of the desk like some macabre paperweight was the body of a small blonde boy, thin, and pale. His limbs had begun to stiffen. The mouth was slightly parted, and the eyes were slightly open and cloudy. The legs were neatly duct taped together at the ankles. The arms were also duct taped at the wrist and pulled up over his head. On a chair by the desk there was a battery-operated lantern. It was giving off a dull orange glow like a flashlight with weak batteries. Elliot wondered why the killer would have left a lamp burning.

Corpses with open eyes always distressed Elliot. "*Look at you*," they always seemed to say, "*it's over for me, but you flaunt your life in my face, as if you deserve it more than me*." Elliot found himself superstitiously looking for some spark of post-mortem animation in the corpse.

The chamber was only a small part of the massive underground complex. The facility was catacombed with other smaller rooms, which at one time contained everything needed to survive a nuclear attack. There were dining areas, sleeping quarters, and just about everything needed to keep all the essential personnel warm and cozy while the world above was reduced to radioactive top soil.

Elliot was reminded of one of the 'Planet of the Apes' movies, the one where the apes - much to the horror of the movie's intrepid hero - had found the last atomic bomb, which they were keeping around and worshipping as a god.

He had never experienced anything quite like the underground world of the missile complexes. Even if there hadn't been a dead kid thrown into the equation, he would have still been a little unsettled. *If you bury any animal in a hole long enough, its bound to come out changed.*

Sally was on the other side of the chamber. She was making a rough sketch of the scene. He wished she were by his side.

He forced himself to detach and look closely at the body. He didn't know how the coroners and forensic types did it. It wasn't human or animal nature to want to spend too much time around the dead; but if you wanted to learn their secrets, you had to get up close and personal where the dead could whisper in your ear. Maybe it was easy for the coroners and the others who just processed the meat. The investigator had to see beyond the meat. He had to bring the bag of flesh and bone back to life. Detachment, apathy, acclimatization were the enemies of victimology. The investigator had to give the corpse a personality. He had to learn its loves, see the world through its eyes, give it back its name, give it breath and tears, and learn its vulnerabilities. Then he had to kill it again, slowly, frame by frame.

There were a number of small wounds on the body, horizontal cuts, deep enough to have drawn blood, but not deep enough to have been the cause of death. They were each about an inch long. Forehead, throat, chest, abdomen, and groin area; definitely a pattern in the way the wounds were evenly spaced down the center of the body like the cross stitching on a football.

The body and face were blue, but Elliot couldn't tell whether the cyanosis was from the coolness of the chamber or from the manner of death.

On closer examination, small petechial hemorrhages on the cheeks around the eyes indicated strangulation. But there was no trauma to the neck, no bruising, and no ligature marks. Maybe suffocation. He didn't notice anything in the immediate vicinity that could have been used to suffocate the boy.

Ken had mentioned there was evidence of cannibalism. Elliot noticed it at first glance, but he'd been studiously ignoring it until Sally wandered up from behind, startling him.

"Shit," she said with her customary bluntness, "Looks like we have a biter, huh?"

Elliot didn't answer her. All over the small torso, arms and legs, were clear bite marks.

"I think I'm going to be sick." She said, just to have something to say. She actually had a high tolerance for homicide scenes.

"Try not to puke in front of the help." He said nonchalantly, pointing a thumb at the crime scene technicians. He felt anything but nonchalant. He was sure Sally wasn't going to be sick, but he thought he might.

"You done with your sketch?" He asked.

Sally nodded.

"What say we go up top for awhile, get some air."

They left the chamber and climbed back up the metal staircase in, each silently internalizing and processing the horror to which they had been called to bear witness.

Elliot could hear a crime scene technician's laughter, forced and a little high pitched, echoing off the walls beneath them. Elliot winced. There was nothing like a dead kid to liven up a party, huh? Then he felt guilty for being judgmental. Actually, kids were sacrosanct in the cop world – nobody laughed when a kid died. The technician was likely trying to find an unrelated bit of mirth to help him cope with the scene. His unease stabbed into Elliot's guts. In a way, Elliot sympathized with the man: he couldn't count the times when he'd made some stupid joke while standing over some unfortunate soul whose life had been reduced to a bad punch line, or found some other inane bit of humor that seemed to be the height of hilarity at the time. But even Elliot drew the line when a child was involved.

What kind of people must we be? He didn't know whether it was a positive or negative human trait, to learn to laugh in the face of horror and tragedy.

As they neared the entrance, Elliot was overcome with a vision of the slab sliding across the opening above them, the crescent opening growing smaller and smaller until they were trapped in the darkness. He felt a wave of panic, and fought off the urge to rush through the opening.

He still let Sally exit first. He emerged on her heels, pale and sweating.

"You okay?," Sally asked.

"Yeah, I'm not having such a good day anymore. Looks like I picked the wrong day to stop sniffing glue," he said in a half-hearted attempt at humor.

Sally saw that his eyes weren't twinkling anymore. But this time the mood shift was understandable.

"I'm not having the time of my life either," she said. "Things are getting ready to get real fucking strange, aren't they?"

"I'm thinking, yeah, pretty much. You along for the ride?"

"I guess it beats slamming my tit in a car door."

"You're such a delicate flower."

"Fuck you."

Ken Raymond was still hanging around topside. He wasn't doing anything, but he was doing it well. He was leaning on his Jeep, cleaning his nails with a buck knife. He saw Elliot and Sally emerge and closed the knife with one hand using his thigh. He tucked in back into its carrier without looking-Samurai Sheriff style.

"Could he possibly be any cooler?" Elliot asked Sally when he was sure Raymond could hear him.

"I'm the prince of cool, dick head," Raymond answered for Sally.

"He is, you know," she said.

"You two speckled agents seen enough?"

"For now." Elliot said, then, in a stage whisper, jerking a thumb at his partner, "Sally was feeling queasy."

"Don't even try it, green boy," Sally said.

Elliot noticed the young cowboys were also still hanging around, and were starting to look like the tired scared teens they were. "Has anybody contacted their parents?"

"We tried. No answer."

"I'm gonna send them home."

"Don't you want to talk to them?" Raymond asked.

"Yea, of course," Elliot said in mock indignance, "What am I an amateur?"

"You said it, not me."

"Don't make me kick your ass in front of my partner. I'm gonna get some initial impressions from them, then bring them in for a more in depth session when I'm rested, and they're more lucid. Look at them."

"They are looking kind of tired," Raymond agreed, "and speaking of tired, if you don't need me hanging around second guessing you, I'm going home. I'm going to go eat dinner and hug my kids."

"Do that, man. It was nice seeing you." Elliot turned to walk towards the teens.

"E.T.," Raymond called to his back.

"Yeah?"

"Give me a call sometime. We'll get together, do lunch or something."

Chapter Six

They started processing the scene at about two thirty, falling into a comfortably silent routine. For twelve hours they meticulously noted everything about the scene, from temperature and smells, to the lighting. Elliot photographed while Sally sketched every inch of the enclosed space. With quiet efficiency, Elliot held the tape end to each object in the room as Sally placed the other end against at least three fixed points in the area and called out the measurements. In this way, everything in the room, including the little boys' corpse, was triangulated and documented. Elliot and Sally understood that processing any crime scene, especially a homicide scene, marked the starting point of a journey that could take days, months, or even years. Even the most routine crime scene had to be handled with exact care, and this scene was far from routine. They noted every detail and documented them in such a way as to enable the scene to be reconstructed through words and pictures at a later date, almost exactly as found.

They marked every item they would need as evidence. Once they were finished, the Technicians from the Colorado

Bureau of Investigations (CBI), collected the evidence and prepared it for transport to the lab. Elliot knew how tedious that leg of the journey could be, and he was grateful for the CBI's assistance.

It was one thirty in the morning by the time the CBI techs placed the last piece of evidence, appropriately tagged and bagged, into a plain cardboard box. Elliot checked to make sure the list attached to the lid accurately reflected the evidence inside then watched as a technician sealed it with tape and put his initials on it. The coroner had already taken the body to the forensic pathologist, who would perform his own bit of alchemy to extract any clues about the boy's death.

Elliot and Sally felt and smelt like the walking dead themselves. Elliot wanted nothing more than to eat a three-egg omelet, wash it down with a beer, and sleep for a day. Neither he nor Sally had dressed to spend twelve hours underground. His engineer boots didn't breathe well and he was sure that once he released them from their bonds, his feet would express their dissatisfaction by smelling like bad corn snacks. Even his leather jacket was more fashionable than functional. Sally had it even worse. She was wearing a skirt. But at least her shoes were flats. Sally didn't do heels.

They were both rumpled and dirty. Elliot could smell himself, and his father had always told him, "by the time you can smell yourself, other folks have been smelling you for weeks." He could also smell Sally, sweat and something female, something… pheremonal.

Even once they were on the road heading south into the city with the dry Colorado evening wind blowing through the open window, Elliot imagined he could still smell death in the air. His mustache was holding onto the smell like a wool suit holds the smell of smoke. He decided the mustache would have to go before he ate anything.

Sally was feigning sleep again. Her skirt had shifted to the middle of her thigh. Elliot allowed himself a lecherous thought or two, then felt a flash of guilt that he could think about sex after processing a death scene.

He forced the guilt away, and went back to his fantasy. He wasn't the one who was dead.

Chapter Seven

Later, after he and Sally had dumped their gear at the office and crawled into their respective cars to go their separate ways, Elliot stared at his mustache-less face in his bathroom mirror, critically eyeing his upper lip and remembering why he'd grown a mustache in the first place.

Across town, Sally was giving herself a similar examination. She was looking in her bathroom mirror at the gray bags under her eyes, wondering when she'd grown old, and when she had forgotten how to enjoy life. She was thirty-one. Some days she felt ancient.

Her life had become inextricably tied to her job, and sometime during the past few years she had ceased to be Sally Dupree and had become Special Agent Dupree. She had recreated herself in the image of her profession and didn't know how to undo the damage.

She envied Elliot his duality, the way he seemed to be able to separate his professional life from his personal life. Not that his personal life was something to be envious of: he was divorced, lonely, and drunk most of his off duty time. But it was *his* time. He was able to leave the job behind and enjoy his life of microwave dinners, cheap dates, and network television.

It was almost three o'clock in the morning. Her husband, Dave, who Elliot would only refer to as her 'spousal unit', was sleeping noisily on their king size, extra firm (on account of Dave had a bad back) waterbed. She thought having an extra firm water bed was kind of an oxymoron, but Dave had insisted. Dave was a real estate agent, a good one, but being good had a price. Between the erratic hours she worked as an OSI special agent and the time he spent showing houses and closing deals, they only seemed to see each other in passing. The bad thing was she didn't really mind. They'd stopped connecting long before their careers got in the way.

She was naked, just about to take a shower. She examined herself in the full-length mirror behind the bathroom door. She allowed herself to take a brief inventory; Strawberry blonde hair, small breasts, thin waist, well proportioned legs leading up to wide hips, and what she had been told was a nice ass. She had childbearing hips, but she didn't think they would ever be put to that test. Her maternal instinct had atrophied by the time she was twenty-five, and neither she or Dave had time for children. She wasn't a nubile, young virgin anymore but she still had her good points. She tried a provocative pose in the mirror; back arched, breasts out, lips formed into a sensual O.

She heard a noise from the bedroom, Dave shifting around. She flushed red and stepped away from the mirror, thinking she must be the only person in the world who could embarrass herself when she was alone.

After her shower, she put on a flannel gown and crawled into bed with her still snoring spousal unit. She drifted off to sleep thinking about Elliot stealing peaks at her legs while she feigned sleep. She wondered what he was doing. Probably called up one of his bimbos.

Elliot Turner, saint and sinner; old school special agent, menace to the profession; it all depended on who you talked to. What face would he show her tomorrow?

Sally made it into the office the next morning, shortly after ten. She was bleary eyed and feeling guilty about not making it in by seven thirty - even though that would have given her only four hours sleep.

Elliot was already in. She automatically looked at her watch, figuring she was later than she thought. On his best days, Elliot seldom made it into the office by eight. She figured, after working well past midnight, he would milk the flextime until at least noon.

But here he was, wide awake and not looking hungover. It was too far from the norm to handle without a cup of coffee.

As if his mere presence at this hour wasn't enough, he had shaved off his mustache.

She stared at him incredulously, mouth agape. "My god man," she teased, "You have no upper lip."

"Bite me Dupree."

"I mean, Jesus, what kind of lips are those for a brother? Did you slice it off while you were shaving, or is it congenital?"

"I'm very proud of my lips, they're Turner family trademarks." He unconsciously rubbed his fingers over the naked space where his mustache used to be. He was very conscious of its absence, especially since his upper lip seemed unaccountably cold without it.

"Your *lip*, you mean you're proud of your *lip*, 'cause you only have one."

"You're feeling froggy this morning," he paused and looked her up and down, "Did you get some last night?"

"Not unless your talking about left over meatloaf. Why

are you here so early anyway? You tired of getting last pick of the donuts?"

"I'm just trying to make the world safe for democracy."

"You can start by firing your decorator." She said, casting a curious eye at the wall behind him.

"Oh, yeah," he said turning his attention back to the wall. "Look what the crime-scene fairy left us. The photo guys must have stayed up all night." Elliot had pictures of the crime scene tacked up on one wall in a grisly collage. He was practicing a brainstorming trick he'd learned from some cop movie. *Art imitates life, and life imitates art.*

He had a notebook in his hand and was free-associating, writing down ideas and images as they came to him. So far he had written:

Boy
Cannibalism
Patterned wounds
Semen
Ritual
No ligature marks
Petechia/suffocation? Strangulation?
No defense trauma
Victim drugged?
Tape
Lantern

"I talked to Tony Coleman from the FBI this morning. You know, that guy we met last year at that thing," He said closing his notebook. With cops and agents there was always a *thing;* some task force, seminar, convention, pistol shootout, or golf tournament. Even if you'd never met someone before, you could always say you had, at *that thing.*

"Yea, Tony from that thing," she said, nodding and smiling.

"Anyway," Elliot continued, "they've decided to let us run with the case. Of course, they're going to monitor the investigation, and they reserve the right to push us aside if they change their minds."

"Of course." Said Sally blandly. They both knew the FBI would run their own investigation independent of the OSI, and as soon as one of the agencies developed a good suspect they would push them completely aside.

"FBI's waiting for us to fax them a Violent Criminal Apprehension Program (VICAP) detail sheet. I told them I would fax it as soon as I had the medical examiner's report."

"VICAP is going to help us with a profile?"

"Uh huh, they figure this wasn't a one time good deal, and the killer's done it before."

Sally sighed and said, waving her hand in the direction of the photos, "Yeah, your garden variety murderer doesn't usually start off with that level of ritualistic mutilation on his first try."

"I figure the same thing but with a twist." Elliot grinned at Sally and twirled a pen around his fingers while he waited for her to take the bait.

"Ah, a genuine Elliot Turner twist, I've heard of them and always wanted to see one."

"Are you having jest at my expense? Cause I'd hate to have to slap you around."

"Promise?" She walked over to his desk and perched on the corner. She suspected Elliot was about to launch into one of his long sermons about a topic of acute interest to him, so she decided she better get comfortable for it.

Elliot turned serious, "I think this is one of my icemen.

I called Steve Drake, and he agrees. He's coming in to conduct cognitive interviews of the cowboys."

"Shit," Sally rolled her eyes heavenward and said, "There goes the neighborhood."

Steve Drake was the Regional Forensic Consultant (RFC). RFCs were the OSI's super sleuths. They kept agents in the field abreast of all the latest forensic toys available to support an investigation.

The OSI was a small organization and everybody seemed to know everybody, some in the biblical sense. Sally knew Drake well. She had dated him before she got married. She thought he was an asshole.

"You never told me what you had against Steve," Elliot said.

"He's an asshole."

"Is that all?"

"Isn't that enough?"

"Well...we go way back, so try to be nice."

"Way back, riiiight," she said. "I will if he will." Then, changing the subject, "What's up with this icemen thing?"

"It's a personal theory of mine. I haven't given it any thought in awhile. Actually, Drake and I used to get drunk and turn it into a kind of investigative hypothetical exercise. If you're interested, I'll dazzle you with my profiling acumen."

" Sure," Sally said. "I'm not doing anything but trying to solve one of the most horrible murders I've ever seen, but I haven't been dazzled in a while, so go ahead – knock my socks off." In spite her sarcasm, she noticed a gleam in Elliot's eyes that she could only translate as motivation and give-a-damn, and she wanted to hear what he had to say.

"You've heard most of this before," Elliot began. "So, just bear with me for a few minutes. Obviously, the accepted school of thought is that there are basically two serial killer food groups: the disorganized killer and the organized killer. The disorganized killers are, in scientific terms, crazier than shithouse rats. They are the guys who are directed by their dogs to kill all blondes, or redheads, or women who resemble Marilyn Monroe, or whose names began with the letter 'J.' They convince themselves they need to wear foil caps and eat spleens to make them immune to alien mind control rays. Luckily, disorganized killers are so fucked up they tend to get themselves out of the gene pool without protracted investigations. They leave neon trails of evidence, are often delusional, and once their psychosis finally takes total control of their feeble minds, they can't operate for long in regular society. More often than not, they end up wandering around the street, sporting their foil beanies, wielding a bloody knife, chewing on a mouth full of spleen, and spouting gibberish about the aforementioned space aliens."

Sally smiled despite herself. She knew all of this already, but she enjoyed Elliot's flare for descriptive absurdity.

"I'm not concerned with the disorganized killer, and I don't particularly care for the term 'organized'. I like to think of the majority of these freaks as regular guys with unusual fetishes," here Elliot speared her with his most professor-like gaze," or, in other words, "paraphiles." He made parenthesis in the air with his fingers.

Sally nodded gamely and fixed a look of genuine interest on her face to encourage him, not that he needed it.

"I, however," he said with a flourish, "prefer to think of them as regular guys with an unusual fetish. By no means does this make light of the heinous nature of their crimes, but I believe that labeling them with too much criminal profiling jargon causes the average investigator to look too far beyond the problem. They are fetish killers, they are sane, and, for the most part, well adjusted individuals. Somewhere along the line they acquired a taste for death, its smells, and textures, or the feeling of power they feel when stealing the life spark from another human being. But it's still just a fetish." Elliot paused here for dramatic effect before delivering his coup de grace with a certain amount of relish, "Some men like their women tall, some like them thin, some like them buxom, and *some*...like them dead."

"Wow." She said, making her eyes wide with wonder.

"Screw you, Dupree." Elliot continued undaunted, "The thing with fetishes is that the fetish target group is finite, and most people driven by a particular fetish are aggressively promiscuous within that target group. Variety is paramount. So, for the gent who favors lots of women with huge breasts, if he didn't travel around, the well-o-huge breasted babes would soon run dry."

"Really? There's a well-o-huge breasted babes out there?" Sally feigned incredulity.

"Yes," Elliot acknowledged reluctantly, "but you have to have a membership. Anyway, for those who like to kill, the killing fields quickly become too dangerous for the hunt; and they have to move on. But, whether you are a ladies' man or a fetish killer, the military offers the perfect lifestyle to help perfect the art of the hunt. On the average, Air Force personnel are reassigned every three to six years. Just like the incorrigible lounge lizards of the seventies who tried to choose occupations based on their chick appeal, fetish killers are drawn to the military for similar reasons. The military offers a structured lifestyle that almost guarantees a no cost change in hunting grounds every few years - with regular pay raises, and free medical/dental. Who could ask for anything more? And that," Elliot concluded, "is why I call my hypothetical, calculating killers, who join the military to travel and kill with impunity, "icemen".

"Hmmm, interesting...I can see your point." Sally conceded, "Now that you mention it, I read somewhere

Ted Bundy and Jeffrey Dahmer had some connection with the military."

"Exactly!" Elliot said, excited by her acknowledgement, " Bundy had ROTC, and Dahmer was in the Army for two years. However, Bundy and Dahmer, while categorized as organized, were not icemen in my book; at least not Dahmer. Bundy is debatable. Near the end, he may have wanted to get caught."

"You see," he continued, warming to his topic, "icemen are not delusional. They know what they are doing is wrong. They do not kill as a result of some deep-seated emotional trauma. They just like it. They don't want to get caught, and consequently, they aren't getting caught. But they must exist."

"Kind of like black holes." Sally said. "You only know they exist because of their effect on the space around them."

"I wouldn't know a black hole from my ass," Elliot goaded, then smiled.

"Why are you smiling?" Sally asked, already dreading the response.

"I was just thinking, now that I think about it, my ass actually *is* a black hole."

Sally didn't smile.

"You know," Elliot explained, on the verge of spinning off into a juvenile tangent about his backside, "because I'm..."

Sally cut him off. "I get the analogy, it's just not funny. Can we move on?"

"Okay," Elliot begrudgingly gave up his sophomoric train of thought, "I think the killer is a local or a GI, because he knew about the silos. My money is on him being a GI, because the term "local iceman" is an oxymoron. Icemen don't stay in one place long enough to become local. So,

I think were looking for a military member, who is in a position to know about the silos."

Sally grimaced. "Word of mouth being what it is, and young GI's being as adventurous as local teenagers, that narrows our search down to approximately every GI on the base."

"I didn't say it would be easy," Elliot said. He realized that he really wanted to solve this case. He'd forgotten what it felt like to actually care about a case. He had boxed himself into his ever-narrowing cynic's eye view of the world and had grown comfortable and secure in that box. His philosophy was simple; the world was basically fucked up. Shit happens in an imperfect, fucked up world. Sometimes, as an investigator, he was tasked to find out why it happened. Of course he knew why...it happened because the world was fucked up. He went through the motions anyway.

Maybe it was because this case fell in line with one of his personal theories. Maybe he needed an excuse to rise out of his slump; or maybe it was that shit shouldn't happen to a little kid, who hadn't collected enough karmic baggage to become a meaty plaything for some evil fuck head. Whatever. Sometime during the night Elliot's little chicken heart grew three sizes and he was starting to care again. He was surprised to find that he welcomed the feeling.

Chapter Eight

He blamed generation X (Didn't everybody?). Young recruits had no respect for authority, and discipline was non-existent. His service had become a corporation run by incompetent bureaucrats, and infiltrated by snot nosed youth who questioned authority just to get out of an honest day's work. He had been in the Air Force for thirty years and did not like what his service had become.

The Air Force had always had a reputation of being soft compared to the other branches of the military, and he was finding himself increasingly unable to champion his beloved Air Force's tarnished reputation without feeling like a hypocrite.

He was getting ready to retire, and he was afraid. But it wasn't just the anxiety of leaving a lifestyle that he loved and excelled at; he was afraid for the state of his Air Force. Each day he watched airmen change from soldiers into bureaucrats. Even the base he was currently assigned to was scheduled to be closed and become an "administration base" in about a year. Another example of the Clinton Administration's efforts to cut the deficit by closing military bases. The fact that he had been assigned to a dying airbase hadn't been lost on him. His war machine was becoming the war country club. But for all his dissatisfaction, military service was all he knew. He was going to be lost without it. The routine stress of military life kept his body strong and his mind focused. These days he was a desk monkey, a FAG (Former Action Guy). He ran an office instead of a field unit, but he was still required to make major decisions on a moment's notice. They weren't life or death decisions - at least not on duty - but they kept him sharp.

Some days he thought the killing was the only thing that kept him sane. The killing. How long had it been a part of his life? Twenty years? More? It was his only vice. A man could allow himself one or two vices. Couldn't he?

Sometimes, when he had a good one, reliving the event was almost as pleasurable as the real thing...almost. It seemed as if the pleasure increased exponentially each time he felt that delicious final quiver, as a body tried futilely to draw the life force back into itself. In the beginning it just felt good. Now it was nirvana. It was a wonder he managed to stay in control.

But he was always in control of himself and his surroundings. His apartments were always immaculate, a reflection of the ordered life he lived. A man needed to have control over his actions and his environment. He needed structure. Where there were no guidelines, there was anarchy. Sometimes, however, a man needed to let go and unwind.

He was unwinding right now. He had a lock of blonde hair in his right hand. He brought it to his nose while masturbating himself with the other hand. He could still smell the child, so clean, so pure, so trusting...definitely a good one. He could almost see the boy's pale skin, unblemished by age, without even the faintest trace of pre-adolescent hair.

The boy had been so calm, even bound at the hands and ankles. But he always did have a way with kids. When he took the tape off the boy's mouth, even though it must have hurt, he didn't cry out. He'd just looked at his tormentor sadly and asked innocently, "Are you going to hurt me mister? I'm tired of playing. Can I see my mommy?"

"Your mom, yeah," he had said distractedly, pawing himself and licking the boy's face, because licking the boy's face, somehow, seemed appropriately evil. "I think the bitch is better off without you."

Then he began the pressure. The boy started to cry, but there was no sound. With each breath he tried to take, his killer, like a boa constrictor, pressed down on his abdomen, using both hands and a small pillow that he had brought along for the occasion.

Tears streamed down the boy's face. His eyes were open wide, the fear and the pressure on his abdomen causing them to bulge from their sockets. But there was still no sound. His mouth opened and closed, opened and closed, like a fish out of water, trying to draw air into lungs that refused to inflate. Then even the mouth stopped moving. The body began to shudder as if in orgasm, and then it was still.

Now came the knife and the blood. Oh god the blood, so thick, so clean. He covered one of the larger wounds with his mouth, making love to it with his tongue, and then... the other thing. The wound was warm, and the blood was so sweet...

He had ejaculated in his pants while sucking on the wounds and then again on the body as he admired his work.

Now, he could feel himself cumming again, the semen landing on his bare thighs, warm and thick. He took some tissue from the nightstand and wiped the semen off of his pale muscular legs.

There were times when the logical career military man in him reminded him that the longer he continued with his sick pleasures, the more likely he was to get caught, but stopping was out of the question. How could he live without the blood? It made him feel alive. He wasn't insane. He was addicted. He acknowledged his addition like a chain-smoker or alcoholic. He knew his actions were horrible, his predilections perverse. But what was he supposed to do? It felt so good, and he was pretty sure there was no serial killers anonymous organization.

Of course now he had to deal with his own incompetence. In his haste to get on with his loathsome pleasure, he'd forgotten trash bags. How could he have forgotten to bring the trash bags? Well, he hadn't actually forgot them. He just didn't check to make sure he had enough left in the box. Imagine that. Over the years, disposal had become such a routine that he'd let himself grow complacent, and complacency bred mistakes. He made a mental note to make out a new checklist to standardize his kill kit, so that he could stay on task during his next excursion. Shit, he must be getting old.

He had killed, sodomized, and consumed the soft parts of a small child. The scene had been discovered. Any other person would probably be stressing out. He was fascinated to find he was enjoying the situation. He thrived on stress and had immediately assessed the current situation as survivable. He didn't waste time berating himself. He had simply made a mistake. He wouldn't make the same one again.

* * *

On his way back to the silo with trash bags and a diet soda, he'd spotted the sun glinting off the windshield of a truck. He was still easily half a mile out. He didn't know what to make of the reflection, but it was close enough to the silo to warrant caution. His instincts told him to proceed slowly, and he always listened to his instincts.

They called this area of the missile fields the flatlands, but they were far from flat. They were littered with small hillocks decorated with brown foliage. Natural land depressions, and gullies carved in abstract patterns by decades of flash floods, provided plenty of natural cover.

He found a gully deep enough to conceal his truck from prying eyes, parked the truck, and worked on figuring out the best course of action. He decided, before he jumped to conclusions, he should get a better look at what was going on. He was probably just being over cautious. He finished his soda, grabbed a flask of water and his binoculars from the truck, and took off at a slow jog in the direction of his silo.

He didn't think he had anything to worry about. The silo was well concealed. He wouldn't have been able to find it himself if he didn't have access to the civil engineer's surveyor's maps on the base. But there was no such monster as being too cautious.

When he was about three hundred yards out, he stopped running. He was at the base of a hillock, and knew from prior excursions and survey maps that his silo would be visible when he crested the hill.

Binoculars slung across his back, out of the way, he low crawled up the hill using his knees and elbows. The tan, stoney soil was covered with rough blades of buffalo grass and blue grama, making it an unforgiving landscape to crawl over. He was wearing khaki pants, combat boots, hat, and gloves, all in desert hue. He was confident that from the silo, if anyone were around, he would appear to be no more than a natural land formation. The sun was high and to his rear; low enough to blind anyone looking in his direction from the silo, but not so low as to silhouette him against the apex.

He was enjoying himself. He missed the subterfuge, the adrenaline, the spying. He'd always preferred the field to the office, and there were times when he regretted making rank as fast as he did. But he embraced the office life, and didn't run off to go camping and hunting, or to play paintball games like the other FAGs and survival freaks. He didn't want anyone to think him strange. Instead, he kept fit by running and playing racquetball like a good desk warrior.

Feeling nostalgic, he unhooked his binoculars and, making sure the lenses were properly hooded against any stray glare, he focused in on his silo.

He hadn't really expected to see anyone, but there they were. He'd watched the two young cowboys working on the slab. He was assailed by a host of questions. First and foremost, how did they find the silo? What were they trying to do? Had they seen him earlier? If so, is that what peaked their curiosity? They obviously recognized the entrance slab for what it was. Most of the local residents knew about the missile fields. They didn't seem to know about his maintenance shaft entrance. If they did, they wouldn't be trying to haul the primary slab away.

He had picked his silo, not just because it was segregated from the others. He'd also discovered that it had a number of easily accessible, small, maintenance shaft entrances buried under the dirt. The smaller entrances were about the size and shape of a manhole cover. They had all been welded shut.

The preferred silo access for the local teens and curiosity seekers were the main entrances, because they were visible from above ground. Four years back, he had spent three evenings, working with an acetylene torch, breaking the welds on two of the maintenance shaft entrances. He worked at night and in the early hours of the morning when he would have been least likely to be spotted by some stray patrol vehicle or curiosity seeker. If he had been approached and questioned, he would have passed himself off as another souvenir seeker. He completed his work unmolested, and had made sure to cover his private entrances with dirt and dead sagebrush. He hadn't been worried about anyone finding or tampering with the main entrance, because this complex was so far off the beaten path, and well concealed in a natural land depression. It was the perfect *sanctum sanctorum.*

Apparently, he had been wrong to assume the silo complex would be perfect. Nothing was perfect, even a silo as far out and well camouflaged as this one. Pity. The silos had offered one feature that he'd gotten plenty of use out of, the abandoned missile shaft. The missile shafts were well over two hundred feet deep. Years of flood run off had filled them with stagnant water. He couldn't remember how many bodies he'd dumped into the shaft over the past three years. Alas, the best laid plans of mice and men...

He had watched Darryl and Clayton; laughing, drinking beer, adjusting their tow rope, and whooping like a couple of rodeo riders as their truck lurched and bucked and spun its wheels, seeking some firmer purchase beneath the sandy top soil.

He considered his options: He could kill them. That would be fun. But, judging from their ages, they probably had families who would miss them if they weren't home by dinner. Then, by nightfall, every redneck in the area would be out here searching for them, maybe even before he had a chance to clean up. He could approach them as an authority figure, cop or ranger or something, point out that they were tampering with government property and shoo them away. That approach seemed feasible, but he hadn't packed any authority figure disguises; and if he pulled some half-assed ruse that they didn't buy, he would have shown them his face. At this juncture he was invisible.

The worst-case scenario was, they entered the silo-*why the hell did he leave the lantern on*-and found his chamber and the body. What was there to connect him to the scene? He'd left no fingerprints anywhere. Of that much, he was certain. There were bite marks and semen. With only semen, the cops had to know where to start looking, he was certain that his DNA wasn't on file anywhere. If he were actually caught they would have an open and shut case with the bite marks and the semen. But again, they would actually have to know where to start looking.

In the end, he decided his best option was to wait and see what developed. The best-case scenario was, the teens would exhibit the short attention span common to males of their age, tire of their game, and go away on their own accord.

No such luck. Darryl and Clayton hadn't gone away. They managed to drag the slab far enough across the opening to where there was a hole large enough to climb through. From his vantage, he had watched calmly, his mind working overtime, as they disappeared into the silo, armed with flashlights and beer.

Oh well, twenty years without a hitch was not a bad run. Hell, it was bound to happen. Things were so complicated in America. Snatch a kid in America, and it was a fucking national crisis. He knew people in Thailand, the Philippines, and South America, who he could call and have a kid delivered to his doorstep. No questions asked. C.O.D., don't bother to return them. If the child isn't there in thirty minutes or less, we'll take 50% off.

The cowboys were only inside for about thirty minutes. When they exited the silo, he looked for some indication they had discovered his chamber. He didn't need any of his formidable observation skills. They popped out of the silo visibly shaken and pale. One dropped to his knees by the entrance and spewed what was left of the six-pack he had for lunch. The other just stood by the truck as if in a daze. His partner joined him when he was finished retching, wiping vomit off of his chin. He watched their exchange. It was a panicky pantomime that reminded him of a silent film. It made him smile. The jig was up. Fancy that. They stopped talking suddenly, as if it occurred to them that the killer might still be around. They surveyed the area, 360 degrees, wearing expressions of open-mouthed fear. Their expressions reminded him of one of the old Abbott and Costello films; something like, 'Rednecks Meet the Mummy'. He laughed out loud.

They reached into their truck and each grabbed a rifle. The smaller cowboy also grabbed the microphone to their CB radio. Fuck. A radio, Who'd a'thunk it? They obviously weren't going anywhere now.

He packed his binoculars away, backed slowly down the hill; and chuckling to himself, jogged back to his truck. The game had just taken an unexpected turn. He didn't mind, it felt good to have a real problem to solve.

Obviously, he would have been content to continue pursuing his chosen form of self-gratification in complete anonymity, but shit happens. He had always prepared for this eventuality. In truth, having one of his playthings discovered before he could dispose of it and completely cover his tracks, was not worst-case scenario. Worst-case scenario would have been some unlucky person wandering in while he was violating a corpse. That would be a bad thing. This was survivable. All of his emergency protocols were in place.

Chapter Nine

"The Denver Police, missing persons unit just called. The boy's name is Josh Bennett," Elliot was talking to Sally and the commander, George Devine. Devine was taking notes. Devine always took notes when Elliot was speaking. Elliot thought he did it just to make him uncomfortable. It didn't. But Elliot was well aware that whatever he said could and would be used against him at a later date.

Some who had worked with Elliot thought he was one of the best agents they'd ever met. Some thought he was a bullshit artist, taking up valuable office space. Devine was part of the latter camp. The truth was, Elliot had been in the organization long enough to have been both super agent and problem child at one time or another. These days he was somewhere in between. He didn't know why Devine despised him so much, but was sure it would come out sooner or later. It always did.

"Why this kid anyway," Sally asked?

"That's the question, isn't it?" Elliot said. "The killer could have known the kid either through personal association or random extended stalking, but my gut tells me he came to the mall fully prepared to snatch any kid, and Josh drew the short straw. Either way he was well prepared.

Devine scratched something on his pad. The commander's dislike of Elliot didn't completely cloud his objectivity. He realized Elliot had had a number of high visibility, if bizarre, successes in the past. He didn't like Elliot. In fact, he thought it was downright creepy the way he sometimes seemed to know things. He'd tried to talk to Elliot about some of his past cases; but Elliot would just smile that creepy, holier than thou, superior smile of his and say, "some things can't be taught." What the fuck was that supposed to mean? He knew Elliot had killed a man in Idaho and that there was some controversy surrounding the killing. Whenever he queried headquarters on the subject of Elliot Turner, his call was routed to the OSI liaison office at the National Security Agency (NSA). The response was always the same - that was when he actually talked to a person as opposed to a voicemail; 'The Elliot Turner investigation was strictly need-to-know'. He would be contacted when and if he were needed. Well, from what he had seen, Elliot Turner was nothing special. He was just this guy; but he was lucky, and if any of that luck was going to shine on this case, Devine was damned sure not above basking in its glow.

"The mother," Elliot was saying, "is Anne Bennett. She lives at 2409, Havana Street, Apartment 14B. I know the area. It's the Oak Village Apartments. She filed a missing persons report on the 18th of March. That was a Tuesday, two days before the body was found. Classic scenario; She's out shopping in the Aurora Mall, turns her attention away from the kid to do a little window shopping and, bam. The kid's gone. She looks for him herself. When she doesn't find him. She reports it to the Denver Police Department. They probably don't work the missing persons report as aggressively as they could, because she's recently divorced. They figure the father could have snatched the kid, and they concentrate their efforts on him. Of course, when they find the father, he doesn't have the kid, and he has an iron clad alibi. Now they're back at square one, passing out pictures of the kid at the mall, and trying to find out if anyone saw anything. They're going to start running a 'crime stoppers' spot on the news this evening."

"Have you contacted the mother?" Devine asked.

"Done. She's coming in first thing tomorrow morning."

"Are you keeping the FBI in the loop?"

"Consider them looped, boss."

"Right now we're the primary agency," Devine said. "I would like it to stay that way even if we develop a good suspect."

"You mean when we develop a suspect. Right boss?" Elliot said.

"Whatever. If this shakes out well, I don't want the feds waltzing in here and taking the credit."

"You know," Elliot said. "I really don't care who gets the credit. I was just hoping we could catch the guy and fuck him up." Devine's eyes narrowed to slits, and he looked like he was going to say something. "Did I say 'Fuck him up?,'" Elliot asked innocently. "I meant catch him and bring him to justice." Elliot nodded seriously.

Elliot was one of the *get 'em* guys. Every law enforcement agency and police department had *get 'em* guys. At times the law was a slippery, amorphous, creature, hiding in a gray uncharted place where the boy scouts feared to tread, least they exit with their careers in tatters.

The *get 'em* guys were those cops who strode confidently through the gray areas with little or no concern for how they would come out. When they came out unscathed, they were heroes. If they were less than successful, they were an embarrassment, and sequestered away in some hole until the stench of their failure blew over.

Elliot lived his life by thinly veiled mysticism and fairy dust philosophies. He had an instinctive grasp of sub-culture and cult mentality. Elliot understood that human insight couldn't be found on the evening news. He embraced the fact that all men and women had an equal capacity for good and evil, and an equal capacity for understanding both. The dichotomy was the nature of the beast. He didn't try to fight it. He tried to live it. Ever the closet meta-physicist, Elliot believed a universe of understanding could be found on the head of a pin. Moreover, he knew he need look no further than himself to gain an understanding of human behavior, no matter how bizarre. One man sufficiently self-actualized, and able to objectively examine his own fears and motivations, could understand the fears and motivations of individuals never met. Most humans were loath to admit they actually understood the dark side of the human animal. It was almost as if admitting the understanding meant acknowledging their own darker nature. All humans were naturally empathic; but rather than admit to understanding their fellow man, they sequestered themselves behind walls of prejudice and lived in blissful ignorance of the primal human condition. They would rather die than walk a mile in another's shoes and admit to understanding what made their fellow homo sapiens tick. Conflict was preferable to compromise or understanding. People loved to say, *'I don't understand how he/she could do something like this or that.'* Elliot understood.

Elliot was widely respected as an undercover agent with an uncanny ability to infiltrate the tightest clique. Black, white, other, whether the target was a narcotics ring or black marketers, selling off government surplus, Elliot could be counted on to look inside himself, to examine the head of the pin and find uncomplicated social access to his criminal target. The path to justice was not always a straight line. However, he was quite comfortable walking the winding path with those engaged in criminal activity and ultimately bringing them to some semblance of justice. What made this man steal? What made this man kill? What made this man desert the profession of arms, and to where might he run? Elliot knew. Elliot had certain...skills. Elliot was the *get 'em guy* guru - until he got the wrong guy; and now he belonged to George Devine, but with ownership came the understanding that the boss would have to suffer a little insubordination.

Denver was Elliot's hole, not so much the area, as the position. Lowry AFB was in the process of being closed down with in the year, as part of the military's cost reduction program. Being assigned to a closing base was not a career enhancing assignment, but rather someplace to put the less useful members of the armed forces in order to get them from under foot. He was coming out of the not so glamorous world of undercover narcotics operations. He'd had a string of successful, and one not so successful, operation. Headquarters, and his last commander- still trying to get the stench of Elliot's last failure out of his reputation - decided George Devine was just the person to re-assimilate Elliot into mainstream OSI.

Devine was a mean-old-white-guy in training – apprentice to the OSI uni-mind. He knew about Elliot's reputation for doing the unorthodox, and he wanted no part of him. But he had no choice. He had the distasteful task of keeping Elliot on a short leash until Headquarters figured out what to do with him. Trying to train Elliot was not unlike trying to leash train a house cat. Elliot would chew his arm off before he conformed.

If Elliot was a *get em guy,* George Devine was a *weenie boy.* That was Elliot's private term for those timid conservative agents; who spent so much time pushing paper, planning, refining, and preparing for an infinite number of contingencies; so much so, that they invariably lost their window of opportunity. It was Elliot's personal philosophy that it was good to have a plan, but at some point you just had to act.

Elliot accepted the *weenie boys* as a necessary evil, one of those flaws that made the jewel of society so priceless. Lord knew he didn't want the job. Plus, as long as they stayed in their places, behind desks, in conference rooms, or playing with their computers, they weren't so hard to stomach. The problem was, they seemed to have a knack for getting themselves into positions of upper management. Once there, whatever spice they lacked as individuals, they tried to compensate for with their professional positions. Many of them sincerely thought they were in charge by divine right, and were imbued with competence by virtue of their position. When you tried to run what seemed to be a pretty good idea up the road to higher headquarters, it had to have sufficient momentum to make it over a *weenie boy* speed bump. Elliot referred to the speed bump level of management as the *bozone layer.* If Elliot was the *get 'em guy* guru; George Devine was lord of the *bozone layer.*

Chapter Ten

Elliot sat looking at 'The Mother', Anne Bennet, wondering how he was going to extract a detailed narrative of her son's life, and the events leading up to his untimely death, without seeming like an uncaring robot. It had been almost a week since Darryl Bartot and Clayton Taylor discovered Josh's body in the abandoned missile complex. Sally could have told him that he didn't have anything to worry about. He was one of the most caring investigators she had ever met. He just tried hard not to show it for some reason.

They were in the plush and narcissistic surroundings of the Commander's office. Devine had an I-Love-Me wall that was as oppressive as a shrine. It was a gaudy collection of degrees, certificates, plaques, and pictures, all paying homage to his favorite subject...himself.

Elliot couldn't use his own office to interview Anne Bennet, because he didn't think the pictures of her dead son tacked to his walls would go over well. But, he refused to take down his grisly mural. The pictures allowed him to re-visit the crime scene every morning. It was the first thing he saw when he walked into his office and the last thing he saw when he left for the evening. Each morning he hoped that some previously overlooked detail would jump out at him. He refused, however, to interview a woman, who had just lost her only child, in the austere confines of one of the interrogation rooms. Using the Commander's office was also Elliot's way of demonstrating to Devine that no agent was more important than the people they were sworn to protect; and if Devine got pissed off in the process, Elliot considered that a pleasant fringe benefit.

Anne Bennet was a brunette. She had olive skin, and a wide Mediterranean mouth. Josh must have inherited his blond hair from his father. She was pretty, but she didn't carry herself like she was aware of it. She wore a gray business suit, which was a half size too tight, but her upbringing had taught her that women in suits were taken seriously. She oozed vulnerability. That was her main attraction. Any man, upon seeing her, would want to shield and protect her, or maybe he was projecting his own knight-in-shining-armor complex. She would have been radiant if her features weren't drawn in grief. She had a faraway look in her eyes. Occasionally she would glance up at him, but she wasn't seeing him. Elliot knew she was remembering her son.

Sally was assisting him by taking notes. She was no more comfortable with interviewing the survivors of victims of violent crime than Elliot. No investigator was really comfortable with it. Sally was just no good with people. She wanted to be, but didn't have the touch. Elliot had the touch. He instinctively understood their fears and needs. Sally knew Elliot had a gift. More often than not, it was a gift he used to piss people off. However, when it came to interviewing victims, or anyone who had been kissed by tragedy, nobody did it better than Elliot.

For his part, Elliot was grateful, as always, for Sally's presence. Anne Bennet's grief was so palpable that it sat like a rock inside his gut. He knew he wouldn't be able to detach himself from her pain long enough to conduct a thorough interview. Sally had no such curse; and because she couldn't crawl inside a victim's head and feel their pain, she sometimes came across as uncaring. Elliot knew that wasn't the case. Sally was every bit as compassionate as he, but her emotions didn't get in the way of her professionalism. Her detachedness was her security blanket. He needed Sally around to keep him on track and ask the difficult questions, the questions he knew would reconstitute Anne Bennet's sorrow and render him useless for anything but comfort. Elliot knew Sally's underdeveloped bedside manner stemmed from a compelling need to rush victims through their grief and get to the heart of the story. The faster the victims got to the details, the faster the real investigation started and the more likely they were to bring the perpetrator to justice.

Anne was taking her time. It was almost as if she felt telling her story slowly would change the outcome. Elliot moved his chair closer to her, sensing she would find strength in his closeness.

Sally watched, envying his compassion. It was one of the things that attracted her to him. Usually he kept it well hidden.

Anne stopped talking. She'd come to the difficult part of her story and was waiting for grief to relax its hold on her throat. She closed her eyes tightly to stem the flow of tears, but some still managed to break free and run down her cheeks. She made no attempt to wipe them away. Elliot respected that. She had every right to her tears. The loss of her son wouldn't break her, but it would change her. The ordeal would make her hard around the edges, and her view of life would be jaded for years to come.

* * *

Anne could still see Josh clearly when she closed her eyes. She was wondering how her life had come to this. Was she a bad person? Had she been a tyrant in a previous life? Was it because of the divorce? Was she the victim of a vengeful Catholic god?

What kind of god would have had her stay with Josh senior? She'd only left him after finally deciding she could no longer tolerate his infidelities. The decision hadn't been easy, but the hurt was nowhere near as profound as she imagined it would be. She'd quickly found herself among the ever-growing ranks of single parents. But there was life after Josh senior. At least there had been. She hadn't curled up and died, at least she hadn't then.

If anything, after the divorce she'd felt revitalized. For the first time in her life she'd been in control of her own destiny. She and Josh had been moving on to new horizons and Josh senior could be damned. Hell, the way he carried on, he was probably damned already.

She remembered the night she left. Josh senior came home late that night. He was always late. Anne had stayed up late reading a romance novel and was feeling... amorous. She was eagerly, and a bit shamefully awaiting his return. She heard his keys in the door and got out of bed to greet him as he entered the bedroom. She was wearing a carefully selected negligee (red of course) that displayed her good points and dressed up her bad ones. Josh senior had been drinking. He was cranky, and smelled of cigarettes, sweat, and scotch. He also needed a shave.

At first when she'd hugged him and pressed her silk encased body next to his he resisted, complaining that he was tired. When she dropped to her knees and pressed her face against the front of his pants she could feel him growing interested.

If she hadn't been feeling so pathetically needy, and

hadn't been trying desperately to save her marriage the scene would have been comical: The young housewife in the faded red negligee, on her knees in front of her smelly, ex-jock, pig, of a husband, trying to blow some spice back into their marriage.

She undid his belt with her teeth (she'd read that men liked that sort of thing) and pulled his pants down around his ankles, which added to the overall absurdity of the scene. She pulled down his underwear, trying to ignore the track marks. Nothing could ruin a mood like thinking about scrubbing track marks out of smelly underwear. He was semi-hard already. She leaned forward, preparing to fellate him back into being a faithful husband.

The first thing she noticed was the smell, the smell of sex and latex. With his penis mere millimeters from her face she could see long blonde hairs wrapped around its base, contrasting with his dark pubic patch. Anne was a brunette. Not that it mattered. She hadn't been close enough to his manhood to leave her own hair there in a long time.

She left her body for a moment, and was able to look as an outsider upon the scene unfolding before her. She saw a not unattractive woman (carrying some extra pounds, but nothing a month of aerobics couldn't fix) on her knees in front of an oafish, bore, of a man well past his prime. She was on her knees getting ready to wrap her lips around a penis decorated with another woman's hair. Shit, she was on her knees, like he was an object to be worshipped.

She thought about doing a Lorena Bobbitt on him. Instead, she stood up and took a step backwards. She returned to herself, and in front of her stood a fat man; back against the bedroom door, sporting a fading look of lust and wilting tumescence.

She laughed at the absurdity of it all. Then she cried at the absurdity of it all. She went to a closet and pulled out a suitcase. Behind her the fat man stumbled through a litany of apologies, and excuses as flaccid as he had become. She had ignored him and continued to pack and heal.

She took Josh and returned to her childhood home in Denver.

In the months that followed her leaving Josh senior, she learned to love being a mother again. She and Josh had been inseparable. Josh didn't exhibit any of his father's pig-like tendencies. He was friendly and inquisitive, gentle and trusting. He had all the traits that should have led to a happy and productive childhood. Instead they lead to his death. He would have been a good man. She should have instilled in him a healthier distrust of strangers.

Now her world was dark and empty, and filled with sorrows, and strangers who said they wanted to help her. How silly of them to think they could help. Were they gods? Could they bring her son back to her?

Everyone was so very understanding. They were understanding when they said they would do everything they could to find her son. They were understanding when they said they may have found her son, and he wasn't alive. They were understanding when they lead her to the viewing room. They were understanding when she identified her son, laid out on an efficient looking metal table, draped in an efficient white shroud. What a contrast to the colorful sheets in his bedroom. She was so proud to have found a job allowing her to afford the two-bedroom apartment and to decorate Josh's room with all his favorite cartoon characters. Oh, but they were so understanding and efficient.

There was an understanding Doctor with a fucking understanding look on his face, all ready to sedate her when her chest locked up, and her stomach grew tight, and her legs refused to support her weight. He had held her while grief forced the bile from her belly. Lucky her, she hadn't eaten breakfast, wasn't sure if she'd ever be hungry again. He had stroked her hair and said he understood, and everything would be all right. Well...Josh was everything, and he most definitely was not all right. He would never be *all right* again. They understood nothing.

Josh senior had flown in from Phoenix and efficiently handled the funeral arrangements. Always the passive aggressive sadist, he'd gently reminded her that, if she hadn't left him, Josh would still be alive.

Then there was this strange one, this strange black man with the haunted eyes that betrayed the tough guy facade he tried to project. Were those tears? He didn't seem efficient, but she felt inexplicably that "he" understood. Only he didn't seem to know what to do with the understanding. He felt her sorrow, but didn't seem to realize that simply understanding-really understanding-was enough.

Elliot handed Anne a tissue. When she accepted it, he rested his hand gently on her shoulder. Anne grasped his hand and squeezed, acknowledging the gesture, showing she knew he understood. Sally watched and felt an irrational twinge of jealously.

Elliot let Anne ramble on, not wanting to interrupt the natural flow of her memory. This was the hard part. By remembering events leading up to Josh's disappearance, she would also be thinking of a thousand things she could have done differently to prevent the abduction. Elliot noted she only talked about 'the abduction'. She didn't address the fact that Josh was eventually found dead. It was too soon for her to let him be dead.

Elliot glanced over at Sally, who was also trying to look sympathetic, but was only managing to look pained. Anne had been rambling on about what a good little kid Josh was; and Sally was beginning to fidget, twirling her pencil between her fingers. Elliot said a silent prayer that she wouldn't say something like, *"I understand he was a swell kid, but could we skip ahead to the moment when you realized he'd been snatched?"*

"Take your time," Elliot said to Anne. "Tell me again about the mall."

"I don't know what you're looking for," Anne said.

"Me neither," said Elliot almost sadly. "But I'll know it when I hear it."

"Okay," she said, looking into his eyes. They were dark brown and rimmed with lashes that she suddenly noticed were very lush and thick. She suddenly realized she didn't want to look away from his eyes: they seemed to pull her in, and she wanted to be pulled in. "Okay," she repeated, "I believe you will."

She sat up straight and composed herself. She had repeated her story so much, now she spoke by rote, "Josh was abducted on the 18th. It was Tuesday. I do secretarial work for a temporary employment agency, which is good for me because temp jobs are compatible with my hours. I'm going back to college. But I was off that Tuesday.

"Josh had a doctor's appointment-allergies. After we left the doctor's office, I took him to the mall for lunch and ice cream. We ate at the Scarborough Tavern. It's not really a tavern. They have a bar and everything; but during the day it's pretty much a family place, and they have sundaes."

"Do you remember what your server looked like?" Elliot asked.

"Not really, young girl, silly hat. All the waiters and waitresses wear these silly looking jester caps. Josh loved them..." She paused, and Elliot thought he was going to lose her again.

"Do you remember her name?" Elliot asked.

"No."

"After lunch what did you do?"

"We went to the big toy store in the mall. Not the one with all the commercials, but the other one."

"Jack and Jill's?"

"Jack and Jill's. That's its name. I bought Josh one of those robot action figures from that cartoon, Robo Warriors 5000. He'd been bugging me about one for weeks," she smiled. "I'm glad the last thing I did for him made him happy," she said misty but still composed.

"Did you talk to anyone in the mall?" Elliot asked.

"Yes, strangers were always coming up and telling me what a beautiful little boy Josh was, but no one really stands out."

"Any men?"

"No."

"Then?" Elliot prodded gently.

"I figured I'd do something for me for a change. You know?" She asked, clearly needing his acceptance.

"I know. Sometimes you have to treat yourself." Elliot said.

"We walked around the mall for awhile. Then I went into 'Leslie's'.

"The women's clothing store?"

"Yes, there's one of those four sided mall benches outside of the store with a fountain in the middle. Josh would have been bored sitting outside of a dressing room waiting for me, so I set him on the side of the bench facing the store. I could see him from just about anywhere in the store, and he could see me. Even if I couldn't see him, Josh isn't...wasn't the type of kid to just wander off.

"I found some things I liked and wanted to try on. The sales lady said she would keep an eye on Josh while I was in the dressing room.

"I went into the dressing room. The saleslady must have got busy with another customer, because when I came out, she was ringing up someone on the register. I didn't see Josh on the bench, so I put the clothes on the counter by the cash register and went to get him. I figured he got caught up playing with his toy and moved to the side of the bench facing away from the store. But he wasn't there.

"I looked for him for about thirty minutes. Then I went to the mall security office. They looked for him until the mall closed. I can't tell you how hard it was to leave the mall without him.

"After the mall closed that evening at about nine o'clock, I went to the police station-the one on West Colfax. I filled out a missing persons report then went home. I didn't sleep much. I really haven't slept much since."

"Could his father have snaa...uh, abducted him?" Sally asked. "Were there custody issues?" Josh senior had an alibi and wasn't a suspect, but Sally wanted to re-visit Anne's thoughts on the subject.

Anne gave a very unladylike snort. "His father...?" She said, as if it was the most preposterous idea. "His father doesn't care about him. He hasn't made any attempt to talk to him since the divorce. Hell, I've only talked to him twice this past year, and he only asked about Josh once."

"Have you dated since the divorce?" Sally asked.

"Just to the movies two or three times," and then she added almost shyly, "nothing serious or sexual, and Josh never saw any of my dates. I always dropped him off at a friend's place."

"Is there anyone, a relative maybe, who Josh would have recognized as safe?"

"No. Just his father; but truthfully, Josh recognized everyone as safe. He was the most trusting kid you ever met. I killed him by being naive, didn't I?" She started crying again.

"No." Elliot said, probably a little more vehemently than

necessary. "You raised a loving child, and an evil man took him from you. You couldn't have predicted it, and it's not your fault."

"If not mine, whose?" Anne asked under her breath, not intending Elliot or Sally to hear.

"Someone who we're going to catch and...bring to justice," Elliot said, as much to himself as to Anne. Both Sally and Anne noticed his eyes had clouded over.

Chapter Eleven

More death. Elliot sighed. At least this setting was more clinical, and as such, marginally more tolerable than a stagnant room at the bowels of the earth.

The pathologist's lab was everything it should be; sterile, organized, smelling of antiseptic and...potpourri?

"Gives the place a little ambiance, don't you think," the pathologist, Brent Sheldon, asked, seeing Elliot sniffing the air.

"Yea, ambiance," Elliot said. "Completely takes my mind of the guy with his guts hanging out on the table behind you."

"Oh, him," Brent said absently, "Drive-by."

"Oh." Elliot said, "but of course."

"Hey, Sally!" Brent said as if noticing her for the first time.

"Hey, Brent. What's up?" She wasn't as squeamish as Elliot. Both she and Elliot were wearing white, paper, lab coats; but Sally had pulled on a pair of surgical gloves and was walking around the dissection table poking about. "Look at this," she said, pointing at the penis of the cadaver.

"What?" Brent asked, thinking she was going to make some insightful investigative observation.

"Its just like a real penis, but smaller." She grinned. Brent blushed; and Elliot noticed, not for the first time, how young the pathologist looked. It seemed he was getting older, and everybody else was getting younger.

"Don't touch that," Elliot said to Sally. "You don't know where it's been. You got the report on the Bennet kid," he asked Brent.

"Bennet kid?"

"Yea, Josh Bennet. That's his name," Elliot said. "You working on any other dead kids for me?"

Brent walked over to a gray metal desk in the corner of his office. It was just like the one that had been Josh Bennet's not so final resting-place. Jesus, Elliot thought; who makes those fucking ugly gray desks, and what makes the government want to buy them. Was there some kind of rule against buying furniture that looked nice?

There was a stack of files on the desk. Brent pulled one from the center without looking. "This was a tough one to read," Brent said, smiling. "I actually had to do some research."

"I'm sure he was honored to provide you with the challenge," Elliot said bitterly. "We talked to his mom this morning. I bet she'd be tickled too."

Brent looked at Sally. "He's on the rag today. Ain't he?"

"Yeah, well...You know," Sally shrugged.

"Anyway, come here." He motioned Elliot and Sally over to the desk. He moved aside a half-full coffee cup, and a partially eaten donut so he could spread out some pictures from the file.

"I'm sure you noticed the petechiae on the face and

in the eyes." Brent said, rummaging through the pictures looking for a close-up. He found one and handed to Elliot.

"Thanks," Elliot said, "but I have my own." He didn't take the picture. Sally took it and studied it as if she hadn't been looking at similar pictures everyday when she walked into their office where Elliot's collage still decorated the office walls.

""Petechiae," Brent continued, "but no other indication of suffocation or strangulation; no edema, no ligature marks, no pharyngeal or hyoid bruising. When I opened him up, I noticed there were also petechiae on the walls of the abdominal cavity." He went back to his file, looking for autopsy pictures of the abdominal cavity. This time Elliot took the pictures. Sally studied them over his shoulder.

"Do you see them?" Brent asked.

"Yes," Elliot said. The pictures were 5 x 7 inches, color glossies of very good quality. Elliot could clearly see the pin-prick hemorrhages concentrated on both sides of the abdominal sack where small capillaries had burst as if under some central pressure. "Okay," Elliot deadpanned, "You're the man. You're so smart. You're a genius. What's it mean?"

"You ever hear the term burking?" Brent asked.

"Burking, as in 'to burk'?" Elliot asked. "No."

"I've heard of it." Sally said.

"Okay, you're smart too," Elliot said. "What is it?"

"I think it means squeezing the air out of someone. Is that it?" She asked Brent.

"Exactly," Brent said. "It was named after a Swedish guy, William Burke. During the 1800s, Burke perfected the art of-like you said-squeezing the air out of people. He needed a relatively non-traumatic way to kill people so he could sell pristine cadavers to the medical schools. Apparently, he worked with an assistant. They would get the victim drunk then take him to some secluded spot. The assistant would hold the victim down; and Burke would sit on his solar plexus, keeping the diaphragm compressed so the victim couldn't draw a breath."

"So the kid was squished?" Elliot said, genuinely impressed.

"Burked," Sally corrected.

"Whatever," Elliot said, "You've got to be an evil motherfucker to have a type of killing named after you. How long would it take to burk someone?"

"Not having burked anyone recently, I couldn't say." Brent said.

"You know, you're a very funny, for a guy who cuts people open for a living."

"I try."

"What about the cuts?" Sally asked.

"The cuts were just kind of there." Brent said.

"Another clinical term *just kind of there.*" Elliot said. "You are a real Doctor, aren't you?"

"You know what I mean," Brent said. "Outside of the pattern, there was nothing particularly noteworthy about them. There were five cuts in all. They were each about an inch long and a quarter inch deep. The boy was probably freshly dead when they were made, because there is indication of anti-mortem pooling, but not the flow you would expect from a living wound. None of the cuts were deep enough to be life threatening. I swabbed the area around the cuts and sent the swabs up to the lab. The results, as well as the toxicology report should be done by the end of the week. Oh, there was also a sticky substance on the face."

"More semen?" Elliot asked.

"No, it was tacky like glue, probably from tape, we'll know at the end of the week."

"You do good work," Elliot said, "I don't care what Sally says about you."

"You know, semen isn't that sticky," Sally said.

"Well, I guess you're the expert," Elliot said.

She ignored him.

"Anything else?" Brent asked.

"You forgetting something?" Sally asked.

"Oh, the bites, how could I forget them?"

"Well, I can see how that could happen," Elliot said with more than a trace of sarcasm.

"Anyway, " Brent continued, "We swabbed all of the bites, some of them were pretty deep, and we had plenty of saliva. We'll have no problem with DNA."

"Can I get a copy of your report?" Elliot asked.

"Come by tomorrow. Bring cash," Brent said grinning.

"How 'bout a check."

"From a federal agent? You must be kidding. Oh, one last thing," Brent's face turned somber, "The bites were made anti-mortem. He wanted the boy to suffer. I don't want to tell you how to do your job, but you may want to catch this sick fuck sooner than later."

"Right," Elliot said, "Take a memo. Make the horrible case a priority. Anything else?"

"Just catch him, man," Brent said.

For the first time, Elliot saw a crack in the young pathologist's game face. He walked over and gave the young pathologist a gentle man-squeeze on the shoulder. "We're on it," he said, but he didn't feel particularly "on."

Chapter Twelve

He was wearing one of his favorite hunting outfits, penny loafers, polyester action slacks (a little too high), white socks and a plaid polyester shirt (open at the collar showing the white T-shirt underneath). He had on his military glasses; the Buddy Holly style everyone called "birth control glasses". There was a bulge in his pants...the pocket. It was the tie he would have worn to work, but had taken off to seem more casual. He hadn't actually worn the tie. It was just one of those many little details he prided himself on. Attention to detail; nothing done half-assed ever amounted to anything. He had a jacket balled up in on of his hands and fidgeted with it as if trying to find the most nonchalant way to carry the unnecessary burden. Whether hunting deer, or rabbits, or humans, it was essential to have the right clothes for the job, *clothes made the man.* The hand inside the jacket held a nasty looking knife with a wide flat blade. For only $29.95, it was just what the discerning huntsman needed to complete his ensemble. The knife was used for skinning large game animals. *The right tool for the job.* He thought of the outfit as his Joe-average-white-guy-waiting-to-be-a-victim look.

He was in one of the low rent neighborhoods off of West Colfax Avenue in Denver. These neighborhoods reminded him of some of the barrios in the Philippines, or depressed areas in any number of third world or developing countries. He was the bait and he'd just hooked himself a meal (figuratively speaking...kind of).

He had caught the attention of someone lurking in the shadows of the urine-perfumed foyer of a housing project that had never been new. He hoped it was a young thug. Most of the street criminals seemed to be very young these days. They just weren't living long enough to become full-grown menaces to society. The young tough in the shadows was no exception. He coughed into his hand to stifle an involuntary chuckle. There was nothing like a green apple, plucked from the tree of life while hard and sour. Here was one who wasn't going to have the opportunity to ripen and become a skilled blemish on the ass of American society. Hunting in these areas was nothing like snatching a tasty suburban pup. This was more like weeding the undesirables from the herd.

The green apple was Alonso Procter. He was sixteen years old. He was angry. He was watching his prey. An easy mark: a white dude, middle age, didn't walk like a cop. Ugly eyeglasses, high-water pants, white socks...white socks? He deserved whatever he got. He looked like a first time John looking for some pussy. First time Johns had first time John money. If he was looking for a girl he was in the wrong part of town. Alonso shook his head: Fucking out of touch pervert, figured just because the neighborhood was poor and black there would be a *ho* on every corner. Well, John, looks like you the only one getting fucked tonight. He put his hand inside his pocket, emboldened by the feel of the

9mm he'd "borrowed" from one of his girlfriend's father's sock drawer.

Alonso was pretty. That's why he was angry. It was his curse. He looked younger than his sixteen years. His caramel skin was smooth and unblemished. His eyes were hazel and dreamy. He had full sensual lips and curly brown hair. If he were dressed in drag, he would be an exotic beauty with heart stopping looks, a 'Crying Game' candidate. He wasn't comfortable with his condition and would have gladly swapped it for a more menacing visage. He had no shortage of girlfriends-probably had more than his share. He was overcompensating to prove his masculinity-but the boys in the hood were still merciless in their persecution. With his mind he knew it was jealously. With his emotions, the taunts of "pretty boy" and "Miss thang" gave him ugly homicidal thoughts. Deep down he hoped them homicidal thoughts would harden his angelic countenance, maybe make him look a little more like an evil angel and less like a faggot.

He was about to take his first step towards self-improvement. He hoped. If he earned himself a reputation for fucking people up, the taunts would eventually die down. People would say, "Don't mess with Alonso. You know that white dude who got fucked up on Lincoln Street, behind the Quick Mart...? He did that." If the guy had money, that would be good, but mainly, Alonso just wanted to start causing mayhem so he could get on with his life.

There was little to no traffic at this time of the evening, just a stray car here and there. Alonso and the unfortunate white guy seemed to be the only ones out on the street. Of course, the streets were actually teeming with life, the homeless and the forgotten, hunkered down in the putrid depths of any number of alleys and abandoned buildings. Alonso followed his mark, trying to stay about half a block behind. He was waiting for him to get to Hamilton Street. There was an alley there where he could jack him in peace.

At the corner of Hamilton Street, the man stopped, giving Alonso time to catch up. He looked around as if he wasn't quite sure where a civilized gentleman with discriminating taste might find a *ho.* There was a working streetlight on the corner. He was confident-even at this deserted hour-whatever the junior thug was planning, he would not try anything in the light.

Alonso sensed his victim was conscious of his presence and decided that continuing the stealth act would be conspicuous. He walked boldly up to the light and met the unlucky John's hesitant gaze with his own smooth, steely, criminal glare (which he'd been practicing in the mirror).

The killer was momentarily taken aback. Not by the smooth, steely, criminal glare-although it was impressive. At first he thought his would be robber was a young woman, dressed in baggy pants, big shirt and football jacket. He quickly realized his green apple was just an incredibly beautiful young man, as beautiful as any he had taken in Thailand or the Philippines. He felt the beginnings of a painful erection. The blood lust was dancing around in his head in delightful abandon. This was a bad night to be an incredibly beautiful young man. The gods were smiling on him tonight.

When he'd started this hunt, he had planned on a quick thrill kill to relieve some work frustration (sometimes he did that). Suddenly, his evening plans had begun to take on new and creative dimensions. When the gods tossed you a bone, you had to make bone soup.

"Hey, you okay?" Alonso growled. His steely gaze had scared this motherfucker speechless. The bitch was flushed with fear. Alonso almost felt sorry for him. Almost.

"Yes, I'm okay," he managed. "I seem to be lost."

"Bad night to be lost, motherfucker." Alonso pulled back his shirt flap to reveal the purloined 9mm, and a smooth muscled midriff.

"I don't have much money on me," he stammered, not feeling the least bit threatened, and finding it terribly erotic the way his green apple thrust his little pelvis out to display his weapon. He added quickly "If you promise not to hurt me, I have more cash in my car." He could tell from the look in Alonso's eye and the thrust of his chin that the kid actually meant to cause him harm. *Isn't that special? They're so cute at that age.* He coughed into his hand, concealing a grin. He hadn't been much older than Alonso when he'd killed his first man for god and country. *I would have been his first,* he thought. *Well I'm proud and honored to have almost been a part of such a major step in your life.*

Although Alonso's primary mission was senseless violence, only a fool would overlook the easy money aspect of the operation. Anyway, he was feeling fearless; and while he knew spending too much time with someone you were going to fuck up was dangerous, no old white guy was going go try anything on him. Plus, this guy wasn't much bigger than him, and Alonso had the gun.

The hunter was parked in an alley six blocks away. He was driving one of his unmarked hunting vehicles. He had two. This one was an old model, beige, rusting, Crown Victoria. The other was a truck. He drove neither to work during the day. No one had ever seen them...and lived. They were not registered in his name.

They walked leisurely back down the street towards the alley. The street was still deserted, and the area was far from being well lit. Anyone passing on the road would pay them no attention. He walked slightly ahead of his tormentor and managed to look nervous. Alonso was confident, almost cocky. He was secure in the fact that he was in control of the situation. Every few yards Alonso would nudge him a little, just a reminder that he was still there. It wasn't necessary. He was acutely aware of Alonso's presence just off of his right hip. His senses were firing out of control. He could feel Alonso's breath. He imagined he could also hear his heartbeat. He could definitely hear his own heart fluttering excitedly, and he marveled that he was able to maintain his control and not force Alonso into the nearest alley for the quickie kill that had been his original goal. A man was nothing without self-control.

By the time they arrived at the car. He was breathing heavy, and Alonso could see the beads of sweat forming on his brow and the nape of his neck. Alonso hoped the old fuck didn't have a heart attack before he kicked his ass. He had no way of knowing that his prey had been running at least five miles every weekday morning for more mornings that Alonso had been alive. He wasn't much taller than Alonso, and had always been slight of build, but he was a machine. Beneath his polyester hunting clothes was the lean body of a career soldier. Not a bureaucrat who fancied himself a military man, but an old school snake eater still full of piss and vinegar and killer instinct.

He'd spent his formative years in the Air Force as a combat controller. High altitude, low off, first in, last out, no support; He knew caution but he didn't know fear.

Motherfucker was so scared he was about to shit his pants. Alonso nudged him towards the car. He fumbled with his keys. He dropped them; and then quickly, nervously, knelt down on one knee to pick them up. The car disappointed Alonso. He was hoping for a newer model, figuring he would take the car and the money. It was a late model four-door sedan of indeterminate make or model. It looked like a cop car, painted beige or gold. Alonso couldn't tell in the light. It had rust everywhere. At least it had tinted windows. That was cool.

The hunter retrieved his keys and stood up, smiling sheepishly, self consciously brushing off his pants. He opened the driver's side door, and climbed inside, feet and butt sticking out comically. Alonso laughed. "Back out real easy motherfucker. I don't wanna hav'ta bust a cap in your ass." He was thinking about pistol-whipping this motherfucker like the cops in the movies.

He eased himself out of the car. It wasn't' easy because he was using both hands to hold on to a wad of bills, which had been stuffed in his glove compartment.

"I don't know how much is there," he said. "I keep some cash around for emergencies."

"Like you're driving down the street, and suddenly got to get your dick sucked. Right? You can't fool me motherfucker. You were out looking for a bitch. Well, you're in the wrong neighborhood. Ain't no bitches selling pussy in this neighborhood. Only thing you find is this." Alonso quickly took the gun out of his coat pocket. His hand was steady. The sudden movement startled his intended victim, who dropped the money. Alonso looked down. The hunter struck quickly. He had been standing directly in front of Alonso. He stepped to Alonso's left. As he did so, he reached out with his left hand, grabbing, twisting, and breaking Alonso's right wrist. Even before the gun, which had been in Alonso's right hand, hit the ground; or Alonso's scream of pain and surprise had a chance to escape his delicate lips, her chopped down, closed fist, on the side of the youth's neck. The blow simultaneously broke Alonso's collarbone and rendered him unconscious by compressing the brachial and carotid nerves.

Sloppy. He hadn't meant to do that much damage; at least not so soon. Alonso was on the ground, writhing, and semi-conscious. There was a high-pitched keening sound coming from the back of his throat. He sounded like a little girl; hurt and mewling like a trapped and tired animal, which was definitely a turn on. He crawled quickly back into the car-not looking so comical this time-and retrieved a roll of duct tape from the glove box. He wrapped the duct tape around Alonso's head, three times around, covering his mouth and chin, cutting off the keening sound. Alonso looked like he was wearing a metal mask that started just under his nose. Alonso was breathing rapidly now, snot bubbles running out of his nose over the mask of duct tape.

He worked methodically, no wasted movement. He taped Alonso's arms together, assessing the wrist damage, taping the arms at the elbows down to the wrists, so the good arm served as both restraint and splint. Then he reached down and with the finesse of a rodeo cowboy wrapped a length of tape around Alonso's ankles, binding his legs together. He bundled Alonso into the back seat. Alonso's eyes had cleared. They were looking at his captor. They were full of terror and pain. He'd wet himself. His would be victim now looked ten feet tall. He met Alonso's eyes with his own eyes clouded by lust. He remembered a line from a movie, that seemed to fit the situation; "You know," he drawled in his best back woods accent, "I hadn't really noticed it before, but boy..." he paused and licked his lips. "You sure do have a purty mouth. Looks like I found me a bitch after all." He unconsciously reached down and adjusted his crotch, where his briefs were unsuccessfully trying to bind a painful erection.

Alonso knew he was already dead.

He secured Alonso's limp body on the back seat with the seat belts, and scanned the area around the car for anything he might have dropped. He didn't want to be on of those guys who left his driver's license or something at the scene of a crime.

On his way back to the warehouse apartment, while stopped at a red light on east Colfax Avenue, a hooker tapped on his window.

"You want a date?" She asked when he cracked his window.

"No thanks," he said politely. "I already have one."

Chapter Thirteen

Sally hadn't slept well. She'd had a fight with her spousal unit the previous evening, and now she was feeling cranky, and hormonal. She was in a men-are-pigs kind of mood. She was having a rare moment when she wasn't looking forward to her complicated relationship with her partner, at least without first downing a cup of coffee.

When Sally walked into the office, her partner was not at his desk. She'd seen his car outside, so he had to be somewhere. She wondered around the building, looking in the usual places: the kitchen and the coffee pot, Devine's office, and the men's bathroom. Finally, she peeked into the conference room.

Spread out on the conference room table were various articles of women's clothing; bra, black stockings, shoes, skirt and blouse. All the clothes smelled like smoke, beer, sweat, and shame, as if someone had spent an evening of heavy activity; dancing, drinking, and general debauchery. Before the clothes were shipped out to the lab, they had to be air dried to prevent any perishable fluid evidence from putrefying during transit.

Elliot was standing next to the table, holding a pair of dingy panties mere fractions of an inch from his face. He was inhaling deeply, his eyes closed.

"What the fuck are you doing?" Sally was incredulous, the cup of coffee forgotten. Elliot started and dropped the panties onto the table. He smiled at her, not the least bit guilty.

"I'm helping Jerry with his rape case."

"And how is violating a defenseless pair of panties helping Jerry's case?"

Elliot rolled his eye, "Amateur. You can tell a lot from the smell of a victim's panties. You should try it sometime."

"Who is the victim?" Sally asked.

"Actually, it was one of Jerry's informants. He's in the interview room with Fred taking a statement from her."

"Oh, Jerry," Sally said. Jerry Fleming wasn't a bad guy. He was just investigatively challenged. Nothing ever seemed to go right for him. If one of his informants was raped, it would undoubtedly be as a result of a Jerry Fleming fuck-up. "What's the scenario?" She asked.

"She was targeting a low level marijuana dealer. The guy was supposed to be having a party. So, Jerry sent her in to check it out," Elliot said.

"So far so good. What's the catch?" There was always a catch or snag or bit of blatant oversight with Jerry.

"When she got to the party, she found out she was the main attraction. There were no other females there. She has a reputation for being promiscuous, border line nymphomaniac with a terrible case of slut-itus; and she's about as smart as a box of hair. Dealer figured he would get her high, put some drinks in her and have her service his friends. Which, apparently, she gladly did."

"Where's the rape come in?"

"Well," Elliot perched on the edge of the conference

table, "now she's worried about being pregnant." He looked down at the pile of clothes and a stillness stole over him. All the bravado and devil-may-care melted away from him. Sally thought she had never seen him look so peaceful. When he spoke, his voice was steady and clear, "That and she doesn't want Jerry to find out that she's been stealing his money to buy marijuana and the occasional gram of cocaine. Last night, she discovered that the neighborhood weed dealer had managed to score some grade-A coke, and she just couldn't resist. She blew the whole wad that Jerry gave her, snorted the coke, then tried to earn the money back by screwing his friends." Elliot looked up and smiled, the old Elliot was back. "Jerry briefed the JAG and the he thinks there's a case here."

"And why would our illustrious Judge Advocate General think there's a case?"

"Because, she hasn't admitted to what she did yet, and she says she was too fucked up liquor and rock and roll to know what she was doing. And as we all know, if you have sex with a woman, and you know she's too fucked up to think coherently, it's rape," he said, with a flourish of his hands, as if to say *viola*.

"Well, if she hasn't admitted that yet, I presume you found some remarkably incriminating evidence in this well worn pile of clothes that tell the whole sordid tale." She took a long sip of coffee. It was putrid, and tasted like decades of scorched coffee grounds.

"No, other than a semen stain or two, I haven't found anything concrete, but it seems like the obvious explanation."

Sally nodded, typical Elliot to pull something like that out of his ass. "Fair enough, but what's that got to do with you sniffing her panties?"

"You can tell a lot about a girl from the smell of her

panties. In her case, she was ovulating, and had a lot of garlic for dinner."

Sally recognized when Elliot had gone back to bullshitting her. She decided to just roll with it. Usually, when he went off on a tangent, it amused the shit out of her. "You know, I ovulate a lot and like garlic, too, but that doesn't make me a candidate for rape; it just makes me a little bitchy and a lot smelly."

Elliot nodded in silent agreement with her assessment of the effect ovulation had on her. He went on, "No, but combine that with the fact that she is a borderline nymphomaniac and you've got yourself a recipe for disaster. Between the dope and the ovulation, she was probably more interested in procreation than recreation – and she certainly wasn't focusing on the task at hand: collecting evidence for Jerry to use against the bad guys. Basically, she was in heat. There is no case here. Once she finds out she's not pregnant - and she's not - and when she sees all of the legal crap she's gonna have to put up with; she' gonna fess up."

"You can tell all that from smelling her panties? So, now you have super senses or something, like that guy on TV?"

"No, nothing like that. My senses are no better than any person off the street. But sometimes smells and tastes and textures help me to get a feel for a situation." Elliot smiled and took another whiff of the panties. Elliot closed his eyes and tilted his head back in thought as if he were at a wine tasting. His senses were immediately infused with the smell of musk and smoke...garlic...and something more primal. Among other things, Elliot was a sensualist. Physical sensations, taste, smell, touch, awakened his perceptions. Elliot used his senses the way Pavarotti used his voice, or Tiger Woods used a putter. He embraced the world. He drank it in. He ate it, smelled it, and rubbed it on his body. The resulting by-product of his sensualism was that he'd developed a keen memory for sensation over the years. He recognized tastes and smells, textures, and sounds. He knew what the air looked and smelled like before rain or snow. He could smell when a person was angry or afraid. He could feel when a jury was getting ready to turn left or right. "Hey, isn't garlic a natural aphrodisiac, how ironic is that?" He smiled.

"Why is everything sexual with you?" Sally asked.

"It's not all sexual. We just happen to be talking about a rape case. It involves sexual stuff; and let's face it 70 percent of what we do is sexual, but that's another conversation."

"A rape isn't sex."

"Whatever."

Jerry Flemming walked out of the interview room with his informant, the victim, in tow. Elliot hid her panties behind his back.

"Morning Jerry," he said. "What's happening?"

"Guess you heard," he said to Sally.

"Yea, tough break," Sally said, looking at the informant; about 5' 2", brown hair, oozing eighteen year old sexuality.

"We have to take a potty break," she said, and giggled. "I had spaghetti with lots of garlic in it last night. I love garlic, but it makes my tummy icky." She touched her stomach, which was bare. She was wearing a half-shirt and jeans shorts. Her belly button was pierced. Elliot could still smell alcohol coming from her pores. She giggled again and then followed Jerry out of the conference room, heading for the bathroom.

Sally rolled her eyes. She suddenly felt the need to fill the ensuing silence, but really didn't want to talk about this case anymore. "Let start tagging and bagging this stuff, shall we?"

"Sounds good to me, but leave the bags open for now, some of these things aren't dry yet, and even though they can dry in the paper bags, if they're still too damp, they can mildew or rot and ruin anything evidentiary, just in case I'm wrong." Elliot smiled. He and Sally started filling out evidence cards and attaching them to brown paper bags. They worked in a comfortable silence, each knowing what to do as they handed one another evidence, bags and tags. They were nearly done when Jerry walked back in the room, rubbing his bald head which Sally thought looked alarmingly red.

"What's up Jer?" Elliot asked, putting down his black, government-issue pen. He looked at Sally and she thought she saw the beginnings of a smug smile.

Jerry sighed, and put his hand on his hips and stared hard at the ground. He was dressed in Jerry business casual: short sleeved, stripped shirt with brown dockers. He started pacing.

"She just admitted she wasn't raped. The little bitch has been stealing my money and using it to buy drugs."

Elliot tried hard, but failed, to look surpised. "Well, isn't that what she's supposed to do with it?"

Jerry shot him a dirty look, "Yes, but she's not supposed to *use* the drugs. Anyway, she went to the party, snorted a bunch of coke and willingly participated in group sex. She just said she was raped when she realized she had neither drugs nor money to give me after the party."

Sally glanced at Elliot and raised her eyebrow. "That sucks, Jer. Sorry to hear it." She shoved the bag of "evidence" she had been working on away from her and stood up.

"Now I've got to explain all of this to the JAG…and Devine."

"I don't envy you there, buddy." Elliot said, in his most sympathetic voice.

"Yeah, thanks." Jerry turned and stomped out of the room.

Sally regarded Elliot, "That's a pretty good bit of deductive reasoning, there, partner. Actually, it was a very accurate guess, panty sniffing not-with-standing. So what is it? You got the ESP or something?"

Elliot fidgeted uncomfortably. He couldn't tell if she was being serious or not. He decided to just go for it and see how she took it. "Sometimes I know what people are feeling. Sometimes I can almost feel what people are thinking. It's hard to explain, and sometimes I get these feelings of déjà vu, but they're more than that. I kind of...almost...might have ESP, sometimes."

There, he'd said it. He watched her face to see how she would react.

"Um hmm...", Sally remained carefully neutral.

"When I get that feeling, like I've been here or done that, I can hang onto it for a couple of minutes or a few seconds, predict what's going to happen one or two minutes after that 'been-there-done-that-feeling.' It's worthless most of the time. Like, if you're sitting on your ass watching TV – something I've been known to do - thirty-seconds or two minutes into the future, you're probably still going to be sitting on your ass. So, who cares? But if that feeling strikes while you're getting ready to kick a door in, it could save your life. The telepathy, for lack of a better word, works better with people I know well, and I usually have to be near them. Even then it's still like a weak radio signal. Sometimes it's clear, but usually it is barely perceptible. Emotions are different. I feel them strong."

Sally was actually shocked that he was telling her this: she hadn't really expected him to share. She wasn't certain how to respond, but she wanted to remain open and not shut him off.

As she struggled for an appropriate response, Elliot tried to connect with her emotions, but he had never been able to read her, which was not unusual; some folks were just "closed" to him. After an uncomfortable moment of silence, he plowed ahead, "If it makes you feel better, forget the whole thing. It's mostly useless anyway."

She grinned lopsidedly, trying to break the tension, "Well, this just shows what a loser you are. If I had that kind of ability, I'd live at the casinos. Surely you could use this ability to get filthy rich?"

Elliot appreciated what she was trying to do and decided to accept her face saving gesture, "Actually, I do make a killing at the casinos, but I blow it all on booze and dirty magazines."

"Ha! Figures. Let's go solve some crime." she said. Even though she had taken it in stride, her expression was guarded, and Elliot knew things had changed between them. They always did.

Chapter Fourteen

The cognitive interview was a relatively new technique in law enforcement; but in the short time since its inception, it had proven to be more accurate and reliable than forensic hypnosis. The theory behind cognitive interviewing was simple and sound and Elliot, being a connoisseur of all things off the beaten path, had been following the technique for years. He was well read on the subject and had the opportunity to practice it on fellow investigators at a recent law enforcement seminar. It was no substitute for the real thing, but he thought he could handle a session without adult supervision if he had to.

During the cognitive interview, the interviewer helped the witness recall in vivid detail a specific block of time. It was similar to hypnosis in that the interviewee entered into an almost trance like state, but the cognitive interview trance was nowhere near as deep as forensic hypnosis. The witness was guided through the past event by the interviewer who walked him slowly through the process. The interviewer helped him to recall everything that may have happened during that block of time; not just the event itself, but unrelated thoughts, smells, feelings, etc. Pertinent witness observations often attached themselves to those unrelated memories and feelings. Elliot thought it was just the coolest shit.

During their initial interviews both Darryl Bartot and Clayton Taylor recalled seeing a handful of cars on the road leading to the missile fields, and fewer still meandering around the silo area. Nothing unusual, no particular colors, styles, or license plates had fixed in either of their minds. Elliot suspected that their own names probably didn't fix in their minds on any given day. He didn't delude himself into believing anything would come of the interviews; but he didn't want to write off any potential lead, no matter how unlikely.

While he was toying with the idea of conducting the interviews himself, Sally-always the voice of reason-talked him into waiting for Steve Drake, the Regional Forensic Consultant. Sally convinced him that- no matter how confident he felt- he should get someone who had more than just textbook knowledge of the technique to conduct the interview. Sally had issues with Steve Drake, but his competence wasn't one of them. Elliot also knew and respected Drake, so he didn't need much convincing.

True to form, shortly after Elliot decided to call Drake, the Commander, George Devine, wandered into his office.

"E.T. we need to talk." The commander never said, "Hello Elliot", or "Can we talk?" or anything that might be construed as a pleasantry.

"Don't tell me," Sally said, "You found his upper lip, right?"

"What?" Devine blinked at her. Then furrowed his brow, frowned, and ignored her. Anything that did not compute simply got ignored.

"Never mind." Sally said.

"E.T. I just wanted to tell you that if you have any half-baked idea about interviewing Darryl Bartot or Clayton Taylor without an RFC, you'll be explaining to headquarters on your way out the door about how you decided to promote yourself to forensic consultant and ruined this case."

"Well," Elliot said, "if you feel that strongly about it, I'll call him immediately."

"Do that." Devine turned and walked out the door, satisfied at having put Elliot in his place once again.

Elliot watched him leave, thinking that George Devine lived in a strange, sad, little world.

* * *

They decided to interview Darryl first because he seemed like the brains of the pair. He chewed tobacco, and wore cowboy boots, jeans, and had the obligatory big shiny brass belt buckle; but Elliot's redneck meter wasn't pegging. Darryl seemed to have a little depth behind his eyes. He was now waiting patiently in the lobby.

The only thing that kept the OSI waiting room/lobby from looking like the waiting room of the average dentist's office was the two inch thick bulletproof one-way mirror in front of the reception desk. The organization had paid a small fortune for the bullet proof mirror and then set it into a wall that wouldn't have stopped a flying spit ball. The walls were covered in soothing sky blue wallpaper. They were decorated with multi-colored, abstract prints, of tasteful design, donated by someone's wife a few years back. There were two dark blue sofas, which went impeccably with the wallpaper. The sofas were covered in some corduroy fabric with a zigzag design that, for some inexplicable reason, felt really nice to run your hands across. There was a coffee table in front of one of the couches with the latest editions of popular news, entertainment, and hunting magazines, donated by the agents in the office (in the men's bathroom there was a collection of old girlie magazines, also donated by the agents in the office).

Darryl Bartot was sitting on one of the couches reading a hunting magazine, absently running a hand over the fabric on the arm of the couch and feeling much better than any man should feel while caressing furniture. Every now and again he would pause to spit tobacco into a soda can. Elliot was on the other side of the one-way mirror watching him. The fact that he was reading comforted Elliot. Although, Elliot thought, chewing tobacco was a fairly disgusting habit.

He'd had a partner who chewed tobacco. Both he and his partner had preferred the same brand of diet soda. After almost having one disgustingly unfortunate incident, Elliot trained himself to always look twice before he reached for an open can of soda, even if he was certain it belonged to him. It had been years since he'd picked up that soda can, still warm with spittle and tobacco, feeling as if there were something alive and gooey inside. He still hadn't kicked the habit of always looking twice.

Darryl was seventeen years old and enjoying his fifteen minutes of fame. He and Clayton had been on the news the night they discovered the body. The Channel 6-news chick, who was even sexier in real life, had interviewed them. He felt like a cop by association. The whole experience already had him thinking about applying to the police academy when he graduated high school. He figured he was going to have to get used to seeing dead people and all; but for the most part, he thought he would enjoy the job. He'd always been distrustful of cops-cowboy generation "why" was still generation "why" and inherently distrustful of authority-but everyone he met had been cool, even that black guy, although there was something about him that didn't seem quite…natural. None of the cops had laughed at him-at least not to his face-or chastised him for puking. His old man would have called him a pussy.

Elliot meandered back to his office where the RFC, Steve Drake, was reviewing the Bennet file, preparing for the interview. He stopped at the Commander's door. Devine was on the phone, back towards Elliot, bitching about something. Elliot gave his back the universal 'you're number 1' sign and continued on.

Elliot respected Steve Drake. They had been in the same class at the OSI Academy and had actually managed to stay in touch over the years. Drake had been well respected as a street agent and had gone on to become a forensic consultant. Their successes on the streets almost mirrored one another, but while Elliot's methods were sometimes violent, erratic, and always strange, Drake operated in a bubble of detached efficiency that Elliot found enviable. Steve Drake had class and culture, and he carried it well. Elliot was a jeans man. Drake was *Armani.* Elliot drank beer. Drake sipped on well-aged scotch. Drake was classy but not pompous, and Elliot liked him.

Drake set the Bennet file aside when Elliot walked into the room. "Good work so far." He said.

"Um." Elliot perched on the edge of his desk and picked up a small bag of Cheeto's, tore it open and began to crunch loudly.

"Gonna tell me what happened in Idaho?"

"No."

"You still sane?" Drake asked.

"Reasonably." Elliot said.

"I guess it doesn't matter," Drake said. "You wouldn't be the first agent to go functionally insane." He picked up the Bennet file. "You think this bit of nastiness is one of your icemen, huh?"

"I'm hoping it is and hoping it's not?"

"You might be right." He opened the file and pulled out a picture. "Guys a real fucking sicko."

"Is that a clinical term?" Elliot smiled.

"No. I think the clinical term is something like *personus sick phukus.*"

Sally rushed into the office. She looked like she had something to tell Elliot. She saw Drake and stopped short. She said to Elliot, "Let's talk later." She gave Drake a perfunctory nod, turned and walked out.

"Nice ass," Drake said. "I don't think she likes me anymore."

"Don't hate her because she's astute." Elliot said around a mouth full of cruncy, salty goodness. He stopped chewing. "Wait, did you say 'anymore'?"

"Yeah, you know we used to date?"

"You and Sally?" Elliot asked, looking momentarily surprised before a lecherous grin spread across his face. "What happened? And don't spare any of the gory details, I can handle it, I'm a professional."

Drake laughed, "Nothing happened. We dated, and then we stopped ," he paused, "and then it got awkward."

"Oh, well, that explains it." Elliot turned his attention back to his cheetos.

"Explains what?"

"Why she hates you. I'd hate you too if we'd been dating, and then you dumped me unceremoniously with no explanation because I got too serious and you couldn't handle it."

Drakes smile stayed fixed on his face, as if he was trying hard not to let it drop.

"I thought you didn't know what happened." Drake said, mildly.

Elliot carefully chewed and swallowed before answering.

If he had been paying more attention to the conversation, and less attention to his Cheetos, he would have been more careful about blurting out the thought that had popped into his head: the very clear realization of exactly what had happened between Drake and Sally, which he had mistaken for one of his own thoughts. He understood now it hadn't been his thought at all. Elliot put on his best shit eating grin, his safest 'awe shucks' demeanor.

"Hey, man, don't hate me because I'm a good guesser, and you're such a predictable loser."

Drake's smile relaxed into something more natural, "Hey, not speaking of Sally...I didn't realize George Devine was the Commander here. What's it like to work for one of the golden boys?"

"Fuck George Devine," Elliot said.

"That good, huh?"

"He's an android," Elliot said. "No guts. No creativity. No instincts. He sincerely believes there's only one right way to do everything and everything else is wrong. One way! As opposed to the hundreds of different possibilities that you and I take for granted."

"You said 'You and I'. I'm glad you think I've got guts and instinct. I'll sleep better tonight."

Elliot ignored the sarcasm. "He's got none of the things that separate technically proficient investigators from great agents."

"Like us, right?" Drake asked smiling.

"You know what I mean. He's so concerned with looking good for the politicians, that he'll either slow me down or get someone killed."

"Don't you think you're being melodramatic?" Drake asked.

"No. I don't. I've been there. Melodrama is for amateurs and rookies. I'm telling you like it is. Someday, when I'm king, I'm going to round up all the androids in this fucking agency and unplug their asses."

"You done?" Drake asked.

"For now, but I'm sure I'll find something to tirade about later."

"What happened in Idaho?"

Elliot ignored the question.

"Whatever. When I'm done with the cowboy let's go get a beverage or two."

"Fucking A. Let's shall," Elliot said in a fair British accent. "You can tell me all about the fair maiden Sally Dupree, and what you did to make her hate you."

"It's not like that at all," Drake said.

Chapter Fifteen

The OSI didn't use the word interrogation because it had such negative connotations. It was a benign bit of political correctness that started long before political correctness was *chic*'. The organization was well aware of its 'big brother' stigma and tried to stay neutral and objective in thought and deed. Being the bastard spawn from the unholy union of military and civilian bureaucracies, the OSI had a centuries old pool of euphemistic jargon from which to extract the appropriate verbiage to disguise its deeds.

Unclear talk was so inherent in the organization that it was used even when its actions and motives weren't questionable. OSI Agents didn't shoot to kill; they shot to stop, making sure to hit the center of the thoracic cavity (and then one to the head if the aforementioned 'stopping' was not achieved). They didn't interrogate; they interviewed. However, a respectable percentage of weaker willed suspects killed themselves or enrolled in therapy after the experience. They didn't coerce or blackmail or manipulate; they found a common commitment that helped identify a person's self esteem orientation, and focused him/her towards the mission goals (Elliot preferred to think of this process as *punking out some loser for the greater good*). Whatever you wanted to call it; the OSI could definitely hold its own with any other government acronym when it came to mind-fucking someone into submission. Actually the men and women of the OSI were mind-fuck masters and proud of it.

The interrogation (interview) room was usually in mind-fuck configuration, one small chair and a table for an assistant interviewer to take notes, and two equally uncomfortable chairs, facing one another, one for the lead interviewer, and one for the interviewee. The room had been re-configured for the cognitive interview. They'd moved out the assistant's table and chair and put in a comfortable leather easy chair (taken from the Commander's office at Elliot's insistence). This left one small chair in the room for Drake, positioned on the right side of the easy chair near Darryl's shoulder, from where he would guide the process. The room was now in mind-fuck-light configuration. The interview was being audio and video taped, but Elliot would still observe and take notes from behind another one-way mirror.

* * *

Darryl's cognitive interview was actually going better than they expected. He turned out to be a pliable subject, quick to slip into the relaxed almost trance-like condition desirable for the interview.

Darryl explained he and Clayton went roaming the flatlands almost every weekend. Most of the time they were alone, but sometimes they brought their girlfriends. They always brought beer and guns. Elliot felt a chill at the thought of the two teenagers, armed to the teeth, drinking driving, and raising hell out in the flatlands. It was an American tragedy waiting to happen. Because it was spring break they had been out roaming on a Thursday.

The day they found Josh Bennet's body, they were sans girlfriends but had beer and guns aplenty. They each had their own .22 caliber rifles; and Clayton, in addition to his Dad's truck, had also absconded with his father's .45-caliber automatic. At 17, both Clayton and Darryl, like so many young men living in the mid-western United States, were skilled marksmen and seasoned hunters. With their rifles, they figured they could bag some small game. The .45 was to practice blowing apart whatever random shit they could think of. They had planned on making it a late evening, dressing and cooking whatever small game they found, drinking beer and bonding; just a couple of cowboys on the open plains, living out their wonder years in blissful ignorance of the evil that had taken root in their playground.

On the day they found Josh Bennet's body, Clayton and Darryl had both mentioned seeing other trucks out in the silo area; but nothing stuck in their minds. Elliot hoped the cognitive interview would bring out some detail about the vehicles they'd seen. So far they had nothing. At the very least they might be able to identify other adventurers who might have seen something that day. Elliot made a mental note to contact Channel 6 news and have them add the fact that they were looking for anyone who might have been in the missile fields that day to the crime stoppers spot.

Elliot and Drake had already agreed that the perpetrator would probably be driving a truck, either a pick-up with a shell or a sport utility vehicle. It would be something that would blend into the area, nothing flashy. They crossed their fingers hoping Darryl would remember such a vehicle. They weren't disappointed.

"How are you doing, Darryl?" Drake was asking. Drake was wearing his glasses. He usually wore contact lenses. Elliot thought the glasses made him look like Darryl's psychiatrist, especially with the way the room was set up. Drake had a legal pad of his own and was taking notes. Couldn't have to many fucking notes, Elliot thought.

"I'm doing just fine sir. I like this chair," Darryl said.

"You were telling me about the jack rabbit you saw," Drake said.

"Yessir, biggest fucking rabbit you ever saw. Looked like a kangaroo. I mean, I never saw a kangaroo in real life; but I bet it would look almost the same. Anyway that fucker was taking off to our right like there was no tomorrow, but I had him lined up. I was leading him just a little. You ever eat rabbit, Mr. Drake? Taste like chicken." Darryl laughed. Drake smiled. "Then Clayton hits this ditch. Man, I thought I was going to drop the gun out of the fucking window. I banged my elbow on the door pretty bad, and we stopped to take a look at it and have some lunch."

"What did you have for lunch?"

"I had a ham sandwich and a juice box. We try to bring a little something to eat just in case we don't bag anything. Good thing to."

The conversation went on like that for about an hour, just a couple of good ole boys hanging out, with Drake wandering patiently through Darryl's memory, asking a question now and then to pull out details as they rose to the surface. In the observation room, Elliot had stopped taking notes and was trying to throw a pencil and make it stick into the soft soundproof tiles on the opposite wall. He was getting pretty good at it. After he grew tired of that game he found something interesting in his nose. He was working at it with a fingernail when Sally walked in.

"Oh, that's attractive," she said.

"Want some?" Elliot asked still digging.

"No thanks. I just ate."

"Your loss," he said, extracting his finger and wiping something on his pants.

"You know," she said, "if you're not self conscious about doing that in front of me, we spend far to much time together."

"Doing what?" Elliot asked.

"Forget about it...How are we doing in there?" She asked, pointing at Drake through the glass.

" 'We' are fucking boring me to death," Elliot said. "By the way, how come you never told me you dated Steve Drake?"

"It's ancient history. You never asked."

"Does he have any weird bedroom habits that I could bust his balls about?."

"I'd never tell you, Jesus! What kind of question is that?"

"It's a partner question. We're going out for drinks after this thing. Do you want to come?" Elliot asked.

"Ooh, drinks with my asshole ex-boyfriend and my semi-telepathic, psycho partner...How could a girl resist?"

"Hey," Elliot put his finger to his lips, and said in pig Latin, "icksne on the elepathicte talk."

Suddenly... "Oh shit, Oh shit, O shit," Darryl said from the other room. "There was something." "What do you see?" Drake asked calmly.

"A big brown fucking truck, like a suburban or something. Yeah, it was a suburban, a beige one. I caught it out of the corner of my eye while we were working on the slab. I remember thinking it was going to come all the way over to us. We thought it might be one of the Fish and Wildlife rangers, and we were going to get in trouble. But it turned off the road while it was a ways out. Shit, I'd forgot all about that. It didn't seem important."

"Everything is important," Drake said. "Did you see it again?"

"No, and after that we managed to open up the silo. You know what happened after that." Darryl said.

"I know, but let's run through it again," Drake said.

Chapter Sixteen

Lots of purple neon, subdued lighting, clientele' that ranged from cyber-punk to boots and leather; the "Zenith" bar could best be described as an alternative, techno, biker bar.

"Nice place," Drake said to Elliot, while eyeing up a pale waif with expensive looking breasts, wearing (and wearing well) a black leather mini-skirt, with black lipstick and sporting a fashionable nose ring connected to one of the five in her left ear. "You come here often?" Drake asked Elliot. He was shouting to be heard over the music, which sounded like it used to be rock and roll.

"It's not much," Elliot shouted, "but it's home."

"Is it always this smoky in here?" Drake shouted, his voice cracking.

"Yeah, I love that."

"But you don't smoke."

"I'm addicted to second hand smoke."

"Next time I pick the bar," Sally shouted. "I keep expecting to see Han Solo."

"Don't knock it until you try it," Elliot said, surveying

the room affectionately. "These are some of the most non-judgmental, open minded folks you'll ever meet."

"Yeah," Drake said. "It's hard to be holier-than-thou when you've got pierced genitalia."

"Live a little," Elliot said. "One night with that one," he pointed at the pale waif in the mini, "and your yuppie days would be over. She'd cure you of your *Armani* habit forever. What are you guys drinking?"

"Scotch, Glen Fiddich if they have it," Drake said.

"I'll have a white wine spritzer," Sally said.

"Shhh," Elliot put his finger to his lips and looked conspiratorially to his right and left. "They'll kill you for that kind of yuppie speak in here." He waved the bartender over. "Hey, Greg..."

"Elliot Turner," The bartender, Greg, said recognizing him. "What's it been, about a week? How's Tammie?"

"Sadly, no longer a part of my life. But what a ride." Tammie. Twenty-two years old and dumb as a rock. Elliot found an x-rated memory clip and scrolled leisurely through it while Drake and Sally tried to think up acceptable drinks.

"What can I get you folks?" Greg asked.

"Three of your finest glasses of brown liquor," Elliot said; and to Sally, "And I know what you're thinking, but Tammie wasn't a bimbo. She was free spirited."

Sally frowned, "Actually, that wasn't what I was thinking."

Their drinks came. Elliot raised his glass. "I want to make a toast," he said. "Since I've been know to drink to excess, I should probably say a little something now while I'm sober and lucid. I heard this somewhere and always wanted to say it to my friends: "May the best of your past be the worst of your future."

They touched glasses. "Greg," Elliot called over the din of bar, "Keep 'em coming. We're going to stay for awhile."

"By the way," Drake said. "Exactly what are we drinking, what is this brown liquor?"

"It's the cheapest rail bourbon money can buy, or maybe it's corn whiskey with brown food-coloring. I'm not really sure, but you'll get used to it, and maybe even learn to love it. I plan to wake up tomorrow smelling of cigarettes, this deliciously cheap bourbon and shame. I hope you can join me for part of the ride."

Elliot was sitting between Sally and Drake at the bar. Now he moved his stool back from the bar so he could address them both. "Okay, we're going to be a three person team for the next few weeks or months. So this is our obligatory bonding session. You know, clear the air, group hug thing, and maybe the beer gods will enlighten us about our case."

"We don't really have to hug you, do we?" Drake asked.

"Only if you feel you have to," Said Elliot. "Keeping your distance won't break my heart. Speaking of hugging; the fact that you two kids used to an item, bumping uglies, making the two headed monster, doing the horizontal mamb..."

"Elliot..." Sally said.

"I acknowledge the menace in your tone, and I digress." Elliot said. "My question is: Is your past going to affect how we work as a team?"

"It didn't' then, and it won't now," Drake said.

"Ditto," Sally said. "He's an asshole, but he knows his shit."

"And I can't think of any other lesbian I'd rather work with," said Drake.

"Fuck you!"

"I love you both, man; and it's not the booze talking," Elliot said, swiping at a non-existent tear. "Greg," he called, "another round for me and my yuppie friends."

An hour later all three were considerably more relaxed. They had switched to beer, and Drake and Sally agreed that the Zenith was a lot more palatable after a few drinks.

"You guys ever watch the nature channel on cable?" Elliot asked, slurring a little.

"I love that nature shit, man." Drake slurred.

"Yeah, nature is awesome," Sally agreed.

"Anyway," Elliot said. "I was watching the nature channel and they were having like a special spider edition." He managed to say "special spider edition" without slurring it, which was no small feat after numerous shots of brown liquor. "Then they started talking about these banana spiders, and it pissed me off."

"I can see how that would happen: banana spiders piss everyone off," Drake said, taking a large gulp of beer.

"Well, they were talking about how the banana spider is probably the most dangerous spider in the world."

"And..." Sally was used to these types of conversations from Elliot, even when he was sober. He'd get to his point eventually.

"Well," Elliot said. "Do you think they could have given the most dangerous spider in the world a more innocuous name? That's just what I would expect from a bureaucrat scientist."

Drake asked, "What would you have them call it?"

"Calling it a banana spider implies...I don't know, that it eats bananas or something. They should call it 'The Most Dangerous Fucking Spider In The World, With-A-Yellow-Spot-On-Its-Back.' He looked at Drake and Sally. "You see?"

Sally laughed, "You've got a point – that is a much more accurate description."

"Exactly! The scientists and bureaucrats never call things what they are, no matter how dangerous. They prefer to be cryptic and misleading. Case in point: Our killer." Sally was beginning to get some glimmer of what Elliot was getting at, but she decided not to interrupt. "Our guy is a banana spider," Elliot continued, "the most dangerous spider in the world. We call him an organized serial killer or a homicidal paraphile, but he still has basic spider needs, and can be squashed like a regular spider."

"I'm sure I don't follow you," Drake said.

Elliot to Drake: "Take you and me, your average corn nuts off the street..."

"Just us corn nuts," Drake said, "thanks."

"Don't mention it. Anyway, we're just a couple of regular guys. We like chicks. We're proud to be heterosexual, and sometimes we masturbate, you know, beat off, spank the monkey..."

"I know what masturbating is." Drake said.

"With a personality like yours, of course you do," Sally said to Drake. Then to Elliot, "I knew you'd get around to something sexual."

"That's still the topic *de jour*," Elliot said. "Anyway, Drake, what do you think about when you masturbate?"

"Usually Sally," Drake said.

"Try to take this seriously, would you." Elliot said. Both he and Drake looked at Sally and laughed.

"Thanks a lot," she said. "Sometimes you guys are so juvenile, like a couple a school boys."

"I'm sorry," Drake said, not looking the least bit sorry. "So Sally what do you think about when you masturbate?" Drake asked.

"Fuck you," Sally said, "I don't know why I put up with you guys."

"You love it," Drake said.

"Okay, kids..." Elliot said. Drake and Sally obviously weren't going to resolve their personal differences in one evening.

"By all means continue," Said Drake.

"Yea, I'm getting tired." Sally shot Drake a contemptuous look and turned her stool to face away from him.

"Where were we?" Said Elliot.

"We were beating off," said Drake.

"Yea, beating off, spanking the monkey, engaging in a little self gratification...Hey!" Elliot paused as if hit with a major scientific insight. "I just realized, chicks don't have any colorful colloquialisms for masturbation." He looked at Sally with such lecherous curiosity that she felt herself blush. Elliot was one of the few people who could make her blush, probably because he had more than just words in his arsenal. "Maybe I just haven't done my research," he said. "How 'bout it, Dupree, you chicks have a pet name for whacking off? Plucking the bud. Stroking the cat... something colorful?"

"Is this really important?" Sally asked. She was never sure when Elliot was having jest at her expense, but he was probably the only man she knew who she let get away with teasing her. She didn't even let her husband take those kinds of liberties. It was like she was back in high school.

"It's not important, but it should get me through some lonely nights," he said.

"Pervert."

"Well, if you're not going to oblige," Elliot said. "Any way, masturbation 101; Hi my name is Elliot..."

Sally and Drake in unison: "Hi Elliot."

"...and I beat off. But I don't just beat off. No guy just

beats off. It's like a ritual. You have your favorite place, your favorite lubricant, and of course, your favorite material. I personally prefer my naked pictures of Nancy Reagan."

"You're a sick disrespectful motherfucker," Drake said, "...I love you man."

"I've heard it all before," Sally said. "What's your point?"

"Do you know how hard it is to find good naked pictures of Nancy Reagan? She's got a small and very exclusive following. You can't pick them up from behind the counter of just any old Quickie Mart."

Drake joined in, finally realizing where Elliot was going. "Nor, if your thing is kiddy S&M can you go to any old porn shop."

"Tell him what he's won, Sally," Elliot said gleefully. "Mister Drake has realized that, when our banana spider is not burking and cutting up little kids, he might like a little literature in that peculiar genre' to fill the void..."

"And since it's a very exclusive genre", Sally finished. "We need to find out where sick fucks of similar ilk go to partake of kiddy S&M literature."

"Which means," Elliot said, "surfing the web and hitting the porn shops. We're going to change our work hours. We're going to become vampires, and wander the streets during the fringe hours."

"The fringe hours?" Drake asked.

"Absolutely, there is a time of night, usually between 2am and 4am, depending on when the bars close, when the only people on the streets are cops, crooks, and perverts."

"You can fill two of those blocks by yourself," Sally said.

Elliot ignored her. "Anyway, we need to hit the streets during those hours and see if there's anything in this city that would appeal to a freak like our killer, such as underground S and M clubs, Satanist gatherings-and by the way, Denver has it's share of Satanists-or porn shops that cater to connoisseurs of the bizarre."

"There's only one problem with your theory," Drake said.

"Do tell," Elliot said defensively.

"Well, you can get all of that stuff off of the internet."

"True, but the feds have the kiddie porn stuff wired, and most sickos know that they could be surfing into a trap; and these guys are tactile. They want something they can rub on their body and hold under their nose."

"Sometimes you kind of scare me, man." Drake said.

"Sometimes I kind of scare myself." Elliot waved at the bartender. "Greg, one more for the road. There is evil afoot, and we have work to do."

Greg brought three more beers. He leaned over and whispered to Sally, "Has he always been this weird?"

"You don't know the half of it," she said.

As they talked, Elliot, noticed a large, loud, drunk a few stools down. The drunk was not only large, he was also fit, like a yuppie on steroids. He was wearing an expensive suit, tailor-made and cut to highlight the hours that he spent in the gym. He was pounding on the bar, not to get the bartender's attention, but to punctuate some incredibly insightful point he was making about "fucking democrats." His tie was askew, and there were beads of sweat on his exceptionally cruel upper lip. The bartender, Greg, was also keeping a wary eye on the not so friendly drunk. Elliot hated loud drunks, and this one felt mean. Loud, mean drunks tended to be unpredictable. He didn't like unpredictable, and Elliot could also spot a bully from a thousand paces. As if on queue, the drunk noticed Elliot, Sally, and Drake, but mostly he noticed Sally. He smoothed an unruly lock of hair out his face, jerked his tie to the left, leaving it askew on the left side vice the right side. He stumbled off his stool and began to amble towards Elliot's group. Sally and Drake weren't functional drunks like Elliot, and they had the disadvantage of having their backs to him, and didn't see the approach. Elliot called their attention to the approaching problem.

"Hey," Elliot said. Sally and Drake turned towards him. "Don't look now, but I think Sally has made a friend."

As Sally turned to look over her shoulder, the drunk forced his way into their little group and hit her with his best line. "I sure hope you're not with one of these guys, because you're the best thing I've seen all evening."

Sally slurred, "Really, that's sweet, but I am with these guys, and I'm also married, but thanks for playing."

Undeterred, the drunk pressed on, "Look, my name is Randy, and as fate would have it, I'm married too. So what say us married folk leave these two and go have a private party?" He put his hand on Sally's shoulder.

Elliot started to get up, but he caught Sally's eye and he could she clearly wanted to deescalate the situation.

Sally shrugged Randy's hand off of her shoulder, and said. "Randy, you're drunk, "no" means no; and I'm a cop, and these guys are cops, and you should never touch a lady without asking, now please step the fuck off."

Randy removed his hand and said, "Oh, I get it, too good for a guy like me. Well miss cop, I'm a lawyer, and a good one, and it's your loss bitch. I got to take a piss anyway." He staggered off to the bathroom.

As he left, Elliot felt a flash of emotion from him, ugly, primal, and dangerous. Elliot knew instinctively that, as long as Randy remained drunk he was a danger to everyone around him, especially women. He decided to take the drunken lawyer out of the game long enough for his primal rage to die down. Elliot stood up.

"Now where are you going," Sally asked.

Elliot smiled, "He reminded me that I've had to go tinkle for the last half hour myself."

Elliot made his way quickly through the crowd and caught up with drunken Randy at the urinals in the men's room. Elliot made sure the bathroom was empty except for him and Randy, and took up position at the urinal next to him. He looked pointedly at Randy's crotch in violation of all urinal etiquette, and said, "Wow, my friend doesn't know what she's missing."

"What?" Randy said.

"You're penis, man," Elliot smiled, "That's a nice one, if I do say so myself."

"What the fuck?" the lawyer said, his drunken mind trying to keep up with whatever Elliot was doing.

"Hey, no worries," Elliot said. "A couple of guys like us should be able to admire each others penises, don'cha think?"

Randy's brain caught up with his mouth. "I'm gonna kick you're ass faggot!" he said.

"Well, toodles , big guy," Elliot said quickly exiting the bathroom, and hoping Randy was drunk enough and homophobic enough to take the bait. He didn't have to worry, as soon as he made his way back to Drake and Sally the big lawyer came thundering through the crowd towards him, eyes ablaze.

Sally saw the lawyer shouldering his way through the crowd. "Uh, Elliot," she said. "Did you say something to that guy? Cause he's coming fast and he doesn't look happy."

"I'm sure I don't know what you are talking about," Elliot said, wrapping a cloth bar napkin around his hand.

The lawyer grabbed Elliot by the shoulder and spun him around easily. He yelled in Elliot's face, "I'm gonna kick your ass, faggot." He pulled back his arm almost comically, but Elliot knew that if that big meaty, comic, fist hit him, it wouldn't tickle.

Elliot held up his left hand, the one without the napkin wrap, "Whoa, there, big guy, am I to understand that you want to hurt me physically in some way?"

"You understand right motherfucker," The drunk spat, "I'm gonna fuck you up."

Elliot looked at Drake and Sally, and a couple of random bar patrons. "You guys hear that?" He asked. Everyone nodded.

Elliot put everything he had into a right hook, which took the drunk by surprise. It connected perfectly on the side of his lower left jaw. The lawyer's head snapped back at an odd angle, when it snapped back to the front his eyes were glazed, and he slumped to his knees.

Elliot looked at the crowd, "Are we all in agreement that that was self defense," he asked? Everyone nodded. He knelt down and quickly took the lawyer's pulse. "He's fine, folks. There's nothing to see here."

Greg the bartender, who Elliot had always assumed was standing on some kind of raised platform, had come around the bar. He was easily almost 7 feet tall. He lifted the big lawyer onto a stool with no discernible effort. He looked down at Elliot and said, "I've got this, E.T., I suggest you and your friends call it a night."

"I hear you, man," Elliot smiled. "We don't want any trouble."

Chapter Seventeen

The killer was sitting in his warehouse apartment reading the newspaper and ignoring a TV sitcom. On the worn coffee table in front of him were the remains of his dinner; the teriyaki chicken and vegetables he had thrown together, and a glass half filled with ice and diet cola.

He liked the spacious warehouse apartment much more than his assigned quarters on the Air Force base. That was a good thing, because there was a possibility that his Air Force self would have to disappear, and then he would have to become his other self permanently.

He'd been following the Josh Bennet story on the news. The authorities were at a total loss. If they'd had anything substantial to go on, they wouldn't still be airing those annoying crime stoppers spots-*only you can bring this man to justice.* He chuckled.

Parked in one corner of the warehouse was the truck he used to transport Josh Bennet to the missile silo. It was an old, beige suburban he had picked up at a government auction as his alter ego. The suburban was his first fail-safe. It was one of two disposable vehicles. He knew he might have to get rid of it soon. But he still had the other two cars. He owned three vehicles. The suburban and the car he'd used the night he snatched Alonso were registered under two different names. He'd picked up the other car at a Denver Police auction. The car he drove to work each day, a white Japanese compact, was registered in his Air Force name, his birth name, but he was feeling less like that person every day.

There were worse fates than retiring to the warehouse as his other self. He'd grown to like Colorado and Denver in the five years that he'd lived in the city and on the Air Force base. His hunting grounds were by no means dry, and he had no plans to leave. The boy had been a mistake. In hindsight, the risk of getting him out of the mall had been an unnecessary thrill. He knew he couldn't stop himself, but for now he was going to have to limit his killing to the abandoned and the forgotten, the dregs of the city who wouldn't be missed. He couldn't snatch any more mainstream kids...for a while. Especially since he'd lost access to his disposal area. He still didn't know what he was going to do with Alonso, who was currently taking up space next to a box of steaks in his large freezer. He couldn't keep him there forever. It was so stocked with food; frozen steaks, chicken, and other frozen goods, that he could only fit one body in it at a time-even a small one. He was going to need some extra freezer space soon.

What an unexpected treat his green apple had turned out to be. He had taken every liberty a man still in his prime could possibly take with such a beautiful prize. He had sodomized, bit, and sponged bathed-Alonso had a couple of accidents- his prize repeatedly for a full three day weekend before the teen's mind snapped and he had to kill him. Then, like he did with all his victims, he had made the cuts and drank the blood. He imagined he could still feel Alonso's life force. He was sane enough to question whether or not the blood was actually re-vitalizing him. But in the end it really didn't matter. The blood was sweet and it felt so good to suck on the open wounds.

Now that the heat was on, even punks like his green apple were probably too mainstream. He'd have to go back to the dregs and the occasional male prostitute from Denver's City Park. Sometimes, if they were young enough, he could pretend that they were pure. Maybe he should go back to women. He couldn't remember the last time he'd taken a woman. It might be a nice change.

Chapter Eighteen

It was raining; and from the looks of the non-existent horizon, the deluge was just beginning. Elliot was staring out the small window of his office. The dark, irrational (sadistic), voice deep inside his psyche punished him-unjustly-by pointing out that it would probably rain forever. That was a bad thing; cops always died in the rain. They also died in the sunshine, but always in the rain. If it was raining, somewhere, some time, or in some alternate dimension, a cop was dying.

Elliot was a devout sun worshipper. He thrived on blue skies and sunshine. In the spring and summer months he was invincible; his body a living, breathing, solar cell, soaking up the bright ultraviolet rays and redistributing them as productive energy. Early in his career, he had been stationed at Minot Air Force Base, North Dakota. The winters were sub-zero. The snow was abundant, and Elliot was miserable. If he hated anything, it was the snow and the cold. Cabin fever didn't begin to describe the torment he endured during those cold hard years (both of them). In those days his tireless, mean spirited, inner companion, reminded him that the summer would never come, and that he would never be able to leave North Dakota. He knew there were people who thrived in cold climates every bit as much as he thrived on the smell of sun baked flesh, and boat drinks, more power to them.

Being so helplessly at the mercy of the weather gods, he looked forward to retiring to someplace warm year round, where the skies were always blue, and there was always a gentle breeze to dry his brow. He imagined a place where the beer was always so cold it had those little ice chips in it. It was a simple, hokey, vision; but it was his happy thought. It got him through the tough times and rainy days. Staring out at the rain; but seeing blue skies, he felt calm and alone.

Unfortunately, he wasn't. He was in his office with Sally and a small wiry fellow named Fred Shaw. Sally was always welcome company; which was a good thing, considering they shared an office. Shaw was an annoying little fucker: in addition to having an infuriatingly condescending air about him, he couldn't seem to stop picking at some kind of festering sore on his cheek.

Shaw was the Regional Computer Crime Investigator, or, as the cool kids called them, an "RCCI", and he looked the part. He was to computers what Drake was to forensics. He was dressed in RCCI casual, black wingtip shoes, white socks, two inches of which were visible between his shoes and the bottom of his pants while standing, and a plaid shirt with no tie. Unknowingly, he had achieved the perfect Joe-Average-White-Guy-Waiting-To-Be-A-Victim look.

Elliot had called Shaw in to help him look for anything on the internet which remotely resembled kiddy S&M. Shaw would then help track down any connoisseurs of those web sites. They might be wasting their time, Elliot knew, but they were going through the right motions.

Shaw was looking through a folder containing documents

Elliot had sent to his office requesting RCCI support for the Bennet case. He was shaking his head, absently picking at his sore, and making a clicking noise in the back of his throat that was irritating enough to make Elliot's eyebrow twitch. Every now and again, he would look up at Elliot with an expression that managed to successfully convey amusement, disdain, and pity that Elliot was so hopelessly uninformed about the intricacies of cyberspace. He didn't see Elliot as a seasoned investigator so much as a barely functionally illiterate dinosaur.

It had been over a month since finding Josh's body, and they didn't have any leads of substance. Sally was at her computer writing up all the dead end leads they had accomplished, using Elliot's notes to put together a preliminary report on the case.

She wasn't so absorbed in her work that she hadn't noticed the tick developing behind Elliot's eyebrow. She would have recognized it as the autonomic manifestation of him making a supreme effort not to say something rash or kick the shit out of someone. She usually saw it when he was dealing with the Commander or especially rude suspects.

Shaw was sitting at Elliot's desk. Elliot had moved away from the window and was sitting on the opposite side, one leg thrown up on the desk, the sole of his shoe facing Shaw (He'd heard in some countries it was rude to point the bottom of your shoe at someone). Elliot knew what the RCCI thought of him and was trying desperately to hang onto his happy thought. He needed Shaw, and he didn't want to ruin any RCCI support by polarizing him with any rash statements, so he satisfied himself by showing him the bottom of his shoe, which seemed to be the right level of disrespect.

To Elliot, computers were the magic windows that made pictures and words. Cyberspace was the astral plane, and the only persons who could easily access it and make it work for them were cyber-shamen. They knew the spells. They had the incantations. The problem was; the uninitiated had to first sacrifice some pride on the alter of the shaman's intellect. This could be the most important case in his career, and he told himself he would kiss as much shaman butt as necessary to get the product he needed.

Elliot had a sound theory, and it looked good on paper; but he had no idea how to make it real. The theory was simple: Josh Bennet was not a first time kill for their iceman. The killer was in the military, probably the Air Force. His first kill was probably as a young GI. The best place to kill and go undetected was Southeast Asia. Elliot believed a good many icemen learned to kill for pleasure in Southeast Asia. He wanted a listing of all personnel assigned to Air Force Bases in the area, who had served more than one tour of duty in Vietnam, Thailand, or the Philippines from 1965 to present. He excluded Japan, because of its first world status and relatively sophisticated law enforcement system. Once he had that listing, he needed another listing detailing where each individual had been assigned since his (of course it was a *he*) Asian tours. When he knew where each individual had been assigned, he or the RCCI would contact police and investigative agencies in those areas and obtain a listing of all unsolved disappearances or homicides involving pre-adolescent males. Those individuals who were stationed in areas with a high incidence of unsolved disappearances or homicides coinciding with their assignments would be his primary suspects. When he had a list of primary suspects, he would review case files obtained from those jurisdictions and figure out where to go from there. Simple...not.

The kinks in his plan were infinite. There was no concrete evidence to indicate the perpetrator was in the military, and unlike the movies, all law enforcement organizations didn't have some super computer with Hollywood's ubiquitous omni-database from which to pull the raw data. He would be contacting busy police organizations and asking for a manual search of inactive case files going back over twenty years; and he would be asking based on a gut feeling and a pet theory, actually more gut feeling, but he had no idea how to get that across.

He wanted the RCCI to design a program to sort and catalogue the volumes of information he hoped to collect. He was asking for a database similar to the FBI's famed VICAP program, but focusing on cities near military installations.

Shaw looked up from the folder, disgusted by the incompetence of computer neophytes like Elliot, who thought it was sufficient to simply provide him with a layman's list of parameters needed to catch a man who might not exist. The scheme involved searching and creating a variety of different databases, untold man-hours; and there was no guarantee he was even on the right track.

Elliot took a deep breath and let the RCCI's disdain wash over him. He knew he was asking his organization to authorize him to spend an exorbitant amount of money, and RCCI man-hours, on the hunch of an agent some would consider a drunken madman. There were people in the organization he could contact for support - drunks and madmen most of them - who might help him to vocalize and legitimize his theory, but he needed Shaw's backing and was loath to call in markers prematurely.

Shaw, who saw in Elliot everything wrong with investigative society, was looking at him again. "Do you have any idea what you're asking?" Shaw asked.

"Yes and no," Elliot said. "I was hoping you would have a handle on the finer points."

"This is going to take lots of money and probably more

of my time than the organization is willing to spare." Shaw said.

"I know that part," Elliot said, already not liking where the conversation seemed to be headed. "Can it be done?"

"Of course it can be done, but you haven't convinced me you're on the right track."

"That's a 'yes' huh?" Elliot said.

"Listen. Let me be honest." Shaw said. Elliot hated it when folks said that. "This is a long shot," Shaw continued, "and I don't think you know what you're doing." He lifted the folder and dropped it like it was a spoiled piece of meat. "This is all smoke and mirrors. I know you're famous for that. You throw some verbiage at us and hope we'll jump on the Elliot Turner bandwagon just because you used to be some kind of hotshot undercover agent. I'm not a fan. I'm not impressed, and you're going to have to do better than this."

Elliot lost his happy thought.

Sally saw it happen. She had stopped typing when Elliot's eye tick locked up in mid-spasm, and was preparing for the inevitable. It happened quickly.

She had seen Elliot in action before, once when a suspect had resisted arrest. Drunk or sober, Elliot's reflexes were almost preternatural. He'd let his stamina atrophy-preferring drinking over running-but his ability to move quickly from a standstill was almost frightening. He moved so fast she didn't think his rational mind could keep up with his actions. At those times he reminded her of an animal, primal and unpredictable.

She thought about how gentle he had been with Anne Bennet, and wondered if Anne would have been so soothed by him if she had ever seen the primal side. Then she felt ashamed for allowing herself to go there, knowing there was a little jealousy behind the random thought.

Elliot had launched himself across his desk and was sitting on the desk facing the RCCI. He was sitting directly in front of him, feet on the arms of Shaw's chair, leaning down, predatory. His face was next to the shaman's left ear. He could have been ready to kiss him. His right hand rested gently, and dangerously on the little man's right shoulder. He looked like a large bird of prey or a vulture trying to pick out the soft spots.

"Listen to me," Elliot whispered, and then moved his face away from Shaw's ear so the shaman could see his smile; so inappropriate for the situation.

Shaw looked into Elliot's eyes; eyes bright, manic, and untouched by his smile. In a flash of alien insight he realized the rumors about Elliot Turner were probably true; Elliot was dangerous. Elliot had done things.

"Listen to me," Elliot said again, and the smile disappeared. "Over on that board," Elliot gently cupped Shaw's chin in his hand and turned it toward the collage macabre decorating the wall by Elliot's desk, "...are the remains of what used to be a small child. You got kids?" He didn't wait for an answer: the RCCI had two children. "A man - an animal - took that little kid and cut him up, but cutting him up was too easy; it didn't satisfy his fucked up libido. First he squeezed the air of him, then he took that little boy's body and used it like a woman. You understand? While he was using that dead little boy's body like a blow-up sex doll, he drank from the kid's open wounds, and chewed on him." Shaw tried to look away, but Elliot's grip was firm. "I don't know why he did what he did, but I know it turned him on because there was semen all over the body. Do you hear me? He cut up a little kid and spooged on the corpse. He's done it before. He will do it again. I'm not okay with that. I want to catch him. You're going to help me." He spoke as if to a small child. "I don't know what bug crawled up your ass, but that kid didn't put it there; and I'm not the guy who used to steal you lunch money. I'm much worse. I need your help." Elliot would never lay a hand on a fellow agent, but he tried to project a feeling of threat and malice into the RCCI's head.

Elliot let go of Shaw's chin and climbed off the desk. He stared at the RCCI, who was sweating profusely. Elliot could smell his fear. It made him happy. He didn't smile.

Shaw couldn't shake the feeling that he'd just experienced one of the most potentially volatile situations in his sheltered life.

"Will you help me?" Elliot asked, the threat still palpable.

"I'll do what I can," Shaw said uncertainly, still weakly feigning defiance, but scared shitless. *What just happened? What just happened?*

"You know," Elliot said. "I think you mean it." He smiled amiably at Shaw, winked and shot him the single-barrel, cocking his thumb over his index finger.

The RCCI begin to collect his things, keeping one eye on Elliot, as if he were a mad dog, temporarily placated, but who might decide to charge at the last minute. Elliot watched him watching him. Shaw finished collecting his things and scuttled out of the office.

Elliot looked at Sally, who had contented herself with watching and analyzing the scene for future reference. "Why is it never easy." Elliot asked, not expecting an answer.

She answered his question with a weak shrug. Elliot didn't see it. He was looking at the collage. "Do you spell *spooge* with a 'j' or a 'g'?" she asked.

Elliot held up his middle finger, giving her he non-verbal universal two word reply.

"Is that your IQ or your sperm count?" She asked.

“It’s my sperm count, but he’s a big motherfucker. I keep him locked in a cage in my apartment. Wanna see?”

“You know, I love you, man,” she said, because she thought he needed to hear it, “...and it’s not the booze talking.”

“Yeah,” he said. “Me too. Ain’t it weird.”

Chapter Nineteen

"I heard what happened with Shaw," Steve Drake was saying.

"Surely, I don't know what you're talking about," Elliot said, waving him off.

"You can't just go around terrorizing people," Drake persisted; "Especially fellow agents, and don't call me "Shurly."

"I didn't terrorize him...much," Elliot said. "Anyway, he's a *weenie.* He deserved it."

"A *weenie?*"

"I'm trying to stop cussing, clean up my act a bit," Elliot said.

"Oh. What did you do to him exactly?"

"I appealed to his sense of decency," Elliot said, digging in his pockets, looking for change. They were in downtown Denver canvassing adult novelty stores, also known as porn shops. "Do you have a quarter?" Elliot asked, giving up. "I want to call Sally."

"What's wrong with your car phone?"

"Fucking batteries are dead. The cigarette lighter doesn't

work." Elliot said, shooting a dirty look in the direction of his government owned vehicle.

"I thought you were trying to stop cussing?"

"I haven't found any good euphemisms to use with inanimate objects...Just give me a fucking quarter." Elliot said.

"Whatever. Tell Sally I said 'hello'."

While Elliot called Sally, Drake found a bench, took out his handkerchief to brush the pigeon shit off, and settled in to watch the downtown ballet. *Hookers and bums and crackheads, Oh my!*

So far, every one of their leads had gone bust, but Drake couldn't argue with the fact that the RCCI, Shaw, had been amazingly compliant these past few days. Elliot had done something to turn him into a tireless cyber-hound. Everyday he was in the office by seven o'clock and surfed the web, RCCI-style, until early evening. Sometimes he didn't even break for lunch. When he left, red eyed, in the evenings, Drake would catch him throwing the occasional furtive glance towards Elliot. He was like a whipped dog looking for his master's approval. It was more than a little creepy, but neither Elliot nor Sally seemed to notice.

The long hours surfing the net hadn't paid off. Shaw had found some interesting web sites that gave the agents in the office no end of perverted amusement. He'd even found what could be construed as a kiddy S&M web sites on a Japanese web porthole, but they didn't seem to jive with their iceman's tastes. They'd tagged the sites anyway and passed them over to the FBI. They managed to find a handful of the web site customers; one guy in a wheelchair, some high school geeks, but no one who matched their profile.

Porn shop patrol wasn't doing any better, although Elliot seemed to be in his element, rubbing elbows with the freaks and dregs of society, bullshitting with shop owners, and pawing the merchandise. It almost seemed as if Elliot were more at home with the dregs than he was with the most respectable members of society. Drake, however, was learning what a hopelessly sheltered life he himself had been leading. He found himself constantly saying things like, *No way! There aren't people who like that, are there?! I just don't understand how...*They'd visited more than a dozen shops, but older white guys seemed to be a large chunk of the porn shop customer demographic, and none matched their military variable.

Shaw had also worked some magic with the Department of Motor Vehicles (DMV) computer and found about forty-six privately owned suburbans. None were registered to military members. There were about ten agents in the office, including Elliot, Drake, and Sally. The task of tracking down the suburban owners and interviewing them had been divided amongst them. Forty-one people had been interviewed in the past month. All of them had alibis or didn't fit the profile. Five were unaccounted for; meaning they could not be found at the addresses on file at the DMV. They had enlisted the aid of the Denver Police Department, who were stopping suburbans, and checking the drivers against the DMV list provided by Shaw.

Drake couldn't shake the feeling that they were missing something. *Yea, the bad guy!* Elliot's behavior was also becoming an issue. He couldn't recall seeing Elliot act so... unsure. That was it, Elliot Turner was unsure of himself. He was putting up a good act, but he was far from the E.T. of old. . Elliot had always been one of those people with an easy unaffected star quality. He had average looks, average height, and was definitely no slave to fashion, preferring T-shirts and jeans, as opposed to the required suit and tie. But he had presence. Whether Elliot Turner had been a special agent or a store clerk, when he walked into a room people noticed. He had an aura about him that made a person think that, no matter what Elliot happened to be doing, it was simply the coolest thing. Of course, after they got to know him, most folks just thought he was weird. Weird or not he still had that bigger than life presence, and that easy confidence that was...missing. Drake hadn't really worked with Elliot since before Idaho. Elliot had lost something since then. Drake thought they were going to need that something back if they had a chance of solving this case.

Elliot came back from the pay phone while Drake was pondering Elliot's recent lack of that old Elliot Turner *ja ne sais quoi.*

"I think they like you," Elliot said, shooing away the pigeons that had congregated around Drake's *Gucci* loafers. They were either expensive shoe aficionados, or they were waiting for a handout. Elliot dropped down on the bench beside Drake, ignoring the pigeon shit on his side.

"What did Sally say?" Drake asked.

"Business as usual, no new hits on the suburban. Shaw is working overtime, but nothing on the net. Devine is looking for a way to blame me for the kid's death. Same shit." Elliot said, his face contorted between a smirk and a smile.

"Did you tell her I said 'hello'," Drake asked.

"Yea, she said 'fuck you'."

"All I said was 'hello'."

"She said it was the way you probably said it."

"She's such a heartbreaker," Drake said.

"You know," Elliot said. "You still haven't officially told me what happened between you two."

"I'll tell you mine, if you tell me yours. What happened in Idaho?"

"Maybe someday, man," Elliot said.

"Ditto," Drake said. They watched the pigeons and the other denizens of the inner city for a little longer.

A homeless man wandered past, and Elliot gave him a dollar. "Karma," he said to Drake.

"Yea," Drake responded. Down the street a BMW screeched to a halt; gold rims, television antennas, tinted windows.

"There's something you don't see everyday." Elliot said.

The passenger door opened up and a hooker, dressed fashionably in shiny, gold, ass hugging, spandex, and a halter-top barely containing her ample cleavage, was ejected. Some unseen citizen inside tossed a waist length fur jacket out after her. "I'd be upset too, if I couldn't get it up motherfucker!" She yelled, kicking the car as it sped off. Elliot and Drake watched the mini-drama unfold. This was so much better than network TV.

"You know," Elliot said. "I would pay them to do this job."

"It does have its moments doesn't it?" Drake asked rhetorically. "You know," Drake said tentatively, dreading what he had to say, but figuring a dose of reality might shock the old Elliot into showing himself. "Whatever you want to call our perpetrator; serial killer, parapheliac, sicko fuck bag, iceman...You might not have one."

"One what?" Elliot asked.

"One what!" Drake echoed. "You always do this. You know what I'm going to say before I say it. But if it's something you don't want to hear, you play stupid. If you want me to spell it out I will. Your pet theory might be fucked up; and if you start tunneling blindly towards it, and this turns out to be something completely different, you could irreparably fuck up this investigation. You've sacrificed some of your objectivity for your own press. You may need to broaden your scope, even if it means giving up on your prized theory. Did it ever occur to you that this might just be some sick asshole, who happened across the kid in the mall or something. You're trying to create a small violent offender task force, and terrorize Shaw into designing databases, but you're forgetting your basics."

"What we're doing is pretty basic," Elliot said defensively.

"I'm not saying everything is wrong. I'm saying we should be doing more of some stuff and less of other stuff. Right now you have a dead kid. You know someone killed him. All the effort you're putting into proving that unknown someone has killed before is of very little consequence at this juncture."

"You think I'm taking the wrong track?" Elliot asked, then added, "I knew it was just a matter of time before all that forensic consultant shit went to your head..."

"Shut up and listen," Drake said. He knew from experience that the best way to handle Elliot was toe-to-toe, in his face. "I think your iceman theory has merit. I did the first ten times you explained it to me. I still do. Actually, it's not even a unique theory."

"The hell you say," Elliot said sarcastically. "Somebody stole my theory. Say it isn't so."

"Don't be a dickhead...A number of criminologists-some before you were born-have published volumes on the subject of sexual sadists being criminals and sadists not because they're crazy but because it feels good to them. You're trying to catch this guy by figuring out who in your target group assigned to this base was assigned to other bases around the world when similar unsolved cases occurred, right?"

"Yea, and," Elliot's arms were crossed in front of his chest unconsciously warding off what he perceived as Drake's attack on his investigative expertise.

"I've got to tell you, the whole thing gives me a headache."

"You've got something better?" Elliot asked.

"Why yes, yes I do. That's what I've been trying to say. You might even like it if you weren't busy playing E.T. against the world, trying to be the hero and avenge the lady in distress." He saw Elliot's eyes cloud over at the thinly veiled reference to Anne Bennet, and thought he detected a twitch over his left eye. From talking with Sally, he suspected that Elliot was more than a little taken with Anne, and wondered if he'd gone to far.

Elliot uncrossed his arms. "Don't let me fuck this up, man." He said. That definitely wasn't the old Elliot talking.

"You're putting the cart before the horse," Drake said. "Because the crime is so much bigger than life, you're looking for a bigger than life solution, which incidentally goes against your banana spider hypothesis. If you look closely, the killer left a fucking warehouse full of evidence, saliva, lamp, tape, methodology, and semen. The list goes on. It just might be possible to find him through good clean old-fashioned investigative work. No fancy theories or miraculous insights. Of course I realize you used to be the miraculous insight czar, but maybe in this case you don't have to pull a miracle out of your ass. You call your hypothetical fetish killers 'icemen'. That's another misnomer. It's completely out of line with your own theory. Your 'banana spider' is a regular guy. I'm thinking he made some regular guy mistakes. Hell, his first mistake was leaving the body behind; a nice fresh corpse. It wasn't exactly in disposal configuration was it? It wasn't wrapped in plastic, buried in quick lime, put in a box, or dismembered, none of that shit. I don't think he was done with the kid, but for some reason, he went away. I think he had every intention of coming back; but before he could, cowboys Bob and Neil stumbled across his killing ground before he had the chance." Elliot was listening now. Not quite so defensive. Drake was verbalizing some of his own ideas, which hadn't quite managed to coalesce.

Drake continued, "You can't be expected to be the expert on everything. Hell, your thing was drugs and undercover operations last time I checked. Street stuff. I'm here because I'm good at the nuts and bolts thing, conventional investigative activity. Let me do my thing, and you do yours. Look at the evidence again, then go talk to people. People are your thing. Do it alone if you have to, especially if there's some reason you would rather not have witnesses. But keep it out of the office. You might have temporarily cowed Shaw, but that was just luck. He could have made whatever happened between you and him an issue. What I'm saying is don't get all complicated and textbook on me now. That's my job. You go to the streets and work some of that E.T. magic. I'll be here to make it legal and help you with the big words."

"That was some speech," Elliot said.

"Whatever. You savvy what I'm getting at?" Drake asked, serious.

"Yeah, work my magic and leave the grown up investigating to you."

"Hey, you said it, not me."

Chapter Twenty

"Check this out," Sally said. She tossed a computer printout on Elliot's desk. He had been staring intensely at his computer screen. Sally figured he was playing a game. Elliot simply wasn't that intense when he was doing actual work at his computer.

"What's this?" Elliot asked, tearing himself away from his game of solitaire.

"It's your first list of suspects, compliments of Fred Shaw."

"Little fucker's worth his weight in gold when he's properly motivated, ain't he?" Elliot said picking up the list.

"Lighten up," Sally said, "He's not so bad. Here's the Reader's Digest version of what you're holding," Sally said. "There are fifty-three names on that list that meet your parameters. That is fifty-three persons, now assigned to Lowry Air Force Base or Buckley Air National Guard Base, who served more than two tours in Vietnam, Thailand, or the Philippines between 1965 to present. About 30 of those spent most of their time in the Philippines before they closed. Am I right to assume you didn't really want the younger troops?"

"Yeah, I figure we're looking for a crusty older GI." Elliot said.

"Good, the other twenty three on the list are senior Non-Commissioned Officers, who actually did time in Vietnam and Thailand. Five out of those twenty three are Chief Master Sergeants."

"Isn't your list a little biased? You've only got enlisted guys there."

"Ahh, you noticed. That's because the officer list is a little shorter and decidedly more exclusive," she said, taking a folded up piece of paper out of her jacket pocket. "I've written five names on this list. They're all full bird Colonels, and one Brigadier General who made the cut: they served a bunch of time in various Southeast Asia garden spots. We are now in the political zone, and of course, there's the other problem."

"What's that," Elliot said, going over both lists, whistling whenever he came across a heavy hitter.

"Your theory," Sally said.

"What about it now?" he asked defensively.

"You've got no real reason to talk to them. In your mind they're suspects because your gut and your hypothesis says they are. But there is no real evidence linking them to any crime. Remember, usually we look for a little thing called "evidence," she made quote signs with her fingers," linking a person to a crime. The law doesn't recognize your theory. Unless you've read about some obscure case law involving proactive profiling of serial criminals, you're getting ready to step on your dick, and the boss says it's my job to point that out to you as necessary. Check me out...I can predict that and I'm not even psychic." Sally said.

"You think we can talk to Drake about coming up with

some reason to conduct Behavioral Analysis Interviews of the Chiefs and Colonels?" Elliot asked.

"I don't know the legalities, but I'm assuming that you don't just start interviewing Colonels and Chiefs as potential suspects in a homicide, without having a damn good reason. I believe in your gut, but on paper, it's real thin. This could get real political and real ugly," Sally said. "You don't just start dragging these guys in without something tangible to show when the congressional complaints start coming in. You know we can't make this happen behind Devine's back. He's going to have to buy off on it."

"I'll handle Devine," Elliot said a lot more confidently then he felt.

"Can't you just look the list and do your thing?" Sally asked.

"I don't just do my thing," Elliot snapped, frustrated. "Remember, unless it's auditory, visual, tactile, or olfactory, I have no real control over it. The other 'things' just kind of happen. I don't have a fucking crystal ball." Over the years, Elliot had tried to control his ability. He'd even tried the two "M's"; Meditation and Marijuana (the marijuana of course before entering the Air Force). He'd had some success (very limited and during the marijuana years) but measurable control always eluded him.

After the Idaho incident, he had been tested by a team of specialists - no name types who said they were with the NSA...whatever. He tried to guess cards and see symbols and read minds. They told him he had been marginally successful. He didn't know what that really meant. He did have one measurable clairvoyant episode (he correctly predicted one of the no names would get a call from his wife).

In the end, the NSA was able to confirm to the OSI that Elliot was indeed a low level clairvoyant with negligible psi talents. Overall, they weren't impressed…they'd seen better apparently. However, their findings were enough to convince the organization that Elliot hadn't blown Hatchet's face off just for fun.

Elliot once again thought that he shouldn't have told Sally anything. He didn't mean to take his frustration out on her. She didn't mean any harm by her off handed comments, and she had no way of knowing what a constant source of frustration his errant talents were. They were there when he didn't need them; and - the Idaho incident aside - they weren't there when he did.

"Well, excuse me," Sally said testily, plucking the two lists from his hands.

"Look...Sally," Elliot said. "I'm sorry. It just doesn't work that way. I can't turn it on and off. I wish I could. If I could, I'd tell the fucking world and get myself one of those psychic hotlines." Sally had grown quiet. Elliot softened his tone. "I'm sorry I snapped at you. I really shouldn't have shared anything with you, but you're like my only friend. When I retire, incidents in my career will go the way of UFOs and Project Blue Book. I'm like this freak, too freaky to let go, but not freaky enough to be really important. I guess I snapped at you because I had to vent. After the organization found out - and I won't even go into that story - they had the same attitude as you...and they knew better. They had me tested. They knew I couldn't turn this thing on and off. Still they were always trying to get me to do this or that, and when I couldn't produce; they gave me this *what are you good for* attitude. I'm a damn good agent, and I was a damn good agent. The OSI didn't hire me because I had this 'thing'. They hired me because I could do the job. I'm not some kind of freak. I'm an OSI special agent, and don't need any fucking psi talents to find this guy." He looked like he was going to say something else. Then, all of his frustration vented, he slumped down in his chair to sulk. Good speech, he thought. He hoped he'd convinced Sally. Because, he wasn't sure how competent he would be without a little help from his unreliable psychic friend.

"I should be the one apologizing," Sally said. "Remember, your revelations change nothing between us, right? You're still one of the best friends I've ever had. So, 'you' make sure this thing doesn't come between us. I'm always going to have your back, even when I don't." She walked behind his chair and hugged him around the neck.

"I actually understood that, Dupree," Elliot said.

"We're gonna do this. We're gonna catch the first, pure, grade A, evil motherfucker to be caught by the OSI in modern history. Come on," she said, tugging him out of his chair. "Let's go get famous."

Chapter Twenty-One

Elliot was in the gym pumping away on the stair climber machine. He was thinking about Anne Bennet; thinking about the way her hair smelled when he'd pulled her close during the interview. The knight in him was always attracted to women in crisis; and Anne, having just lost her only son, was most assuredly in crisis. Her grief was magnetic, her vulnerability intoxicating. Elliot always felt more comfortable being the hero, saving the damsel in distress, than he did just being Elliot Turner, thirty something and needing someone with whom to spend a lonely evening. With Anne it was a dangerous condition. Nothing could tilt an investigator's objectivity like getting the hots for a victim or witness.

Did he want to solve this case because he sincerely cared about the injustice done to a little kid, who was too dead to care one way or the other, or did he want to be the hero? If he cast himself in the mode of the hero, recreating himself in Anne's gratitude, what would he do when she no longer needed a hero? Deep down he was certain that his marriage had died because his wife, who had entered the marriage a basket case, had finally started to get her shit together. She didn't need the hero anymore, and he had gone off looking for someone who needed saving, spending more and more time in the field away from home. Finally, they had simply drifted apart. Was there a part of him that needed a woman that needed him, and created herself through him? Even though that wasn't what he wanted? Why did *life* have to be so complicated?

Since the divorce he'd had countless trysts with women, some whose names he couldn't even remember. He'd even had a couple of steady relationships ("Steady" meant more than three dates). He never once stopped to ask himself what any of the faceless women thought about him as a person. He hadn't cared what they thought. Hell, if they were sleeping with him, they didn't find him totally unpalatable. Even if they did, they were little more than entertainment, exercise. They carried about the same importance as a good game of racquetball, or an interesting movie on television. Anne was different.

He felt himself drawn to her, probably for all the wrong reasons; but nonetheless, the feelings were there. He cared about what she thought of him. *Of course, he wanted her to see him as the hero.* He was, after all, busting his balls in the gym for the first time in almost a year.

He looked down at the LED display on the stair climber, certain he'd been pumping away for at least half an hour. He'd been exercising for barely ten minutes. He stopped at the fifteen-minute point. The room was spinning and he could taste his breakfast working its way back to the light. There was a large woman pumping at the stair machine next to him. She was easily thirty pounds overweight, but very cute in the face. When Elliot first hopped on his machine he had looked at her pumping away and thought; Hmm, cute fat chick. Now, as he sat down by his machine in a puddle of sweat, and she showed no signs of tiring; he thought he detected a look of smugness on her puffy cheeks. She was like that little pink rabbit with cellulite; she just kept on going. He looked at his watch as if to say, "*I sure wish I had more time to work out. Fifteen minutes just isn't enough for me.* He grabbed his towel and took the walk of shame back to the locker room.

Elliot showered, dressed in his usual jeans and T-shirt, and headed back to the office. When he walked into the office he shared with Sally, he noticed her purse on a chair, and Drake's rental car keys on his desk, but they didn't seem to be anywhere around. He wandered around the building, and found them eating lunch in the conference room.

Sally was eating a salad out of plastic bowl. Drake had a double cheeseburger as big as his head. He had a paper towel stuffed in his shirt collar like a bib; *couldn't have cheeseburger juice on his silk, tailored, shirt.* Drake took a huge bite of the burger as Elliot walked in. Grease and catsup ran down the back of his hand. Elliot eyed the sandwich with blatant covetousness; *one day I, too, will dine on cheeseburgers and fries.*

Drake knew Elliot was trying to lose weight (Elliot was far from overweight, but recently he'd noticed the beginning of the thirty something tire around his waist). Drake would eat anything and still look like a corporate lawyer. Drake saw Elliot eyeing his burger. He held it up to Elliot, knowing he was dieting. "Oh...man...mmm," Drake said, waving the burger around as he spoke. "This has got to be the best cheeseburger I've ever tasted. You gotta try one. I mean, this is the mother o' all cheeseburgers. It's 90% lean beef, bacon... why it's the *Armani* of double bacon cheeseburgers. Wanna bite?" He held the burger out at arms length then pulled it back. "That's right; you're trying to diet." He laughed.

"Leave him alone," said Sally. Being in constant battle with her hips, she could sympathize with anyone dieting.

"Yea," Elliot said. "Leave me alone before I kick your ass."

"Well," Drake said. "If your gonna kick my ass, at least let me finish this heavenly burger, and my thick and creamy chocolate milkshake," he said, slurping noisily. "If I die with bacon on my breath; I die a happy man."

"Bite me," Elliot said, grinning. "I'll be a cheeseburger eater again one day, and you'll be sorry. You know, it's nice to see you two kids getting along, breaking bread together and all."

"I was in here first," Sally said.

"Yea...well, you've gotta crawl before you can walk," Elliot said. "Any earth shattering developments while I was out getting buff?"

"Possibly," Sally said; "We were talking about the disposal issue."

"Disposal?"

"Yea," Drake said, mouth full of burger. He swallowed with an audible 'gulp' sound. "Remember what we were talking about the other day. How the body didn't seem to be prepared for disposal?"

"Uh huh." Elliot said sitting down by Sally and reaching for a tomato in her salad.

"Get your own, " she said; but she didn't stop him.

"What do you think our boy was going to do with the kid's corpse?" Drake asked. "We've already established that he probably wasn't going to leave it there."

"However," Sally said. "Wouldn't you think taking the body into the silo was risky enough? Why run the risk of being seen taking it back out?"

"...and," Drake added. "Those complexes are huge."

"You think he was going to leave the body somewhere in

the complex." Elliot said, "and in about thirty seconds you're going to reach into your briefcase and pull out blueprints of the silo complex."

"You're going to have to show me how you do that someday." Drake said.

"Lucky guess," Elliot said, looking at Sally.

"I don't just think he was going to stash the Bennet kid in the complex somewhere," Drake said. He wiped his hands on his makeshift bib, and opened his briefcase, which was on the table next to him. "If your theory is correct; and we have to assume that it is since we've put so much fucking work into it."

"Thanks," Elliot said.

"Anytime," Drake said. " Anyway, if this guy is a serial killer, or iceman, or whatever; he's probably killed before, right? If he is in the military and has been stationed in this area for awhile; he's probably killed in the missile complex before, and disposed of the other bodies in there." Drake spread moved the remains of his lunch aside and spread the blueprints of the missile complex out on the table.

"Where'd you get the blueprints?" Elliot asked.

"Ahh," Drake said. "He doesn't know all and see all. While I was out picking up that delectable cheeseburger, I paid a visit to the base civil engineer's office... Look at the size of this thing," He said, spreading his arms out over the blueprints.

"I guess we're going back out there," said Sally. "Shit, it's going to take us a week to search that place. He could have stashed other bodies anywhere."

"No," Elliot said. He was leaning on his elbows, peering closely at the blueprints. "If there *are* other bodies; they're in here." He pointed to what looked like a long cylinder, three floors deep, on the left side of the blueprint.

"Oh, man!" Drake said. "The missile shaft. The fucking

missile shaft! You could dump a hundred bodies inside one of those things."

"You know what I'm thinking." Elliot said.

"I'll go brief Devine and change my clothes." Sally said.

Chapter Twenty-Two

Until he found another permanent disposal site, the city's dumpsters were just going to have to do. He was tired of seeing Alonso's well packaged corpse haunting his frozen vegetables; and it wouldn't be the first time he had to relay on local sanitation workers to dispose of his refuse. It was a nice evening for a drive so he decided he would take the suburban and make the two-hour drive down to Colorado Springs. He could dump the body somewhere along the way, or find a dumpster in town. He was looking forward to the drive and he could kill two birds with one stone. There was a little steak house in Colorado Springs that he had tried once, and was eager to try again. They made a prime rib that practically melted in you mouth.

He had the window down and the radio tuned to 94 FM, KSOF (Kiss Off), soft rock. God, he loved Denver. It was nothing like the small town in Oklahoma where he had grown up. That was part of the appeal. He hated that town. Even growing up in Gainsville, pop. 1,000, he knew he was a city boy at heart. Small towns weren't rustic, or homey, or quaint; they were just small. Plus, Gainsville, Oklahoma was hopelessly ill equipped to contain his evil.

He couldn't wait to leave home. At seventeen his parents (*losers)* were only too happy to sign whatever waivers were needed to allow him to enlist in the Air Force well before his eighteenth birthday. He hadn't even finished high school. He'd earned his General Education Diploma (GED) in the Air Force and gone on to earn a four-year degree in psychology.

The war in Vietnam had just been getting set to wind down in 1969, but the bodies were still coming back. Other parents cried as they put their boys on the bus bound for the processing station in Oklahoma City, off to help keep the world safe for democracy against the new yellow peril. His folks waved him off happily. He could still see their stupid grins; Good by son, *you sick evil motherfucker,* don't forget to write. No more complaints from the neighbors about their mean spirited son kicking the shit out of Bobby Joe, or harassing Becky Lou. No more dogs turning up dead because they had the poor judgment of barking at him. He never saw them again. If they hadn't birthed him, their lives would have been a complete waste.

He kicked ass in basic training. He'd always been athletic and in above average physical condition. This, and a natural ...meanness, didn't go unnoticed by his drill instructors. They urged him to try out for the combat control program. He excelled. Combat Controllers were some of the Air Force elite. Like Navy Seals or Force Recon Marines, Combat Controllers were always first in the thick of things and last out. He graduated at the top of his class. When they shipped his unit off to Vietnam, some of the controllers were nervous. He just hoped they had saved some gooks for him. Vietnam, was full of war, death, and destruction. It had been nirvana. Then there were the women.

The women were a most unexpected, but pleasant, surprise, petite, exotic, and willing. He couldn't get his hand on a tit to save his life back in Gainesville; but not for lack of trying. In the Nam he could buy a piece of pussy for the price of a six-pack. He bought plenty.

By the time he was nineteen, he had been in Vietnam over a year. He'd found his niche, and had no intention of rotating out. He had killed with impunity in the name of America; and for R&R (rest and relaxation) he had the girls. Before his twentieth birthday he had experienced every form of heterosexual pleasure known to man. Then he got creative.

Sadly, once he got creative, and word got out amongst the girls that some of the things he liked went well beyond the ol' slap and tickle (to much slap, very little tickle, and some bite) the girls weren't so eager to play. He had to get increasingly more aggressive if he wanted a little companionship, practically dragging girls out of bars. Soldiers dragging girls from bars weren't an odd sight in Vietnam, and no one questioned his actions because he was known to be a good soldier and a certified badass. Sometimes they cheered him on. He quickly discovered that he actually like it best when he had to drag them off. The less consenting the better. Those were swell times. It was during one of those non-consenting times when he finally went *all the way*. Oh, what a magic evening that had been.

Long before he went *all the way*, he had a habit of biting the girls a little to hard during sex. They didn't like it, but he always paid top dollar. They stopped soliciting his business when he started drawing blood. He, of course, found he liked the taste of blood...a lot, and the way they squirmed underneath him while he was hurting them, drove him crazy. He realized he wanted more than they had to give. Long before his first pleasure kill (his first social kill; war kills didn't count) he realized he was going to be doing a lot of killing for pleasure. He'd said it aloud in his mind; *I am a man who likes to kill women. Hmm, I guess I'm okay with that.*

He probably could have gotten away with killing one of the bar girls in his regular stomping grounds in Vietnam. But even at nineteen, he had a firm understanding of the importance and the art of discretion.

Pattya Beach, in Utapao, Thailand, was the Disneyworld of Asia, one of the hedonistic capitals of the world. Anything a person wanted to have done to him or to do to someone else could be negotiated in Utapao. In WWII, Tokyo was the place for GIs to go play. During Vietnam, it was Pattya Beach. He took his first R&R there in 1971. It was his first hunt.

He had two weeks of leave. The first week he spent learning the area; which bars were the most popular, which girls were diseased, who were the players and pimps and madams and drug dealers. Then he avoided those people and those areas. He was looking for something outside of the regular GI pleasures. During the second week that something found him.

He had been on the outskirts of town, still in Utapao, but off the beaten path. He was watching a Thai boxing match. He loved the ferocity of the sport, two boys trying to kill each other, just to be able to work the crowd for tips and feed their families. Small town Thailand had small town Oklahoma beat any day of the week. He'd become a fan of Thai fighting after only a couple of days in Utapao, had even stepped into the ring once after being invited up by a cocky young local champion. He'd stepped boldly into the ring (He was a combat controller and none of these fuckers could touch that). He got his ass kicked. He was handed his pride and his jaw on a stick. But after that he was respected as an insider, and became a staunch fan of the sport.

He had been leaning against a pole in an open air bar near the beach watching the fight when she found him.

"Hey, GI," almost a whisper. He turned and saw in the shadows outside of the bar a small Thai beauty. She couldn't have been more than thirteen years old, but she already had the eye, the ability to look at a man as if he were different and special and not a carbon copy of every third GI in town.

"Hey, yourself," he said, all full of nineteen year old cool. "What's your name?"

"Suzy," she said. All the girls were Suzy.

"Of course it is," he said smiling.

"Me love you long time GI?" she said. It was more a question than a statement.

"Not if I love you first," he said, ignoring the puzzled look on Suzy's face, and holding out his arm. Suzy had taken his arm and wandered ignorantly, docilely off to her slaughter.

He took her back to his hotel room. It was also off the beaten path. For his first time, he was flawless in his execution. The pleasure had been nothing less than exquisite...ethereal. Damn it had been good. Over the years, he had moved on to other pleasures; but that first planned and deliberate kill would always be magic. When he was done, he had dumped the body unceremoniously into a large trashcan at the back of the hotel. He returned to Vietnam the following morning a changed man.

Chapter Twenty-Three

Gloria Sanchez couldn't have picked a better evening to die. Of course, had she known she was going to die, she probably wouldn't have felt quite the same about the gorgeous twilight. But, ignorance is bliss, and Gloria couldn't remember the last time she'd seen such a beautiful night.

Sometimes Denver had the kind of skies normally reserved for the middle of the desert on the clearest nights. This was one of those nights. There wasn't a cloud in the sky. The pregnant moon was encased in a halo of light. She could see the surface clear enough that, had she been an astronomer, she could have named the geological formations on the lunar surface.

She was alone, parked by the side of the rode on the outskirts of town. She wasn't afraid to be by herself. Actually, she'd grown to like it. Gloria was one of those people who could genuinely enjoy her own company. She decided to enjoy the evening up close and personal, so she got out of her cruiser to lean back against the hood. She hated the way a patrol car could isolate a person: a hulking beast of metal acting as a barrier between and the fresh air. The only thing that could possibly make a night like this even more magical was Eddie.

Eddie Johnson was a paramedic. A hero. He looked the part. He was 6' 3", blonde, with blue-green eyes. He was one of those fortunate blondes (like Malibu Ken) who tanned without burning, and his body...Gloria felt herself grow warm just thinking about his strong legs and muscular torso. If he had a hammer and horned cap, he could be Thor. She was in love with the god of thunder; and oh man... thunder...did he ever. Life was good.

Eddie was working the graveyard shift. She envisioned him running up and down interstate 20, sirens wailing, pulling accident victims from the twisted metal that used to be a car with his bare hands. Okay, maybe she over romanticized him. But he did look like Thor. She figured they would get home at about the same time. She didn't plan on going straight to sleep. As much as he turned her on, the attraction wasn't just physical. Eddie was the most understanding, patient man she had ever met. He had a gentle way about him one wouldn't expect in a man so large. Then there were his eyes. Eddie had poet's eyes. Had he been here with her, he would have appreciated the sheer untainted beauty of the universe laid open before them. His eyes were kind and dreamy, and seemed designed to see the natural wonder in even the smallest things. Eddie was so masculine; he didn't have to be macho. The best thing about Eddie was that he loved her back.

In the seven months since they'd met, their relationship had developed from casual friendship, to the occasional movie date, to being one inseparable entity, bound by love, and 'like'. Gloria had been in love before. 'Like' was a much more elusive beast. When the passion died - and it would - there had to be 'like'. Gloria loved and liked Eddie. If they hadn't been lovers, he was the type of person she would want to have around just for the company and conversation.

Gloria leaned back against her car, the hood still warm from the engine, and breathed deeply of the night air. She closed her eyes and let the open plains sing to her.

Then she heard a car approaching. She'd patrolled this stretch of road often enough that, in the five months she'd been working this sector, she could count on two hands the cars she'd seen on the road after midnight. Route 19 was one of those seldom-used highways that had been put out of business by the big four lane super highways. It really was the road less traveled. As the headlights drew closer, she could see it wasn't a car but a truck. The truck blew past her. No. It wasn't a truck. It was a suburban, a beige suburban. What had she heard about a suburban?

The driver saw the police cruiser parked by the side of the road while he was still well up the road. His high beams had picked up the reflective POLICE lettering on the trunk of the black and white patrol car. Speed trap? No. Then What? Some bored patrolman stretching his legs or taking a leak by the side of the road. Then he was past. Not a policeman, but a policewoman. She seemed to be interested but not overly so. She gave him the passing glance anyone on a lonely road - even a policewoman - might give a lone truck on a seldom used road in the middle of the night.

Suburban! During her shift briefing, her Sergeant had mentioned that the Air Force was looking to question suburban owners, who might possibly have information about that kid found dead in the missile silo. Gloria hopped in her car, relieved to have something to break the monotony of night patrol in this sector. Because she was riding without a partner, she figured the Sergeant, in an act of *kindness* born of chauvinism, had given her the boonie sector to keep her safe. Chivalry was not fucking dead. Gloria Sanchez could take care of herself. They just wouldn't let her do it.

She called dispatch: "This is unit 12. I've got a brown suburban, northbound on nineteen, over."

Dispatch: "Ten-four Unit 12, uh, is he doing something wrong?"

Everybody is a comedian at this time of night, she thought. "Negative. Our friends on the airbase have a bolo out for Suburbans. I'm gonna do my bit for Uncle Sam."

"...Ten-four. Don't be a cowgirl 12."

She caught up with the suburban about four miles down the road.

He saw her pull up behind him. Guess the policewoman is curious after all.

Gloria called the Suburban's license plate into the dispatcher. After a few minutes, the dispatcher came back the stats: the DMV had the vehicle registered to Lester Phillips of 212, Darcy Avenue, in Aurora and the National Criminal Information Center had no wants or warrants. Mr. Suburban was just a lonely citizen on his way to Colorado Springs. Gloria figured she would stop him and asked if he'd been contacted by anyone from the airbase. If he hadn't, she would get all his pertinent information and put him in touch with somebody. *Maybe that black guy she met last year at that thing.* Then her good deed would be done. She flashed her lights for the truck to pull over.

Chapter Twenty-Four

The Sergeant didn't say exactly what the Air Force wanted to talk to this guy about. Best play it by the book, Gloria thought. There would be time for apologies later.

He saw the lights flash in his rearview mirror and pulled off on the side of the road. What could she possibly want? He hadn't been speeding. Broken tail lights maybe; No. He was almost compulsive about preventative maintenance on his vehicles. He checked the oil and other fluid levels every week and gave them tune-ups every 4000 miles. There were no red lights or stop signs to violate on this stretch of road. Maybe she was lonely; *Pardon me, have you any Gray Poupon.* He grinned.

Gloria Sanchez brought the police cruiser to a halt behind the truck's rear bumper. She called in the stop.

She called into dispatch, "Unit 12."

Dispatch: "Unit 12 go ahead."

"Hold me out with the Suburban at mile marker 63. I'm going to have a friendly chat with the driver."

"Ten-four, Unit 12. Do you need a Ten-twenty?"

"Negative Bobby, I've got this – no back up needed."

Beside, Gloria reasoned, by the time back up finally got to her location, the traffic stop would be over and then she would have taken two Units out of service on one call.

"Ten-four Unit 12...out."

Gloria switched over to her loud speaker and called out, "Please put both hands out the window where I can see them." When she saw his hands, she climbed out of her patrol car and, hand discreetly on the butt of her weapon, approached the truck in its blind spot.

He couldn't see his policewoman, but he knew exactly where she was. He could hear the gravel on the shoulder of the road crunching under her boots. What could she possibly want? He asked himself again. Could somebody have seen him take the boy from the mall?

Taking the boy had been a work of art. So he thought. But now, he was wondering if had been worth the risk. Had he gotten sloppy in his old age? Was he going to go the way of some of the others in his homicidal tribe? Was he going to start taking unnecessary risks? Was there a part of him that wanted to get caught...? Nah. He most definitely did not want to get caught.

The boots crunched to a stop outside and to the rear of his window. He heard, "My name is Officer Sanchez. Do you know why I stopped you?" Why would I ask that? Gloria thought. He hasn't done anything.

Why do they always ask that, he wondered? "I don't know officer," He said. "Was I speeding?"

Gloria didn't answer his question. She had already slipped into police officer, stopper-stoppee, cat and mouse mode - *I'll ask the questions here.*

"Nice truck," she said. "suburban?"

"Yes, can I ask what this is about?" Had somebody seen the truck?

"I pulled you over because there are some people who

want to ask you some questions about your truck. Has anyone from the Air Force base contacted you?" Air Force base? Had to be the OSI. What would the OSI want with him? No. Not him...the truck. Somebody had seen the truck! He had to get rid of the truck...tonight, and the cop.

"No, ma'am," Gunther said. "No one from the base has talked to me."

"Can I see you driver's license?" Gloria asked. She wanted to make sure it was the same as the name in the DMV records.

Gloria had moved to just outside his window, and he could see her face. She was attractive in a female cop kind of way. Long, dark brown hair pulled back into a bun at the base of her neck, light brown skin, and very pretty dark brown eyes. Not his flavor anymore.

"My license is in my glove compartment," he said. He still had his hands out of his window and was starting to feel silly.

"Okay," said Gloria. "I can see you now. You can pull you hands in." She had quickly assessed him as being harmless. He was in his early forties, plain looking, and had a military style haircut; short on the sides and a little longer on the top, like a Marine.

He reached into his glove compartment. His Lester Phillips license really was inside, but there was a gun in there also. The trick was to get the license without letting the cop see the gun. He tried to keep the glove compartment shielded with his body, but Gloria caught a flash of the gun in the moonlight coming through the passenger side window.

"Is that a gun, sir?" She asked, alert again, but lots of folks had guns these days.

"Yes it is Ma'am," he said quickly and as polite as possible. *Ooh, quick eyes. You're a credit to your profession, officer.* He grinned.

Was he grinning? Gloria didn't know why she hadn't noticed it before, but there was something not quite right in this guy's eyes. Was he high or something? "Could you step out of the truck, sir?" She said.

"Certainly," he said. The he stepped on the gas and the truck lunged forward.

Gloria jumped back, momentarily stunned. Shit! She hadn't told him to turn the engine off. She remembered she had the gun. "STEP OUT OF THE TRUCK NOW!" She yelled at the retreating truck.

He stopped about 25 feet forward of Gloria after his initial burst of speed. Now, he jerked the truck into reverse and angled the rear end towards Gloria.

Gloria saw what he was doing even as the truck started to move. She fired two quick shots into the rear window. Both shots missed their mark. This is not happening, she thought. Nothing ever happen on the stretch of road. How could things go so bad so fast?

She had been back peddling towards her car while she fired, and the suburban backed towards her. She turned quickly and sprinted the remaining distance to her car, conscious of her flashlight and other equipment slapping against her legs. The door to the cruiser was open. She reached the car and dove inside. The suburban's rear bumper rammed the door as she tried to pull her feet into the car after her. The door slammed shut on her left ankle, crushing it.

Gloria had never felt such pain. The pain in her ankle was excruciating. The intense pain burned quickly up her left side. She could actually feel the pain in her neck, back, and arms. She grabbed her radio and shouted; "OFFICER NEEDS ASSISTANCE...OFFICER NEEDS ASSISTANCE..."

"UNIT 12, IS THAT YOU!?" Dispatch responded.

Gloria could feel herself going into shock. She felt like an outsider watching the scene unfold before her. A part of her watched calmly as the suburban pulled around, preparing for another ram.

"UNIT 12, YOUR STATUS? ...UNIT 12? ALL UNITS, RESPOND TO MILE MARKER 63. OFFICER NEEDS ASSISTANCE. RADIO SILENCE UNTIL RADIO CONTACT IS RE-ESTABLISHED WITH UNIT 12. UNIT 12, YOUR STATUS?...GLORIA, DAMMIT. CAN YOU HEAR ME?"

The suburban didn't ram her. It pulled up along side of the police cruiser. The driver was looking down at Gloria. Her left leg was hanging out of the door. The foot was barely attached, hanging from a string of tendon. There was a steady pump of arterial blood from the stump.

Gloria tried to point her gun at her tormentor. She realized she had exchanged the gun for her radio microphone. She could still hear dispatch calling from the far end of a tunnel: "UNIT 12...UNIT 12...UNIT 12...COME IN, 12!" She noted calmly there was a gun pointed at her, but couldn't focus on why that was important. Then she remembered. She brought the microphone to her lips, her eyes on the handgun that had become her world. "This is unit 12. . .Gloria," she said. "Officer down."

The world exploded. Mercifully, Gloria had lost consciousness from the shock and the blood loss. She didn't feel the bullet rip through the side of her throat at a downward angle. The bullet exited her armpit and lodged in the passenger door. She died under a beautiful, bejeweled, Colorado night sky, which was indifferent to the little light that winked out of existence on the little planet drifting slowly around an adolescent star.

Chapter Twenty-Five

While Elliot, Sally, and Drake prepared to go spelunking in a man made cavern, detectives Margaret Madison and Jason Wright were puzzling over one of the strangest and most disturbing crime scenes either had ever seen; made more so by the fact that one of the victims was a fellow law enforcement officer.

The patrol car where Gloria Sanchez lay dead had been roped off with yellow crime scene tape along with the tan suburban with the dead body in the back seat. Sanchez had one leg hanging out of the door, the foot almost completely torn off. She'd also taken a bullet through the neck. The driver of the suburban, obviously their prime suspect was, of course, nowhere to be found.

From the large blonde paramedic, who seemed almost catatonic, slumped against the door of the patrol car, to the forensic vans, to the television crew who were starting to show up; the scene had all the makings of an unwanted media circus.

The first two police cruisers arrived about thirty minutes after the life force that had been Gloria Sanchez was extinguished. The paramedics had arrived about fifteen minutes after that. They were all too late.

The officers on the scene, Davis and Beale, had watched the ambulance, sirens wailing, screech to a stop. They had already checked the car. There was no rush. The ambulance driver jumped out of the ambulance and rushed over to the patrol car. Big guy, Davis thought; looks like a Viking.

The Viking, Eddie Johnson, paramedic, hero, sometimes god of thunder – at least to Gloria - rushed over to the patrol car. He could already see a leg hanging out of the door. *Gloria's leg?* This was her beat. *Please, God, don't let it be her!* But a part of him already knew. She could still be alive. Right? She had to be alive. Pay no attention to the two policemen already on the scene, somber and sad, and not acting as if there was anyone alive and in need of medical attention. She had to be alive. He had a surprise for her.

He'd squirreled away half of his last three paychecks for the surprise. He'd only known her for seven months, but she was *The One.* No woman had ever made him feel the way Gloria did. She was smart. She was funny. She was athletic and independent. She was quick to laugh and easy to be with. She was in love with him...She was dead.

Eddie looked in the window of the patrol car. He felt his throat constrict. His eyes became teary as if they refused to allow him to see what was in the car. Out of habit, he had reached into the car to feel for a pulse. Her skin was cold. *See! It couldn't be Gloria. Her skin was never cold.* Even when it was cold outside, Gloria seemed to radiate like a furnace. This would have been the morning. He had it all planned: He was going to make her breakfast in bed (after they finished their morning business). Then he was going to hide the engagement ring under her napkin. On bended knee, he would tell her; *You are my best friend and my soul-*

mate. Without you I'm nothing. Please marry me. He could feel the ring in his pocket. *What do I do with it now?*

Eddie's partner, Mike Smith had gone to the back of the ambulance to get their trauma kit while Eddie checked the victims for vitals. They'd done this dance a hundred times. His large partner was not checking for vitals, he was slumped by the side of the car, crying like a child. He had a jeweler's box in his hand. He looked somehow smaller, not at all like the god of thunder, but like a man whose spirit had been snapped like a twig. Mike looked inside the patrol car. Was that Gloria?

"Oh man, Eddie...Oh man, I'm sorry," Mike whispered. He had knelt beside his partner and put his arm around him. With each sob that wracked his body Eddie Johnson seemed to grow even smaller.

Detectives Margaret Madison and Jason Wright watched Eddie. He had long since stopped crying. Now, he was sitting on the ground next to the patrol car. Someone had thrown a blanket over his shoulders. He was rocking back and forth, clutching something to his chest. He look like a large, blonde, bear, guarding his fallen mate.

"I guess we should start doing the detective thing," said Detective Margaret Madison.

"Why don't we wait awhile," said Wright.

"We really should get this over with before the sun is too high," said Margaret

Wright looked at her and then looked at Eddie, grief stricken, crazed, his paramedic's uniform barely containing almost three hundred pounds of functional muscle. "You want to tell him to move," asked Wright.

Detective Madison nodded, "Maybe we can wait just a little while."

Chapter Twenty-Six

Okay that wasn't much fun at all. He was safely ensconced in his warehouse apartment in the Denver industrial center. He had run all night, which was no small feat considering he'd been easily 20 miles down highway 19 when he had his ill-fated encounter with Officer Gloria Sanchez.

What the hell had she been doing out there anyway? There was no criminal activity on that stretch of road (present company excluded), no drug dealers, no whores, no serial traffic offenders. No sir, nobody but us killers.

After he'd put a bullet in the police bitch, he had taken off running across the open plains. But first, he cleaned out the suburban's glove compartment. That hadn't taken long. The only thing in there, besides the gun, had been the vehicle insurance and registration showing the suburban registered to Lester Phillips. He then took a rag and wiped down every surface he could reach. He knew he was leaving behind hair and fibers, but there was nothing to be done about that. He didn't have any way to clean in that kind of detail.

As of tonight, Lester Phillips was dead. He'd only existed to purchase, register, and insure the suburban.

Officer Sanchez said people from the Air Force wanted to talk to him, or rather the owner of the truck. The OSI must have somehow managed to link the suburban to the missile silo or the mall. Snatching that kid had definitely been bad juju.

Now the police had the suburban and his green apple's thawing body. The connection between the two crimes was set in stone. What did it mean to him?

Between the two boys and the cop; having the suburban told the cops that there was one person responsible for three deaths in less than two months. It wasn't the most he'd ever killed in such a short time, but the others remained lost in the shadows of his past; a fraction of the faceless and nameless who went missing every year.

They would be pulling out all the stops now; especially with a dead cop in the equation. He had killed one of-their-own. That was a big 'no no'. Was killing the bitch really necessary? Had he panicked? Choked? Maybe.

He'd left them with two bodies in one shot. It didn't get much hotter than that. Alonso's body was clean...kind of. If they cut him open - and they would - they would find his semen, which would match that found on the Josh Bennet. No problem. He was still anonymous and invisible. He'd also given them a bullet, but that would tell them nothing without the gun for comparison. Even if they had the gun, it didn't matter. He'd used the 9mm that he'd taken from Alonso.

He had remembered to wipe down the truck. However, wiping a suburban clean was nothing like wiping off a lamp or a doorknob. If he missed any prints, they would find them. How long would that take? Days? Hours? Maybe it was time to disappear.

Okay, NO MORE KILLING...at least not until this blew over. That could take awhile. He could handle it. He'd once gone a whole year without killing anybody. He was just going to have to find another hobby or something, maybe go back to school, and get his master's degree in abnormal psychology. Yeah, he could handle that. It'd be like a Mexican taking Spanish.

That had been some run, almost 25 miles, in work boots. He was pretty pleased by that. *You are still one tough motherfucker.* He had cleaned up the crime scene, and run a marathon across moonlit plains, and through the city. He'd just finished the serial killer triathlon. Not without a price, though, his feet were swollen and blistered inside his boots, and he was going to lose a couple of toenails. But going it on foot and getting a few blisters beat the alternatives: he could have driven the suburban back into town, of course the cops would have been looking all over for it. He was sure the policewoman had called it in. Staying in the suburban meant running the risk of having the cops chase him down and kill him while he resisted arrest, which he had been prepared to do. No sir, not going to happen. He could have just sat there with his thumbs up his ass and waited for them to come get him. On second thought, maybe he didn't choke. He'd instinctively made the right decision; just like he'd been trained to do.

Good thing it was a weekend. If this had all happened during the week, he would have never made it into work on time. He was sitting in his usual spot, on the couch in front of the television. He started working on the laces of his combat boots. He feet were so tender to the touch that he contemplated just cutting the boots off. But they were his favorite boots, and he didn't feel like breaking in a new pair. He worked the boots gently off each foot. When he peeled his socks off, they were lined with his skin.

He cleaned his feet, covered them with dollops of antibacterial cream, then wrapped them in gauze. He was dehydrated from his run and starving. He made himself drink a half-quart of water and a sports drink before he allowed himself to even think about solid food. Then he settled into the couch to wait for the news.

He didn't have to wait long. The death of Officer Gloria Sanchez was on every local channel. The Channel 6 news chick was on the scene. Conservative brown skirt, yellow shirt, hair professionally wind blown; she had that gleam in her eyes that news people get with they know they have a scoop:

"Good Evening, I'm Melanie Rivers with Channel Six news..."

"Good Evening, Melanie," he said to the television.

"We're on a desolate stretch of highway 19 at the scene of a most tragic and bizarre crime. Early this morning; Officer Gloria Sanchez, two years with the Denver Police Department, was shot and killed during a routine traffic stop, apparently by the driver of the truck you see behind me." The camera shifted away from Melanie Rivers and panned in on the suburban. "Authorities are still looking for the driver, who fled the scene on foot."

"That he did," he said out loud, examining his bandages.

"...In a surprising and unsettling twist, patrolmen responding to Officer Sanchez's final pleas for assistance, discovered the body of an unidentified black male in the back seat of the truck."

"Authorities believe this horrific scene could have some connection to the kidnapping and murder of five year old Josh Bennet, whose body - you will recall - was found in one of the Air Force's abandoned missile silos during March of this year. Local police are reluctant to call this a serial crime, and Air Force Officials have declined comment at this time."

"All that we know for sure is that this is one of the most egregious acts of violence to assail our city in recent history. Stay tuned throughout the day for more updates. I'm Melanie Rivers, and this has been a Channel Six News Special Report."

"Looks like I'm famous," he said to his empty apartment. "I don't think I like that at all."

Unlike many of his kind, he took no pleasure in seeing his crimes attract media attention. He had never been this close to discovery. Although he had done plenty of backstopping and all of his protocols and fail-safes were in place, he'd also been lucky. He hated relying on luck; luck ran out.

Chapter Twenty-Seven

Elliot, Sally, and Steve Drake headed out to the missile fields at around five o'clock that morning. They missed the morning news and were oblivious to the events currently being presided over by detectives Margaret Madison and her partner, Jason Wright. They arrived as the sun began peeking beneath horizon: a gentle, pink ribbon pushing against the navy blue shade of night. They clustered around the round, 4-foot in diameter, concrete slab, pulled aside where the cowboys had left it, inviting anyone who dared access to the missile maintenance shaft. Even in this remote area, some local residents, disturbed by the loss of an innocent life, had deposited teddy bears, cards, and flowers around the entrance. They stood for a moment, not wanting to disturb the monument. Finally Drake stepped forward and began carefully removing the gifts. Elliot and Sally helped him.

They climbed down the shaft and made their way to the scene of the crime. After an initial glance to be sure nothing had been disturbed, they pulled out the map and inspected it with their flashlights. Elliot didn't need the map. He felt an insistent tugging in the pit of his stomach.

As Sally and Drake turned the map this way and that, he swung the flashlight beam into the corridor to his left. It was grey and square, the concrete floor fading into the darkness beneath exposed pipes and concrete walls, painted with streaks of dark rust the color of drying blood, and white lime deposits.

Sally stepped next to him holding the map, "That way." She said, pointing in the direction he was facing. They started walking. The corridors connecting the silos ran for miles. They walked in silence, not wanting their voices to bounce off the walls. Elliot led the way, as Sally checked their progress on the blue prints, but she needn't have bothered since each turn he took led them in the direction of the nearest silo. Their boots crunched on debris littering the floor, and splashed through the occasional puddle. The entire place smelled like rust, metal, and mud. Finally they arrived at a door with the numerical designator "11" above it.

"Here we are." Elliot said. He turned the doorknob and swung the door open. It didn't make a sound. He frowned. Sally began to move forward, but he stopped her. "Why didn't it creak?"

"What?"

"The door, it didn't creak. If no one has been down here in years, it should be rusty as shit. It should creak." He was looking at the hinges. He stood on his tiptoes and shinned the light into the creases of the door. The plates were discolored with age, but the hinges themselves were shiny with use. Someone had lubricated them.

"Holy shit." Drake said behind them.

Elliot looked down at the doorknob and instantly regretted not wearing gloves. Each of them was carrying backpacks with a full investigative kit in it. Elliot dropped his bag, opened it and pulled out his finger printing kit. He regarded it for a moment, then put it back in the bag.

"What are you doing?" Sally asked.

"Doorknobs are hard to get prints off of with tape. It crinkles. Let's just remove the knob and have the lab techs hit it with glue." Elliot suggested. Epoxy glue, when made into a mist, attached itself to the oils left behind by the touch of a human hand on any surface, regardless of its structure.

"Ah," Drake said, "good idea." He pulled out his Leatherman and took Elliot's place in front of the door. Once he had removed the knob, they placed it in a paper bag and secured it in Elliot's backpack.

They turned their attention to the silo room. It was large, with the cylindrical silo situated in the center, surrounded by metal spiraling stairs. The top of the silo was flat and open. Next to the opening, attached to the end of the stairs, was a maintenance platform. Looming overhead was the silo dome, which opened to the world above. In the event of a nuclear attack, that dome would open like a gapping maw to spew forth the missile beneath.

Without needing to speak, they fanned out: Elliot taking the left, Drake the right, and Sally the center. All of them had pulled out their weapons. They performed a sweep of the room, each keeping the others in their peripheral vision. They converged on the opposite side of the silo. Satisfied that no one was in the room with them, they returned to stairs and ascended them to the platform. They peered over the edge and shone their flashlight beams downward. Years of flood run off had filled the missile shaft with stagnant water.

"Fuck." Sally said.

The flashlight beams refused to penetrate the inky black of the waters' surface. Elliot felt mesmerized by the shinning liquid. He felt as though he couldn't drag his gaze away. It was telling him a story and he wanted to listen…if it weren't for Sally's fingers digging into his bicep and shaking him in the most annoying way possible.

"What!?" he snapped.

"We've been talking to you for about a minute." She was pulling him away from the edge, and looking tense. "Let's go back up top, and figure out how to deal with our water problem."

Elliot suddenly felt like he could breathe again. "Yeah, okay, good idea. This place sucks anyway."

"Yeah," Echoed Drake, who was watching him with barely concealed concern.

Not knowing that significant events involving their case were unfurling not too far across the plains, their main concern of the early afternoon was trying to figure out what to do with the water in the missile shaft.

"We could send divers down," Drake said.

"It would take a special kind of diver to want to get in that water," Elliot said.

"Yea," Sally said, "...a special kind of stupid diver." She looked pointedly at Drake when she said 'stupid'.

They were eating lunch on the hood of their unmarked government sedan. Sally, demonstrating the foresight and practicality that often epitomized her sex, had insisted they pack a lunch in coolers in anticipation of a long day far from the convenience of a drive through.

"Have you ever noticed," Elliot said, mouth full of ham sandwich, "...these cars make better tables than they do cars?"

"Let's have it pumped," Sally said

"Well, that was easy." Drake said sarcastically. "I'll just go get the industrial strength pump out of the trunk. Where are we supposed to find somebody to pump out a whole missile shaft? It's not like pumping out a flooded living room or basement."

"You...will...always...be...an...asshole," Sally said to Drake. "I figured we would use the Base's Civil Engineers. You might have thought of that too, if you weren't an idiot." Then to Elliot: "What do you think?"

Elliot had drifted off again. He'd crawled into that dark corner of his mind where the weird shit happened and the world outside became the fantasy. He'd been in and out of that state since they'd returned to the missile fields. Elliot knew with every fiber of his being there were bodies deep in that water: a lot of them. Drake and Sally didn't know what he was doing, but they knew he was doing something. Drake, not being privy to Elliot's *secret,* decided he was understandably preoccupied.

Sally figured, correctly, the he was hoping that returning to the crime scene would shake up his erratic 'talents'.

Elliot was staring intently at his sandwich as if he'd never seen a slice of ham before. The ancients read tea leaves; Elliot was reading ham on white.

"Earth to Elliot," Sally said, tossing a piece of foil at him.

"Huh?" Elliot looked up. His eyes were clouded over. He looked at Sally as if he didn't recognize her. He closed his eyes and shook his head. When he opened them, they were bright and alert.

"You find anything in that sandwich besides ham and cheese?" Sally asked.

Elliot held his sandwich out at arms length, and eyed it critically, "Ah...the universe on the head of a pin," he said, "...a serial killer in a sandwich." He was grinning, but Sally thought his eyes looked serious.

"Try not to be too weird today, okay." Sally said.

"So what do you think about this whole pumping thing?" Drake asked Elliot.

"I can say that I am unequivocally in favor of the 'pumping thing'," Elliot said. "What's the pumping thing? It sounds dirty, sorry I missed it."

"Pumping the water out of the missile shaft," Sally said. "We were talking about pumping out the shaft..."

"She said 'shaft'," Drake said giggling.

"Kiss my ass, Drake," Sally said.

"It's a good idea," Elliot said. "If the Civil Engineers don't have the equipment for it, most construction companies have mobile rigs that could handle that volume of water in a few hours." Sally looked at Drake and stuck her tongue out at him. Drake gave her the 'finger' and wandered of to find a private place to relieve himself.

"I wish I were a guy." Sally said. "My eyeballs are floating."

"I suggest you get into this whole outdoors thing," Elliot said. "It's going to be another long one."

"Aren't they all," Sally said, scanning the plains for a 'private spot' of her own. "Did you get one of your...you know...*flashes*, or something?"

"No," Elliot said. "No *flash*, but I can smell death in the water. There's something down there. I'm going to call the office and get Jerry or one of the other guys to get an industrial pump sent out here."

Sally had made a mental note of which direction Drake had gone. She walked off in the opposite direction. Elliot hopped off the hood and got into the drivers' seat. He turned the car on, plugged the bag phone into the cigarette lighter, and called the office. The Commander, George Devine, answered the phone. *Oh great!* He thought.

"What do you want, Turner?" Devine greeted him.

Top of the morning to you too, boss, you prick.

Elliot explained what he needed, and Devine said he would get someone right on it. *God forbid he should pick up a fucking phone and do a little investigative work himself.* Devine also brought Elliot up to speed on the Officer Sanchez situation.

While Elliot talked with the Commander, Drake returned and busied himself cleaning their picnic remains off the hood of the car. Sally came back and hovered next to the open window, listening to Elliot's half of the conversation and trying to figure out what was taking so long to arrange for a pump.

Elliot was drumming his fingers on the steering wheel, telephone to his ear, shaking his head saying things like; "Yea...uh huh...hmm...I see...uh, uh...yea. We're on it. No. No, about two hours? No, we're fine. We're big kids, we can handle this. Okay. Bye." He hung up the phone and got out of the car.

"Devine?" Sally asked.

"Yeah."

"What'd he say?"

"He said the pump truck should be no problem. It should be here in a couple of hours. But there's more. Go get Drake."

Sally was going to tell him to stop being so cryptic; but she saw he was drifting inside himself again, and let it alone. Elliot walked over to the silo entrance and sat down on the concrete covering. Sally and Drake came over and sat down beside him.

They looked like three thirty something year old kids, sitting on a curb, wishing they had something to do. Elliot was chewing on a toothpick, frowning, lost in thought. He had a stick and was using it to coral a stink bug. Drake was tossing pebbles into the sagebrush, not aiming at anything in particular. Sally was fidgeting. Finally, she said; "Well...?"

"Oh, sorry." Sometimes Elliot forgot that other people couldn't read *his* mind. The news about Gloria Sanchez was monumental. She had seen his suspect, and he must have left valuable evidence behind. He started to feel an excited glimmer of hope that this might be the break they needed.

"The local cops found the suburban we were looking for," Elliot said.

"Did the suburban's owner see anything related to our case?" Drake asked.

"I have no doubt what so ever that he saw everything." Elliot said

"That's great!" Sally said

"He saw everything because he was the fucking killer," Elliot said. Both Sally and Drake screwed their faces into question marks, but neither said anything. Elliot gave his pet stink bug one last flick and continued. "A cop-female-pulled him over early this morning. He managed to ram her with the fucking suburban and put a bullet in her."

Sally groaned, "Is she dead?"

"Yeah, she's dead. She managed to call for backup before he shot her, for all the good it did. Fucker was smart enough to realize she might have called for backup, and he probably had a better chance on foot. He abandoned the suburban and disappeared on the open plains.

"This is starting to sound like a bad movie." Drake said.

"Yes, well, if they make this into a movie, I want Bruce Willis to play me," Elliot said. "He's cool."

"He's also white," Sally explained patiently, as if to a very slow child.

"Oh, I see how it is," Elliot said grinning; "If I was a white guy, you wouldn't have a problem with Bruce playing me."

"If you were a white guy, this entirely pointless conversation would be moot. " Sally said.

"Oh," Elliot said. "Anyway, that's not all. There was a body wrapped in plastic in the back seat of the suburban."

"Holy Cow!" Drake said. "What are we doing here?"

"We're going to finish what we came to do," Elliot said. "The Denver Police are on the case. They've assured Devine that they'll keep him in the loop. Oh, and - surprise, surprise - the Feds want a piece of this now."

"Do we know who in Denver Homicide is going to honcho this on their end?" Sally asked.

"You know Margaret Madison?" Elliot asked.

"I think so."

"Well, I think she's lead investigator. She's good but kind of a cold fish."

"What makes you say that?" Sally asked.

"I asked her out to a movie last year at that conference thing, and she wouldn't give me the time of day."

"Maybe it was your breath," Drake said.

"Maybe it was your Elliotness," Sally said.

"Whatever," Elliot went back to toying with his pet stink bug, who had been loitering around, soaking up the conversation and reveling in his new found domesticity.

Chapter Twenty-Eight

It took almost three hours for the septic truck to arrive. Elliot crawled into the back seat of the car to take a combat nap. Drake and Sally passed the time alternately arguing about their previous relationship and ignoring each other.

"You know," Sally was saying. "A pig in a designer suit is still a pig."

"That's profound," Drake said, brushing a patch of dust off his sleeve. "When ever you come up with one of those little sayings; I asked myself how I could have dumped such a clever woman."

"You did not dump me. I dumped you."

"Did not."

"Did to."

"Did not." They went back to ignoring each other.

Shortly before the truck arrived, Elliot peeled himself out of the unmarked government sedan/picnic table/bedroom and wandered over to where Sally and Drake were sitting, firmly entrenched in the ignoring each other portion of the evening, adrift in their newly visited mutual loathing.

"Raymond's coming out here," Elliot said.

"Inside information?" Sally asked, tapping her index finger against her temple.

"Car phone." Elliot jabbed a thumb in the direction of the sedan. "What have you two crazy kids been up to?" He asked absently, not really expecting or listening for an answer.

"Strolling down memory lane," Drake said. Then to Sally, "Was it as good for you as it was for me?"

"Don't… start!" Sally said through her teeth, the threat naked.

Elliot was staring off at the horizon, brow furrowed, deep at work on some Elliot Turner inner mystery. He looked at Drake and Sally, his expression almost comic in its I-have-something-important-on-my-mind configuration. "What do you guys think of Anne Bennet?"

"What?" Sally asked. Anne Bennet? He pulled that one out of his ass. "I think she's the mother of a victim in a high profile case. That is the context you meant; right?"

"You don't think there's something special about her?" Elliot asked.

"I don't believe your sitting here mooning over the mother of our victim." Sally said. "You know, I'm starting to get disgusted with the whole male animal experience."

"Special? Like one of Jerry's kids, right?" Drake asked. "I agree with Dupree. I don't want to hear about any feelings you may be developing for Anne Bennett. The only thing special about her is some whack job killed her only child. Tell your feelings to stand down."

"Definitely," Sally said. "She could be involved somehow."

"She's not," Elliot said defensively.

"We all know that," Sally said; "but we don't know that. She's too close to the case and the limelight. Don't go stupid on us."

"I wasn't saying I was going to do anything," Elliot said. "I was just sharing my feelings. You know? Another time and another place, maybe...

"Next time you want to share something," Drake said; "warn us, so we can wear protection; dark glasses and rubber gloves or something. Because in the future, I don't want to get any of what you're sharing on me." Sally giggled in spite of herself.

"Try to have a fucking moment with friends," Elliot said, almost pouting.

"Are you pouting?" Sally asked. "Because that's a trick reserved for lesser men. "

"I'm not pouting," he said pouting.

Drake joined in, "Looked very pout-like to me, definitely pout-esque; and I'm more than a little ashamed to have witnessed it."

Drake stood up and smoothed his jeans. He patted the dirt off his butt and checked his tie. *I can't believe he's wearing a tie out here.* Elliot thought. Even Drake's jeans, after a morning on the open plains, were still crisp.

"Is that your friend?" Drake asked, peering off into the distance to where a plume of smoke was visible.

Elliot could just barely see the light bar on top of the Sheriff's truck. "Ah," he said, shielding his eyes from the late morning sun. "Hail the comet Ken Raymond. I must depart this earthly shell and go say to him 'whatsup' in the galactic tongue of our forefathers." Elliot walked over to the unmarked government sedan and waited for Raymond to pull up.

"He's so weird sometimes," Sally said as much to herself as to Drake, who answered her anyway.

"Yeah, but he's going to make us famous. You know he's done...things."

"So I hear." They walked over to wait with Elliot.

Ken rolled to a stop in a cloud of dust. He stepped out of the truck before the cloud dissipated, thus ensuring he'd have to walk through it; the hero emerging from the open plains. He paused, let the dust settle, and looked back over his shoulder for no particular reason. But the gesture allowed the sun to catch his jaw at the perfect angle, making him look like a young Lee Majors. Elliot didn't think Ken was ignorant of the effect.

Elliot walked over to him smiling. "You are so cool you should have your own theme music. You know? Hero music, something appropriate for a high plains drifter like yourself."

"I missed you too, man," Drake drawled. "Especially at night: the missus won't take it up the ass like you do."

"This a social call?"

Like an intrusive CB transmission on an FM radio, Elliot suddenly picked up an intense and unexpected telepathic flash from Raymond, Officer Gloria Sanchez, slumped on the dash board of her patrol car in a pool of coagulating blood, the left side of her neck turned to hamburger by an exiting hollow point slug. At least Raymond was thinking it had to have been a hollow point.

"You okay, man?" Ken asked. "You just went ghost white, which is no small feat because you're black."

"You are, you know," Drake said, not wanting to be left out of the snappy banter. "I'm Steve Drake." Drake held out his hand. Raymond took it and gave it one firm pump, looking Drake in the eye. Drake met his gaze in the time honored cop version of two dogs sniffing each other's asses.

"Nice to meet you," Raymond said. "How'd you come to be hooked up with these two regular agents?"

"I went to the OSI Academy with Turner, and Sally and I used to do it."

"Fuck you Drake," Sally finally found her cue. "Drake's our Regional Forensic Consultant. He's here to help us with the big words and keep us straight."

Raymond noticed Sally didn't deny the 'doing it' comment.

"Good luck," Raymond jerked a thumb at Elliot. "This one's as twisted as they come."

"Yea I know. Fortunately; I'm also his therapist," Drake said, "and he's coming along just fine. We've almost got the bed-wetting thing licked. Don't we, E.T.?"

"Drake thinks that, once I get over my thing for small furry animals, I can be a productive member of society again. Every day in every way, I'm getting better, and better and...hey, is that a squirrel?"

Sally interjected, "If you guys are done - and mind you, I don't want to spoil your fun - mind if I asked why you're here, Ken? Not that I could ever get enough of that jawline."

"Ken just came from the other crime scene," Elliot said.

"Wow, figured that out all by yourself, huh?"

"That's why I'm a Special Agent, and you're a hick cop."

"Oh, and here I thought the special meant you couldn't read. But seriously I did just come from the other scene and...shit. This just keeps getting stranger. I mean...shit... man...shit." Ken leaned back against his car gathering his thoughts. Now he was the sensitive vulnerable high plains drifter. He noticed Sally's expression go all gooey at Raymond's sudden sensitivity. Elliot thought *Note to self: be more sensitive. Chicks like that.*

"I knew Gloria Sanchez," Ken said.

"Is that the officer who was killed?" Sally asked, using

the exchange as an excuse to place a sympathetic hand on his bulging bicep.

"She grew up around here. She was only twenty-two years old. She'd been on the force about two years. All she ever wanted to be was a cop"

"Man." said Drake.

"That's not the worst part. Her boyfriend is a paramedic. He responded to the scene. He was so torn up they had to sedate him."

"Oh, man," Sally said. Elliot and Drake gave 'oh man' sounding grunts. Guy speak. With one grunt the managed to say, "Oh man, if that happened to my girlfriend I don't know what I'd do. That is so depressing. Life is sooo unfair." To Sally they just sounded like non-committal grunts, and it reaffirmed her disappointment in the male of the species.

Elliot changed the subject, eager to break the melancholy and flee the realm of Gloria Sanchez. "Why are you here anyway?" Elliot asked. "Did you just want to play news boy? Don't you have some vandals or shoplifters to roust in Mayberry?"

"Not at all. My streets are safe from vandals and common rabble, and while I don't have any jurisdictional juice in all this weirdness, it is happening right in my back yard so I want to keep an eye on it. When I left the other scene, I called your office to talk to you about it, and your boss said you were out here. So I says to myself...'self, Why don't we go see what speckled agent Turner and his purty little investigative maul-that's you Sally-are up to."

"You forgot me," said Drake.

"Didn't know you'd be out here but you are a might purty yourself, in a prison kind of way. Are those jeans Armani?"

"And he's witty too," said Drake. "We're waiting on a

truck to pump the water out of the missile shaft. You gonna hang around?"

"A truck like that monstrosity?"

There was a large truck in the distances rumbling slowly towards them. With the large oval cylinder on its back, it looked the basic oil and gas truck.

"Show time boys and Sally," Elliot said.

Chapter Twenty-Nine

Eddie Johnson, paramedic, sometimes god of thunder, had been sedated and guided off to valium Valhalla, leaving homicide detectives Margaret Madison and Jason Wright free to do their thing, which seemed to involve a fair amount of tut tutting, grimacing, and saying 'hmmmm.'

Officer Gloria Sanchez's death presented no major mind twizzler for the detectives. She had been shot through the neck and her foot had been almost sliced off at the ankle by her car door after being rammed by the rear bumper of the suburban. They had taken paint samples from both the patrol car and the rear bumper of the suburban. But they were just going through the motions. They both could read that part of the crime scene like a book.

The body in the suburban was another story altogether. It presented what was known in the detective world as a gin-you-wine mystery.

Alonso's almost thawed and gamy corpse had been transported to Brent Sheldon's lab. There it had been carefully unwrapped by the young pathologist. The green trash bag that was his death shroud had been carefully placed in a cardboard box. It would be sent to the crime lab and processed for latent prints.

Detectives Madison and Wright were in the lab with the pathologist. Alonso's body was displayed on one of the stainless steel examination tables. Brent hadn't cut him open. He was still doing the exterior exam. He was walking around the table with the detectives following him single file like medical interns as he dictated into a micro-cassette recorder.

"Denver police case number 93187280: I'm conducting the exterior examination of an unidentified black male, John Doe 89. I estimate him to be approximately sixteen years of age. John Doe 89 was found under unnatural conditions, wrapped in plastic trash bags in the back seat of a truck, believed to be used during the murder of Denver patrol officer, Gloria Sanchez. Cause of death appears to be a violent realignment of the uppermost vertebrae..."

"Somebody broke his fucking neck," Wright offered his medical expertise.

"Shhh," Margaret Madison silenced her partner. "I can't take you anywhere," she whispered.

Brent clicked off his micro-cassette, "Do you both mind...?

"Sorry," Margaret whispered. She made a zipping motion across her mouth and smacked Wright on the shoulder. He gave Brent a sheepish smile and copied Margaret's zip.

Drake turned his recorder back on. "Subject has been deceased for an undetermined amount of time due to the apparent refrigeration of the body. There is no other major trauma to the body. However, there are several horizontal lacerations, each about three centimeters long, and five millimeters deep. The wounds run in a vertical pattern down subject's body." Drake clicked his recorder off again.

"Hey, I didn't say anything," Wright said.

"You two may want to talk to Special Agent Elliot Turner from the Air Force OSI." Brent said.

"Turner, Turner...where do I know that name?" Margaret asked.

"He's the lead investigator on the Bennett case."

"Dead kid in silo?"

"That's the one. By now everybody's determined the guy driving the truck was probably the same guy who killed the kid. But one of the things we withheld from the press was that the Bennett kid had wounds just like this on his body."

"You know Elliot Turner?" Wright asked Margaret.

"Now that I think about it, yeah. We've met. Matter of fact, he came on to me last year at that thing."

"Came on to you?"

"Yeah, he made a pass at me"

"What'd he say?"

"He asked if I wanted to go to a movie with him some time."

"That's not a come on," Brent said.

"It's the way he said it."

"How'd he say it?" Wright asked.

"It was like, 'Hey babe, how 'bout a movie-wink-and then he undressed me with his eyes."

"He really said 'hey babe?" Brent asked.

"No, but he was thinking it, and I felt naked when he looked at me."

"He really winked?" Wright asked.

"No, but there was an implied wink in his voice."

"I think you were projecting," Brent said.

"Whatever."

"If I were a chick, I'd think he was attractive," Brent said.

Wright looked him up and down. "You going all homo on us doc?"

"No, hey, I was just saying...you know? Elliot's okay. I mean he's like a cross between Denzell Washington and Mickey Rourke."

"You can't cross those two," Margaret said.

"Why?"

"Because Denzell is Black and Mickey is white."

"Exactly," Wright said. "Actually, I met him too. He seemed okay."

"Then you'd go out with him?" Margaret asked.

"Are you crazy?" Wright said, laughing. "He's a creepy motherfucker."

Chapter Thirty

The truck was making a suck-gurgle-slurp-squish-slop sound; a metal behemoth feeding on some delectable filth. One orange hose – which Elliot liked to think of as the suck-gurgle-slurp, unit - had been lowered into the missile shaft via the winding metal staircase. It spiraled down the length of the stairs and wound serpentine through the entrance chamber of the underground complex and three sub-chambers until it reached the top of the missile shaft. The other hose - the squish-slop unit - was regurgitating the filth from the shaft into another truck. Elliot hoped they would reach the bottom soon before they needed another truck.

They had run into a number of logistical problems with the pumping process, which had seemed relatively simple in the beginning. First, there was the monumental effort of running the hose through the missile shaft. It would have been more convenient if they could have opened the silo doors: but they weighed several tons a piece, and the mechanism to open them didn't work unless the silo was active and you had launch codes. Then they needed to get the second truck when one of the pump truck operators pointed out that pumping it into the nearby creek bed (as Drake suggested) might be construed by the great State of Colorado as environmental contamination of some sort – on account of the whole *nuclear* aspect of it. The water smelled like raw sewage and...something else. Elliot had a good idea what the something else was, and it wasn't nuclear waste.

The pump operators, two Air Force civil engineers in BDU's, were busy monitoring the pressure gauges attached to the valves on the truck. They were wearing white paper surgical masks. Elliot, Sally and Ken Raymond were also wearing masks. Everyone looked slightly out of place; big kids playing doctor, except for Drake. With his blue blazer, power tie, and starched jeans, Drake simply looked like a hip young surgeon.

Elliot's couldn't shake the feeling of dread that had attached itself to his spine; and the feeling increased with each stream of filth the belched forth from the hose into the giant belly of the truck the engineers called a "water buffalo". The smell of filth and - now he was certain about the other something...putrefaction…and the electric tension emanating from the others was edging him towards the feeling of detachedness which usually preceded one of his episodes. He knew what they were going to find. His mind latched onto an image of the mass graves from the holocaust during the Second World War. The image coated his mind like a living blanket of psychic sludge, its tendrils worming in and holding tight, tainting his own memories; making him see what he didn't want to see. Mutilated corpses floated before his eyes, blank stares and grins of rictus.

Elliot closed his eyes but the images persisted. He was nudged out of his vision by a loud, hollow, slurping sound. It sounded like a child (a big one) trying to capture the last dregs of a milkshake through a straw, only multiplied a hundred fold.

When he opened eyes Sally was staring at him, looking intently into his eyes, with a worried look on her face. Drake was standing behind her. He was looking at the two pump operators, who were walking hurriedly around the truck, turning off generators and closing valves.

"Looks like we're about ready." Drake said without much enthusiasm.

Sally was still staring intently at Elliot. "Is it bad?" she asked.

"On a scale of one to heinous; it rates a heinous plus six," Elliot said.

"Are you okay?" Sally reached out and touched his cheek. The tenderness of the gesture didn't escape Drake's notice.

"Tell you a secret," Elliot said. "I haven't been okay in months." He looked at the silo entrance. "Let's do this."

The pump operators displayed none of the normal human morbid curiosity for things grotesque or out of the norm. Some inner voice told them that what was in the shaft went well beyond normal rubber-necking entertainment at a car accident. Without saying a word to each other, they'd come to the mutual agreement that sticking around was simply something they weren't prepared to do. They'd smelled the water spewing out of the hose. Whatever was in the shaft smelled as bad as their usual pump jobs, but different. The difference went beyond weird different and was kissing up on evil different.

With Elliot as a guide, they had climbed down into the missile silo complex to position the hoses properly. Now they were thankful that they could simply crank up the hoses with a wench. They watched as the hose wound around its spool, hoping it didn't snag on anything that would make them climb back into the silo. After the hose was fully retracted, they waited by their truck for further orders: no doubt hoping Elliot would relieve them of duty and allow them to go on their way.

Elliot and crew silently climbed into the silo, once again into the mouth of evil. The stench of wet decay assaulted them when they reached the chamber which connected the missile shaft to the service chamber. In addition to providing concealment for the grisly booty at the bottom of the shaft, the water in the shaft had acted as a filter for the putrescence which now drifted freely throughout the silo. The masks they wore were ineffectual against its cloying presence.

Elliot heard Sally make a gagging noise, and even Drake's bubble of detached efficiency had caved in under the odiferous assault. In the flashlight beam, Drake was drawn and pale. His normally tanned skin had gone an unhealthy gray.

They made their way towards the maw of the shaft. This close to the pit, they didn't need Elliot's extraordinary senses to tell them what they were sharing their space with. They were all familiar with the smell of death, and this close to the freshly drained shaft the air was ripe with eye watering, sickly sweet smelling gases which had started their evolution as caustic human fluids.

When they reached the shaft, Elliot and Drake shined their flashlights into the hole. Sally and Ken grasp the circular raised wall of the shaft and followed the beam to the bottom. The air in the shaft was so thick with putrid mist that it seemed to slow down the lights descent.

Once the light reached the bottom something green and glistening (many somethings green and glistening) greedily captured the light and began to play with it and pass it back and forth between them.

"This is too much!" Ken said. The sheriff backed away

from the hole, retching. None of the others turned to watch. Their attention was trapped by the pit. They gave him his privacy as, against the wall of the chamber, he began to efficiently evacuate every particle of the ham and cheese omelet he had for breakfast.

"How many do you think there are?" Sally finally asked. Her eyes were watering, and Elliot didn't think it was because of the foul air. The bottom of the pit was lined with not quite man-sized bundles wrapped with duct tape.

"More that twenty; less than a hundred," Drake said.

Elliot was silent. He was seeing the holocaust images again, superimposed over the human shaped bundles in the pit. This was nowhere near the scale of the Nazi death camps, but it was every bit as horrible. The plastic bags made it somehow just as evil, not worse, but a disregard of human life every bit as terrible in its deliberate nature as the death camp atrocities.

"Well," Elliot said calmly. "This little slice of evil is going to ruin the evening for a bunch of people." Then he turned and threw up too.

Chapter Thirty-One

There were 29 bodies. Even the pathologist, Brent Shelton, well accustomed to the bizarre and grotesque, was unsettled. The bodies were in the same disposal configuration as that of Alonso Proctor, found in the suburban. But while Alonso's body had been relatively fresh, the bodies in the shaft had had time to ripen. They'd grown soft and squishy in their plastic cocoons, marinating in their own fetid juices.

When Brent skillfully cut through the green plastic and peeled it aside to display the first victim (Silo John Doe #1), the outer layers of skin split and sloughed off onto the plastic in a gooey pile. The sub-dermal fat followed, dripping onto the piles of skin like yellow tapioca pudding left too long out of the refrigerator. *Well that's just about the most horrible thing I've ever seen,* he thought.

It was 12:00 am-the witching hour. The bodies had been delivered to him at around 11:00 p.m. He'd been getting ready for bed earlier that evening when a shaken up Special Agent Elliot Turner called to give him a heads up on the terrible discovery. He'd popped a couple of ephedrine tablets to stay awake, a habit he'd had since his college days - not that they were that far behind him. He found a pair of wearable jeans from the only-worn-once pile in his closet, and rushed to his lab.

29 bodies! Brent looked down the row of plastic shrouded bodies. There were six examination tables in the room all six held the discarded playthings of an entity surely too evil to be called human. The rest of the bodies were on ice. Brent had contacted the pathologist's offices in Colorado Springs and Oklahoma City for assistance. He expected the Colorado Springs pathologist to arrive in a couple of hours. The Oklahoma City pathologist would be on the first morning flight into Denver. *This is what I have to show for one to many Quincy reruns as a kid*. Brent marveled at how quickly *Quincy* could turn into *The Twilight Zone*.

* * *

Elliot was pacing back and forth in the wide corridor outside of Brent Shelton's laboratory, the expectant father waiting for the birth of a lead. He had accompanied the bodies to the laboratory. However, his dead body meter was pegged out, and he couldn't force himself to enter the lab, even though curiosity was killing him. He assumed Drake and Sally felt the same way. Neither was making a move towards the lab. The corridor had been converted into a makeshift lobby, presumably for squeamish cops. There were a couple of uncomfortable chairs, a soda machine, and a snack machine. Drake and Sally were sitting on two of the chairs, for once they were too caught up in their own bubbles of private horror to bicker. They were sharing a supper of shock, candy bars, and diet soda. Ken Raymond had fled to his domestic sanctuary long before the shaft disgorged its last loathsome package. Elliot envied him.

"When it rains it pours, huh?" Detective Margaret

Madison wandered up behind Elliot, disrupting his pacing.

"Brent asked us to talk to you about the kid we found in the suburban."

"Why, was he burked?" Elliot asked, knowing exactly what Margaret wanted to talk about.

"Beg your pardon?"

"You know, suffocation by squishing. Didn't Brent explain it to you?"

"I don't know anything about that," Margaret eyed him suspiciously. Now she remembered what she hadn't liked about Elliot; No matter what he was saying, it was as if he was having some private joke at her expense. "Brent wanted us to talk to you about the cuts." She handed him a picture of a young black...boy?

"Is this a boy?" Elliot asked.

"Pretty, huh?"

"If that's your flavor, he's a little young for me," Elliot said, taking a closer look at the picture.

Drake walked past them zombie like and entered the lab. He grunted a greeting at Margaret as he walked past. Elliot watched him go.

"Personable fellow," Margaret said.

"We've had a long day," Elliot said in Drake's defense.

"Look at the cuts," Margaret moved behind him where she could see over his right shoulder. She leaned over his arm and pointed at the picture with her right hand. Her chest brushed against his arm. Elliot wondered if she was as conscious of the contact as he.

"There were cuts just like this on the Bennett kid," he said.

"That's what Sheldon said...oh, I'm sorry. Have you met my partner, Jason Wright" Wright had been hovering silently, watching Sally do battle halfway down the corridor with an old style pull handle candy machine and swearing under her breath. Now he turned his attention to Elliot and held out his hand.

"I think we've met," Jason said.

"Last year, at that thing, right?"

"Had to be. How've you been?"

"Tired, confused and generally freaked out," Elliot said.

"You too, huh?" He looked over at Sally. "That's your partner isn't it?" Sally was bending down in front of the machine, unconsciously displaying her posterior in its best light. Jason thought it was a fine posterior.

"I think so too" Elliot said just loud enough to be heard.

"What?" Jason asked.

"I didn't say anything," Elliot said.

From across the room Sally muttered, "fuck." and kicked the candy machine in frustration. Jason walked over and said something to her under his breath. Sally stepped aside. Jason jiggled the change return lever a couple of times and said something else to Sally. She pointed at a candy bar (her second of the evening). Jason braced one hand on the machine and jerked the handle like a lawn mower cork. They heard the *thunk* of a candy bar dropping into the catch tray.

"He's always been mechanically inclined," Margaret said.

"Um," Elliot said, looking at Alonso's picture. *Cuts...something about the cuts. Just like Josh Bennett. Neck. Chest. Solar Plexus. Lower Abdominal. Groin. NeckChestSolarPlexusLowerAbdominalGroin. Neckchestsolarplexusabsgroin.* Elliot had closed his eyes but he still had the picture held up to his face. To Margaret, it looked like he was examining the picture through his eyelids.

Sally and Jason walked over. "What's he doing?" Jason asked. Margaret shrugged.

Sally said, "Who knows. He does that sometimes."

"Does what?" Jason asked.

"You know, weird shit in general. You get used to it."

Jason leaned over and whispered in Margaret's ear, "He *is* a strange motherfucker, isn't he?"

Elliot was looking at the cuts on Alonso's body. His eyes were still closed. The incisions floated free of the body on the black satin behind his eyelids, *neckchestsolarplexusabsgroin*. As he watched, each cut seemed to open up and glow with its own color *neck, chest, solar plexus, abs, groin; blue, green, yellow, gold, red.* Elliot gave a sharp gasp and opened his eyes to find everybody staring at him.

"Oh man," he said. "Did I fall asleep? It really has been a long day. I have got to get some sleep. What are you guys staring at anyway?"

"Are you okay?" Sally asked.

"Just peachy. Hey, any of you guys ever meditate?" More blank stares. "Never mind. So, what does Denver's finest think of this whole situation?"

"I'm too tired to think," Margaret said. "Why don't we all-especially you-go try to get some sleep? Let's meet at my office tomorrow."

"It's a date," Elliot said, his smile about twenty-percent too lupine.

"No," Margaret said. "It's a meeting." She plucked her picture from his hand, and walked into the lab to tell Brent she was going home.

"Burr," Elliot said hugging himself. "She went ice-queen on me real quick. What's up with that?"

"She thought you were kind of cute," Jason said. "Then

you did that whole falling asleep on your feet thing and it fucked with her mind. She doesn't handle weirdness well. The ice-queen act is her was of expressing her disappointment at finding out you're as damaged as the rest of us."

"Wow, she thinks I'm cute, huh?" Elliot said.

"Don't mention it." Jason walked towards the lab to joint Margaret.

"Hey," Elliot said before he disappeared through the door.

Jason paused, "Yeah?"

"There's a guy in a really nice blazer and jeans in there..."

"I saw him."

"Could you tell him we're ready to leave now."

Chapter Thirty-Two

The Denver police department was nestled inside the confusing maze that made up the Denver judicial complex; almost a whole city block of modern gray, steel reinforced, concrete, and mirrored rectangles of glass showing the Denver sky to itself. The complex also housed the courthouse, city jail, and the District Attorney's office.

Madison and Wright worked in the homicide unit on the fourth floor. Their Office, with its view of the Denver skyline, and expensive looking blue, faux leather furniture, looked more like some corporate executive's office than the stereotypical detectives' bullpen.

Elliot and Sally walked in, glanced around, and in good Special Agent fashion, tried not to look impressed.

Margaret Madison looked up from her desk when they walked in. "Hi," she said, "You guys go first."

"Hey nice digs," Elliot said. He decided quickly that Margaret's tone had a little too much command in it for him to do anything she ask without first giving her some frustration. He and Sally had just walked in, and here Ms. Ice Queen homicide dick Madison was ordering them around even before any pleasantries were exchanged. *I don't think so.* Elliot decided Margaret could use an etiquette lesson.

"Pardon me," Margaret said.

"I said 'nice digs,' your office is much nicer than ours."

"What's that got to do with anything?"

"Nothing," Elliot smiled. "It's just customary to begin this kind of business meeting with a little gratuitous small talk. I say 'nice digs,' than you say, 'Thanks, it's nothing special. Then I say, 'Hey, it's got our office beat. Then you say, 'Can I get either of you a cup of coffee?' Then Sally says, 'Sure,' and I say, 'No thanks. I'm trying to cut down.' Then after you or Jason, whoever is coffee bitch today, brings Sally her cafe' latte' - that's how she likes it - you smile and say something like; 'Maybe you guys should go first", at which time I regale you with our tale of murder, intrigue and evil."

Margaret was a women used to giving, not taking, direction. She opened her mouth, undoubtedly to administer Elliot the requisite tongue lashing. Then she closed her mouth. She tried to start again, but nothing came out. Finally, she settled on the ever-reliable dirty look. She glared at Elliot just long enough to make him squirm, and huffed out of the office.

"You just had to start something, didn't you?" Sally said.

"She started it." He looked at Wright. "Didn't she?"

"Leave me out of this man," Wright said, then added; "You, of course, realize that any romantic designs you may have had for her are now completely off the table?"

"She's not my type anyway."

"What is your type?"

"Drunk, slutty, barely able to mask the smell of stale beer, cigarettes, and desperation."

"Figures," Wright said.

Margaret walked back into the office carrying a cup of coffee. "Here's your fucking coffee Special Agent Dupree. I was thinking, if it's not too much fucking trouble, maybe you guys could tell us where the fuck you are with your fucking investigation."

"I thought you'd never fucking ask," Elliot said cheerily.

Margaret took a notebook off of her desk, sat down and glared patiently at Elliot. Her anger was so focused that Elliot could taste it like warm bile in the back of his throat. Some people just couldn't handle a little snappy banter. "I don't suppose you'd accept my apology," he said.

"I don't suppose," Margaret was unflinching.

"I'm sorry."

"I'm glad."

"Well, okay," Sally said, intervening. "Now that we've kissed and made up, let's get this show on the road. Oh, and Detective Madison, thanks for the fucking coffee." Margaret grinned in spite of herself. She liked Sally. Sally, for her part, had no intention of drinking the coffee, as she strongly suspected Margaret had spit in it.

"Do you have your pictures?" Elliot asked, all business now that the fun was over.

Wright pulled an accordion folder out of a very trendy brushed steel filing cabinet. "Tab H," he said, handing it to Elliot.

Elliot took the folder and thumbed to Tab H. He found the pictures of Alonso's autopsy and spread them out on the desk. Then he pulled pictures of Josh Bennet's autopsy out of his briefcase and spread them out next to the pictures of Alonso. "Visual aids," he said. "We'll come back to them. What do you know about our case?" He asked.

Margaret made no attempt to answer the question. Wright offered, "Pretty much what we've read in the paper and what they've been telling us during our shift briefings: About a month ago, some juveniles found a dead kid in one of the old missile fields. You guys didn't have any suspects; but you were questioning suburban owners, because one of the juveniles thought he saw a suburban. To be honest, I thought your case was dead in the water, because the suburban angle was pretty weak. Well," he corrected himself, "it was weak until two days ago. Looks like Officer Gloria Sanchez died to break your case. You've gotta catch the fucker now."

Elliot thought Wright's tone was almost accusatory. Then he decided his own guilt was coloring his perceptions. It hadn't escaped his notice that Officer Gloria Sanchez might have inadvertently sacrificed herself for his case. He figured he would add that to the already voluminous pile of karmic goo that kept him awake at night. "You're right," he said. "The Sanchez case might just point us in the right direction. Right now our regional Forensic consultant, Steve Drake..."

"That's the guy in the nice blazer, right?" Jason interrupted.

"Yeah, him. Anyway, he's at the FBI lab with the truck. He's working the fingerprint angle. He's also trying to enhance a filed down vehicle identification number with Special Agent Tony Coleman. They haven't found anything yet. Drake will call me if they do. Right now, what I'm concerned with are these cuts.

"Last night I asked if any of you meditated; transcendental meditation, or any new age stuff, because while I was..." he paused, "...looking at the pictures, I realized there really is a discernible pattern. Not just because the cuts on Josh Bennet's body are similar to the cuts on your guy, but because the cuts were made over key *chakra* points."

"Chaka what?" Jason asked.

"*Chakra,* c h a k r a. Have you ever heard of *chi* or *ki?*"

"That's a martial arts thing," Margaret said. Her professionalism had replaced her anger, and she decided she was talking to Elliot again. "It means inner strength."

"Actually, it literally means blood, air, or energy. But the basic concept is: Your *chi* flows along specific paths throughout your body. When your *chi* is flowing freely in harmony with your mind and body, you can tap into incredible reserves of strength and energy. There are hundreds, thousands, of *chi* meridians, energy switching stations, throughout the body. We would have to study acupuncture for years to even begin to understand and chart them all. But there are six primary meridians that every amateur martial artist - that's where I fit in - or weekend guru knows about." He pointed at Josh Bennet's picture, "...neck, chest, solar plexus, mid-abdominal region, and groin."

"What's it mean to us?" Jason asked.

"It's just another piece of our puzzle," Elliot said. "Our profile already suggests our bad guy is a white male, in his late thirties or early forties, who is in the military, and served time in Asia. The fact that he is into martial arts, eastern religion, or meditation will help us narrow our focus."

Margaret spoke up, "White? Male? In the Air Force, Really! What do you think you are? Some kind of profiler?"

"No," Sally said. "He thinks he's some kind of psychic."

"Don't you start too," Margaret said. "Let's try to be serious for a few minutes. Turner, explain yourself."

There was that command voice again. Elliot ignored it this time. He figured Margaret needed to lord it up over him to save a little face. Actually, she thought she needed to lord it up over him because she thought he was a flake who needed some direction to stay focused. Unfortunately, she was entirely unaware that he had deep seeded issues with authority figures, and anything that smacked of command inspired instant insubordination. Had she known that, she might have wondered why he chose to join the military.

"Okay," Elliot said, "White, male, because they're always white male. Historically, most of your really sick fucks have been white males. But I'm willing to concede, based on the fact that your victim was black, that the race thing could go either way at this stage, but not likely. Late thirties or early forties because it takes time to evolve into the kind of casual fetish killer we're dealing with. I'm betting on forties because of the military angle."

Margaret interrupted, "*Casual fetish killer?* You're making this up as you go."

"Am not," Elliot said in an adolescent voice, teasing.

"Elliot," Sally said sharply.

He looked at Sally and smiled. "What I mean is," he started again, "If we take Josh Bennett out of the equation for a second, we're left with Alonso Proctor and the other bodies found in the missile shaft. All of those bodies were neatly disposed of. Our guy obviously took his time, wrapping and taping and packaging. When I say *casual,* I mean that's how our killer's attitude seems to me. You know...calm, nothing but a thing, nonchalant. I get the impression that, whether he's washing his car or wrapping up a dead kid in a plastic bag, his attitude is pretty much the same. Like his things-to-do list reads; pick up laundry, buy bread, wrap up dead kid and take him to silo, call mom. He's been doing this for so long it's become routine. You see?"

"I think I do," Margaret said. "I feel pretty much the same. The guy is too savvy to be a novice. You don't just kill a cop, leave a truck and a body behind, and disappear into thin air."

"That brings us to the military angle," Elliot said. "I had

already decided the guy was probably military because he knew about the missile silos."

"Everyone growing up around here knows about those things," Jason said.

"Exactly," said Elliot.

"You're loosing me again," said Margaret.

"Like Jason said; everyone growing up around here knows about the silos. If you were a killer, and you had grown up exploring those damned things, knowing they're pretty much open game for any teenager, would you use them as our little house of horrors, if you wanted to ensure your privacy?

"Our guy knew about the silos, but he didn't have the corporate knowledge to realize they're not off limits to the public, even one as far out as his. I figured he knew about the silos, but the mere fact that he felt comfortable using one to do his dirty work in, said he was relatively new to the area. That screamed military."

"That is probably the thinnest theory I've ever heard," Margaret said.

"It is pretty weak, man," Jason added. "People move into Denver every year by the thousands. We're in the middle of a population boom."

"But your average transplanted businessman doesn't know about the silos," Elliot said. "He just doesn't walk in those circles; kids with a need for adventure, or military guys. In hindsight, it sounds pretty weak to me too. But I had this whole theory about fetish killers and the military, and I really wanted this case to prove that theory. I was beginning to doubt my thinking, but little things are starting to reinforce my thinking.

"For instance; the way our bad guy cut and run after the Sanchez killing. He was trapped. He must have known or assumed Sanchez had called in his truck, and the police would be looking for it. At that point, the truck, even though fast transportation, became more of a liability in its visibility than an asset. Our bad guy recognized that immediately and cut his losses. He knows the truck can't be traced back to him, so he went with the unpredictable and took off on foot. Efficient. Military. On foot, through the desert.. fast...military. He was using an old government suburban. Suburbans might as well be urban Hum Vees. Military.

"I felt that any killer in the military probably would have got his taste for killing in Asia, specifically, Vietnam, the Philippines, or Thailand. The whole *chakra* thing, a common point of many eastern religions, reinforces my thinking."

"I was in the Philippines when I as in the Navy," Jason said. "The Philippines is a predominately Christian and catholic country."

"Good point," Elliot said. "But the Philippines is on my list because of the open prostitution."

"I don't think prostitutes create killers," Margaret said.

"That's because you're only familiar with America prostitutes," Elliot said. "They're not as disposable. But I'm not saying that the prostitutes of those countries create killers, and I mean no offense when I say they are not as disposable, but if you every spent any time in the third world, you would know how cheap the lives of the poor and disenfranchised can be to the local constabulary. The death of a prostitute or two, or three, or ten, might go completely unnoticed. A paraphiliac would thrive in that environment. Our guy was probably a killer – or had the predisposition - when he went over there. Southeast Asia just provided him with a venue to explore his needs."

"That's sick," Margaret said

"Give him time," Sally deadpanned. "I'm sure he can top it."

"Reality is stranger and sicker than fiction," Elliot said. "In the Philippines, during the seventies, there was such a high incidence of prostitute murders and disappearances around the Marine and Air Force bases that the Philippine government asked base officials to do something about it"

"Why would they think base officials could do anything about it?" Margaret asked.

"I can answer that," Wright said. "Any of the local soldiers could tell you that many of the deaths were GI related. If a prostitute got pushy in a relationship, or turned up pregnant, there was an unspoken acceptance to rough them up a little to get them off of your back. Some of the roughing up got out of hand. One of those expose' new shows did a special on GIs and hookers in the Philippines. The focus was on the youth of some of the prostitutes. Soldiers were shacking up with girls as young as eleven and twelve years old. In some cases the girls' parents knew what was going on. But the soldiers were helping the families with food and basic living needs. The expose' didn't create the outrage in America that it should have; probably because a lot of politicians had been young GIs in Vietnam or the Philippines themselves, and their own personal skeletons wouldn't let them make waves about the issue."

"Now," Elliot said. "Take the Philippines at its worst, multiply by ten, and you've got some places in Vietnam and Thailand. A lot of soldiers in those areas developed tastes that were a little more...exotic than heroin and hash. Hell, they've still got fishbowls in Thailand today."

"What's a fishbowl?" Sally asked, knowing she wouldn't like the answer.

Elliot too knew she wouldn't like the answer. Sally was a border line feminist; and on top of that, she was sometimes surprisingly naive' about some of society's stranger kinks. "A fish bowl is a sex bar. You walk in, and it's a regular bar with waitresses, drink menus, and all that shit; but one wall of the bar is all glass. On the other side of the glass is a room full of women just kind of sitting around..."

"Naked?" Sally asked appalled.

"No, not naked. Not normally. Usually, they're wearing evening gowns or swimsuits. Each girl has a button with a number on it. After you've got a couple of drinks in you, and you're feeling a little...amorous; you can call a waitress over. You give her the number of the girl you want, and they bring her to you."

"And American women complain about being treated like sex objects." Margaret said to Sally, who harrumphed in agreement.

"Actually it's good work if you can find it," Elliot said. "It beats working the streets. Fishbowl girls are well taken care of."

"You keep telling yourself that," Sally said. "I won't even get into that debate with you."

"Anyway," Elliot said. "In the world of fetish killers; I think a fairly high percentage of those who we don't catch - and let's face it; we've probably only caught less than one percent - are in the military. Being in the military keeps them mobile, and the Air Force is probably the most mobile service."

"There are a lot of big companies that move their employees all around the world." Jason said.

"Yea, but not as frequently. Look. I'm not saying my theory is fool proof. But right now, it feels right."

"Let's entertain your theory," Margaret said. "Could your guy have recently retired from the military? A guy who just got out of the military would still fit you profile, and the significant life change might spark a killing spree. Have you checked your database for recent retirees in, oh...say, the past five years or so?"

"No."

"Don't you think we should?" Margaret asked.

She was right, of course. Elliot scanned her face for some hint of smugness at his oversight. He couldn't find any. He conceded to himself that on an emotional level, Margaret was probably more mature and professional than he was. "Yes," he said. "I think we should, and...about earlier; I apologize again. I was out of line."

"Already forgotten." Margaret lied. He was still on probation.

"What are you guys gonna do now?" Jason asked.

"Jeez," Sally said. "The question is where to start. We've got leads into infinity."

"We're going to continue to work the Alonso Proctor angle," Margaret said. "Maybe he had habits that could have put him in touch with the killer."

"Good luck," Elliot said, "but I'm pretty sure Proctor was just in the wrong place at the wrong time. I've been criticized for the way I do things..."

"Say it isn't so!" Jason interrupted in mock surprise.

"...But I've always found that sometimes coming at a problem obliquely can open up new avenues."

"You have an angle in mind?" Margaret asked.

"Maybe," he said. "Sally and I have gotta go see a lady about some chakras."

Chapter Thirty-Three

Colfax Avenue was Denver's major artery, running the length of the city from east to west. There was no item or service which couldn't be procured on Colfax Avenue. If a person wanted to buy a new car or a little something for the monkey on his back, he could travel down Colfax until the desired item was located and acquired for a nominal fee.

Like any major thoroughfare in any major city, Colfax had its respectable areas and its take-your-chances-after-dark areas. Elliot was visiting the *Abyss* bookstore which was in a take-your-chances area, nestled snugly between an adult video rental store and a head shop.

Elliot knew both the head shop and the movie house well. He frequented the head shop to keep on top of the latest trends in narcotics paraphernalia. As far as the dirty video rental store: well, a man had to have a hobby. Sally, to be expected, was not familiar with the area. But Elliot would have been surprised, and delighted, to learn that she enjoyed the occasional adult video, but she left the hunting and gather of such items to her husband. Elliot would not have been surprised, however, to learn that she and Dave had not engaged in any naughty business in a very long time.

Neither the shop nor its proprietor was what Elliot expected. He figured an occult bookstore would be dank, dusty, and poorly lit. On the contrary, the smell of incense permeated the place; no doubt masking the smell of formaldehyde, eye of newt, and all of the other things every layman knew witches needed to perpetuate their dark art.

The shop was neither dank nor dusty. It was well lit, and the atmosphere inside was clean and cheerful. To Elliot it felt like a Christian Science bookstore. Except instead of books on an unrealistically happy family life and scripture interpretation, the shelves were lined with books on Satanism and witchcraft. There were also crystals, tarot cards, and other arcane merchandise. Elliot was fascinated and found himself wishing he had ventured in sooner. Especially when he saw the proprietor.

She had auburn hair, which fell to just past her waistline. She didn't wear it in any particular style, content to just tie it back, and let its health and condition make its own statement. Elliot was immediately taken with her in a less than noble manner, and had to make a conscious effort to keep his mind on the matter at hand. Lately he couldn't seem to keep his mind off of women and booze.

Sally left Elliot to deal with the proprietor. She really had no idea what Elliot thought to accomplish by coming here, but she was curious just the same. She wandered around the shop looking in books and picking up crystals while Elliot made his way to the counter.

Elliot bent over a display case, trying to look engrossed in selecting a crystal pendant, watching the proprietress out of the corner of his eye, and thinking she was definitely his flavor, when she wandered over.

"You seem a little lost. Can I help you with something?

You know, different crystals have different properties. You could pick one and become rich; or you could choose the wrong one and end up with a terrible case of space herpes. Maybe you should let me help."

"Actually," Elliot said, "I'm not in the market for a crystal today. I'm Special Agent Turner with the Air Force Office of Special Investigations. We talked on the phone." He showed her his badge. Elliot had called the shop earlier. He'd been feeling uncharacteristically professional and calling ahead, for a change, seemed like the right thing to do.

"Special Agent Turner, Special Agent Turner," she chanted his name as if it had some hidden meaning to her. "I'm Blair Edgewater. I don't think I've ever met a real Special Agent. You're something a little different, aren't you? You didn't sound black on the phone."

Elliot was delighted with her bluntness. He didn't take her comment to be bigoted in any way. He knew she was pulling his chain to see how he would react. He respected that in a person. Most people would have found it politically incorrect to be so forward with a stranger. He also recognized the fact that she noticed immediately that his speech was not typical for where he grew up. Sally, who was standing nearby, perked up to hear the answer. He moved closer to get a better look at her face and to see how she would react when he invaded her comfort zone. It was a trick he used with women in bars and suspects to access their sense of self, and attitude towards him. He couldn't read her face, but felt that she was involved in some private joke at his expense, which was usually his schtick, *I'll do the joking here missy.* Her fragrance was strong but not unpleasant or overpowering; sandalwood, with just a hint of something clean and distinctly female underneath. He found that he didn't care if she was having jest at his expense, as long as he could stick around and savor her scent.

She saw through his trick immediately, and moved closer to him, turning his game around on him. They were close enough to kiss, and her presence overwhelmed his sense of self. He felt himself flush. She sensed her victory and moved back a couple of inches but remained close enough to keep him within her sphere of influence.

Smiling, Elliot said, "I had to take speech therapy as a kid for an impediment, and it ruined my ebonics."

"Where did you grow up?" She asked, leaning over and giving him an impressive view of her cleavage. At that point, Elliot would have answered anything.

"South-East D.C."

She looked impressed, "I'll bet you got your ass kicked a lot for sounding like that."

Elliot knew immediately that he was not dealing with an airhead in a new age shop. Even Sally was impressed from the incense wrack: she didn't even know that. The proprietess was smart and observant. "I did, until I learned how to defend myself," he said.

"I'm glad it worked out for you. So what does an Air Force Special Agent do?"

"What does a Special Agent do?" He repeated her question. "Well, basically we catch bad guys, help ladies in distress, dodge bullets, and generally go about making the world safe for democracy, peace, justice and the American way of life. If we're lucky, most days the world is safe by five o'clock, and we go have a beer."

She looked at her watch. "It's four thirty-five now. I close at five, and I have a feeling you need more than a couple of minutes. You have two choices; the beer or me." She leaned forward giving Elliot another whiff.

The innuendo was not lost on Elliot, or Sally who marveled at the effect he had on total strangers. Elliot found himself forgetting his planned line of questioning, and thinking that if the light were just right he could actually see through Blair's blouse.

"I'm dedicated to protect and serve, and if making the world safe for democracy requires me to work well into the evening, then beer be damned, and let the bad guys tremble, because Special Agent Turner-call me E.T.-is on the job. Of course, you are more than welcome to accompany me while I attend to the beer thing."

"I don't do beer, but if you will spring for a shot or two of something...stiffer… we might be able to save the world together."

Elliot was in love; and if he wasn't in love, he was aroused, which was the next best thing. Sally felt compelled to wander over, mostly out of a mild case of jealousy.

"Hi." She held her hand out to Blair, "I'm Special Agent Sally Dupree."

Blair smiled pleasantly at her and shook her hand, "Nice to meet you. Are you his partner?"

"Yes, we're working on a murder case which may have some occult elements, and this seemed like a good place to educate ourselves." Even though Sally didn't know exactly what Elliot thought about the chakras and this case, she felt compelled to introduce herself so as not to feel completely irrelevant in this exchange.

"Ah." Blair said, "You know, there are a lot of freaks and weirdos out there who think the occult is evil, and therefore appropriate to incorporate into criminal activity. By no means, however, does adherence to occult practice mean one is mentally unstable or prone to criminal activity."

"Of course not, but we are required to investigate were the evidence leads." Sally smiled sweetly, an exactly mirror of Blair's. Sally's pager beeped. She checked the number and suppressed an annoyed sighed. "Excuse me. Do you have a phone I can use? It's a local call."

Blair nodded, "Sure, it's in the back." She pointed behind her through a curtained door.

"Thank you." After Sally disappeared, Blair turned her attention back to Elliot.

"I have about twenty minutes before closing," Blair said, "and while you're definitely my cutest customer, you're not my only customer." Across the shop there were two teenage girls dressed in black, floor length, cotton, dresses. They were wearing black lipstick. They each had shoulder length black oily hair; and their pale complexions looked like they would melt in the sun. The pair was eyeing up a book of spells, trying to look like serious witches. Blair saw the look of amusement on Elliot's face, winked at him and walked over to offer her assistance.

Sally emerged from the back room, her face pinched.

"What's up?" Elliot asked.

"I forgot I've got a boring real estate agents dinner tonight with the spousal unit. He was calling to remind me I needed to get my ass home and make myself presentable so as not to embarrass him among his friends and all their perfectly manicured trophy wives."

Elliot grimaced, "Sorry to hear that. You can take the car, I'll find my own way home."

Sally was instantly angry, but tried not to show it. She was angry because she wanted to go out and have fun with Elliot rather than go home to Dave, for whom nothing was good enough. Instead, she knew Blair would be his companion tonight. She had no choice, however, and so she nodded and mumbled a petulant "Thanks."

She waved to Blair on her way out.

* * *

After Blair locked up the shop, they left by the back door and wandered one street up through an alley. They came out on Hollywood Avenue, and Elliot marveled at how Denver neighborhoods could change from block to block. One minute you were watching your back in fear of being mugged; the next you felt underdressed. Blair's shop was not in the best of neighborhoods. But when they emerged from the alley, the streets were lined with well-lit storefronts and trendy yuppie bars.

They walked down the street making small talk and trying to pick a good bar. Blair was entertaining and well read. Elliot didn't have to contribute too much to the conversation. She talked about everything from current events to satanic rites. Elliot thought he detected something strange about her manner. Then he decided it was probably just the situation in general. Anyway, he had always found himself strangely attracted to intelligent quirky women. In Blair's case, there was also her ample bosom, which was like having an extra side of bacon. Most of the bars they looked in were full of white shirts and red striped power ties, young professionals stopping by their favorite spot after work for happy hour. All the men looked like Steve Drake, and all the women looked like competent young female lawyers.

"See anything you like?" Blair asked, still playing the innuendo game.

"At this point anything with beer and bar food is perfect. I'm getting hungry. But all of these places are so…," he spun around once with his arms spread, "…respectable. Isn't there something just a little less corporate around here? Yuppies frighten me."

Blair laughed, and snorted. Her laugh was real, not the standard, polite, insert-laugh-here variety. "You too, huh? I always thought that people like that, always trying to get ahead, drinking and partying with folks they don't even like, were kind of pathetic. They don't understand that it's all dust in the end."

"He who dies with the most toys wins…nothing," Elliot said sardonically, and he realized that Blair had quickly become less of a sex object and more of "real" person, intelligent, and genuine. He also realized she was a genuine sensitive. She wasn't the first he'd met, and he was leery of them as a rule. They always treated him like a lost cousin or wanted to talk about the problems of being sensitive and bond with him. Elliot had never been a joiner. He was a private person by nature, and being around others like himself made him self-conscious.

They walked silently down the street. There was a steady flow of yuppies moving up stream towards the respectable bars. Elliot and Blair moved against the tide, Elliot scanning bar fronts, focused, as if picking the right bar was the most important mission on the evening. Blair walked silently by his side lost in thought. He hoped she wasn't trying to read him. His thoughts were less than gentlemanly.

Elliot glided to a stop in front of an appropriately disreputable looking watering hole and announced proudly, "This is it."

"You've been here before?"

"A hundred times in a hundred different cities."

The bar had a large window facing the sidewalk and the street. But they couldn't see inside. The window was decorated with neon beer signs and opaque from years of cigarette residue. The smell of stale beer and cigarette smoke clung to every surface, including the patrons, who - in keeping with the overall motif -were working hard at looking dangerous.

Elliot walked in, took a deep breath, and sighed happily. Blair, who'd always been proud of her blue collar roots, found herself clutching her purse a little tighter and reminding herself to take out her car keys with the pepper spray on the key-chain.

"Cool, huh?" Elliot said.

"It's not exactly what I would have picked. I can feel eyes crawling over my body."

"Those are my eyes," Elliot said. "I'm sorry. Let's get a booth. You'll feel more comfortable."

They found a corner booth. It had ripped red vinyl cushions covering the bench seats, and the table was sticky with the remains of the previous occupant's bar food. Blair sat down, feeling more trapped than comfortable. When they were settled in, and had ordered their drinks-beer for Elliot, and the house scotch for Blair-She looked at Elliot and said, "Okay, let's put our cards on the table. You are aware that you're sensitive, aren't you?"

"Well, I have always been in touch with my feminine side. Actually, I'm touching it right now." He smiled.

"How long have you known?" She pressed, ignoring his attempt to side step her question. "It's more common than you think, you know?"

"I know," Elliot said. "Look at all the psychic hotlines."

"You're hiding behind your jokes," she said. "That tells me you're not really comfortable with the situation."

"You're right. I'm not. Do you think we could change the subject?"

"Okay, for now, but if I'm going to help you out with whatever it is you want, you're going to have to be a little more forthcoming. It's not everyday a psychic Special Agent working for the Air Force and his blank partner shows up on a girl's doorstep bearing a cryptic request for assistance. Sue me. I'm curious."

Elliot frowned, "Blank partner? What are you talking about?"

She leaned forward, her eyes searching his face, "Sally Dupree. She's blank. She's a psychic black hole."

For the first time, Elliot felt a little annoyed by what he perceived as an attack on Sally, "So? Most people have no psychic ability."

She laughed and shook her head, "No, it's not that she doesn't have the ability, it's that she can't be read, tracked, or sensed by a psychic. You've never noticed that before: that you can't read her?"

Elliot was startled for a moment. He'd never actually thought about it. He thought he could sense Sally, but if he really considered it, he realized that with her, he did a lot of guessing. "Well, I'm sure Sally is readable – I've just never tried. Regardless, I'd rather not get into it tonight, okay?"

She thought about it for a second. "Okay, not tonight. So, Special Agent Turner, what can I do for you?"

"How are you with dead things?" Elliot asked.

"I guess we'll all be dead things eventually. I'm okay enough."

"Good. I want to show you some pictures." He took two pictures of Josh Bennett out of his coat pocket and laid them on the table in front of her. The bartender, who also seemed to be the cook and the waiter, sauntered over with their drinks. He set their drinks on the table and paused to look at the pictures. The cigarette in his mouth didn't even twitch. They might as well have been looking at a newspaper. He walked away his mind already on his next order. "I love these places," Elliot said, watching the bartender's back. "Nobody asks any questions."

"What am I supposed to be seeing here?" Blair asked.

"Looks at the cuts."

"Nasty."

"No. Look at where they are."

Blair studied the pictures some more. "You want to give me a clue?"

"Think *chakra.*"

"Hey, you're right. The cuts correspond to *chakra* points."

"As an authority on things metaphysical or paranormal, I need to know what that means to you."

"Nothing really, whoever killed this kid has probably dabbled in the occult."

"I figured that. What if I were to tell you that there was saliva found in the cuts?"

"Saliva?"

"I think whoever did this drank from the wounds."

"Vampirism?"

"You tell me. Have you ever heard of anything like this? I think our bad guy drank from the wounds. But I don't think he was after the kid's blood, so much as his *chi.*"

"A *chi* vampire. Do you really work for the Air Force?"

"Not a real vampire. Not even a vampire. I think we are looking for a guy who, for whatever reason, thinks there is something to be gained by drinking blood from those areas. I want to know where he would have gotten that idea."

"This is out of my league, but I've got a friend at the university who eats this stuff up. Can I talk to him and get back to you?

"I don't know. Is he on the up and up? I'm not going to read about this in the paper tomorrow, am I? You know, something like *Air Force Looks For Chi Sucking Vampire?* That would be bad for my reputation.

"I get the feeling that you don't have the best reputation anyway."

"I'm serious."

"I think he can keep a secret. He's my father."

Elliot took out his wallet and handed Blair a business card. "My cell phone number is on the back. Call me anytime, okay?"

"I'll do that. We're not done here are we?"

"Only with the business portion of the evening."

Chapter Thirty-Four

Melanie Rivers, managing to look both perky and solemn, sat behind the commentator's desk staring into her teleprompter. The screen behind her proclaimed in blood red letters, SERIAL KILLER! In smaller letters, scrolling across the bottom of the screen was...6 NEWS SPECIAL REPORT.

"...Late last night Air Force officials discovered the grisly remains of over 20 unidentified bodies in the same abandoned missile silo where the body of five year old Josh Bennett was found a month ago. Investigators have not released a formal statement. But our sources tell us the FBI, Denver Police Department, and investigators from the Air Force Office of Special Investigations, have formed a multi-agency task force, and believe this to be the work of a serial killer."

"Such an ugly world," The killer said to himself in mock horror. "What kind of fiend would kill cereal?" He chuckled to himself.

It was only a matter of time now. Pretty soon someone

without his best interests in mind would be knocking on his door, at least they would be knocking on one of his doors. He'd tried to be thorough, but there simply hadn't been enough time to ensure that the suburban was completely free of fingerprints. If they were there, he had to assume they would find them. Once the cops had his prints it would be a simple matter to run them through some military database and then run him to ground. How many times had he been fingerprinted during his military career, three or four?

He'd even been arrested once for driving under the influence. That had been years ago, and he hadn't had a drop of alcohol since. But once was enough. His fingerprints were in the law enforcement system.

The story of Josh Bennett, Alonso Proctor, and the bodies in the missile shaft were on every channel. One bit of carelessness had turned him into the most despised and sought after person in modern history, *gonna be tough to pick up chicks when this gets out.*

He was still invisible, but the fruits of his labor were the top story in every country around the world. He had to disappear. No, he had to die. He had passports and bank accounts in more than one alias name. After all these years, it was time to go back to the Philippines or Thailand. God, he missed the Orient. The thought of living out the rest of his years in some warm, humid, uncomplicated, city in the far East, complete with hot and cold running young boys, helped him to focus on the matter at hand.

He would kill his military persona, and live quietly in the warehouse apartment until some of the 'silo killer'- as he had been dubbed- mania died down, then he would disappear.

But what was he going to do with himself in the interim? The urge to hunt had never been so strong. If he could just relieve some of the pressure in his head and pants, he'd be able to concentrate. Somebody had to die. Someone needed to give him some blood and fear, and it had to be soon. But no more kids. That had been bad *juju*.

He'd been almost flawless in his execution. Luring the boy away from the bench where he'd been playing had been a study in finesse.

His shopping mall hunting outfit had been markedly different from his white-man-waiting-to-be-a-victim-clothes. His waiting-to-be-a-victim-clothes were designed to help him exude an air of ineptness and vulnerability. In the mall, he'd worn gray overalls and a tool belt. It was his outfit for hiding in plain sight. With a tool belt and overalls he found he could wander freely, through almost any building. With a hard hat added, he was invisible on any city street.

He'd gone to the mall looking to treat himself to something special. He hadn't known what he was looking for, and he had been content to wander the mall pretending to look for ceiling leaks, while checking out the crowd, doing his own special kind of 'shopping'. He would occasionally stop in front of some store, look at its name and then study the ceiling tiles above its entranceway.

During the week, the mall wasn't that crowded. But even with the sparse patronage, no one paid him any mind. He was just another faceless, nameless, maintenance person, and didn't warrant more than a passing glance.

At this time of the day, most of the mall goers were housewives, either shopping alone or with children still too young to be pawned off on the public education system. Naturally, it was the children who interested him most.

He'd spotted Josh Bennett on his first pass. Blue eyes, flaxen hair, lost in the fantasy of his toy cars and action figures, he was a beautiful child, and too tasty to pass up.

Plan A had been to find some young housewife and ambush both her and her kid in the parking lot, or to even follow them home. He'd never taken a child while the mother watched, and he wasn't ashamed to say the thought of it got his juices flowing.

He didn't really have a plan B. It just jumped out at him, and he knew it was right. Here was an unsuspecting piece of cherub flesh left to his own devices in a public mall. If he believed in god, he would have sworn the child was god's gift to him.

His first order of business had been to determine exactly where the child's mother was. He assumed the child was with his mother.

Directly across from the bench there was a Leslie's clothing store, one of those clothing stores that specialized in trendy career women attire. The bench was a four-sided, high-glossed, plank job encircling a water fountain. The opposite side of the bench was facing a tobacco shop and a novelty shop. Even though Josh was playing on the side of the bench facing the tobacco shop, he would have bet money that the mother was in the clothing store.

Even before he acted, he knew he was about to take a very uncharacteristic risk. But he had to have the boy. He walked past Josh. When the boy looked up, temporarily distracted from his toys by his jingling tool belt, he'd smiled his best I'm-mister-safe-handyman-smile, then continued around to the Leslie's Boutique side of the fountain.

He had a good view of the interior of the store. There were dozens of well-spaced, circular clothes racks with trendy business suits, trying to lure in young women with their pleasing pastel patterns.

The dressing rooms were at the rear of the store. There was a lone saleswoman. He'd watched a she delivered a load of suits and matching blouses to the center dressing room and removed a stack that had been thrown over the top of the door.

He'd found the errant mother, and from the looks of things, she would be occupied for a few more minutes. She'd undoubtedly sat Josh on the bench with a good view of the dressing rooms, correctly assuming, if the boy could see where she was in the store, he would content himself to play quietly until she was done. He just loved an obedient child.

There was a 'help wanted' sign by the cash register. That told him that the sales girl was probably working alone, she of the tight ass and retro platform shoes. Help wanted, huh? He wondered what the application process entailed. What kind of questionnaire did they use to ensure their prospects were perfect, trendy, retro, size zeroes? *Is your ass firm yet resilient? Do your nipples get hard just because? Have you ever seen a grown man naked? Were you daddy's little girl? Do you like to be spanked 'till your bottom is red?*

"I'll bet you do," he mumbled to himself.

He walked around the fountain, and when he was once again on the side where Josh sat playing; he took a quarter out of his pocket, smiled at Josh, and threw it in.

"Why'd ya do that?" Josh asked.

It was so easy to excite their curiosity at that age. "I'm making a wish," the killer said truthfully, in his best Mr. Roger's voice. "If you throw a quarter in the fountain, you can make a wish."

Josh furrowed his eyebrows, his pre-adolescent computer mulling over the exchange. He decided quickly that the killer was telling the truth, and then said, "I don't have a quarter."

"Do you want one?" he asked, digging in his pocket.

"Yes please," Josh said, eyes alight with five-year-old gratitude and expectation.

Yes please? What refreshingly good manners. He turned his pockets inside out and frowned apologetically at Josh.

Wanna see me do the elephant, kid? "I'm sorry. I thought I had another one," he said stuffing the pockets back into his pants

"That's okay," Josh said, clearly disappointed.

"I'm really sorry," he said. "I've got some quarters in my office, you want to come?"

"I'm supposed to stay here."

"It's right over there," he said, pointing to the corridor leading to the restrooms and back exit. If Josh had said 'no' again, he had already decided not pursue the issue. "Your mom's still trying on clothes, I bet it's okay. We'll be back real fast, then you can tell her about your wish."

Josh digested this for a second. "Okay," he said simply.

Just like that; 'okay?' A part of him hadn't believed there was any merit in the want-some-candy-little-boy technique. But he was nothing if not prepared.

He had lead Josh into the corridor, and taken him into a janitor's closet. He knew every inch of the mall, it was one of his favorite hunting grounds, but he'd never actually taken any one from there. Up until actually taking the boy it had just been one of his favorite fantasies. In the closet he had bound, and gagged the boy. He'd stuffed him into a large plastic trash can, and rolled him out to the parking lot, where he'd put the boy, trash can and all into his truck. He was certain no one had seen him. He'd taken a risk and beaten the odds. At least he'd thought he'd beat the odds.

He thought of the way the boy's skin had felt and tasted. Even with things going south so fast, he couldn't say that it hadn't been worth it.

Chapter Thirty-Five

"Do you want the good news or the bad news?" Drake asked. He had just come back from the FBI offices with FBI agent, Tony Coleman, in tow. Coleman was now officially in charge of the silo killer-as they had taken to calling it-task force. "This Tony Coleman."

"I think we've met," Elliot said, holding out his hand.

Coleman took Elliot's hand. His grip was firm and dry. He looked Elliot in the eye and smiled. "Last year at that thing, right?"

"Have you met detectives Margaret Madison and Jason Wright?" Elliot asked, hooking a thumb at Margaret and Jason. They'd come by the office to hear Drake's briefing on the evidence taken to date.

"Yeah," Coleman said, without bothering to elaborate. He smiled and nodded at the detectives.

Coleman and Drake were both dressed in slacks and blazers, Drake in his trademark navy blue, and Coleman in tan slacks with a well tailored black blazer. Elliot could still detect the bulge of his shoulder holster underneath the left arm. Together they looked like an advertisement for some well heeled men's clothing outlet.

Elliot was wearing jeans, cowboy boots, and a tight, black, T-shirt. The T-shirt showed off his new lean torso to its best advantage. He'd been burning off excess pounds every evening in the gym. Elliot didn't own a blazer. He had a black leather biker's jacket thrown over the back of his chair. He sat down and put his feet up on the desk. "Bad news first," he said. "Always give me the bad news first."

"There were no prints on the truck," Drake said. "There were no prints on the plastic bags. There were no prints on the lamp from the silo or the tape binding Josh Bennet's arms and legs, or the door knob from the missile shaft access door. The tape itself was common duct tape. The suburban was registered to Lester Phillips, who apparently doesn't exist. It was purchased at a military surplus auction in Colorado Springs five years ago."

"Well that's good news," Elliot said, "More military connection and some indication of how long our boy has been in the area."

"I meant to do that. It's my way of segueing into the good news portion. We have body fluids aplenty, mostly semen, for DNA typing. There were useable samples from both the Bennet kid and Alonso Proctor. Tony's folks have determined we're dealing with the same person..."

"Fantastic work guys," Elliot said sarcastically, giving Coleman a thumbs up. Coleman remained poised and quiet, and Elliot sensed there was more to Tony Coleman than comfortable business attire and the arrogance of a well bred preppy. However, his asshole alarm wasn't ringing, and Coleman's aura was so non-threatening that Elliot found himself mirroring the FBI agent's relaxed manner.

"Don't be a dickhead, Elliot," Drake said. "We need all the FBI juice we can get."

"FBI juice," Elliot said. "Make mine sugar free.

"You don't need to feel threatened," Coleman said. "We're all in this together, and Drake already explained your theory and plan of attack. I'm not a profiler, and this isn't really my area of expertise, but you guys seem to be making all the right moves. I don't see any reason to mess with the program just because the Bureau has exercised big brother rights to the investigation. In other words...chill out, man."

"Chill out, man, really?" Elliot smiled, but he was wondering just *what* was Coleman's area of expertise.

"What can I say," Coleman added. "This case is big enough for us all to get a chunk. I'm on your side."

Elliot once again tried to get a sense of the FBI agent. He believed Coleman had nothing but good intentions, but when he reached with his senses, he couldn't keep him in focus. All he could pick up was that sense of quiet.

"I won't bullshit you", Coleman said. "This is the biggest case of this type in recent history, and the Bureau is throwing money and agents at it that would make your head spin. But there's a funny thing about task forces; they can get so big that they become self-licking ice-cream cones, good to look at but serving no real purpose. The task force can crunch evidence and write profiles until they're blue. They may even find this guy. But my money is on you guys. You, Drake, and Special Agent Dupree," he nodded at Sally, "actually broke this case with instinct and the investigative chemistry that comes from having good partners."

"We didn't break anything…" Sally said.

"I know I didn't," Elliott interrupted.

Sally continued," ignoring Elliot. "This is still an unknown subject case. It's too early to start patting ourselves on the back."

"What you three did was figure out the scope of this

thing. You decided there had to be more bodies, and you found them."

"It was mostly Elliot," Drake said.

"No, he's right," Elliot said. "I've got the smoke and mirrors, but I couldn't focus without you guys."

"All this mutual admiration stuff is touching," Coleman said. "But the bottom line is; you guys are getting things done. My money is on you five bringing this thing to a head, and I want to play with you." Coleman took his coat off, looked around for some place to put it, seemed not to be able to find anyplace appropriately sanitary, then settled on folding it over his arm. "What's our next step?"

"We were going to conduct behavioral analysis interviews on our list of Air Force personnel who fit the profile, but first..." Elliot looked at Margaret and winked, "could I get you some coffee or something?"

Margaret gave him the finger, but now it was good natured. She and Jason had been working with Elliot, Sally, and Drake almost daily, and she'd come to realize that, beneath the weirdness and the tough guy act, Elliot was compassionate, intelligent, and insightful enough that he sometimes seemed to be able to read her mind.

"I don't drink coffee," Coleman said. "It makes me irregular."

"Thanks for sharing that with us," Sally said. "I feel closer to you already."

Coleman smiled. "Actually, before we get into this whole behavioral analysis interview thing; I'd be interested in hearing where detectives Madison and Wright are with their investigation."

"We thought you'd never ask," Jason said. "As you know, we've been working the Alonso Proctor angle, you know, the kid whose body was in the suburban. We've talked to his friends and family members, but they're no real help.

Mostly, what we're getting from them is anger over how we're screwing up this investigation because we haven't found the killer. I'd be happy to turn the fucking thing over to them." Jason paused to gather his thoughts, and like a good partner, Margaret continued where he left off.

"On a hunch," she started, and gave Elliot a look that said, 'see I get hunches, too.' "We went down to City Park, were the chickens and chicken hawks (young male prostitutes and their clientele) hang out. We figured if our guy was into pretty young boys he might have been a City Park regular."

Every day Elliot was more impressed by Margaret's detective skills. She had a keen analytical mind, and working with her was a constant reminder to him that, without his unreliable psychic friend, he was no better than the average good investigator.

"It took some time before the working boys realized we weren't there to bust them," she said. " But when they finally warmed to us and started talking, they gave us information that conflicted just a little with the statistics the missing persons folks gave us. After Brent Shelton finished his preliminary exam of the bodies from the missile shaft, he passed on to us that they were all male..."

"Mutilations?" Drake asked, feeling a little slighted that Brent didn't pass him the information first as a fellow forensics expert.

"Some of the bodies were in pretty bad shape," Margaret continued, "what with being under for so long. But, once Shelton got the hang of opening up the cocoons, while leaving the skin intact, it was clear most of them had the chakra cuts. Anyway, we reviewed our files for homicides matching your guy's MO, pretty boys, patterned wounds, that kind of stuff, but came up with nothing. Which kind of makes sense, because he was hiding the bodies in the missile silo."

Jason continued for Margaret, "Missing persons had the usual stack of cases, but nothing that fit the pattern, no pretty boys disappearing in droves. But when we talked to the boys on the street, they told us that about seven of them have disappeared in the past two years or so. Since most of them are runaways, they figured the boys got tired of street life and found sugar daddies, or reconciled with their folks. I'm thinking something a little more sinister happened to them."

"Good work," Elliot said, sincerely.

"Did any of them recall seeing the truck?" Sally asked, "or did any of their clients seem strange?"

"You mean stranger than the normal grown men who troll the park at night looking for adolescent boys to fuck up the ass or give them blow jobs?" Margaret asked.

"Good point," Sally said. "Scratch that last question."

"Can you bring me up to speed on the behavioral analysis interviews?" Coleman asked.

"We've been working with our regional computer crime investigator," Drake shot Elliot a look. Elliot looked innocently back at him. "Using Elliot's profile, he put together a list of officers and enlisted men, active duty and retired, assigned to bases in the areas who seem to be a good fit."

"We've already got a pool of over fifty names," Sally said. "Which is a very manageable number for BAIs. I've heard of investigations where there were thousands of subjects in the target group."

"Who is going to conduct the interviews?," Coleman asked.

"We all are," Drake said. "You're familiar with process, right?"

"Only on paper," Coleman admitted. "I've never actually been involved in an investigation where it was used."

Sally continued, "Drake and the guys in our psyche unit made up a questionnaire disguised as a criminal information survey. Elliot and I will contact the Air Force guys on the list, and we've sent copies of the questionnaire to the Army Criminal Investigations Division (CID) at Fort Polk They're about fifty miles north of us, but that puts them in our game area. Our detachment in Colorado Springs also has a list of about 20 names. Margaret and Jason will handle the recently retired guys in the area."

"Where do I fit into all of this?" Coleman asked.

"You give us credibility with my boss and unrestricted access to the FBI analytical uni-mind." Elliot said.

Coleman looked almost disappointed. "You want me to run interference while you guys do the fun stuff."

"Uh, yeah, do you mind?" Elliot smiled.

"I guess somebody has to do it."

Chapter Thirty-Six

Sally was sitting to Elliot's left. Her right leg was crossed over her left. From where he was sitting he had a good view of her upper leg, the good part, the part of the thigh right before it turns into ass. Elliot liked that part. Actually, he wasn't trying to look at her leg. He was looking at her notebook, which was resting on her right knee. Her thigh was just a pleasant stop along the way.

She had her notebook canted at an angle that told him she wanted him to read what she had written.

The page was blank except for a single word printed in her neat hand large enough for him to read without straining...ANYTHING?

She was referring, of course, to the gentleman in front of them, the 82nd Support Group commander, Colonel William Gray. They were in Gray's office, an enclave of polished oak furniture and comfortable, leather, high-backed chairs, that would have made Elliot's boss, George Devine, green. From the antique globe with the gold overlay, to the keepsakes from his illustrious past, it was every bit an office fit for a commander, officer, and gentleman.

Colonel Gray sat behind his desk, regal. He was receptive and at ease. On the wall above his head was a 2' x 3' framed black and white photograph, depicting a young Lieutenant William Gray standing on a ladder hanging from the cockpit of his F-4 Phantom fighter jet. He was dressed in a flight suit and smiling confidently at the camera, undoubtedly pleased with himself at having sent some commie to a premature, fiery, grave.

He was the fifth name on their list. Out of the four who they interviewed before the Colonel, three had been so firmly locked in their domesticity that they couldn't find the time to step out for a pack of cigarettes, without clearing it through their respective spouses, let alone find the time to enjoy mutilating young boys. The other was a female, who had somehow found her name on their list.

Colonel Gray was friendly and relaxed. When he moved his arms to accentuate his speech, his gestures were clipped and precise. He was a big man and in incredibly good shape for a man in his late forties, or any other age for that matter. His uniform was immaculate. He had dark hair with just a hint of gray, and an inviting smile. He had the air of a man who was secure enough in his position not to be pompous or pretentious.

His thoughts were also some of the ugliest Elliot had ever encountered. They were vile and violent. On the inside Colonel Gray was a seething caldron of barely contained rage and insanity. Elliot was nauseated being in the same room with him. Could Gray be the man they were looking for? He was certainly not the pillar of the community that his outward appearance suggested.

Elliot wondered if Sally could sense anything. He didn't see how she couldn't. Plus, she was a female, and most women had great instincts for evil (even if they chose to ignore them). If she felt anything, she wasn't showing it. She was calmly going down the list of behavioral analysis survey questions. She gave no indication that the Colonel repulsed her. In fact, she seemed almost charmed.

Gray had a copy of the survey, and as she asked each question aloud; he was filling in his response on the form in front of him.

There were thirty questions on the list. Gray thought he was participating in a community feedback, criminal justice survey. The survey had questions like; do you think there is a problem with violent crime in your area, or do you believe in the death penalty?

Studies had shown that perpetrators of certain crimes tended to answer key questions alike. Once all the surveys were in, Drake and Coleman would sit down with psychologists from the FBI and the OSI and narrow the list down to a more manageable number. Individuals from the second group would be re-contacted. That group would be further paired down until only a handful remained. If they had the right target group, those final few would be their primary suspects.

They would contact their suspects, explain the situation to that group, read them their rights, and offer them polygraphs - unless somebody spontaneously confessed.

Elliot didn't think it would come to that. The more time he spent in Gray's presence, the more convinced he was that they had their man. However, no matter how hard he concentrated, he couldn't pick up any specific thoughts from the Colonel. He just wasn't on the same frequency. Elliot knew enough about his errant abilities to realize they were very much akin to a radio transceiver, and if two radios weren't on the same frequency, they might as well be paperweights.

He was starting to get a headache from trying so hard to focus, and by the time Sally ask her last question, his headache had grown into a blinding migraine. He was barely aware of them saying their good-byes to the Colonel and thanking him for his time.

When they were out of the office and in the parking lot, Sally turned to him and said, "You look like you're going to be sick."

Elliot leaned back against the driver's side door of their sedan. "I had a major headache, but it's starting to fade."

"Want me to drive?"

"No, I've got it." He pressed his hands against his temples for a second as if trying to hold in his thoughts. "You didn't feel anything strange about the Colonel," he asked?

"No, I thought he was a nice guy. Apparently you felt something."

"You could say that," he said, digging in his jacket pocket for the car keys. "I think he's our guy."

"Did you get a...flash or something?"

"Nothing specific, he just feels real bad."

"How bad?"

"Bad, bad, like he just might be an evil motherfucker, bad."

"What are we going to do?"

"Let's press with the interviews, but I'm going to disappear for a while, do some sleuthing into the Colonel's life."

"What am I going to do about the other interviews? Want me to wait?"

"No, don't wait. Take Fleming; there's no way he could fuck this up."

* * *

Elliot dropped Sally off at the Office. He planned on spending the rest of the day dissecting Colonel William Gray's life. He figured his first stop would be the military personnel office. He wasn't expecting to find anything in Gray's military personnel record that would help with the investigation. But the more he thought about it, the more convinced he was that Gray had to be their man. Gray's personnel record would show Elliot the public Colonel Gray. He had no doubt that Gray's file would be anything less than exemplary. But he had to go from the known to the unknown.

After reviewing the personnel file, he planned on going to the base hospital to see if Gray or anyone in his immediate family had a history of mental illness, or reoccurring injuries that could indicate abuse.

Once he had reviewed all of the records, he was going to come up with some reason to meet Gray's family face to face. Maybe he was closer to their frequencies than he was to Gray. If so, he might be able to pull something helpful out of their heads.

He had just pulled into the personnel office parking lot when Blair Edgewater called his car phone. He knew it was Blair even before he answered. He hadn't been expecting her call, but something in him said "Blair" as soon as the phone rang.

He'd been trying to do so many things at once that he'd almost forgot about Blair, which was a testament to his pre-occupation with this case. She was not an easy person to forget. In fact, after their first meeting, she was all he thought about for almost a week.

They had stayed out drinking well into the evening and Blair turned out to be more than just long auburn hair and intoxicating scents. She had a master's degree in philosophy and was a great conversationalist. She was well read and could speak knowledgeably about everything from trends in politics to the best movies to go see. She could also hold her liquor (Elliot found that particularly appealing).

They had flirted and laughed and had such a good time that they decided not to risk ruining the magic of the evening by having bad drunken sex. But both of them knew - and knew the other knew - there was going to be some slightly tipsy, hot, sweaty, monkey-love, in the future.

Elliot answered his phone, and before Blair could say anything said, "Hi Blair, sacrifice any virgins today?"

"If you're trying to impress me, it's working. How'd you know it was me?"

"Lucky guess."

"I'll buy that for a dollar, and I don't know any virgins."

"I'm a virgin," he said. "I'm still waiting for the right person."

"I might know someone who can help you. But in the meantime, I've got some information you might be interested in."

"You found out how may licks it takes to get to the center of a tootsie-pop?"

"I already know that. I'll have to show you sometime. I've got something even better, information on your chi-sucking vampire. Can we meet?"

Boy, can we! "I've got some things to do right now, how about this evening?"

"I'll clear my schedule."

He closed his phone and went into the military personnel office. The record's clerks recognized him and greeted him with smiles. OSI agents had unchallenged access to all military personnel files. The clerks knew most of the agents on sight. Elliot found Colonel Gray's file and carried it to an empty desk for review.

Gray joined the Air Force in 1968. He was an Air Force Academy graduate, and a fighter pilot. His record detailed an exemplary career. He had filled in all the necessary blocks to ensure timely promotions. He'd taken all of the right command and staff assignments, and Elliot figured he was ripe for promotion to General. Basically, Gray's record was exactly what he expected.

The colonel had been married for almost ten years, which meant he had been a young, single, fighter pilot from 1968 to 1983. He had plenty of years to sow his wild oats before settling down. Elliot had a good idea how he sowed his oats.

Gray had served two tours of duty in Vietnam, and had also been stationed in both Thailand and the Philippines off and on during those first fifteen years of service. He had two daughters, ages 7 and 9. His wife didn't work.

Elliot tried to find anything that would show what kind of hobbies Gray had. Was he a golfer? Did he like to read? But it appeared as if the colonel had no interests outside of his career. He didn't even belong to any clubs or organizations. Elliot assumed that was because his interests were of a singularly non-socially accepted nature than the average VFW bingo night activities.

He called his office, and Fred Shaw, the RCCI, answered the phone. These days, Shaw could almost always be found at the computer on Elliot's desk. Elliot only used the computer to type reports and play solitaire. He was amazed at what Shaw had turned it into.

"Hey, Fred," Elliot said.

"Hey, Elliot." Shaw sounded happy to hear from him. They were on friendly terms now. Elliot had felt guilty about the way he'd treated Shaw and had apologized a few weeks back. Shaw had accepted his apology. Since then they'd developed an amicable working relationship.

"Can you access DCII from my desk?" DCII was the Defense Clearance Investigations Index. Anyone who had ever been granted a security clearance in the military, or had been investigated by the Army Criminal Investigations Division (CID), the OSI, or the Naval Investigative Service (NIS) would be in the database.

"What do you need?" Shaw asked.

"I want to run one of the guys from our list."

"I'm one step ahead of you, dude. I've already created files on each person from our suspect list, conducted DCII checks on them, and entered the results in their individual files."

"You're incredible, man."

"It's what I do. Gimme a name."

"Colonel William Gray. Do you need a social security number?"

"Not necessary, I've got him right here. It looks like he's one of six guys who we got positive hits on for being involved in criminal investigations. Four years ago, the OSI opened a case on him for assault. Looks like he was accused of kicking his wife's ass, but the investigation was closed after the allegation was determined to be unfounded. Anything else?"

"Vehicles?"

"One sport utility vehicle and a BMW. What's up with this guy?"

"Just between us, I think he's the one."

"Oh, man!"

"Yea, I know, keep it under your hat for now. Take care." Elliot hung up.

Elliot's gut was insisting that Gray had beaten up his spouse to keep her quiet about something. Maybe she discovered some aspect of his hobby. But Elliot found it hard to believe she would keep quiet if she thought he was killing people. He was going to have to pay Mrs. Gray a visit. First, he decided to let the team know what he planned to do.

Elliot called Sally on her car phone and asked her to find

everybody else. When he returned to the office everyone except Margaret and Jason were already there. Jerry Fleming was also there. Elliot could feel Fleming's excitement. Since Jerry's competence, or rather his lack thereof, was common knowledge; the commander never assigned him any cases of any importance. Being part of the unofficial 'silo killer' sub-task force (Elliot and crew) was doing wonders for his self-esteem.

Shaw was sitting at Elliot's desk in front of the computer, and the others occupied all the other chairs in the small office. Elliot shrugged out of his jacket and took a seat on the corner of Sally's desk. He noted with affection that the team seldom met in the conference room. They seemed to have an unspoken agreement to meet informally in the small office Elliot shared with Sally. They'd become more of a club than a task force.

Tony Coleman had traded in his suit for jeans, tennis shoes, and a university sweatshirt. Even Drake had forsaken suit and tie for a more comfortable polo shirt and jeans. Of course, he was still wearing fashionable brown loafers. Sally had also donned a par of jeans. Elliot really liked that. Her ass was made for jeans.

Everybody was armed. Elliot and Drake wore shoulder holsters. The others had their weapons concealed in fanny packs. He thought they looked like the small team of maverick investigators they were.

"Have you guys noticed how cool we look?" Elliot asked. "I mean if we could solve this case with image alone, it would be a done deal." He looked around. "Were are Margaret and Jason?"

"They had to give their chief an update," Sally said. "They're going to be late."

"Let's start without them," Elliot said. "They can catch

up when they get here. I've got some shit hot stuff. But first, I want to hear what you guys have."

"I've got the bureau's completed profile if you want the highlights," Coleman said.

"Let's do it."

"I don't think there's anything here that you didn't already know or suspect. But it's an interesting read nonetheless. The Bureau thinks we're looking for a white male, age thirty five to fifty..."

"That's some top end," Sally said.

"Yea, but it puts our boy in Vietnam during the war," Elliot said.

"I think that's why they topped it out like that. They're taking your theory a little more seriously than your boss. Anyway," he read from his notebook, "white male, thirty five to fifty, no criminal record, they think he's either in law enforcement or the military. He's well educated. He's homosexual, but he's not in denial. If his sexual needs weren't so extreme and criminal, he'd probably be openly homosexual."

"Not if he's in the military," Drake said.

"I thought it was don't asked, don't tell?"

"That was actually an executive branch hoax," Elliot said. "It's always kind of been *ask* but don't really dig, and don't tell. When the military kicks out homosexuals, it's not a lifestyle thing it's a sodomy thing."

Coleman frowned. Elliot elaborated, "They don't get kicked out for being homosexual, they get kicked out for engaging in sodomy. Sodomy is against military law."

"I see." But the look on his face clearly indicated he didn't. He glanced back down at his file to continue, but stopped. "Wait, what if a heterosexual engages in sodomy?"

"If he or she gets caught, it the same thing." Elliot smiled and waited for the next obvious question.

"Um, how does the military define sodomy? There are a lot of ways to interpret that."

Sally chimed in, "As oral or anal sex."

Coleman's mouth dropped open in disbelief. Sally grinned salaciously at him, "That's right, Special Agent Coleman, at any given time nearly every serving member of the Armed Forces of the United States of by-God-American are in flagrant violation of the UCMJ."

"That's ridiculous. How can that be enforced?" Coleman asked.

"Usually it isn't. Sodomy is only used as a charge if the military wants to get rid of a homosexual, or a heterosexual who has done something else, like screwed a fellow officers' spouse. If they aren't caught in the act, it requires one of the participants to report the other." Elliot answered.

"Oh." Coleman shook his head as if to get rid of the cobwebs. The strangeness of that particular law befuddled him. He went back to something easier to understand, the profile of a sadistic serial killer. "Anyway, if our boy is married, it's to a submissive spouse. He needs to be in control of himself and his surroundings, and he may exhibit obsessive-compulsive behavior. He's socially well adjusted. Don't expect this guy to self destruct."

"We should be so lucky," Elliot said. "Sally, what do you and Jerry have?"

"Not much. We talked to two guys this afternoon, nothing remarkable about them, and we're going to talk to a couple of chiefs tomorrow. One of those guys...let's see," she took out her notebook, "Chief Gunther Demochet, was actually in Vietnam as a combat controller for his first three tours. I bet he has some stories to tell, huh?"

"I'll bet he does," Elliot said. "But, I think we're just going through the motions now. I'm convinced we've found our guy, and we should maybe stray a little from our program and concentrate on him."

"Do you think that's wise?" Drake asked.

"You said my thing was people, right? Well, my gut says this is our guy, and we should single him out sooner rather than later."

"What about the other potential suspects?" Coleman asked.

"I'm not saying we should stop the BAIs. Let Sally, Jerry, Margaret and Jason keep working the questionnaires. Me, Drake, and Tony will go after my guy."

"Maybe you should tell us about *your guy,*" Drake said, still not sold.

"This morning, Sally and I talked to Colonel William Gray. I can't put my finger on it, but something about him didn't sit well with me; so I did some digging into his background.

"He started out his career in Vietnam, and also spent a bunch of time in Thailand and the Philippines which fits our general profile. But there are a handful of other things that seem to point his way too. For instance, Alonso Proctor and 15 of the other bodies in the silo had broken necks, and Josh Bennet was practically squished to death. I figured our guy was no ninety-pound weakling, and Colonel Gray is a fucking monster. It also looks like he may have a history of family violence, you know, keeping that wife of his submissive I imagine. I'm looking into that.

"Our killer has a very unique signature, yet the FBI hasn't managed to get any hits out of the VICAP database. Fred hasn't had any luck either. That tells me that our guy has always been very careful about how he disposed of his victims, which could happen; but you would think he would have made some mistakes in the beginning. A second option is, he perfected his art overseas. I don't think police jurisdictions in third world and developing countries report unsolved homicides to the FBI.

"The OSI office on Guam has liaison contacts with police agencies in Thailand, the Philippines, and even Vietnam. I think we should have them ask their police contacts in those countries about unsolved killings that match our guy's MO. I'll bet their are old timers in some of those places with all kinds of corporate knowledge.

"I can handle that," Shaw said. "That's a lot more manageable than contacting every agency in every jurisdiction where one of our potentials happened to be stationed."

"Yes it is. I'm a little more focused now."

"Do you think we should tell Devine what we're working on?" Sally asked.

"He's the boss," Elliot said. Clearly, he had no intention of contacting the commander. But it was the right thing to do. He knew Sally would take care of that chore.

Devine had actually left Elliot and his crew to their own devices during the past weeks. Occasionally, he would ask for an update on their investigation, but most of his time had been spent at the FBI offices as the OSI representative on the official 'silo killer' task force, or at the base public affairs office sucking up to the media. Elliot knew the commander's apparent disinterest in their activities wasn't a by-product of his trust in Elliot's team, in spite of the fact that they had found the bodies. Devine had no faith in Elliot's theory or Elliot's team of misfit's ability to solve the case. Devine's faith was in the FBI, but he figured Elliot and crew weren't hurting anything with their actions; and if they did stumble on to something, he was in position to take the credit.

Chapter Thirty-Seven

Sally was locking up for the night. She had the check out sheet and was going through the darkened offices checking safes and making sure nothing important had been left unsecured. Bizarrely, the check sheet even listed things like "Coffee pot – off", "Front office printer – off", because God forbid they be left on, especially the printer, because life as we know it on planet earth might end. She opened the evidence closet and checked to make sure the bags of evidence were neatly stowed behind their mesh, wire cages to discourage tampering. She bent down to yank on a pad lock, then stood and turned, checking off the block on her clipboard, and bumped into the figure standing behind her.

She yelped and jumped backwards. He was so quiet that she wouldn't have know he was standing there if she wasn't looking right at him.

"Jesus, Tony, you scared the shit out of me." She brushed a stray strand of hair away from her forehead. When he didn't say anything right away, she began feeling a little uncomfortable. "What do you want, Tony?"

"How is going?" He asked, instead of answering. He was blocking the doorway.

"Fine. It's going fine."

He looked at her for a long time, his face entirely unreadable, as if he was trying to determine the truth behind her statement.

"You're married." He stated.

"Yeah....and?" Sally found she was clutching the clipboard to her chest and she suddenly felt silly. She was a goddamn, lead slinging law woman: why should she be clutching at a clipboard like a schoolgirl caught playing hooky? "Get to the fucking point, Tony. You know I hate all this cryptic shit."

He did know that. Sally was a straight shooter. She told you exactly what was on her mind, and liked it when you did the same.

"You've developed feelings for him. That will cloud your judgment. Your job is not to develop a crush on Elliot, it's to study and report."

"I know what my fucking job is, and I've been doing it. You've received my reports and I think they are very impartial and comprehensive." She dropped her arms to her side and pushed past him into the corridor, partly because her suspicious nature made it impossible for her to have a compromising conversation when she couldn't be certain no one was listening outside the door.

Tony followed her, "Just be careful, and extra vigilant. This case has captured Elliot's attention, and he is transmitting out of control. Our remote sensors have been going batshit for the last few weeks. Some them are spending an unusual amount of time drawing pictures of Elliot, when they should be focusing on Russian mobile missile platforms. We can't get them to view anything else."

Sally felt flushed. "How is that possible?"

"We don't know, but Elliot is sucking so much psychic energy, he's actually jamming our remote sensing capabilities. We've got to put this to bed quickly, so we can get our boys back on track. Last thing we need is the Russians to do something fucked up and we didn't see it because Elliot is pre-occupied with a murder case. Explaining that to Congress would be most awkward."

Sally nodded, "Okay, Tony, I get it. Don't worry about me, I'm on it. Elliot doesn't do shit without me knowing about it. You know, why don't your sensors make themselves useful and tell us who the killer is, that would solve all our problems instantly."

"It doesn't work that way, and besides, we don't re-route national resources for low level murders."

Sally opened her mouth to say something, then closed it again. How could he consider this "low level"? What were government agencies good for if not to safeguard the citizens of its nation? As Sally struggled for a response, Tony turned to leave, then paused.

"So how is your marriage going?"

She shot him a sharp look. "You know how my marriage is going."

He nodded, "Yeah, I know. Well, good night, then."

"Good night." She turned and walked down the hallway, intent on finishing her check list.

Tony Coleman left through the back door, where his car was parked in the gravel lot. As the door closed behind him, he paused and took a deep breath of cool, night air. Talking to Sally had disrupted him. A few breaths and he regained his sense of calm. He looked around the parking lot. Everything stood out in hyper-definition. There were no threats. He walked down the steps and got into his car.

He sat there for a moment. Tony wasn't the average FBI agent. In fact, Tony wasn't really an FBI agent at all.

Coleman was an "observer" for the National Security Group (NSG). The NSG was part of the National Security Agency (NSA). Coleman was one of two agents attached to the PSI Observation Unit in Colorado. The presence of the PSI unit in Colorado was the reason Elliot had been assigned to the OSI office in Denver as opposed to some other hole.

The NSG's primary mission was to investigate all credible psychic occurrences. During investigation of the Idaho incident, Elliot claimed to have experienced a clairvoyant episode. The OSI had been understandably skeptical, but departmental heads at OSI headquarters, and other federal law enforcement agencies, had standing orders to report all claims of paranormal activity involving field agents to the NSG.

The NSG did some digging into his background and uncovered inexplicable activity associated with Elliot Turner on more than one occasion, however nothing as serious at the Hatchet shooting. After he killed Hatchet, Elliot had had no choice but to try and explain the truth behind his actions no matter how outlandish.

They had tested Elliot under laboratory conditions and determined that he was indeed a low level psi-talent. They sent him to Denver, which just happened to be where the observation unit was headquartered, where they could observe him in a non-controlled environment. If Elliot had known what was going on, he would have said they wanted to observe the freak in his natural habitat. He would have been correct in his cynicism.

Coleman had been 'assigned' to the Denver FBI offices shortly after Elliot had been sent to Denver. He'd been an FBI agent before he himself had been discovered by the NSG. So, FBI agent was the perfect cover. The FBI had routine contact with most OSI offices, and as the local FBI liaison contact to the OSI, Coleman could observe Elliot's actions with impunity.

Coleman was also a low-level telepath. As an observer he had been trained to shield his mind from other telepaths. He'd felt Elliot try to probe his mind. But Elliot was more empath than telepath and an amateur. He had no trouble shielding his mind from Elliot's heavy handed probing.

The NSG wasn't interested in Elliot's empathy, and his telepathy was laughable. They were interested in his random bouts of clairvoyance and curious to see if he might manifest any other talents that could be exploited for national security purposes. Contrary to what most intelligence experts believed, computers were not the espionage or counterintelligence wave of the future. The success of intelligence operations in the future would depend on the study and effective use of psychics and clairvoyants. But the federal government couldn't very well advertise a need for psychics in the newspaper. They had to take their subjects where they found them. They were constantly on the lookout for persons already in 'the business' who demonstrated exploitable talents.

The case had been a godsend. Coleman had been wondering how he was going to get closer to Elliot. The silo killer had provided him the perfect opportunity to observe up close and personal how Elliot used his talents on the job (the freak at work and play).

He hadn't been disappointed.

Telepaths and empaths were a dime dozen, but clairvoyants were a rare breed. The Idaho incident demonstrated that Elliot was exhibiting that rarest and most inexplicable talent, the ability to latch on to an existing time-line and ride it into the immediate future. The problem with the future was that it was not engraved in stone, and accurate readings diminished with every second stretching away from the present. The margin for error was infinite.

Elliot was one of the best test subjects the NSG had stumbled across in years. During testing he had been able to accurately extrapolate the existing time-line up to three minutes into the future. It didn't seem like much. But in the age of high speed computers and weapons systems those three minutes could be critical in the executive decision making process.

Psychological testing had shown that Elliot was distrustful, almost hostile, towards authority figures and resistant to change. Coleman's secondary agenda, beyond simple observation, was to figure out how best to convince Elliot to give up the life he had always wanted and come to work for the NSG doing things he probably didn't agree with.

Chapter Thirty-Eight

Elliot called Blair and they agreed to meet for dinner at seven o'clock. After he left the office he went back to his apartment to shower. He couldn't very well meet Blair before he made sure all of his man-parts were squeaky clean. At least he was hoping his man-parts *needed* to be squeaky clean. He suspected he was engaging in the female equivalent of pre-date leg shaving.

Elliot lived in a one-bedroom apartment about five minutes from the Air Force base. The apartment was in an up-scale singles complex, with tennis courts, swimming pool, and gym. He'd picked the apartment because it was close to the base, affordable, and home to about thirty stewardesses. The stewardess thing had been one of the major selling points, but the ones he'd met hadn't given him the time of day. They weren't his types anyway. Most of them seemed to be high maintenance anyway. Elliot had a simple formula for high maintenance women; the chance of bedding them decreased logarithmically in direct correlation with the amount of time and effort they put into clothes and make-up before leaving the house. Blair was low maintenance. She could throw on a sweater and some jeans, run her fingers through her hair and be ready to go.

Blair chose the bar this time, a small Irish pub with quiet clientele and Guinness on tap. It would do in a pinch. He arrived before Blair, and by the time she walked in was well into his first beer.

He figured he and Blair would talk a little business, get partially liquored up and go do something nasty. He allowed himself a few illicit fantasies about her. He was up to about item 61 in his mental *kama sutra* when she walked in with her father. At least he assumed it was her father, nothing like having daddy around to mess up a fantasy. He sighed, caught the waitress's eye from across the room, and pointed to his empty glass. She smiled and gave him the 'okay' sign.

Blair's father was every inch the university professor right down to the bifocals and brown tweed jacket with elbow patches.

Blair spotted Elliot and moved comfortably through the crowd towards him. She stopped twice to greet regulars who called out to her. So, this was *her* spot.

Elliot caught her dad waving to a couple of people also. Okay, this is a university staff hangout. That explained the Guinness on tap.

They made their way to the table and Blair introduced them.

"Dad, this is Special Agent Elliot Turner. Elliot, this is my father."

"Nice to meet you," the professor said holding out his hand. "Call me Robert." The professor had a firm dry handshake. He wasn't frail under his tweed, and Elliot realized he was much younger than the gray beard and bifocals led him to believe.

"Nice to meet you, too," Elliot said.

"You've made quite an impression on my daughter."

Not as much as I'd like to make. "I'm just glad she doesn't think I'm wacko," Elliot said.

"I didn't say that. Do people often think you're... wacko?"

"I don't know. Whacko is as whacko does" Elliot said. Then he thought to himself, '*Whacko is as wacko does?' What the fuck does that even mean?* "Why don't you two sit down?"

They sat down. The waitress brought Elliot's second beer. Blair and the professor ordered beers also.

"Blair tells me that you're interested in occurrences of vampirism and the occult in Southeast Asian societies."

"Uh, yeah, something like that. I'm sure I didn't put it quite as eloquently as you. You make it sound like the topic of some thesis. I was trying to find out where an American GI might get the idea of becoming a chi-sucking vampire. The way you put it doesn't sound so cheesy."

"The whole concept isn't that...cheesy...at all. What do you know about occult practices in Asia?"

"Absolutely nothing. I've done some work in the Japan, the Philippines and Thailand, but what I actually know about their history and culture could fill a thimble."

The Professor seemed to brighten a bit at this. Like any good academic he was pleased to have a clean slate to work with.

"Well," he said. "Luckily, I've done some research on the topic. Actually, I consider myself somewhat of an authority on the subject.

"The Far East is rife with occult mythology. They have everything from demonic possession to vengeful spirits running amuck in small villages. If you've ever seen any modern Japanese animation, you'll have noticed that they can't make a movie without tossing in a demon or evil spirit."

Elliot could tell the professor was gearing up for a lengthy dissertation, and while he was sure the professor had some interesting trivia, he was hoping he would just get to the crux and then go away. He hadn't completely given up the idea of spending some unprofessional time with Blair.

"I'm not really that interested in Japanese or Chinese mythology," Elliot said before the professor could continue.

Elliot received a quick empathic flash of annoyance from the professor. But it was gone quickly and never touched his face.

"Yes, of course," he said. "You're probably eager to get on with the whole vampire thing."

"If you don't mind." Elliot said, trying not to sound impatient. The professor seemed nice enough, and he didn't want to offend him.

"There are a number of vampire myths in eastern mythology, but I think you'll be most interested in those with roots in Cambodia and Thailand. As a people, Thais are fairly peace loving. Therevada Buddhism is deeply rooted in their culture, and they'd rather fly kites and have festivals than make war. Now, I'm not saying it's a completely non-violent society. It's almost human nature to enjoy watching violent activities. Are you familiar with Muay Thai boxing?"

"Yeah, Thai boxing, brutal art."

"Yes, on the surface I guess it does seem like a particularly brutal martial art. But it is so much more than just a style of fighting. Modern Muay Thai is full of ritual, much of it for show. But ancient Muay Thai practitioners engaged in ceremonies that were decidedly more occult.

"Warriors from the hill tribes such as the Hmong,

Yao, and the Khmer in the northern mountains near the Cambodian border of Thailand, believed they could augment their fighting prowess by drinking the blood of slain warriors, both friend and enemy. I should probably point out the blood rituals of that sort have developed in both Africa, Asia, and other parts of the world with no apparent connection."

"I think I see where you're going, professor. But I don't think my perpetrator would have had too much time to spend in the mountains of Thailand with the hill people."

"He wouldn't have to. These days Hmong, Yao, and Khmer are so integrated in the modern Thai society, it's hard to tell where one culture ends and another begins. There are Muay Thai sects in Northern Thailand that are steeped in the rituals of the past. They still practice blood ceremonies, although not with human blood. These days they use animal blood and it's more symbolic, like drinking the blood of Christ."

Blair had been silent, listening to her dad, and drinking her beer. She set here glass down and wrinkled her face in disgust. Elliot thought it was cute. But at this juncture, had she puked on the table he would have thought it was cute. "Yuck," she said. "That can't be healthy."

"I'm sure it's not," said the professor, "but socio-mythology is an important part of any culure."

"So where would my guy get the whole blood drinking idea?"

"Lots of Muay Thai schools take on any one who proves he can handle the training, even westerners."

"When I was in Thailand, I remember some of the local boxers challenging the GI's in the crowd. I was always too chicken shit to get in the ring. But there were always plenty of drunken marines willing to take an ass kicking." Elliot observed.

"The Thais are a very friendly and accommodating people. They would welcome anyone with the right attitude into their school with open arms. You're probably not looking for a drunken Marine."

"What about the Philippines? Any blood sucking cults there?"

"No."

"Then I'm going to go out on a limb and narrow my search to guys who've spent a significant amount of time in Thailand." Elliot didn't think it was necessary to tell the professor he had probably already found his man.

They chatted for awhile about Asia and Thailand. Elliot had traveled extensively throughout Asia and was a locker room authority on the subject. But he was humbled by the Professor's almost encyclopedic knowledge about the region.

At about ten-thirty the Professor, much to Elliot's libidinous delight, excused himself. He promised he'd call if he came across any useful information. Then gave Elliot 'the eye,' reminding him nonverbally that Blair was still his little girl, and Elliot should watch his step.

After he left. Elliot turned to Blair and asked, "Did he just give me 'the eye?"

"Pretty much. He *is* my dad. That's his job."

"I'd better watch my step, huh?"

"Only if you think you have to," she said.

Chapter Thirty-Nine

He had killed at least eight women by the time he met a beautiful young man by the name of Rau Watane. Rau had been his first real love. He introduced the young killer first to the forbidden rituals in ancient boxing, and then to the ecstasy one man could have with another. The killer inevitably figured out a way to combine the two. When he met Rau, the young Thai had been a local legend. He was the most feared boxer in his prefecture.

The war in Vietnam was over. It was 1973, and he never wanted to leave Thailand. He'd been there for over a year and had come to love the country and its people, as much as he could *love* anything.

After his first fateful encounter with the Muay Thai pugilists, he tried to learn everything he could about the art. When he found himself stationed at Utapao Air Base, Thailand in 1973. The first thing he did was find a Muay Thai school that accepted westerners. He was so caught up in the art that he only killed one girl that year.

As was his way with all things violent, he had been a

quick study. After less than two years of intense training, he found himself dominating Muay Thai matches in Utapao.

He had taken a break from training and was actually on a hunt when he met Rau. He'd gone up to Naklua, a small village north of Utapao, in Chonburi prefecture, looking for any young girl he could cull from the herd.

What he found was a town alive with the Loy Krathong water festival. The Loy Krathong was the ancient water festival to honor the water spirits, and the Naklua waterways were packed with floats made from banana leaves and decorated with candles and incense. The village pulsed with magic and he had been almost moved.

He had wandered through town in that state of almost feeling...something, and when he got to the town center; he was pleasantly surprised to find a Muay Thai match about to begin.

It was obvious who the local favorite was. He was lean and well muscled. His skin glowed from the sweat of his warm-up. He was naked to the waist and barefoot. His hair was cut short in the style of the Theravada Buddhist monks, and he was...beautiful.

He watched the young fighter posturing for the crowd, and as the fighter knelt to perform the ritual prayer before the contest, he realized the young fighter excited him like no female ever had.

The fact that he was so attracted and aroused by another man didn't give him pause. He had no need for internal debate. He simply accepted it. If he felt anything, it was a fleeting amusement that he hadn't noticed before how sensuous another man could be. New avenues for the hunt opened up for him, but not this one: He did not want to kill this young beautiful fighter, he wanted to *know* him.

He eased through the crowd until he was next to the ring. The other fighter, clearly a sacrificial lamb and content with his lot, watched quietly from his corner waiting for the fight to begin.

There had been music and drums and a cacophony of excited voices. When the music and drums stopped, the crowd grew quiet. The challenger took his place at the center of the ring. His movements were graceful and fluid. His eyes were focused, his body relaxed. The challenger was clearly a formidable fighter in his own right. But his essence paled next to the other's beauty and confidence.

The object of the killer's lust attacked the challenger. The posturing was over. The young fighter danced across the ring. Even without the drums, the fighters continued to move to their own individual internal rhythms.

The favorite, ferocious and beautiful, launched an initial attack terrible to behold. But the challenger unimpressed calmly sidestepped kicks and parried elbows and fist, without attempting to launch a counter-attack.

For three rounds the beautiful fighter attacked and the other calmly defended. During the fourth round, the challenger threw his only punch of the fight, a single backfist, almost too fast to follow. The fist connected with the aggressor's head with a sound like a gunshot, and the fight ended as quickly as it had begun. The killer's beautiful fighter crumpled to the matting of the ring and lay still. Dead? He knew death when he saw it. He was dead!

The victor turned and walked slowly to his corner. He looked out over the crowd, finding and holding the gaze for a moment that seemed like an eternity. He looked into this quiet warrior's eyes and realized the beautiful fighter had been the sacrificial lamb, and this fighter had taken that beauty in an instant, and with that taking had become more beautiful and powerful himself.

The dead fighter was unceremoniously extricated from the ring. The champion faded, unmolested, through the crowd. Everyone kept a respectful distance from the champion, averting their eyes when he glanced in their direction. The killer followed him.

The victor walked purposely through town until he came to a well-kept hut with a corrugated tin roof. He ducked inside. The killer found a seat on a fruit crate across the road, underneath the low hanging branches of a banana tree, and watched the hut hoping for another glimpse of the strange fighter.

As he watched, two men pulling a wheeled cart walked up to the hut. They pulled a man-sized bundle from the back and entered without knocking or announcing themselves. They exited quickly and rolled away back towards the festival.

He crept around to the back of the hut and was able to peer under one of the corrugated tin shutters. Inside, the hut was illuminated with dozens of candles. There was a small altar in one corner with a single statuette. He didn't recognize the deity. On the floor in the middle of the hut was the bundle. Its wrappings had been pulled aside to display the naked body of the dead fighter. The champion, his back to the window, was also naked. He was kneeling over the body working quickly with what looked like a small dagger. He watched him pierce the body of the dead fighter repeatedly, pausing between each stroke to bend and kiss the body. It wasn't until he finished, stood, and looked in the killer's direction, that the sheen of blood on his face became apparent. The blood was almost black in the candlelight. He hadn't been kissing the body at all. He'd but been suckling at the wounds.

He looked directly at the killer and spoke, and the killer, who'd seen combat, and routinely killed for enjoyment, for the first time in his life, had been startled and almost frightened.

"Have you seen enough, American solider?" he asked in English laced with the singsong accent of the Thai language.

For a moment he thought he must have been talking to someone else. Surely the crack beneath the shutters was not enough to give him away.

The fighter continued as if reading his mind. "You have been watching me long time, American soldier. I hear your breath. I feel you move outside. Come inside!" he commanded.

The killer walked around to the front of the hut. By the time he entered, the champion had already covered the body of the slain fighter, but his face still bore the evidence of his ritual. "Why do you watch me, American soldier?" he asked.

He had regained his composure after his initial shock. "Because I want to be like you," he said simply, realizing it was the truth.

The fighter mulled this over then said, "I'm tired. Come back tomorrow, American soldier."

"What do I call you?" he asked.

"Call me Rau."

"Rau," the killer said. "I am..."

Rau cut him off. "You," he said, "are the American soldier."

He had gone back that next day and as often as possible during his Thailand assignment. With Rau he'd been as happy as he'd ever been. After he killed him, he took away a stockpile of bittersweet memories.

Chapter Forty

Elliot lay awake on his back, hands behind his head, staring up at his bedroom ceiling. Blair Edgewater was snoring quietly beside him, one leg tossed over his thigh, auburn hair buried in his armpit. He could feel the moistness between her legs on his thigh and smell her on his face. They'd had incredible sex, and Elliot was already contemplating round two.

He ran his hand down her spine, pausing to massage the small of her back then continuing on to her buttocks. Blair left the confines of his armpit and walked a string of kisses across his chest. "More," she mumbled tiredly. Elliot couldn't tell whether it was a question or an offer. He erred on the side of his hormones and decided it was an offer. They made love slowly at first, but their gyrations became more desperate as their climaxes approached, each seemingly trying to absorb the other. They climaxed together and fell asleep cradled in each other's arms.

When he woke the next morning, Blair was already dressed.

"Sneaking away?" he asked.

"Time to make the donuts." She said. Elliot looked at her curiously. "Something I said?" she asked.

"No, nothing. I was just thinking about last night."

"Yeah, it was pretty decent, huh? You're not a bad piece of ass. Let's do it again sometime."

"I love an old fashioned woman," he said.

"That'd be me," she said, looking under the bed for her purse. She found it, stood up, and rummaged around inside for her keys. She'd insisted on driving her own car to Elliot's apartment the previous evening, which was a good thing because it was already ten o'clock. Blair leaned over the bed and kissed him on the lips and forehead. "Call me," she said and rushed out the door.

"I'll do that," Elliot said to the door.

He dressed carefully, foregoing his trademark jeans and T-shirt, replacing them with casual slacks, shirt and tie. He planned on talking to Colonel Gray's wife and wanted to look as harmless as possible.

When he got to the office, Fred Shaw was the only one there.

"Good afternoon," he said when Elliot slipped into the office, looking back over his shoulder for the commander out of habit.

"It's only 10:15."

"Yeah, well some people do more by 10:15 than others do all day." Shaw said.

"I'll talk to the boss and ask him to give you a raise." Elliot looked around. "Where's Sally?"

"She grabbed Jerry first thing this morning. They're already out doing interviews." Shaw had been staring at his computer screen, now he looked up and noticed Elliot was wearing a tie. "Oh my god!" he said. "Who died?"

"Don't give me any shit, Fred. I'm gonna try and talk to Mrs. Colonel Gray today."

"Which reminds me", the RCCI said, "Steve Drake called about thirty minutes ago looking for you. He wanted me to stop you before you hit the road and ask you to stop by Tony Coleman's office."

"How'd he sound?"

"What do you mean?"

"Was he like; 'if you see Elliot, tell him I want to talk to him.' or was he like; 'Oh my god! The free world is coming to an end, must...see... Elliot...now, ack, ack, argh!'" Elliot clutched his chest and slumped against the wall smiling.

"It was closer to ack, ack, ack, argh than the other one."

"I guess I'm going to the FBI offices."

* * *

The local FBI office had changed since Elliot's last visit. It was no longer the tightly wound field office manned by dedicated androids in conservative business attire going quietly about their business. Now it was a madhouse, a flurry of activity, with androids in rumpled business suits, shuffling around with manic eyes sunk low in unshaven faces. Every phone had an android stuck to it, and the walls looked like Elliot's collage macabre on steroids.

Elliot was well accustomed to chaos, even thrived on; but there was good chaos and bad chaos. There was the chaos of the universe, the cyclic dance of creation and destruction and all that fell in-between; and then there was the chaos born of man's attempt to control the other. This was man made chaos in its purest ugliest bureaucratic form. Elliot could feel the frustration in the office. There was activity but no direction, and the activity had become more important than the goal.

Elliot saw Drake and Tony Coleman talking to the commander, George Devine, across the room. Devine saw

Elliot and gave him a perfunctory nod, which was about as civil as he ever was to Elliot. Elliot nodded back and went over to join them.

Devine disappeared before Elliot managed to negotiate the maze of desks and laptop computer cords. Coleman smiled as Elliot walked up. "Special Agent Turner," he said, "I present to you the self-licking, ice cream cone." He waved his hand over the room.

"Impressive," Elliot said, "and not just a little bit frightening. What's the big emergency? I was going to try and talk to Mrs. Gray today."

"Don't bother," Drake said. "She's in an office down the hall. The Colonel's in one of the interrogation rooms, and the kids are with social services."

"I have absolutely got to start getting to work on time." Elliot said. "Okay, fill me in."

"We briefed Devine on the Gray angle first thing this morning," Drake said. "He thought it had merit."

"That's a bad thing, right?" The thought of one of his ideas in Devine's hands fill him with dread. He looked from Coleman to Drake and back again to Coleman. Then noticed they were both acting a little sheepish. "This conversation isn't going to get much better is it?"

"Not unless by 'better' you mean Devine's knee jerk reaction to the information."

"Smaller the balls, higher the knee *can* jerk," Elliot interrupted.

"Then your boss is probably an eunuch," Coleman said. "He briefed the task force and put a spin on the whole Colonel Gray thing that Oliver Stone would be proud of. He basically used the old stop-him-before-he-kills-again spin. Next thing you know, they've mobilized the forces, gone out and scooped up the Colonel."

"But we didn't have anything on him yet!" Elliot was

horrified, and imagined his case crashing and burning before his eyes.

"The didn't arrest him. They just wanted to talk to him again. But they were kind of heavy handed."

"And...," Elliot prompted.

"...and he's not talking."

"But," Drake said. "The wife is. A couple of guys met Colonel Gray at his office and asked him to come down for a chat. At the same time, Tony and I figured, since the task force monster had latched on to the Colonel, we would go insulate Mrs. Gray from all that ugliness. We paged you and tried to call you, but you must have been busy or something. There was no answer at your apartment and you weren't in the office."

"I was...working." Elliot said, wishing he hadn't turned off the ringer on his telephone when he was with Blair.

"Whatever. Anyway, Once we explained the situation to Mrs. Gray..."

"What situation would that be?"

"That would be; that the Colonel was under investigation for sexual improprieties with a minor."

"Sexual improprieties?"

"That was my idea," Coleman said. "It's almost the truth."

"It's the euphemism from hell," Elliot said.

"Well," Drake continued. "The misses automatically assumed that the improprieties in question were Colonel Gray's late night excursions with his daughters. She couldn't wait to talk to us."

"Excuse me?"

"Apparently, the Colonel has been diddling both his daughters with impunity. The misses grew a spine a few years back and threatened to turn him in."

"Let me guess; that's when he kicked her ass."

"Bingo. After he beat her into submission she lost her nerve. She forgot about turning him in for shagging the girls. As for her injuries, the doctor didn't believe they were accidental; but she stubbornly stuck by her story of slipping in the kitchen and hitting her face on a counter."

"That's pretty transparent." Elliot said.

"Not really. The Colonel had been thinking ahead. He didn't use his hands on her. He smashed her face into the kitchen counter. That ensured her injuries corroborated her story."

"Nice guy."

"Did the job though. Turned her into a fucking Stepford wife."

"He kept her like a slave," Tony said, not bothering to conceal his contempt.

"She thought about killing herself," Drake said, "but she didn't want to leave the girls alone."

"Why didn't she just pack up and leave?" Elliot knew it was a lame question: they never left. It was just that this time he hoped Drake or Coleman might actually know the answer.

"Come on, man. You've heard this story a thousand times. One; she didn't have anyplace to go, and two; the Colonel said if she left him he'd just track her down and kill her. She believed him."

"What about the case?" Elliot asked, knowing the answer.

"That's the bad news," Tony said. "She keeps a journal. The day Josh Bennet went missing, the Colonel had been gearing up for a three-day diddle-a-thon with the girls. He's got an alibi, Elliot. It's weak, based solely on the wife's journal and recollections, but he's probably not our guy. But we've got to be close, man."

Drake could see the emotions playing across Elliot's

face, anger (probably at himself), confusion, and worry. Drake knew Elliot well enough to assume he was probably entertaining another bout of self-doubt. Before he could disappear too far within himself Drake grabbed him by the shoulders. "Don't even try to zone out on us, E.T. We have work to do."

"I was so certain," Elliot said.

"Whatever it was that made you key in on the Colonel was damn close to what we're looking for. Colonel Gray actually validates your profiling theory."

"How so? I was wrong."

"Only about the nature of Gray's crime. You pulled a theory out of your ass designed to proactively detect sick fucks in the Air Force. We profiled a bunch of people using that theory. It seems logical that, if your theory had any merit, more than one sick fuck would get caught up in the net. The fact that we reeled in Colonel Gray increases the odds of us being on the right track. Yes, our guy is still out there; but he's probably already in our net. This thing is working, man; and you probably saved a couple of little girls' lives. So, might I suggest you put the angst on hold for awhile and get back out in the streets."

"Nice pep talk."

"I should get overtime pay for baby-sitting your fragile fucking ego."

"I'm going to find Sally. Someone should let her know not to drop her guard just yet."

"Sally never drops her guard," Drake said.

Chapter Forty-One

At that very moment, half way across town, Sally was dropping her guard. Sally knew there were some agents who would have resented being shuffled off to do busy work while the A-Team went off to catch the bad guy. She wasn't one of those agents. If Colonel Gray was their guy, and based on Elliot's reactions, he probably was, they were going to have to show something in black and white to explain how they had come to suspect a respected Air Force officer of serial-murder. Elliot's sixth sense wasn't something that could be logically explained in a court of law. She and Jerry were cauterizing the loose ends, so that they could demonstrate they had given every potential suspect due consideration.

The behavioral analysis interview was a well-known investigative tool. The interviews afforded a way to demonstrate to the court that identifying Colonel Gray was the result of well-planned investigative methodology; and that they didn't just pull Gray's name out of a hat, or Elliot's psyche. The investigation was far from over, and while Elliot had promoted Colonel Gray to number one suspect, they still had to tie him to the crime with physical evidence.

In the interim, they had to make sure they gave the other potential suspects the same treatment as the Colonel. She knew they were probably just going through the motions, but they had to exhaust all possible leads. She was almost ninety percent convinced that Gray was their man. That certainty, on top of weeks of tension, caused her to relax her guard.

Jerry Fleming, on the other hand, hadn't relaxed his guard one bit. He was starting to feel like a real investigator, and he was certain this would be the high point of his career. This was why he had joined the OSI. He'd be able to tell his grandchildren about how he'd been part of the task force that caught the silo killer.

They were on their way to the third interview of the day: Chief Master Sergeant Gunther Demochet. He was the First Sergeant for the base civil engineering squadron. They had tried to reach him at his office, but he had called in sick. Now they were pulling up in front of the senior NCO quarters. Jerry thought it odd that a Chief Master Sergeant would chose to live in the small efficiency apartments, but figured he was probably divorced and married to his job - classic lonely guy syndrome. He considered himself blessed to have a solid, happy marriage. He indulged in a few feelings of superiority, and just a little bit of pity, towards Demochet.

Jerry allowed himself a brief fantasy that they were going to apprehend a dangerous felon. He reached under his arm to touch his automatic, which he'd taken to wearing in a shoulder holster like Turner and all the other agents who were far too sexy to wear the standard pancake holster at their sides.

Sally saw Jerry fingering his weapon and smiled inwardly. She thought it was cute, if not a little pathetic, the way he had been swaggering around since Elliot let him play in the reindeer games. Her weapon, usually on her hip for easy access, was tucked into her purse.

* * *

When Sally and Jerry knocked on his door, Chief Master Sergeant Gunther Demochet, AKA Lester Phillips, had been packing his worldly goods into one black duffel bag, and preparing to quietly exit the life he'd known for almost thirty years. The bag was new. He'd gone shopping for a set of luggage, but had come away with two black duffel bags. It was hard to shake all the years of military conditioning. Duffel bags were just so practical.

All he had were clothes and an old radio. He had no need for pictures or mementos. He had saved some trophies from some of his more arousing hunts, but they were at the warehouse. His one true diversion was so all encompassing that he seldom spent money on anything beside food and hygiene items.

Over the years, under assumed identities, he had made some lucrative real estate investments. Even as Gunther Demochet had excelled in his chosen military profession, his alter egos had become quite wealthy. Now Gunther Demochet was about to disappear. He would live out the rest of his life as one of his alias personas. He was actually looking forward to it. He had been feeling increasingly burdened by the structure and civility that was Demochet's life. He wasn't schizophrenic. He just instinctively realized that personality was an excellent disguise. No one who'd ever met him when he was playing at one of his carefully constructed alternate personalities would ever confuse him with the bland Chief Master Sergeant Demochet. Where Demochet was all military (back...straight, chest...out, ass... tight) his favorite alter-ego was friendly and clumsy, quick to laugh and charmingly self-depreciating. The only thing they had in common was that they both liked to make sweet love to pretty, adolescent, dead boys and young men.

Demochet had decided that he'd probably waited too long already. He was going to stop being Chief Demochet permanently after he retired from the Air Force. But now, with the possibility that the authorities might stumble across something that would link him to the suburban or one of his victims, he didn't have the luxury of retiring. Something told him he had to disappear now. Nothing fancy, he would just take all of his stuff from his quarters on base and move into the warehouse apartment until the silo killer fervor died down. Then he'd liquidate his assets and move to Thailand.

He finished packing and then, feeling uncharacteristically nostalgic, paused to take a final look around. The sparsely furnished room had been his home for five years. When he walked out the door, Gunther Demochet would be no more. He sighed and picked up his duffel bag. But before he could leave he heard footsteps on the walkway outside.

He stopped and listened. It was probably jut one of his neighbors coming home early from work. But he didn't want anyone to see him leave. He wanted his disappearance to be mysterious, here one day then gone without a trace. He waited calmly for the footsteps to pass, but they stopped outside his door.

* * *

Senior NCO quarters were in a drab, two story, dormitory building. In contrast to the junior enlisted dorms, there were no signs of life, no hibachi grills guarding the doors, or stereos vying for supremacy. The senior NCO dorms were lonely-guy central. Most of its occupants were divorced career NCOs, or that breed of military man who could never quite connect with anyone long enough to form a lasting relationship. The building was an enclave of broken souls in the anti-climax of their careers, going out with a fizzle not a bang. Some of them would find some level of contentment in their retirement, but many would die of boredom within ten years. Those remaining few would haunt the local VFW, reliving the glory years and waiting to die. Sally looked across at the Junior enlisted dormitory where some young, shirtless GIs, likely shift workers, were drinking beer and goofing off at noontime on a weekday, without a care in the world. She wondered if any of them realized the hollowness the future had in store for some of them.

Sally checked the number on the door in front of them, room 211, home to Chief Master Sergeant Gunther Demochet. She had his bio-sheet in her briefcase; two consecutive tours in Vietnam as a combat controller, two purple hearts, bronze star, and now this, the hotel of broken dreams. This is what happened to many of the heroes who survived: A lifetime of accomplishments fading into obscurity.

Sally had six years left before she could retire at twenty years, and lately she'd begun to wonder if her duties were as fulfilling as she'd expected when she joined.

Interviewing all the senior NCOs on their behavioral analysis list hadn't helped her mood. Most of them lived small unglamorous lives, and when they talked about retiring, she could hear the uncertainty in their voices and see the fear in their eyes. She didn't want to go out like that. She sighed and knocked on Demochet's door. Maybe this one was different.

* * *

It seemed like an eternity since the footsteps stopped outside his door, but less than a minute had passed.

Who could it be? No one ever visited him. He had no casual acquaintances or friends who just happened to drop by. The office wouldn't send anyone to check up on him. They'd call first.

His senses, driven into overdrive by paranoia, told him there were two people outside his door.

When the knock came it was like a gunshot.

Should he risk a look? No. Maybe they didn't know for sure that he was home. But what if it was a dormitory maintenance crew? He'd look silly standing around staring at the door, duffel bag at his feet.

Two? Why two? Cops always traveled in pairs. Could they know? It was possible.

He decided to wait quietly. Maybe whoever it was would simply get frustrated and go away.

Jerry helped Demochet through his indecision. He looked at Sally and winked. "Watch this." He pounded on Demochet's door. "We know you're in there. Come out now!"

"Idiot!" Sally spat. "What do you think you're doing? What if he's in there asleep or something? This guy's not a real suspect, and if he were, you would have just spooked the hell out of him. Our goal is to contact him, establish some kind of rapport, and get through the questionnaire."

"Sorry, I thought it would help."

"Don't be sorry! Just don't ever pull a stunt like that again."

Just then they heard the bolt release on the door. Jerry put his hand on his weapon. The door opened and Demochet stepped out.

He took in everything at a glance; Jerry with his hand under his jacket. Sally looking apologetic. Why? There was no one in the walkway or parking lot. There was smoke coming from a grill over at the junior enlisted dorms, but there was no one tending it.

Demochet looked pointedly at Jerry's hand. "That won't be necessary," He said and smiled amiably.

Sally sized up the Chief. Nothing about him said threat. He was shorter than Jerry and not much taller than her. He was slight of build and seemed relaxed and curious. He was dressed in casual khaki slacks, polo shirt, and brown leather jacket. Sally reached into her purse for her badge, trying to think of something consolatory to say. She moved her weapon aside and located her badge. She was wondering why this situation felt somehow strange, when Demochet hit Jerry in the throat.

Sally caught the movement out of the corner of her eye, but she was too late. Jerry dropped to his knees clutching at his crushed larynx and making a clicking sound as he tried in vain to draw a breath. Demochet was on her in an instant. The way he moved reminded her of Elliot, but where Elliot seemed to be driven by something like barely controlled fury, Demochet was completely detached. He almost seemed to be smiling. Her hand was clutching her badge inside her purse and it would be a full second before she dropped it and grabbed the gun. That second might as well have been a lifetime. Demochet kicked her in the ribs, breaking two, then grabbed her head with both of his hands and twisted. Sally twisted with him, her muscles remembering some snippet of her defensive tactics training, moving with rather than against the torque. The move probably saved her life, but she heard a popping sound in a place that shouldn't be popping. She dropped to the floor of the walkway next to Jerry, who was staring at her with blank eyes.

The scuffle took less than four seconds. Demochet remained hyper-aware of his surroundings during the brief altercation. The parking lot was still empty except for his car and another which he assumed belonged to the two agents. He'd been prepared to have to make a fast getaway, but everything was still quiet.

Sally couldn't move. She knew she was hurt, but she couldn't feel any pain. That was bad. She watched unblinking as The Chief dragged Jerry's body into his room. He came back out and dragged Sally inside, dumping her unceremoniously next to Jerry's body.

There was a black duffel bag at the edge of her vision. As she focused on the bag, just because it was something to focus on, a brown, leather-clad arm bent and removed the bag from her line of sight. She heard the door close and lock from the outside. Before she lost consciousness, she wondered if Elliot knew that he had the wrong guy.

Chapter Forty-Two

Elliot, Drake, and Coleman decided to go to the OSI offices where they could hear themselves think. They were in the elevator on their way down from the hustle and bustle of the FBI suites when Elliot was hit with a jolt of pain, like a hot knife piercing his throat.

"Ugh," he grunted and fell against the elevator wall. He would have slipped to the floor but Drake grabbed him under one arm, and Coleman managed to grab his jacket at the shoulders.

The pain was incapacitating. Elliot's essence literally leaped out of his body in an attempt to escape the pain. Leaving his physical body wasn't a new experience. It happened during times of intense duress and pain. It had happened the night of the Hatchet incident, and one morning after a particularly terrible nightmare he had awakened to find himself staring down at his still sleeping body.

He watched from above as Coleman and Drake eased his body to the floor of the elevator. Drake felt for his pulse and used his thumb and index finger to pry one of his eyes open. Coleman paused and looked up, eyes searching the ceiling.

Then, just as suddenly as he was jolted out, Elliot returned to his body and found himself staring Drake in the eye. He drew in a sharp breath and pushed Drake's hand away from his face.

"That was a little scary," Drake said. "You okay?"

"Yeah, what happened?"

"You had some kind of seizure."

"Has this ever happened before?" Coleman asked.

"Yes," Elliot said. He was in no mood to lie, but he didn't elaborate.

"You know, you should probably get that checked out," Drake said. He seemed sincerely worried. Elliot was the kind of person who would have to have a sucking chest would before he admitted something was wrong.

"Probably," Elliot said. "But not today. We've got to find Sally." Elliot could feel the worry coming off of Drake. All he could feel from Coleman was that sense of quiet.

As they walked out to the cars, Coleman noticed Elliot seemed stiff through the shoulders as if he was recovering from a neck injury. Coleman knew exactly what had happened to Elliot: he'd seen psychic seizures before. He only wondered what had triggered it.

* * *

Elliot had recovered from his seizure by the time they arrived at the OSI office. He'd driven like a maniac through town, and Drake and Coleman had been hard pressed to keep up with him. Elliot pulled into the office parking lot and sprinted into the building. Drake and Coleman were on his heels.

He burst into his office where Fred Shaw sat working in a cyber trance. "Where's Sally?" he asked without preamble, violating his own polite-greeting-before-business rule. Fred heard the urgency in his voice and decided not to point out Elliot's hypocritical lack of etiquette.

"She's at the senior NCO dorms dropping off a questionnaire with...let me see..," he typed something into the computer, "Senior Master Sergeant Gunther Demochet, First Sergeant for the Civil Engineering Squadron." He added, "Former combat controller, two tours in Nam, unmarried, stationed in the Philippines and Thailand, set to retire next year."

The color drained out of Elliot's face. He turned to Drake. "Tell me again where you got the blueprints for the silo."

"Oh shit," Drake said. "The Civil Engineering Squadron."

Elliot rushed out of the office, calling Sally on her radio as he ran. There was no answer. They all climbed into one car.

The senior NCO dormitory was only 10 minutes across base from the OSI office. Once they'd settled in for the short ride, Shaw asked the question that was on both his and Coleman's mind. "Why the sudden panic, and what's so special about this guy?"

Elliot didn't answer him, and for a moment Shaw didn't think he was going to. He seemed to be in what the team had taken to calling 'Elliot's quiet place'.

"It's so fucking clear," Elliot said. He didn't seem to be talking to anyone in particular. The other three men remained silent.

Elliot continued. He wasn't so much responding to Shaw's question as thinking aloud, organizing his thoughts. "The base civil engineer's office has surveyor's maps of the missile fields, and blueprints of all the silo complexes. Anyone with access to that office could become intimately familiar with that area from the privacy of their own home.

"That silo was so well hidden that, our two cowboys aside, you'd almost have to know where to start looking, or you would never find it. Our killer obviously picked that silo for a reason. It was well hidden and at least a mile from the nearest complex. He didn't stumble across it by chance. He was looking for it, or rather, something like it.

"Sally told me that she was going to talk to this guy Demochet, but she didn't say he worked in the civil engineering squadron. She only said that he'd been a combat controller during Nam. First Sergeant is management position. It didn't occur to me that an ex-combat controller would be working anywhere other than a combat communications squadron. I should have spent more time reading the bio-sheets. Senior NCO, three tours in Nam, lived in Thailand, access to silo blueprints, single white male, between 35 and 50...Shit!"

"Okay," Shaw said. "Now we know why he's suspect number one, but why the urgency?'

"Because," Elliot, paused. "It just feels real bad, man."

Coleman noticed Elliot was unconsciously rubbing his throat. He checked to make sure he had extra magazines for his weapons.

* * *

Jerry was dead. Any hopes that he might have survived his injuries were being washed away by the spreading puddle of fluid from beneath his body; dead guy fluids, soaking the leg of her pants suit. She couldn't feel the wetness, Jerry's last contribution to this world. For that she was thankful.

She heard her radio beeping at her from another dimension. She allowed herself a fleeting hope of rescue, but her main concern was trying to stay focused on her breathing, which was becoming a chore because of her broken ribs and the awkward angle at which she lay. She still couldn't feel any pain, and she couldn't move her arms or legs.

It was odd. When she thought of her husband she didn't feel a sense of loss. But the thought of her friends and partners, Elliot, and even Drake, finding her like Jerry, dead-eyed in a pool of piss, made her eyes fill with tears. Her regrets marched through her head, insisting she pay attention to them. She regretted marrying her husband: it had been a hasty mistake and she suddenly realized she didn't love him in the least little bit, and probably never had. She regretted the time she'd wasted with him, desparately trying to manufacture an artificial kind of domestic bliss. She regretted not snogging Elliot, something she had fantasized about at least half a dozen times. She especially regretted that she'd never see him again and engage in their usual pointless, amusing banter. More than anything else, though, she didn't want to die *this* way.

She was starting to lose consciousness when she heard running footsteps outside the door. She could feel the floor vibrating against her ear.

* * *

By the time they arrived at the NCO dorms, Elliot was crackling with anxiety. He was a battery charged to overload, and Coleman thought he could actually see his aura, a halo of barely contained, blue energy.

Elliot jumped out of the car and ran straight to Demochet's room. Drake and Shaw wouldn't have time to think about how he knew exactly where it was until days later.

Elliot didn't bother to knock, and had anyone tried to question him on the legalities of what he was doing, busting into someone's apartment based on a gut feeling he never would have been able to articulate as probable cause, the lecture would have fallen on deaf ears.

Barely breaking stride, Elliot spun and lashed out at the door with a kick that carried the momentum of his run down the walkway. The doorframe split like balsa wood, and Elliot rushed inside. The others figuring, if Elliot was wrong, the damage had already been done, so they drew their weapons and rushed inside behind him.

Elliot wasn't wrong. He wished he were. Sally and Jerry lay sprawled on the floor like some giant child's discarded rag dolls. Jerry was staring up at them, eyes wide and vacant. Drake rushed over to feel for a pulse but they'd all seen death enough times to know that Jerry was beyond help.

Time slowed for Elliot, and he hoped he was having a nightmare. He hoped he would wake up in a sweat, go into the office, and have a good laugh with Sally over his silly dream.

He reached out with his mind and was instantly hit with a wave of sadness, panic, and relief from Sally; although she remained immobile. From Jerry he felt nothing. There was no more Jerry. Jerry was a paperweight. Jerry had left the building. He knelt beside Sally. Her breath was ragged and her neck was cocked at a disturbing angle, but her heartbeat was strong. He leaned over and whispered in her ear, "Zigged when you should have zagged, huh? Well, partner you don't get off that easy. The doctor says you're gonna live."

Sally heard his voice but couldn't concentrate on his words. She knew he was probably making some silly remark, trying to comfort her. She could feel his tears on her forehead and knew what he was trying to say. She found her voice and whispered back, "I think we found your guy, Turner." Then her world went black.

Elliot rode to the hospital with Sally in the ambulance.

Shaw went back to the office, and Drake and Coleman stayed behind in Demochet's room with Jerry's body. They were going to supervise processing the room for forensic evidence. They weren't going to find anything. Elliot had sensed that the room was sterile from the moment he rushed in. Sally and Jerry had been the only signs of life, or at least Sally had been.

He watched Sally sleeping. She'd been sedated. She wore a neck brace and her body was strapped to a wooden gurney to keep it from shifting around during the trip. He'd given up on the notion that he was having a nightmare, and he was contemplating giving in to the depression that had been hovering about since the revelation that Col. Gray was the wrong guy.

In the time he'd known her, Sally had become his best friend and confidant. The occasional innocent flirtation aside, just having her near kept him centered. He actually looked forward to getting up in the morning and going to work when Sally was around.

He didn't have to be a doctor to see that Sally was hurt bad. He believed the clinical term was *fucked up*, as in; *There's your problem miss - you've been fucked up real bad.* The paramedic thought she might have a broken neck, but they couldn't tell until the swelling in her neck subsided. At this point, her extremities didn't respond to stimulus. Unbidden, Elliot thought of that stupid joke: *What do you do with a quadriplegic? Hang him on the wall and call him Art.* Elliot felt sick to his stomach.

Chapter Forty-Three

Now there was no turning back. He knew this day would come, had known since he lost count of the bodies. How many had he killed?

Who cared?

Of course, he had planned on fading quietly out of the military and going on to Thailand to live a life of perversity in some enclave of ex-patriot anonymity. Some of the coastal cities were rife with small communities of German and American ex-patriots who fancied little boys, and no one noticed-or cared to notice-how many young boys wandered into their neighbor's apartment, or whether they wandered out again.

He never thought his departure would be so...interesting. Kudos to the OSI, he'd made one - or two - mistakes, and they'd run him to ground. Now they had a name to go with his leavings. He imagined the name Gunther Demochet would find a place on the wall of the hall of atrocities along with the other more prolific paraphiles and serial killers.

And a little child shall lead them. He'd just had to have a piece of that little suburban brat, and look at all the trouble that caused. The little shit almost got him caught. Almost. But he *had* been tasty.

Oh well. If every thing went according to plan, he would be in Thailand by this time next week. He already had airplane reservations in first class. The reservations were round trip. A one-way ticket gave the wrong signature, it made it look like he was running. There were probably a couple of hundred of America's finest looking to make a name for themselves by catching him. They were undoubtedly watching the airports, looking for people leaving the country who met a certain profile. They would not be expecting a killer on the run to leave the country and then come back.

He was taking the scenic route. His tickets took him to Germany via Philadelphia and then back, just another yokel on vacation. Of course he wasn't coming back. He planned on flying to Thailand from Germany.

Today was Tuesday. On Thursday he was going to drive to Oklahoma City. But tonight he had work to do.

He needed to sanitize the warehouse apartment. He'd already abandoned his one car registered to his true name. Bringing it to the warehouse would have meant leaving a connection between his other alias and Gunther Demochet, should anyone search through the remains of the warehouse after he left. It was unlikely that anyone would ever think to make the connection between the warehouse and Gunther Demochet. But he'd already made enough mistakes. It was time to start paying attention to detail. He planned on driving the other sedan, the one he used to snatch that delicious Alonso Proctor, to Oklahoma City. He'd find some place in the city to abandon it before he left the country.

In the meantime he needed to ensure there would be a terrible fire in the Denver warehouse district within the next week or so.

Chapter Forty-Four

Now that they had a real suspect, the task force was focused – a veritable hive of activity and it was an impressive beast to behold. Elliot's small team had been merged into the new task force collective, and Elliot had been relegated to the position of outsider. Profilers were working overtime trying to predict Demochet's next move, while George Devine was working at blaming Elliot for Jerry Fleming's death and Sally's injuries. Elliot, who blamed himself anyway, didn't care.

Sally's spousal unit spent about two, fidgety, impatient hours a day at the hospital. Elliot had a handle on his visiting schedule and was usually around when he wasn't, sitting by Sally's bedside, basking in his guilt and depression.

Sally was paralyzed, but her spinal cord was intact. They planned on operating on her to relieve some of the pressure. Her doctor thought she had better than a 60 percent chance of full recovery. Elliot didn't know what that meant. He surmised that it meant, should she not recover, the doctors would be able to say, *"Hey, we only said 60 percent."*

When Elliot wasn't at the hospital he was glued to Fred

Shaw's ass, who hadn't been assimilated into the task force uni-mind. The FBI had their own computer geeks and all they wanted from Shaw was his files. Elliot was glad about that, since he needed Shaw to help him with his own efforts. He thought the task force was off track. Elliot had a nagging feeling they needed to focus their efforts on the near East, convinced their killer had a connection to that part of the world and would try to return to it. He and Shaw spent their days examining flight manifests and contacting other OSI offices in an effort to find their suspect.

Shaw still worked just as tirelessly as in the beginning but not because of pressure from Elliot. He was an investigator first and a computer geek second. The case was now a part of his life, and like any good investigator, he couldn't let it go. The computer shaman was determined to see the case to closure.

Elliot was typing furiously at his computer while Shaw studied the day's flight manifests out of Colorado. Shaw glanced over at Elliot.

"Whatcha working on over there?"

Elliot replied, still typing, "I'm sending a support request to the OSI detachment on Guam. They support just about all of the OSI's activities along the Pacific Rim."

"I know. I've helped them out on stuff in the past. Why Guam?"

"They have law enforcement liaison contacts throughout Asia. Most of their time is spent traveling around countries in their area of responsibility just keeping in touch with their foreign counterparts. I'd been planning on contacting them once I found out about the Asian mysticism connection to the ritualistic mutilation of the little boy's corpse. After I keyed in on Colonel Gray as a possible suspect, though, I thought it could wait. I'm contacting them now to ask if they would put the word out among their police contacts that we are looking for any unusual deaths in the past thirty years or so."

"Don't you think that's a little broad?" Shaw interrupted.

"For that part of the world, yes," Elliot acknowledged, "Many places, like Bangkok and Pattya Beach, are the last bastions of hedonism in the free world. There you find crime, corruption, bizarre sex for sale, drugs…you name it. Unusual deaths are probably the rule, not the exception. So, I'm defining unusual for them using Demochet's signature perversions; suffocation by burking, broken necks, patterned wounds, and that whole phallic cannibalism thing."

Just then, Tony Coleman walked in. In spite of all the activity at the FBI offices, Coleman found time to check on Elliot and keep Shaw up to date. Shaw thought that was a pretty stand-up thing to do. He eyed the back of Elliot's headed and asked, "How are things going?"

Elliot stopped typing and turned to face him, "You tell me. We're the ones left out in the cold."

Coleman nodded, tacitly agreeing with Elliot's assessment of the situation, "Nothing. We've hit dead ends. Demochet disappeared. He could be anywhere in the country by now and we have no leads."

"That's a revolting situation."

"It certainly is." Coleman turned to leave, but paused, "If you come up with anything, let me know, okay."

"Sure. And you'll do the same for me, right?"

Coleman smiled and walked out. They both knew he probably wouldn't.

At the end of the day, Elliot went home, drank too much, and wallowed in depression. Blair was spending more and more time at Elliot's apartment during the evening trying to fix his fugue by plying him with herbal teas, sex, and tantric massage; but nothing seemed to work for long.

She was wise enough to realize that Elliot's problem wasn't holistic; it was emotional. The significance of his attachment to his partner wasn't lost on her. Elliot was a gregarious person who liked being around people, but she knew he didn't form emotional attachments easily. She didn't even think he had any real feelings for her. Sally, on the other hand, was a different matter altogether.

Chapter Forty-Five

It had been two days since Demochet's coming out party, and his life, his outstanding military career, and his family, was the top story on every news channel and on everyone's lips. He was on America's Most Wanted. Shit, he *was* America's Most Wanted. He was a celebrity; *Debuting at number one. "29 BODIES IN A MISSLE SHAFT...It's got a good beat, but can you dance to it?*

The media actually seemed to enjoy the fact that he'd disappeared without a trace. Demochet had become the D.B. Cooper of serial killers, and pretty soon he'd be completely home free.

While Elliot sunk deeper into depression, Demochet was sitting calmly in Oklahoma City's International Airport watching a breaking news story.

The channel 6-news chick, Melanie Rivers, having chosen a trendy action-girl ensemble for the evening, was in the warehouse district. A fire raged behind her. Her brow was moist, and her trendy bangs were plastered to her forehead. She spoke as if she were out of breath, presumably from assisting in the battle against the conflagration. She was so unashamedly convincing in her non-verbal faux message that Demochet could almost picture her, khaki vest, comfortable shoes, and Gucci watch, charging hoses and barking orders to the firefighters. God, she was good. Melanie Rivers, media parasite extraordinaire, he was going to miss her.

"Authorities have no idea what could have caused the fire," Melanie was saying, slightly out of breath.

"Just doing my job," Gunther mumbled, casually checking his watch and his tickets for the fourth time.

"It could be hours before the fire is contained. Damages could run into the millions, but the real loss can be seen in the faces of the hundreds of nearby residents, forced to evacuate their neighborhood, not knowing if they'll have homes when the smoke clears." She stopped to wipe what could be soot or tears out of her eyes. *"I'm Melanie Rivers, now here's Ted Roberts with sports."*

Demochet was already settled comfortably into the airport lounge when the fire took hold and raced through the warehouse. He'd used cigarettes to start it. A smoldering cigarette was still one of the world's best, slow incendiary fuses.

He'd placed several cigarettes in trashcans filled with newspapers and other flammable refuse. He put the trashcans near curtains in three warehouse offices near his apartment and let nature take its course. He hadn't set any of the fires in his warehouse apartment…but he had it on good authority that the owner of the apartment wasn't very fire conscious, and his place was a veritable tinder box of flammable wood furniture, tasteful window dressings, linen and paper products. Any stray spark from oh, say, a nearby office building and the place would light up like a match.

Melanie Rivers, eyes full of sympathetic crocodile tears, had returned and was pontificating on the plight of the warehouse district residents when his flight was called.

"...and that's the news," Demochet said. "Good night and god bless."

He was chuckling an infectious little chortle when he walked through the gate. The gate attendant – an attractive young man, but too old for him – thought he seemed to be an odd, but friendly little guy. With the red hair and beard, Demochet reminded him of a leprechaun.

Chapter Forty-Six

One week after Demochet left the country Elliot dragged himself into the office at about eight-thirty. Per the norm, he'd been out drinking the night before. He was drinking alone these days because he'd gone from being a happy-happy drunk to a morose drunk. Blair had grown tired of trying to drag him out of his funk and wasn't returning his calls.

During the night he'd dreamed about Thailand and had seen the hotel where Chief Master Sergeant Gunther Demochet was resting his evil head; but upon waking, he couldn't remember the dream. He was simply left with the feeling that he had seen – and then forgot – something important. The frustration added to his funk.

He sought out Shaw. Shaw had graduated from colleague to friend, but being a friend to Elliot meant knowing how to ignore him when he was in a shitty mood. Unlike their rocky beginning, now when Elliot ranted at him, he took it as a sign of trust.

When Elliot walked into the office, looking like he was ready to pick a fight, Shaw met him halfway. He had information guaranteed to take the wind out of Elliot's sails.

"What's the good news?" Elliot asked, intrigued by the sense of elation coming off of Shaw in big, soothing waves.

"Where do you want me to start?" Shaw asked casually.

"What?"

"I've got good news coming out of my ass." Shaw said.

Elliot just stared. He'd decided to remain quiet and give Shaw the chance to disappoint him.

"First;" the shaman continued, "The task force has come up with at least two unsolved homicides, involving adolescent boys, that match Demochet's M.O."

"Where?"

"Alexandria, Louisiana. He was stationed at England Air Force Base between 1983 and 1986. The two boys went missing about four months apart. Their mutilated remains were found in an abandoned well in 1988. They were identified by their dental records. The FBI's Violent Criminal Apprehension was still relatively new and the information was never entered into the VICAP database."

"So we know he's killed before at other bases. That was almost a foregone conclusion. I hope that's not all of your good news?"

"Nope. My good news is a touch more juicy, and the task force doesn't know about it." He said with a conspiratorial gleam in his eyes. Shaw went back to his desk, sat down with his hands behind his head and stared at Elliot with an I've-got-a-secret smile playing across his face.

"Don't keep me in suspense, man!"

"You have to guess."

"What?"

"Guess."

"I really don't have time for this. How about if I beat it out of you instead?"

"If you have enough time to beat me up, you have enough time to guess."

Elliot made a threatening step towards the shaman. He frustrations meter was set at low tolerance. Shaw only smiled wider. He'd come to realize Elliot was mostly harmless and actually a gentle spirit, especially with those who he trusted; and it was nice to be able to toy with Elliot's emotions for a change, give him a touch of his own annoying medicine.

Elliot could feel something that he could only describe as triumph rolling off of the shaman.

"Come on, Fred, tell me."

"No."

Elliot knew what he wanted but was loath to offer it up. Shaw just sat there looking at him, smiling. Finally Elliot said, "Please."

"Whoa," Shaw said, openly enjoying Elliot's humility. "That must have taken a lot of work."

"You have no idea."

"Well, you said the magic word; so I guess you deserve this; I think we've found Demochet." He paused to let the information sink in.

"Jesus, man, and you're playing games?"

"Don't get your panties all bunched up. We can't do anything about it right now. Plus, we've got to let the task force and Devine know."

"I guess so." If they had indeed found Demochet, there was no way that the commander was going to let Elliot have a piece of the end game.

"However," Shaw continued. "I took the liberty of booking you on the first flight out to Guam and then to Bangkok. You have a rental car reserved in Bangkok, and you can drive to Utapao from there."

"So, he's in Utapao?"

"Kind of, but I'll get to that. I cleared your trip through Devine."

"Now I really am impressed. How'd you do that?"

"I convinced him that there were some dead-end leads to be wrapped up on Guam. The task force thinks Demochet is still in the States. It wasn't hard to convince Devine that it would be a good idea to have you out of his hair for awhile. After you've left, I'll break the good news to Devine and the task force. You'll have a short head start on them."

"Why are you doing this, Fred?"

"Because you're not the danger to humanity that I thought you were. Plus, I don't want Devine to have the opportunity to fuck up this lead. If you're out there, I know we'll have a better shot of getting this guy."

"I don't know what to say," Elliot was genuinely touched by the shaman's display of loyalty.

"You don't have to say anything. Just don't get me in trouble. I didn't do this so you could go to Thailand and be the lone cowboy. I'm a computer guy. I like symmetry. You were there in the beginning. You should be there in the end. If you're already in country, there is a better chance that Devine will let you stick around as part of the team. Notice the emphasis on the word team. Promise me you'll play nice over there."

"I promise, Dad."

"Whatever. Here's what we've got: The OSI detachment on Guam came back with an interesting hit that is most likely Demochet. They uncovered similar cases in Thailand, but the key was of course the bites and the chakra signature. I'll be honest," Shaw admitted, "I didn't expect anything to come of your theory."

"How come everybody always tells me that?"

Shaw looked at Elliot, unshaven, jeans, T-shirt; eyes just

barely on the right side of sanity. "You got me, man; you're the epitome of stability."

"Fuck you."

"Down boy. Anyway, to make a long story short; they put the word out and got a couple of hits. The chief of the tourist police in Pattaya Beach was able to recall two instances of ritual markings like our victims almost 25 years ago. One case was a complete mystery. The other was almost as useless except for one witness who claimed the victim, a local Muay Thai boxer, was last seen with a small white guy. The two cases were clearly connected, but between all the American G.I's and the German ex-patriots in country at the time, the description could have fit anybody."

"Was Demochet in Thailand at the time?"

"Yes." Shaw turned and squinted at the report on his computer screen. "He was stationed at Utapao Air Base."

"Then we've only confirmed what we suspected."

"There's more. The police chief in Pattaya," Shaw tapped something into the computer. "Colonel…Sombat – I think that's how you pronounce it - asked his OSI friends to return the favor. He had a daughter who was killed and raped, probably in that order, around the same time. Her body was found in a trash heap behind a local hotel. He had one clue; an American GI had checked into the hotel the night before. He paid in advance and left during the night. According to Sombat, it was strange that an American GI would use that particular hotel, even stranger that he seemed to be alone. The hotel was well out of the bar district, and they'd never had an American check in before. The GI listed his name as Reginald Hansen. The chief knew the name was probably false, but he ask the OSI to run it through the personnel databases at least three times in the past twenty years."

"Anything?"

"Not worth mentioning. But just for grins, I ran the

name through the Dept. of Motor Vehicles. I got a car and an address. The car was a late model Ford sedan. So what, right? However, there was a Denver address. I called Margaret Madison, and she had a car drive by the address. There was nothing there; at least not anymore. The address was an old warehouse apartment. It was burned up in that warehouse district fire about a week ago."

"Not long after Demochet disappeared, that's an interesting coincidence; but you don't think..."

"Thai Airways shows a Reginald Hansen manifested into Bangkok from Germany three days after the fire. Trans-Globe show a Reginald Hansen manifested out of Oklahoma City to Frankfurt the morning of the fire."

Elliot looked at the computer, glowing in front of Shaw's face. His heart was racing a little. For the first time in weeks, he smiled.

"Thanks, Fred."

"Don't mention it. You've got a plane to catch."

* * *

Elliot went home to pack. He called Blair at her shop. She answered on the first ring.

"Hello?"

"Waiting patiently by the phone for me?"

"I'm sorry, who is this?"

"Look, I've been acting like a real shit lately." "Yes, you have."

"Well, I'm sorry."

"That's it?"

"Uh, yeah. I'm getting ready to go out of town, and I wanted to apologize before I went."

"Is this about the case?"

"Yeah."

"So, this thing is probably about over, huh?"

Elliot couldn't tell if she meant the case or their budding relationship. "Yeah, probably," he said. "Take care of yourself."

Blair hung up before he could say anything else. He'd felt a clear flash of anger from the other end. He thought about calling her back but decided against it. Maybe he'd call her when he returned.

Chapter Forty Seven

Every year, the United States Air Force participated in war game exercises with the Thai Air Force. The OSI normally supported those operations by putting agents on the ground ahead of time to establish some kind of rapport with the local constabulary and determine if there was any threat to the troops by scouting out lodging and social venues likely to be frequented by the off duty military personnel. If the proprietors were openly hostile to Americans, or not so openly hostile where Elliot was concerned, or if there were sensitive cultural issues that would prohibit U.S. personnel from going to those establishments or neighborhoods, they would consider putting the location off limits. Basically, the OSI agents wandered into these places, and if no one shot, stabbed, or poisoned them, they gave it their seal of approval. Elliot likened that particular Force Protection duty to miners using canaries to determine if they'd tapped into any underground pockets of methane gas, but he was an excellent canary.

He hadn't been back to Thailand since before Idaho. It hadn't changed. It was as hot and humid as he remembered.

All the days were hot and humid, what the Japanese called *mushi atsui* (bug hot). Of all the sights, sounds, and smells in Thailand one of his most vivid memories was the ever-present feeling of his shorts sticking to the crack of his ass. The locals didn't seem to mind. He'd read somewhere that the Eskimos had a hundred different names for snow; wet snow, powder snow, hard packed slippery snow, snow that blows up your nose, and so on. He wondered if the Thais had a hundred different names for hot; wet hot, dry hot (seldom used), gonna rain hot, shorts-sticking-to-the-crack-of-your-ass hot.

Then there was the omnipresent shade of the color green, resplendently represented in the flora and the fauna. Everything was green; light green, dark green, almost black green. Even the wild life, one of which was crawling across his wall, were mostly green. He swore some of the Thais themselves had an olive green caste their skin.

The country was undeniably beautiful, especially the women. The spectrum ranged from girl-next-door cute too take-your-breath-away. All of them seemed friendly and eager to please - some more eager than others for the right price.

The problem with Thailand was that HIV was running amuck. Like every other country on the globe, AIDS was fucking things up for everybody. As a man whose balls were at times his only true friends, Elliot felt like a kid in a candy store full of tainted candy. It was Halloween, and he didn't know which apple had the razor blade.

Per Shaw's arrangements, he'd flown to Guam and contacted the OSI agent responsible for maintaining liaison with the Thai Police, Special Agent Robert Pearson. Pearson was short, balding, gone to paunch, and very energetic. Elliot liked him on sight. He was a social chameleon, full of movement even when he was sitting still. He'd mastered a quality found in the most successful politicians, liaison agents, and nightclub strippers; the ability to establish and maintain simultaneous rapport with every person in a large group, and make that person feel like he/she was the only and most interesting person in the world. He spoke no single language fluently, but he was a master of international pigeon and could pull the same stunt working a room full of different languages and cultures.

Pearson had been in Guam for over seven years. He was the agent who responded to Elliot's lead request, and who passed along the name Reginald Hansen. He had a well-established liaison relationship with the Utapao tourist police chief, Colonel Sombat; and he had been eager to accompany Elliot to Thailand.

Elliot and Pearson had been in Thailand for two days when Devine and others members of the task force arrived to participate in finding and extraditing Demochet. Devine had left a curt message for him at the front desk of the hotel, instructing him and Pearson to meet with the task force representatives in the lobby at 0800 hours. Elliot didn't get the message until about 2 o'clock in the morning. He'd been out with Pearson watching some shows that weren't on the family tour stop.

Now it was seven-thirty, and with just under five hours sleep he was trying to get himself in a George Devine frame of mind.

He left his room and headed towards the elevator. Three of the hotel housecleaning staff, Thai beauties from the take-your-breath-away end of the spectrum, were clustered around the housekeeping desk.

They had captured two large rice bugs and were eating them. Elliot had been told once that rice bugs were a delicacy in Thailand. He marveled at how humanity was a master of self-deception: claiming something was a "delicacy" just because millions of poor people didn't have access to anything better. Elliot was quite certain if someone had offered the Thai people's ancestors unlimited access to cheeseburgers they would have become some cheeseburger-eating-motherfuckers and never touched a rice bug again.

Okay, they're eating a bug. Maybe I'm okay with that. One of the three, darker skinned with full lips, possibly of Cambodian descent, looked up from her snack as Elliot walked by.

"*Sa wat de kaa* (hello)," she said, face like an angel, with just a hint of bug juice at the corners of her mouth.

"Sa wat de kap," Elliot returned the greeting, adding the male "ap," and making a successful attempt at not looking revolted. He didn't like bugs or anything that crawled for that matter.

As he strolled by he noticed one of the insects was still alive. Another beauty was peeling the good parts delicately out of its carapace. It was a mean looking creature. Its head was like that of a praying mantis. Its body was large and brown, rough like tree bark with jagged edges. It turned its head towards Elliot, as if it were begging him to end its suffering.

With a small sound of triumph, the beauty conducting the operation extracted a dark green piece of bug stuff and handed it to the third. She eagerly accepted the offering, noticed Elliot watching her, and then – looking every bit the socialite who'd forgot her manners – held the delicacy out to Elliot. She put the morsel near her lips, pantomimed chewing, and rubbed her belly. It was the universal symbol for "*Hello noble savage. Because you are too ignorant to know good food when you see it, I offer you this hunk of bug guts in friendship.*"

Elliot smiled politely and declined. *A jug of wine, a big brown bug and thee;* It just didn't work for him.

She shrugged – the universal gesture for *"your loss,"* and stuck the green mass in her mouth, lips glistening sensually with saliva and bug juice.

Elliot noticed the bug had finally died. He smiled at them again and walked nonchalantly towards the elevator. He could feel the women watching his back with something akin to innocent curiosity.

It was almost eight o'clock on the nose when he stepped into the lobby. The others were already there. Elliot was pleased to see Steve Drake and Tony Coleman had come. The commander, George Devine was talking to Pearson and a blonde gentleman in an expensive lightweight summer suit. Elliot didn't know the blonde guy but recognized him from the FBI offices in Denver.

Elliot nodded to Pearson, ignored Devine and Blondie, and walked over to Drake and Coleman.

"So, this is the new A-team, huh?" Elliot asked, shaking Coleman's hand and clapping Drake on the shoulder.

"Looks that way," Drake said, "but I don't think Devine planned on having you here. He's not happy."

"Yeah, well it sucks to be him. How's Sally?"

"Feeling sharp pains in her feet and happier than a pig in shit about it."

"Excellent!"

"Her husband's with her some of the time. I think they're bonding."

"That's because he likes to see her helpless."

"Don't be a cynic. Be happy for her."

"I am," Elliot said, feeling as jealous as he was happy. He wanted to be the one bonding with his partner. "Who's the guy with Devine and Pearson?"

"FBI," Tony said. "The Asian on the phone at the concierge desk is David Wattane. He's FBI also. He's our translator. His mom is Thai. He's a good guy. The blonde guy is Thomas Dean. I should tell you right now he's got marked prick-like tendencies. He could be Devine's blood brother."

"Nuff said."

As if on cue, Devine detached himself from Pearson and Dean. Elliot figured he wanted to come over and lay down the law. He wasn't mistaken.

"Listen up, Turner," he said, which was as good a greeting as any coming from the commander. "I don't want you here, and my first impulse is to put you on the next plane back to the states..." Elliot was thinking *you and what army,* "However, these two," he gave a disgusted nod to Coleman and Drake, "seem to think you bring something to the game. I disagree. So, you need to know right up front that if you so much as..." He trailed off as Wattane began frantically waving him over to the concierge desk. For a moment Devine looked confused. He looked at Elliot than back to Wattane and then back to Elliot. Finally, having lost his train of thought, he gave a snort of frustration and hurried over to the concierge desk. The others watched in silence.

"Diatribe interruptus," Elliot said. "He hates that."

Drake laughed, "Apparently as much as he hates you."

"It really is good to see you, man. How are Margaret and Jason?"

"Pretty good actually. I don't know how you did it, but Margaret seems to have really warmed to you. She was a little put out that you didn't call and say goodbye. Outside of that, things couldn't be better for them. They were able to close out the Alonso Proctor case, and they're working with missing persons to see if they can identify some of the other victims. They're pretty gainfully employed."

Pearson was still talking to Devine's blond blood brother, bound by the spirit of ambition and over-inflated self worth. Pearson was undoubtedly using his particular gift to feed the FBI agent's ego. He also seemed to be simultaneously talking to everyone in Elliot's small group using facial expressions and eye movements. Elliot once again marveled at Pearson's skills.

As he watched, Pearson gave a genuine laugh at something Dean said, gave him a friendly pat on the back and a strange little handshake. Elliot figured it was probably Dean's secret fraternity handshake. Pearson probably knew a thousand class songs and secret handshakes.

Pearson walked over to where Devine and the translator, Wattane, were talking on the phone. Elliot figured they were talking to one of the local investigators. If that were the case, it was probably one of Pearson's contacts; and Pearson was savvy enough to realize Devine was the kind of pompous ass who could ruin years worth of skillful liaison even working through a translator.

Pearson listened to Devine's conversation for a few minutes. Elliot could see Devine becoming increasingly more frustrated about something, and he could feel the unease coming off of Pearson. Pearson didn't let it show. When it looked like Devine might go into dickhead overload, Pearson stepped in, said something conciliatory to Devine, and took over the conversation. Devine stood imperiously by as if it had been his idea to relinquish control to Pearson.

Pearson finished the phone call and he and Devine rejoined the group. Elliot sensed anger from Devine, and a kind of focused determination from Pearson. There was clearly a problem. Devine was handling it in normal weinee fashion by getting angry, and Pearson was working on a solution.

"What's going on?" Coleman asked Pearson.

"Colonel Sombat's waffling."

"What do you mean, 'waffling'", Coleman asked.

"He thinks he knows where Demochet is, but he doesn't want to tell us just yet. There are capital punishment issues."

"Oh, he'll tell," Devine said, "or we'll bring him up on charges."

"Say, chief," Elliot said, not willing to pass up a chance to exploit Devine's ignorance. "It occurs to me that this is Thailand, his country. Exactly what should we charge him with?"

"You're out of line, Turner," Devine spat and stormed off.

Elliot looked at the group. "Am I the only one who finds that unsettling?"

"What does all this mean to us?" Dean asked, ignoring Elliot.

"It means Colonel Sombat is being pressured by someone to stall us," Pearson said, "probably the government. Sombat's not political. He's a good cop. I think before we throw in the towel," he glanced over at Devine, smoking angrily in a corner of the lobby, "we need to pay Colonel Sombat a visit. Sometimes it's hard to waffle face to face."

"Good idea," Dean said, assuming he was in charge of the situation, "let's leave as soon as possible."

"Actually," Pearson said. "I was thinking you and Devine, being in charge of this expedition, could continue working the extradition issue with the embassy."

"You're right," Dean said. "You get on Sombat. I'll contact the embassy." He walked off to find a telephone.

"That was pure art," Coleman said, watching Dean walk purposely away.

Pearson winked, "Old Jedi mind trick."

Chapter Forty Eight

Colonel Sombat was tall for a Thai, taller than both Elliot, Pearson, and David Wattane, who they'd brought along to translate *'just in case'*. They actually didn't need Wattane. Pearson had known Colonel Sombat for years and he'd let Elliot in on a little secret; Sombat spoke perfect English. He'd just been playing dumb on the telephone for Devine. Bureaucratic idiots were the same everywhere, and after one phone call, Sombat had instantly recognized Devine for what he was. Their primary reason for bringing Wattane along was to ensure Devine and Dean, the wonder twins, wouldn't be able to interface with any Thai authorities outside of the U.S. Embassy until they returned. Without an interpreter, the wonder twins would be incapable of alienating anyone but the embassy staff. Coleman wanted to come along, but Drake convinced him that they needed to spend the day in downtown Pattya doing "research", and checking out the ex-patriot demographic.

Sombat had tired, intelligent eyes set in a kind face. He had a quiet confident way about him, but the bags under his eyes spoke volumes about his current state of mind. He was worried. He was chief of police, responsible for a city that kept itself alive with the international sex trade. He'd seen the human animal at its worst. He could have told Elliot a thing or two about paraphiles whose tastes ran towards the wet and dead. Gunther Demochet/Reg Hanson was not mystery to him. He was a monster and a coward who prayed on little boys and little girls. Of course Pattaya had plenty of little girls and boys and girl-boys, a monster's delight.

He sized up his visitors. Pearson he knew and liked. Pearson respected his country. He always had a sense that he saw beyond the prostitutes and sex clubs and appreciated Thailand for its rich Siamese history and culture. They'd shared many a drink and adventure together, and he considered Pearson more friend than professional contact. But he was still an American, sworn to uphold and protect justice under the American constitution. Pearson was a friend, but he answered to a higher authority than friendship, and therefore, Sombat couldn't completely trust him.

Then there was the half-breed, Wattane. Bangkok and Pattaya were filled with the bastard children of nameless American soldiers and western ex-patriots. Sombat was pure Thai, but being taller than many westerners, he'd always felt a kind of kinship with the half-breeds. Life had found favor with this one, handsome and tall, he had the best of both worlds. Even though he was an American FBI agent, who were notorious for their arrogance, he seemed content to stand patiently by until needed, while Pearson and the black man did all the talking. The patience probably came from his Asian mother.

Lastly, there was the black man. What did they call him, *eetee*? Strange name by all accounts, but not so strange as the man himself.

When Pearson introduced him, he'd given him a warm handshake (held it just a little too long) and smiled at him as if they were old friends. While Sombat ordered tea and exchanged pleasantries with Pearson, *eetee* had wandered around Sombat's office, uninvited, peering closely at the knick knacks and wall hangings. Occasionally, he'd stop at some trinket, plaque, or award, and touch it softly with a knowing smile, as if it had some meaning for him. Eetee reminded him of a man who lived in his boyhood village, who claimed to be a sorcerer. He was actually a monk who'd fallen out of favor with the local temple. He'd always seemed to be smiling at some private joke, but his eyes were sad, clouded with the ghosts of images best left unseen. *Eetee* had those eyes.

Elliot watched Sombat watching him. His psychic friend, always stronger in the east, told him Sombat was a kind man. But beyond the kindness he read weariness, determination, and distrust.

Sombat's assistant, Miss Cheng, arrived with their tea. Cheng was a beautiful young woman, but she took pains-unsuccessful-to hide it. She wore a loose fitting, unflattering, brown, police uniform, really little more than a smock, and her hair was tied in a tight bun, giving her beauty a cruel edge. Elliot watched her disappear through a door at the rear of the office. Sombat invited them to take a seat on the couch. Sombat watched Elliot's gaze follow Cheng out of the room.

"You think my assistant is attractive?" Sombat asked Elliot. His accent gave his English a lyrical quality.

"I think she shouldn't be afraid to be pretty."

"She thinks maybe being...pretty… isn't a good thing for a policewoman."

"She's wrong."

"Maybe, but we all have to live our own lives, make our own choices, for better or for worst." Elliot caught the distinct impression that Sombat wasn't talking about Cheng.

Who? And then it hit him: his dead daughter. The influence of her death wrapped itself around Sombat like a suffocating blanket. Elliot wondered how Sombat could breathe through such a thick cloud of pain and regret. Elliot realized Sombat was hiding something, and that this moment was critical in their efforts to capture Demochet. Elliot relaxed, and with a few slow, deep breathes, cleared everything from his mind. He made himself an empty receptacle and prepared to receive whatever snippet of information Sombat let slip.

"In any event, how can I help you?" Sombat smiled politely and folded his hands on his desk.

Elliot decided on going with the direct approach. "We would like you to help us apprehend and extradite Gunther Demochet, who is currently living in Thailand under the alias Reginald Hansen."

"Yes, I have discussed this with my good friend, Pearson. Of course, I will do anything I can to help. Unfortunately, the extradition issue is out of my hands. It is a political matter." Sombat, who had been looking at his folded hands, glanced up into Elliot's steady stare and suddenly found it impossible to look away. A slow breath that he hadn't realized he'd been holding, slowly escaped from his chest and he felt as though the truth fled with it and now floated in the air, plainly visible to Elliot.

Elliot knew that what he said next had to be exactly right: it had to strike the correct resonance in Sombat's mind. He responded, "He will kill again. He can't stop himself. We need to get him off the streets as quickly as possible. At the very least, can't you take him into custody?"

Sombat hesitated. He didn't want to answer. He felt as though every time he spoke, he was revealing far too much to this man. Decorum, however, demanded an answer, and so he lied, with an apologetic smile, "At this time, we have no legal right to take Reginald Hansen into custody. So far, we have no proof he has committed a crime in Thailand, and your government has yet to provide us with documented proof that his identity is indeed false. Once you have supplied this paperwork, I would be happy to arrest him immediately for entering the country illegally. As for the charges against him in the United States, we will not take him into custody and extradite him unless our government is assured he will not be subjected to capital punishment. Until then, let me reassure you that we have him under surveillance. I am hopeful that this bureaucratic impediment will resolve itself quickly."

The lie was so plainly obvious to Elliot he was surprised the other members of his group weren't gasping in outrage. Although the extradition issue was problematic, Elliot clearly got the impression that it did not preclude Sombat from taking Demochet into custody. Sombat didn't want Demochet arrested, and Elliot suspected he knew why. Elliot wanted to warn him about how dangerous Demochet was, and that attempting to take revenge on Demochet for his daughter's murder was a dangerous game, but he didn't want to reveal that he had devined Sombat's plan.

With every bit of gravity he could muster, Elliot said, "We know Demochet's M.O., we can help you get him. He's become a very accomplished killer over the years, with a keen survival instinct. We should be working together on this."

"Thank you," Sombat said, "but we are a very professional organization and we can handle the situation on our own."

Just then Cheng poked her head through the rear office door. She caught Sombat's eye and motioned to him, thumb and index finger spread apart next to her face, telephone symbol. Elliot picked up a sense of urgency, but outwardly she seemed as composed as ever.

Sombat stood up, "Excuse me, I think I should take this call."

After he left, Pearson looked at Elliot and said, "Well?"

"Well what?"

"What was that little exchange about?"

"I didn't know he was your liaison contact: the one who's daughter was murdered."

"Yeah, he's the one. Why?"

"He just told me he's going to kill Demochet."

Pearson frowned, "I didn't hear that."

"Do you believe me?"

Pearson opened his mouth to tell Elliot he was fucking nuts, but Elliot's calm demeanor made him pause and think for a minute. It actually made sense. If Sombat thought Demochet was the man who killed his daughter, it wouldn't be the strangest thing in the world if he wanted to kill the man who did it. It was just that he'd known Sombat for so long, and he was a strictly by the books cop and an unfailingly honest human being. It hadn't occurred to him Sombat would be capable of stone walling them on this. He sighed, disappointed but resigned, "Yes."

"What do you want to do?"

Pearson shrugged, "Let's see if he invites us to the party."

Sombat came back in. "I'm sorry, can we reschedule this meeting for tomorrow?" He didn't wait for an answer. "Good. Anytime in the afternoon is good for me. My assistant will make arrangements." He turned and strode back through the door. His assistant entered as he exited. Their eyes met for only an instant. Elliot felt the worry pass between them. He stood up and Pearson and Wattane stood with him. Cheng placed her body between the door and the Americans.

Pearson whispered to Elliot, "I don't think we're invited."

"Please sit down," She said in Thai to Wattane, who translated for the group.

They all sat back down.

She sat facing them but didn't say anything, collecting her thoughts. She smoothed her skirt over her knees. Now that the material was stretched tight, Elliot could see the tight muscles of her thighs through the fabric. She saw him looking and flushed. Elliot felt a flash of guilt at having been caught appraising her. He gave an apologetic shrug and a lopsided smile. She let the moment pass.

"Colonel Sombat would not want me to talk to you," she began with Wattane translating. *"But I think he is..."* Cheng paused, *"confused, and I think maybe I need to help him even if that means betraying him."*

There was an uncomfortable silence.

"Well," Elliot said, never have been comfortable with uncomfortable silences. "That was foreboding Miss Cheng, but you have our undivided attention."

She nodded, and swallowed hard. Elliot guessed you didn't need to be psychic to know she was deeply disturbed by what she was about to say. Finally, she took a deep breath, *"I believe Sombat will attempt to kill Reginald Hansen tonight. The Colonel has not made any effort to inform the Thai prosecutor's office about your request. There are currently no political problems with the extradition, because our government does not yet know about it. Colonel Sombat has been looking for his daughter's killer for over twenty years. It is his obsession. He believes Hansen...Demochet...is the killer. The only reason he would secretly surveill the killer and not inform his superiors is to give himself time to take revenge. And it must be tonight. By tomorrow, thanks to the efforts of your team, our government will be fully aware of the situation."*

She paused, then appealed directly to Elliot, "*I believe this would destroy his soul and he would no longer be the man I have come to respect. I hope that you can intervene somehow.*"

Elliot held her gaze for a long moment, reaching out with her mind with his own, and felt the connection take hold. Their minds intertwined in an amorphous swirl of feelings and images. Elliot leaned forward and asked, "Can you give me Demochet's address?"

"*Yes,*" She said. No one noticed that she hadn't needed the translator to understand what Elliot said.

Pearson whistled, deep lines of concern etched on his face, "We'll have to be careful with this one. What you're asking is a tall order, but we'll see what we can do. As an outside agency, I'm not sure we could get your government to move fast enough. Why can't you tell his superiors?"

Cheng looked crestfallen at this news, *"Because the men are very loyal to him, and betraying him would be very... unwise. And I also thought if you could help we could keep what has happened quiet, and try to save Sombat's career."*

Pearson sighed and rubbed his head, "We'll do our best, but we've got to talk this over with the rest of our group."

Cheng nodded, "*Thank you. Please do, quickly.*" She got up and went around to Sombat's desk, where she wrote Demochet's address on a small square of paper.

While she did this, Elliot turned to his companions, "If we wait, it will be too late. Sombat will just end up getting himself killed, and we'll loose our last chance to get Demochet."

"Well," Pearson said," even so, we can't do anything without approval from the Thai authorities, and that bureaucratic process is going to take at least until tomorrow. What do you propose?"

"How about if you jump on that whole bureaucratic-process-thing, and I take a little ride out to Demochet's place and take a look around?"

"I think that's an incredibly bad idea. No good could come of it."

"That's not true. It would accomplish two things. First, I can get a good look at our area of play, which we may need later on. And second, if Sombat sees me sniffing around out there, it may make him hold off on his plans. " Elliot held up his hands to stop Pearson's protest, "I know what you're thinking, and Demochet sees me, it's no big deal: he doesn't know what I look like and I'll act like a lost tourist. Besides, I'm just going to drive past, I'm not going to do anything stupid, like sneak up and peak through his windows."

In point of fact, that was exactly what Elliot planned on doing, but he was sure Pearson didn't want to know that.

Pearson sighed, "I suppose you're going to do it no matter what, so just be careful. We'll see if we can't get a team out there tonight, but don't hold your breath. If you get into trouble, you may not get any back up."

Cheng came back and handed the slip of paper to Elliot. "*Please hurry.*" She said.

Chapter Forty Nine

Gunther Demochet a.k.a. Reginald Hanson sat watching the goings on across the street at the creatively named Young Boy Go-Go Club.

He was having an early dinner in one of the many open-air cafes that littered the Pattaya beach red light district. He sat by himself but he wasn't alone.

There were at least two other kindred spirits in the bar with him, each watching the comings and goings at the Young Boy Go-Go, immersed in their individual perverted evening fantasies. One of his fellow perverts glanced in Gunther's direction. Gunther caught and held his gaze then blew him a kiss. The kindred spirit looked away quickly, afraid and a little ashamed that Gunther could read the perversion his eyes. He needn't have worried. Gunther had his own perversions to occupy his mind, and they were a might wetter and more vile than anything he could or would imagine. Gunther would stack his own perversions up against these amateurs any day.

He was planning the first kill of his new life. With the aid of a local real estate office that catered to western developers and far-sighted entrepreneurs, he'd purchased a home between Utapao and Nakula. It was a modern four-bedroom concrete number with an outbuilding that could be used as a separate living unit for household help. Gunther had other plans for it.

He'd been to the Young Boy Go-Go twice. On one of those occasions he'd flirted with a delicious young half girl/half boy, called a *quatoi* in the Thai language, who obviously had something to sell but wasn't indentured to the club owner. Gunther thought it was swell that the club owner let the young transexual ply his*, or was it her?* wares in the establishment without having to give up his hard earned money. Of course, they probably had some kinky side deal worked out. He hoped the owner wouldn't miss the *quatoi* too much.

After the initial meeting, he had patiently staked out the place for three nights. *Good things come to those who wait,* he mused. He'd had a couple of liaisons since his return, but he'd let his partners live, which left him feeling wholly unsatisfied. No temporary fixes tonight - tonight he would be scratching his itch in full. Yup, there would be full itch scratching going on.

His stray had sashayed into the Young Boy Go-Go not five minutes ago. Tonight, Gunther would take him from his less than glamorous life.

Gunther paid for his meal and walked over to the club. The Go-Go was actually one of the cleaner dens of perversion in Pattaya beach. The front of the club facing the street was almost all glass, painted black from the inside. It looked like it might have been a small department store at one time.

Gunther strode purposely up to the blacked out glass door and went inside. A place like this in America would be in some back alley; and the clientele would sneak in quickly, glancing furtively over their shoulders just in case there was a familiar face about. In Pattaya only the newcomers were furtive. The regulars understood that anyone on this strip had the same agenda, and no one need be ashamed of their predilections. Gunther didn't think even his own unique tastes were completely alien in this environment.

All clubs that catered to the flesh seemed to be cut from the same cloth, or used the same instruction manual for decorating establishments of ill repute. Chapter Fifteen in the flesh peddler's handbook: Interior Design; The walls will be painted black and the only light inside the club will be supplied by a few strategically placed track lights and a glittering disco ball, of the studio 54 variety.

Underneath the disco ball a couple of young boys were doing their go-go thing on a raised wooden stage.

Gunther spotted his stray chatting up a hairy German in a corner booth. He moved underneath one of the track lights and waited for the boy/girl to look in his direction.

His stray had been scanning the crowd while doing something naughty under the table that was causing his German to sweat and breath in ragged gasps. He caught Gunther's eye, and his face lit up. He knew Gunther was a big spender.

Whatever he was doing to his German, he started doing it faster. The German let out a barbaric yawp and knocked over his beer. Before it hit the ground his stray was rushing over to him, wiping his/her hand on a pair of too tight jeans as he came.

"Reg (he pronounced it *Lejj)* where you been?" he asked, shamelessly pressing himself against Gunther's leg.

"Looking for you, darling," Gunther said. "I have a surprise for you."

His stray squealed with glee and pressed himself tighter, "I love surprises (he pronounced it *surplizes*)."

Gunther took his stray by the shoulders and gently

peeled him off his leg. He reached into his pocket, took out a wad of money, and began to count. "You want to come home with me tonight? Maybe you live with me some."

That was as close to a marriage proposal as a young go-go boy was ever likely to get. He squealed again (Gunther thought he'd be doing a lot of that) and reattached himself to Gunther's leg.

Gunther caught the German looking at him from the corner booth. He patted his new acquisition on the butt, shrugged, and headed for the door. The German watched them, indifferent. He wished he could afford a live in.

Two other sets of eyes watched Gunther and friend leave the club. They were Colonel Sombat's most trusted tourist police officers. They'd been watching Reg Hansen for days. It wasn't hard. From what they'd seen, he seemed to be a creature of habit. Every evening he had diner at the same cafe and then spent the evening in the Young Boy Go-Go, leaving with one of the *quatois.* Tonight was no different, except this time he wasn't inside for more than ten minutes when he left with a young boy/girl in tow. Eager tonight. They put in call to Colonel Sombat and then took off after Demochet. They took their time. They knew where he was going.

Chapter Fifty

Sombat stared at Demochet's villa through night vision goggles. He sat in an observation post Sombat's men had set up in the forest surrounding the villa. The monster lived like a rich man, Sombat noted. Demochet's villa, located east of Sukhumvit Highway in South Pattaya and a far distance from the center of the city, was not large, and probably only consisting of three bedrooms. No, the luxury was the large amount of forest area surrounding the property, which provided Demochet with enormous privacy, away from the prying eyes of any neighbors. The property consisted of a quaint, one story villa which faced the narrow road to the south, a pool, and a guest house to the rear. His men had set up the observation post in the wooded area to the west of the house. This precluded them from seeing the front, but it gave them the best view of both buildings.

He handed the goggles back to one of his men, Pratong Lee, and joined his second officer, Pre Chatpnang, in the middle of the small, nylon tent they used as camouflage. Prae Chatpnang squatted on a plastic tarp they were using as a floor and was eating a meal of spicy fish soup and noodles that Sombat had brought with him after they called him to let him know Demochet returned to the villa with a companion. Sombat had handpicked both investigators for this assignment. They were smart and loyal, but above all, they were comfortable operating in that gray area between law and justice.

Sombat stared grimly at the bowl of food on the floor, mulling over his options. He was worried that he wouldn't be able to kill Demochet with his government, the U.S. Embassy, and the American investigators looking over his shoulders. If the bureaucrats got to the monster first, he would become an international celebrity, the man the world loved to hate. He would be interviewed and studied. He would be loathed by all, but he would be alive. Alive wouldn't do, not for Sombat.

It had to happen tonight. The monster had taken a lover, and who knew how long he could keep him? Sombat was actually more concerned with how long the monster would be in his lair than he was with the well being of the boy/girl inside. The *quatoi* had long since lost its childhood to surgery and its abomidable profession, and those who led unnatural lives should expect to die unnaturally.

His men knew the monster's every move, and had even offered to kill him quickly and quietly for Sombat. But he wanted to…no, he had to…do it himself. He vowed not to fail his daughter in death like he had failed her in life. Sarinee hadn't just beautiful and headstrong: she had been intelligent and nurturing, always trying to help the local orphans, brining them food and sometimes money. She would have been a good mother. He knew she and her children would have been a joy to him as he grew older. Now his line would die with him, and all he had of Sarinee was her tortured spirit, which haunted his dreams. But Sarinee had also been a dreamer, who longed to leave the boredom of her life in Thailand and travel to foreign lands. Sombat had refused to support her ambitions, feeling it was simply a phase and that she would turn away from her childish dreams and settle down.

Sarinee was determined to experience life outside of Thailand, and rebelled against her father's predetermined plan of marriage and children for her. She had turned to the flesh trade to try to finance her escape. Sarinee's choice filled Sombat with shame. Her death, however, didn't make him sympathetic to the plight of the young boys and girls and boy/girls whose ambition turned to whoring. On the contrary, he dispised the sex trade and felt nothing but contempt for the young prostitutes who were walking symbols of the lie that had taken his daughter. He hadn't known how to make a headstrong daughter of adventurous spirit happy. And Demochet made sure he would never learn that one lesson.

Sombat went back to the tent's mesh window and, retrieving the goggles from Pratong Lee, trained them on the small guest house where Demochet had taken his quatoi. The curtains were pulled, but there was a light burning inside. Occasionally, a shadow would pass in front of the window. What could the monster be up to? He watched for a few minutes, tracking the occasional movement of the shadows inside the house.

"He seems to be busy in there, doesn't he?" Sombat observed, as he imagined all the horrible things being done to the unlucky boy/girl inside. He pushed the idea out of his mind.

"Whatever he's doing, he's very methodical," Pratong said.

"What do you mean?"

"It's like he passes in front of that window every few

minutes or so, like clockwork." He put a second pair of goggles up to his face. "Look, here he goes again."

They watched as the shadow moved past the window. Sombat looked at his watch, the iridescent dial illuminated in the dim light of the tent. Four minutes and thirty seconds later the shadow returned.

"Something's wrong," Sombat said.

"What?"

"Watch." Sombat ordered, and they sat there waiting as the minutes ticked by. Finally Sombat, who had been keeping track on his watch, said, "He's coming back in five... four...three...two...one." He pointed at the window as the shadow moved across the curtains.

Pratong lowered his goggles and looked at Sombat, frowning.

"How could you not notice?" Sombat asked, irritated. "Like clockwork? It's exactly like clockwork!"

Pratong opened his mouth to respond when a hiss of air, *phwup*, blew through the tent and everything exploded in blood. The part of Pratong's brain that had been formulating an apology hit Sombat in the eye.

Sombat's other eye noticed a pinprick of red light searching the nylon wall outside. It stopped next to Prae's head. The light burped and the side of Prae's head turned to mush.

Sombat threw himself to the floor, groping for his weapon as more bullets ripped through the nylon tent, following his decent to the floor. One of them grazed his scalp. He rolled onto his back fired his gun blindly, emptying his magazine into the hole where the lazer beam had come from. He reloaded automatically and dove through the tent flap into the jungle. He strained to hear any sound from the bush, but all he heard was a loud ringing in his ears as the result of his own gunfire; and without the night vision goggles the jungle was as dark as…well,… a jungle in Thailand at night.

He caught a flash of movement out of the corner of his eye and he turned towards it. A large man rushed out of the trees at him, moving fast. He tried to bring the gun up, but his assailant plucked it effortless from his fingers.

A face materialized out of the darkness in front of him and said, "Dude, I've been looking all over for you."

He recognized the cheshire grin glowing in the darkness before he recognized the voice...Eetee!

"You're bleeding," Elliot said.

Then the bullet that had grazed his scalp finally took its toll, and he passed out.

Chapter Fifty One

Elliot looked down at Sombat, his face taut with worry, and watched the aging police officer slowly regain consciousness. When he finally opened his eyes, Elliot greeted him.

"Welcome back Colonel."

Sombat sat up. He was on an unfamiliar couch in an unfamiliar place. "Where are we, Eetee?"

"In the dragon's lair, Colonel." Elliot waved his hand around at the sparsely decorated living room of Gunther Demochet. Sombat lay on an old fabric couch of the grandma's house variety, and the rest of the room contained a coffee table, a television and, surprisingly, a very nice oriental carpet. Elliot's earlier inspection revealed the other rooms were empty, and the kitchen hosted just a few pots and pans, dinner plates, and assorted cooking and eating utensils. The bedroom had one full sized bed, a nightstand, and a dresser. Like Demochet's dormitory room, it contained only the bare necessities. Elliot thought it looked like a hotel room but without the tasteful window dressing or the cheesy lithographs.

"How...?"

"Let's just say you owe your life to the beautiful, yet frumpy, Miss Cheng. She's here by the way."

"Why?"

"Because, Colonel, everybody and their fucking mother is here. Except of course your two men out in the tent, who seemed to have gotten themselves killed." Elliot, who was almost always smiling, had lost all semblance of mirth as his worry was replaced by anger.

"You're angry."

"Yes, yes I am. I warned you about the danger. You could have had him, man! Now he's gone. What happened?"

"I don't know."

"I could have helped."

"Could you, Eetee?" Sombat looked him in the eye. "I was going to kill him! Were you going to help me do that?"

"I...well…fuck, man, who knows!? Here's your gun." He dropped the nine-millimeter in Sombat's lap. "Miss Cheng's in the kitchen. Don't be too hard on her. If it weren't for her you'd be wondering why you were dead! I'm going back to the other building."

"What's in there?"

"A *quatoi*, or what's left of him…or her…or whatever. Oh, and by the way, it's really great that you sat outside while Demochet butchered that poor kid. I'm sure you told yourself sacrificing one *quatoi* was worth the price of getting a shot at him, but then you just fucked it up and let him escape."

Elliot walked out of the main house, trying to get control of his emotions. He let the door slam behind him. Elliot wondered what he would have done in Sombat's place, and he didn't have an answer for it. Was killing Demochet an option? If there was anyone out there who deserved a big ol'batch of death it was Demochet, and they were in Asia. The rules were different here. Weren't they?

Sombat had lost a daughter to Demochet. On the cosmic, karmic scale that made him master of ceremonies at this party. Sombat made no bones about the fact that he was his daughter's champion, but who did that leave to champion the other victims?

Excuse me ma'am, did somebody order a hero? He was walking the short distance between the main house and the outbuilding, gravel crunching underfoot, when the hairs on the back of his neck gave him a warning tingle. Never ignore a tingle.

Someone watching? He scanned the trees surrounding the Demochet estate, and tried to sweet talk his psychic friend into a useful revelation. Nothing. He strained to hear some movement from the bushes. The night was still.

Where would they be right now if the lovely – yet confused – Miss Cheng hadn't told them about Sombat's plan? They'd probably be sitting in the hotel waiting for a phone call from the embassy while the bugs ate the Colonel and his men.

After Miss Cheng's revelation, Pearson had notified Devine and Dean at the embassy, and went to meet them and wait for the State Department's security liaison to coordinate some kind of action with the Thai National Police. As far as Elliot was concerned, it was a fucking Christmas miracle they'd made it here at all. But in reality, Elliot knew the speed with which the OSI and the Thai police responded was due to the fact that Devine had pitched an epic fit, brought on by his certain knowledge that Elliot, who was on his way to Demochet's house, was no doubt going to do something so catastrophically damaging that Devine's career would never recover from it.

Elliot had to give it to the Thai police, they were good.

Once they mobilized they were as professional a machine as he'd ever seen. Americans and Thais were packed into four functional, black, sport utility vehicles of a make Elliot did not recognize. When they pulled up to the villa, Elliot carried the unconscious Sombat to the front of the house facing the road and was waiting for them . They quickly deployed and searched the house and grounds, declaring the area "clear", even though Elliot felt certain Demochet was somewhere near, if not actually on the grounds proper.

Elliot's arrival at the house had been a tad less spectacular than theirs. He had taken a taxi as far as the main road connecting to Demochet's street. He got out a mile away from the house and casually walked down the road. Before he even got to the villa, however, he had stopped by the wooded area surrounding the property. Something had given him the irrepressible urge to tiptoe through the dense, dark, jungle to find it. He'd made his way slowly, almost blind, listening carefully, but mostly relying on his sixth sense to guide him through the terrain. He had no idea what he would find, or even if he was prepared to deal with it once he did, but he figured he get some sort of "signal" when he needed it.

"The signal," had come in the form of gunfire from Colonel Sombat's duty weapon.

Elliot crouched low and approached the direction of the sound at a light jog. His psychic friend wasn't screaming, "threat." He chose to trust it and took the direct approach. Directly into the gunfire's dying echo. He'd burst out of the jungle right on top of Sombat's surveillance post. The Colonel had been staggering around, dazed, one eye glued shut by his own blood and what turned out to be a piece of Pratong's brain. Elliot disarmed him easily. Friendly fire wasn't the way he wanted to go out. In the distance, Elliot had heard sirens and knew the calvalry were on the way.

He suspected Demochet had also realized this, and had taken the opportunity to make his escape, rather then linger around and try to finish killing Sombat's band of misfits.

After a few hours, the special response team, having found no one to shoot, packed their gear and gone home.

The main house had been clean, but the outbuilding was positively gruesome. He'd gone in only briefly, and quickly left to check on Colonel Sombat, deciding he might need to collect himself before immersing himself in the psychic chaos of the outbuilding.

Dean, Devine, Wattane, and Pearson were having a conference outside of the one door to the building. He nodded to them on the way past and went inside. The smell of human viscera welcomed him back to the nightmare. Drake, Coleman, and a Thai investigator, who he hadn't met, were wandering around the small building trying to make some sense of the slaughter.

Elliot puzzled over the carnage. Demochet was usually a highly organized, sane, fetish killer: an iceman. All of the evidence up to this point, from Josh Bennet, to Alonso Proctor, to the carefully packaged bodies in the missile silo, indicated that preferred his killing tidy. Demochet was a killer, a cannibal, and a paraphile of the first order; but he was a neat one. He'd been killing in the silos for at least four or five years. A detailed, forensic, search of every inch of the silo using everything from ultraviolet light to detect body fluids, to luminal, the chemical used to detect trace amount of blood, yielded nothing more than the evidence in Josh Bennet's death chamber.

He always killed clean, burking his smaller victims and snapping the others' necks. There was simply no indication that he had ever engaged in the kind of disorganized carnage decorating the outbuilding. But what did they really know about the man? Maybe this was an aspect of his paraphilia that they'd never seen. Maybe he'd gone so long without killing that he got carried away. Or maybe the reality of who and what he was finally drove him insane. Maybe he'd finally graduated from iceman to disorganized sick fuck, which was a scary prospect. There was nothing more frightening than a sick fuck with nothing left to loose. He'd be like a wild animal, cornered, desperate, and armed with an automatic weapon.

Steve Drake and Tony Coleman were bent over the biggest piece of what was left of the *quatoi.*

"Hey guys," Elliot said. "Let me know if you find his spleen."

Coleman looked up, "What?"

"Nothing. You notice anything strange about this scene?"

"Yeah, it's a little more...," Coleman paused, searching, surveying the blood splattered walls and stray chunks of flesh laying about, "frenetic than the other scenes."

"Frenetic?" Elliot asked.

"Yeah, what were you thinking?"

"Same. Matter of fact, that's exactly how I'd describe it." He turned to Drake, "What's frenetic mean, anyway?"

Drake ignored the question. "You think we lost him again?"

"Hard to say," Elliot said, "Did we ever really *have* him?"

"What do you make of this?"

"I'll tell you in a second. Didn't I see an arm laying around the last time I was in here?"

"It's in the bag already."

"Did it have defense wounds?"

"Yes."

"Let's go have a look."

The unfortunate *quatoi* was in a number of pieces. Three

main pieces and a lot of little chunks carved out of his more meaty parts, to include his breast and their respective silicon implants. The three main pieces were a torso with the legs and the left arm still attached, the head, and the right arm.

Some assembly required, Elliot thought.

The head and arm were in a body bag waiting to be reunited with the big piece.

Elliot, Drake, and Coleman walked over and knelt beside the open bag. Elliot pulled a pair of rubber gloves out of his pocket. He put them on. Then, grimacing, he bent and pulled the arm out of the bag.

The arm had seen better days. It probably yearned for those times when it could scratch its balls, caress its breasts, or clutch another man's penis tenderly in its hand. Alas, now it was pretty much just a hunk of flesh, hamburger, no longer svelte and smooth to the touch. The fingers were flesh hanging off of bone. The arm itself, previously without blemish, was now slashed and gouged and bloodied.

"Are those enough defense wounds for you?" Drake asked Elliot.

"Let me paint a picture for you," Elliot said. "All of these years Demochet has been so careful. He lived a dual life, scratching his itch whenever the mood took him. He wasn't worried about getting caught. He literally lived his life as two or three separate people. Hell, if he'd ever been caught doing something naughty in his Reg Hanson persona, the authorities might not have even made the connection to Sergeant Demochet. But then he makes a mistake. For whatever reason, maybe he's getting old; he snatches Josh Bennet and proceeds to make a number of small – but significant – mistakes. He leaves Josh's body unattended and after it's discovered, he continues driving the truck he'd been driving on the day he snatched him. Maybe, like so many other sick motherfuckers, there is a part of him that wants to get caught, but not because of the wolfman syndrome."

"Wolfman syndrome?" Coleman asked.

"Yeah, you know," Elliot effected a dramatic falsetto and waved his hands, still holding the *quatoi's* arm, around to pantomime hysteria, " '*stop me before I kill again*'. Demochet doesn't want to be stopped, but living two lives has got to be tedious; and he's having much more fun as Reg Hanson. He probably planned his escape years ago. He comes to Thailand and becomes Reg Hanson. Now he doesn't have the baggage of a second persona. But it was having that second person that kept him careful. He stalked this *quatoi* like he's probably stalked all of his victims over the years, but it's been almost three months since he scratched his itch. Now he's eager and careless. Let's assume our friend in the bag has been working the streets most of his young life, at least long enough to buy some breasts. He's not stupid. Demochet underestimates him. Maybe he doesn't bind him tight enough, or watch him close enough. Hell, he might have even unbound him, figuring fright would keep him docile."

"I'm thinking he didn't bind him tight enough," Drake interjected.

"Why?"

"Take a look at the wrist on that arm." Elliot suddenly seemed to remember he was still holding the arm and held it up in front of his face. The wrist wore a bloody abrasion like a bracelet. "The other arm's just like that," Drake said, "and we found a bloody loop of duct tape near the torso. It looks like he worked at the tape until it was loose enough to slip off."

"Good," Elliot said. "So Demochet, true to form, duct tapes his arms, but while he's off putting on cologne or ironing his smoking jacket – or whatever wackos do to get ready for this kind of sick shit– his date works himself loose. Demochet saunters back in with his smoking jacket, ascot, glass of cognac, and big fucking knife, only to find his *quatoi* cornered, afraid, and more than a little put out that this evening's cornholing was going to go horribly wrong. He puts up a fight. He's no match for Demochet, but he does manage to really piss him off. Basically, there's no real change in Demochet's psyche. He just got mad."

"Good story," Drake said, "what are you getting at?"

"Demochet hasn't self destructed. He's out there somewhere, just as dangerous as ever, trying to figure out how to salvage what's left of his paradise. I'm thinking that the most dangerous man we've never met is somewhere trying to figure out what to do about us."

"Wouldn't it make more sense for him to worry about getting as far away from here as possible?" Coleman asked.

Elliot nodded and handed the arm back to Drake. "It would, but I don't think he is."

"Why not?"

"I don't know. I just can't shake the feeling that he's still lurking around here. And I don't know why. There must be something here he wants." Elliot rubbed the back of his neck, thinking hard. The feeling that he was missing something crucial kept nagging at him. It was the same feeling you get when you remember you forgot something, but can't figure out what. He looked up from his ruminations. Whatever it was, he was suddenly certain it was not in this room. He needed to return to the main house, and walked out without further explanation to his friends.

When he entered, it was as he'd left it, only Sombat and Cheng were sitting on the couch having an intense conversation, which they cut short when they saw him. He gave them a curt nodded as he looked around the room. His eyes drifted across the furnishings. It wasn't here. He turned and walked back to the bedroom. The feeling was stronger here: that half remembered thought just shimmering on the edge of his awareness. He stood completely still and breathed. His eyes fell on the night stand. He went over to it and opened the drawer. Inside there was Kleenex, some spare change, and a set of keys. He looked under the night stand. Nothing. He went back to the drawer and removed all of its contents. He ran his fingers along the bottom, then tapped, but the sound was unremarkable. Finally he yanked the drawer out of the stand and looked on the bottom. Still nothing. Undaunted, he returned to the interior and began to claw at the bottom edges of the drawer until his fingers found purchase and he was able to pry the plywood up. Underneath was a thin, false bottom, and inside was a legal sized manila envelope. He opened it and spilled the contents on the bed. It contained an Irish passport and several neat stacks of one hundred dollar bills. He opened the passport. The face of Gunther Demochet smiled up at him.

Elliot put them back in the envelope, and tucked it into the waste band of his pants, concealing it under his shirt. He walked out of the bedroom.

"Is anything the matter?" Sombat asked.

"No, everything is fine. I'll go see if they are almost finished out there." Elliot passed Devine and the other guys, presumable on their way into the main house to check up on him, on his way out. They looked confused, but didn't follow him. When he got to the guest house, Coleman and Drake were outside waiting for him.

"Did you find what you were looking for?" Coleman asked.

Elliot gave him a triumphant grin, "As a matter of fact, I did." He pulled the envelope out and showed them the passport. "It's his evacuation kit. A fake passport with the name...." he checked the passport"...Robert Finley, and a shit load of money."

"Wow."Drake said, "How did you find that?"

"Two parts luck, one part awesome investigative intuition. But more importantly, we now know there's a good chance Demochet will come back here to get this. All we need to do is pounce on him when he arrives." Elliot curled his hands into claws and imitated the pounce movement of a cat.

"And when will that be?" Coleman asked.

"What am I? Psychic? But we should put our heads together and figure out how to leverage this so we don't fuck up what may be our last opportunity to get him."

"Alright. Let's go back in, I think the lab tech is just about finished. We can talk inside."

Chapter Fifty-Two

If he'd been a religious man he'd say God had it in for him. Well, at least he was still free. Of course, he shuddered to think about where he would be if he hadn't spotted the cops in the woods. All it took to tip him off was a flash of moonlight on metal where no metal had any business being. Maybe God didn't have it in for him. But the OSI definitely did.

He had to admit a grudging, growing respect for them. It was the same group from Denver. He recognized the preppie from the civil engineering squadron. The black guy he had seen around the Air Force base in Denver a few times. He didn't dress like an OSI agent - probably thought of himself as some kind of maverick. The others were all "Elliot Ness" wannabees, stamped-out-frozen-patties. Even the Thai investigators looked alike.

He'd been careless again, and his new live-in had slipped his bonds. What's more, that little quatoi proved to be a good fighter: not gifted but good enough to walk the back streets of Utapao confidently and unmolested.

What a waste!

What a rush!

It had been like taking Rau all over again. He'd been angry and excited and probably got more than a little carried away. In the end his *quatoi* had ended up a bit more squishy than he normally liked his victims to be.

When all the wet work was over, he'd been on his way to the main house to take a shower and get some cleaning supplies when he'd seen that tell tale glint. He continued on to the main house, but he didn't shower. The dried blood on his face from his brief, slippery, marvelous, encounter with his guest, made for excellent camouflage. He'd walked back to the outbuilding completely aware of his surroundings, all of his senses tuned to that area in the trees with the unwelcome glint.

The guesthouse contained all of the tools he needed to carry out his sick, twisted fantasies, and it also included two packs of survival gear and weapons. Once back in the outbuilding he changed into jungle BDUs from the first package. The second package contained a silenced Heckler and Koch, MP-5 submachine pistol with a laser sight. He set his rotating security light on five-minute intervals and crawled out of the guest house bathroom window to find the source of the glint.

He would have finished off all the cops if the black guy hadn't distracted him. He'd had a bead on the last guy and was about to finish him off, when he saw movement to his right. It was the black guy, slinking through the woods. That momentary lapse in concentration had given the Thai cop the chance to shoot back at him. He'd had to take cover and try to find a new position. As he was doing so, though, he heard the sirens. He figured he didn't have the luxury of hanging around much longer, so he took off through the woods to his neighbor's property where he watched the little Thai commandos secured the area around his house.

They set up high-powered lights around the perimeter of his estate. Every other light was aimed outward into the trees, turning the jungle into day in a fifty meter perimeter. After that, he snuck back onto his property and found an ideal observation position in a tall mango tree just outside the reach of the artificial day light.

He watched everything through a pair of compact, high-powered binoculars. The lenses were polarized and covered with black nylon. No stray glints there. After the lights were in place, the Thai SWAT team packed up and left. If they were anything like their American counterparts, they were going back to their bullpen to debrief and analyze their actions, leaving the clean up to the investigators.

Now the only persons remaining were the Americans and three Thai cops, and one of the Thais was injured. Gunther had started thinking of the injured Thai as *the one that got away*, like he was a big fish or a deer. Of course, since he was still on the property, he hadn't really got away.

Demochet had already decided he was in a survivable situation. All things not being equal, it was unlikely that every FBI or OSI agent had the skills or the wherewithal to track him across the globe. Nor did he put much stock in the Thai's ability to find him once his finished his work this evening. It was probably safe to assume that the mind or minds responsible for this inconvenience were currently crawling around his property under his watchful eye, trying to dissect his stuff and figure out their next move. All he needed to do was wait them out. When he was certain the cost was clear, he would return to the house and retrieve his fake passport and money and make a clean get away.

Satisfied with his plan, he perched and watched in relative contentment. It was sort of watching a slow, but interesting television show. The black man came back from the house for the second time and approached his friends, who had congregated outside the guesthouse. His contentment turned violently to horror as the black man pulled his manila envelope out of the back of his pants and showed it's contents to his companions

How the fuck had he found it? His heart pounded hard in his chest as he realized that his last chance at escape was currently in the hands of the people who had managed to track him half way across the world. He was thoroughly and completely fucked without that passport and money. There was no way he would be able to hide from the police without it and getting caught was now a virtual inevitability.

Unless, of course, he got the documents back and killed everyone who had seen them. He considered it for a moment. It had intriguing possibilities. Not only was it really his only option at the point, he thought he might actually enjoy the challenge of taking out that many people at once. He smiled. It was good to have a plan – indecision was for the weak minded.

He crept down from his tree and skirted the circle of light to the rear of his property, low crawling through the dense jungle until he had a straight shot to the rear of the outbuilding. The bulk of their force was still hovering around there. Once he dispatched them, the *one who got away* would be routine cleanup.

* * *

Inside the guesthouse, Elliot, Drake, Coleman, and Pearson discussed the relative merits of letting the Thai police in on the passport and when. They made sure they were well out of earshot of the Thai coroner. They were split down the middle, with Coleman and Pearson wanting to hand over the document, and Elliot and Drake wanting to hold onto it for a while. They finally agreed to take it back to the hotel, make a photocopy and then turn it over.

"I don't think there's anything more we can do here," Drake was saying.

"Good, I need a cigarette," Pearson answered. He took a long, almost sad, look at the little Thai coroner, scooping up the smaller chunks of the *quatoi,* putting them in separate bags. He walked outside and lit up a clove cigarette, a habit he'd picked up from young European tourist during his wanderings through Asia. Elliot and Coleman followed him out and sat down beside him on the steps in front of the outbuilding. Elliot put his face in his hands and sighed.

"That bad, E.T.?" Pearson asked.

"Remind me to go back to being just another fuck-up when I get back to America."

Pearson laughed, "Good luck with that. "Fuck-up" is a noble calling. Much more satisfying than going back to take credit for tracking down the single most prolific serial killer in military history."

Just then, Devine, Dean, and Wattane walked back from the main house, deep in serious conversation. Devine nodded to Drake, "Where are we with the crime scene processing?"

"Almost done," he answered.

"We'll go talk to him." Devine said, clearly not satisfied with the answer.

"I'll go with you." Drake said and fell in behind the group, figuring he could keep Devine causing an international incident.

* * *

Demochet pulled himself soundlessly through the outbuildings bathroom window. He duck walked over to the bathroom door. The door was slightly ajar. There was a pencil thin sliver of light bisecting the small room. He squatted next to the door with the MP-5 resting across his knees, muzzle pointed towards the crack.

From his position he had no trouble listening to the conversation in the next room. He counted five voices, four American, one Thai. Full house, he could use that to his advantage.

* * *

"Ask him when he'll be done," Devine ordered. The translator didn't care for Devine's tone. Matter of fact, Devine was really starting to chap his ass. But he figured the sooner they wrapped up, the sooner he could catch up with Elliot and Pearson, who were definitely the fun guys, and go have a beer. He walked over and touched the little Thai coroner on his shoulder.

"How much longer, sir?"

"Not much longer now, friend. Certainly your impatient American friend realizes that these things take time."

Wattane gave him an understanding smile in response.

"Well?" Devine asked.

"Soon," Wattane said.

"What's the hold up?" Dean asked.

"There's no hold up," Drake said coming to the translator's rescue, "and I have to say, I find your impatience embarrassing."

"Beg pardon," Dean and Devine said almost in unison. Drake decided that Elliot was right, Devine was a rather disturbing personality, and Dean wasn't much different. Where did law enforcement organizations find these people?

"Look around you," Drake continued. "This is a complex crime scene. It's a little more involved than just separating the small, medium, and large pieces. What we have here is a big, wet, jigsaw puzzle, and if we don't do this right the first time, it will be just that much more difficult to match up the pieces once we move them. I'm sure you will both agree that when it comes to reconstructing a violent crime scene, pieces are most important. I'm appalled that I have to waste my breath explaining this to you."

Dean gave Drake a hard look trying to read any blatant disrespect on his face. Drake stared back impassively. "I'm going to the bathroom." Dean said.

"Isn't that part of our crime scene?" Wattane asked.

"It's okay," Drake said. "We're done in there. It's clean." Drake was actually relieved that Dean decided to leave the room.

* * *

Okay Mr. Killer, Mr. Man...time to make the donuts! Demochet smiled, took a deep breath, and prepared for the fun to begin.

* * *

Elliot bummed one of Pearson's clove cigarettes. He was busy savoring the sweet smoke when the tingle came again. But the tingle rapidly escalated to a full blown electric shock that hit him in the middle of the spin and shot up to the back of his head. He jumped straight up as the certain knowledge that Demochet was inside the guesthouse materialized inside his brain.

"Fuck! Demochet's in there." He spun and dashed for the house.

Coleman saw the change come over Elliot and recognized it immediately as one of his 'episodes'. He drew his weapon as Elliot reached for the door. Pearson, initially puzzled by Elliot's incomprehensible outburst, didn't realize anything was amiss until he heard the scream.

* * *

Dean pushed the bathroom door open and was greeted with an image that would haunt him for the rest of what was left of his life. The bathroom was occupied, but one look at the occupant and Dean's bladder took care of business without waiting.

Demochet stood in front of the toilet, bathed in light. His face was crusted with blood. He was grinning. He stood still as a statue. He could have been a statue. Even the laser light from his MP-5 was motionless.

Dean, haunted, screamed like a girl. Demochet responded by shooting him in the face.

Elliot and Coleman burst through the door, with Pearson on their heels. Elliot's psychic friend came through with them. It was back with a vengeance, hyped up on ecto-steroids and holding him firmly in the twilight zone. He ran through the room caught up in the juxtaposition of what was and what was going to happen. His psychic senses showed him the room in double exposure, only one of the images was taking place half a heartbeat in the future superimposed over his regular vision.

Dean was obviously toast. He lay splayed out and twitching in front of the bathroom door, one leg across the threshold. Gunther's MP-5 had taken off half his face. He lay gooey side up, one eye akimbo, the other looking at nothing. Elliot didn't need to look to know Demochet was stepping out of the bathroom. He knew he was going to shoot Drake. Elliot didn't break stride, but tackled Drake at the midsection. Demochet's bullet, meant for Drake's heart, went through his shoulder instead as they fell.

Elliot rolled away from Drake and came up to a crouch, looking for Wattane. A constrictive sense of panic in his gut told him Wattane was next, but he was too far away from the translator to do anything about it.

Wattane was diving for the front door when Demochet's MP-5 spit at him, tearing through his spine and exploding his heart.

If Elliot was in the twilight zone, he was in the cheap

seats. The future lay before him in DVD quality but only a half second at a time. He could see clearly what was about to happen but he was powerless to intercede.

Demochet turned his weapon towards Elliot, but he didn't move.

He's not going to shoot me, he thought.

A shot rang out from the front door.

Ms. Cheng?

Compared to Demochet's silenced machine pistol, the report was deafening. Demochet's gun flew out of his hand in a spray of blood, his right hand a mass of blood and bone. He dropped to his knees. Elliot used the opportunity to close the gap between him and Demochet. He launched himself at the wounded killer.

Mistake! He should have just shot him. What was he thinking? Elliot moved quickly. No changing plans now. Anyway, beating Demochet down with his bare hands seemed like the right, and more satisfying, thing to do.

Demochet, still on his knees, spun, and pivoted on one knee. He swung his right leg around in a short arc easily sweeping Elliot off his feet.

Ms. Cheng shot at Demochet again. The bullet went wide. But it distracted Demochet long enough for Elliot to stand up on one knee and shoot an elbow strike to the back of the killer's head. Demochet struck out simultaneously with his good hand. Elliot's elbow connected with a sound that could have been another gunshot. But even as Demochet lost consciousness his backfist broke Elliot's nose. The world slowed again.

The room smelled of gunpowder, sweat, blood, clove cigarettes, and fresh jungle air, all vying for scent supremacy. The blood and gunpowder were winning. Elliot's head was spinning. Most of the blood he smelled was pouring out of his own nose in a steady stream.

Ms. Cheng was still standing in the doorway, gun hanging listlessly by her side. The translator lay dead in front of her and Elliot could hear Drake behind him groaning and cussing. Groaning and cussing was good.

Dean wasn't twitching anymore.

Coleman, Devine, and the little Thai investigator were untouched, taking cover in various corners of the room.

Demochet lay face down next to Elliot, immobile, taking shallow, ragged breaths. Maybe he'd die of sleep apnea before he came to.

Devine was shaking like a leaf. His eyes were wide. His pupils were dilated and unfocused. "Is everyone okay?" he asked. A ridiculous question, since it was obvious *everyone* was not okay. When no one answered he asked again. "Is everyone okay? Is everyone okay? Iseveryoneokay? We need to make sure everyone is okay. SOMEONE CHECK EVERYONE. MAKE SURE THEY'RE OKAY!" His voice was starting to crack. Elliot didn't need his psychic friend, who was still lurking about, to tell him that the commander was about to come apart at the seams. He was in his own special twilight zone.

Demochet woke up. He didn't move. He didn't change his breathing. *Okay, the black guy can fight. Good for him. How many had he killed? Judging by the voices and footsteps, not enough. Shit. Well there was always plan B. Who was he kidding? There was no plan B. Plan B was pretty much going out in a blaze of glory. Why not? He could take at least two of them with his bare hands. Oops, his bare hand.* Demochet tried not to chuckle. Maybe *he could even get a gun. He just needed someone to come close.*

Devine gave Demochet just what he needed.

"Somebody restrain that man," Devine said, pointing at Demochet's prone body. The sound of his own commanding voice reciting his litany of how everybody should be checking everyone had reassured him, and he decided he was taking charge of the situation quite nicely, "and then make sure everyone else is okay!" With the danger clearly over, and his initial panic subsided, the buzz of adrenaline in his system made him feel positively giddy. As he talked he strode confidently towards the killer's limp body, handcuffs in hand, clearly preparing to do the restraining himself.

He kneeled down, preparing to shackle the unconscious killer, which in his mind would make him the one to make the apprehension. At least that was how he planned to write it up in the report...and the organization newsletter. Of course, Turner had helped.

Gunther could hear Devine's handcuffs rattling. He felt Devine's footsteps against his cheek and judge his distance by the scrape of the soles of his shoes.

Plan B here we go. Wait for it. Wait for it!

Elliot was trying to stem the flow of blood coming out of his nose and ignore Devine, when the clear impression that Demochet was not unconscious filtered through the pain. He looked up as Devine knelt next to the prone killer, completely unaware that Demochet was planning to kill him with a flat hand palm strike to the bridge of his nose, which would drive the bone straight into his brain.

An oldie but a goodie, Elliot thought as he lurched towards Demochet's prone form.

Before he could get to them to save Devine's worthless life, Demochet's head jumped as if punched by an invisible hand. Elliot heard the gunshot a nano-second later. He turned towards the sound. Colonel Sombat stood in the doorway, 9mm in hand, looking amazingly sane for a cop who had just shot an apparently unconscious man in the head. He lowered his gun and slumped against the door jam. The lovely, yet frazzled, Ms. Cheng hovered by his side.

Demochet hadn't moved a muscle.

Devine stared at Sombat, wide-eyed. He looked at Demochet's leaking corpse. He looked like he was about to say something, but Elliot cut him off.

"He was going to kill you, boss."

Coleman put an arm around Devine's shoulders. "He really was, you know."

"You're all going to stick together on this, aren't you?" Devine asked.

"Yes, yes we are," said Pearson with a certain amount of disgust. He was tending to Drake's shoulder, applying pressure to the wound.

Devine shook off Coleman's arm and brushed past Sombat into the jungle night. Maybe the twilight zone wouldn't be out there.

Chapter Fifty-Three

Melanie Rivers, wearing her I've-got-a-secret look and feeling every bit the young upwardly mobile news chick, interrupted the regularly scheduled program for a special report:

"Hi, I'm Melanie Rivers, and this is a Channel Six special report. Late yesterday evening in Utapao Thailand, Thai investigators, working with U.S. officials in country, tracked down suspected serial killer, Air Force Senior Master Sergeant Gunther Demochet. However, Demochet, who was using the alias, Reginald Hansen, was killed resisting arrest prior to capture. Thai police have not released the details of the incident.

"Demochet is believed to be responsible or more than 30 killings in the Denver area, including the rape and murder of five year old Josh Bennett of Aurora, and 15 year old Alonso Proctor of Denver.

"Air Force officials could not be reached for comment. However, Denver police, still morning the death of Officer Gloria Sanchez, who was gunned down by Demochet prior to his disappearance had this to say..."

Sally clicked off the television with the remote control. She didn't attempt to put it back on the nightstand next to her hospital bed. Retrieving it had been enough of a chore. She had feeling in all of her limbs, but her doctors said she was probably looking at months of physical therapy before she could get back to work. She thought she could use the vacation. Anyway, there were things she and her spousal unit...Dave... needed to talk about: like a speedy and amicable divorce.

Case closed! Donuts made. She wondered what Elliot was up to. He'd probably stop by to fill her in on the details when he was through debriefing and could break away. She thought she probably should have a T-shirt made that said. *'I survived being Elliot Turner's partner...sort of'*. Well one ride was more than enough for her. She hoped his next partner - that is if Elliot's career survived whatever weirdness undoubtedly went down in Thailand - faired as well.

Epilogue

Jack Norton had been in the OSI for eighteen months, which basically meant he was just coming off of the probationary training period mandatory for all agents, which meant he was a rookie. He didn't feel like a rookie. Probation was over. Now he was a full-fledged OSI Special Agent and damned proud of it. Good thing too, because there was a big world out there that needed saving.

Norton was an agent George Devine would be proud of. He was good rational, logical, android stock. Insert tab A into slot B and...*viola,* bad guys practically put themselves in jail. Norton figured his future was so bright he had to wear shades. He had big plans for the OSI.

Yessir, he was special and his boss, who also had android like tendencies, treated him like he was special. At least he had until he found out Special Agent Elliot Turner was being reassigned to their small New Mexico detachment. Now the boss didn't give him the time of day. The boss had been sequestered in his office with his secure telephone glued to his ear since receiving news of Turner's impending arrival. Funny thing was, he seemed excited but not particularly happy. Maybe agitated was a better word. He' managed to liberate the boss from his preoccupation long enough to ask what all the hubbub was about. What was it about Special Agent Elliot Turner that seemed to have everyone's panties in a ringer? The answer had been singularly unenlightening. "Elliot Turner does things."

THE END